Being a nobody isn't Duncan Alexander's lif(
him. He has a nondescript job, a few good
content. That's until one fateful trip to San Jo
"Called" to meet the mysterious Juliet de Exter. Juliet is a beautiful,
wealthy, powerful Immortal who is undertaking The Calling—a search
for a human to join her world of Immortals. Inexplicably, Duncan's
calling is more dangerous than any of the Immortals, even Juliet, ever
thought it would be.

There is more to this nobody, this only child of long-deceased parents,
than anyone thought. When Duncan experiences uncontrollable dreams
of people he doesn't know and places he hasn't been, Juliet and the other
Immortals worry. Soon, his visions point to a coven of long-dead
witches. The dreams also lead Duncan to his one true love. How will
Duncan navigate a forbidden romance with an outcast Immortal? How
will he and the others keep the balance between the Light and Dark,
survive vicious attacks, and keep the humans from learning who they
truly are? More importantly, who is this implacable foe Duncan keeps
seeing in his dreams?

A NineStar Press Publication

Published by NineStar Press
P.O. Box 91792,
Albuquerque, New Mexico, 87199 USA.
www.ninestarpress.com

The Calling

ISBN: 978-1-947904-86-6

Printed in the USA
First Edition
January, 2018

Also available in eBook, ISBN: 978-1-947904-79-8

Warning: This book contains sexually explicit content, which may only be suitable for mature readers, and scenes of graphic violence.

THE CALLING

M.D. Neu

Acknowledgements

This book would not have been possible without the support and encouragement from these amazing people: Linda P., Caroline O., Angela S., Adelene G., Felisa L., Barbara R., Arlo H., William (Bud) H., Matthew D., Teresa F., Steven R., Randall K., Marnie S., Laura S., Jeanette L., Ernesto V., Arthur S.

You guys are fantastic. Thank you.

Chapter One

WHAT IS DEATH?

I once believed there was only one definition: your body stops functioning, your soul leaves and what's left turns to dust. That was what I thought, until it wasn't.

I've discovered when you're a nobody, the world can be an amazing place if you want it to be. Your life can change in a heartbeat and not make the least bit of difference to anyone but you, or so it would seem.

That was my case.

I'm by no means whining or complaining. I had a job, a small place to live, and friends, but no real family, and that was something I desperately missed and wanted. My life wasn't bad and I was happy. However, I was just a random person, one of the many faces you see on the street and never glance at twice. It was dull. Of course, as with me, the majority of society didn't know our world had hidden secrets, unseen by most.

The other important thing I want you to realize about me is that before I met her, I wasn't a lucky man, not with money and certainly not with love. I made enough to live on, but never enough to take fancy trips. My idea of travel was staying at home and watching movies. That was my price range. And as for love, it was forgettable.

The day my life changed was like all the others, until it wasn't. It was August 19. The year isn't important. But we had finished celebrating the Olympics, and in a few short months, the country would be picking between the lesser of two evils for president.

I sat at an outdoor café in Santana Row. I'd spent the afternoon going on a tour of the Winchester Mystery House. Once my stomach had started to growl, I decided to grab a bite to eat.

I had come to San Jose, California for a vacation that I couldn't afford and didn't particularly want to take. Why San Jose? Why not San Francisco or Monterey or Vegas or Yosemite? To be honest, I don't know, but it's like everything inside and around me pulled me there. Out of the blue, I got emails from the San Jose Visitor Bureau. My dreams were filled with images of the city and the surrounding hills and mountains. It seemed that old song, "Do You Know the Way to San Jose" by Dionne Warwick constantly played. Still, San Jose isn't the place most people consider for a ten-day vacation, especially someone alone who had never been to the Bay Area before.

Despite my apprehension, from the moment I arrived, I immediately felt at peace. I'd never been this calm or relaxed anywhere before, not even at home. There was another reason for me coming here, one I didn't understand yet, at least not on a conscious level.

I would find out why soon enough.

I don't want to get things out of order, so back on point. I sat at this Italian-style outdoor café watching people walk by, enjoying the scent of roses and vanilla that filled the air. The aroma tickled the back of my brain. I smelled it everywhere, which should have been my first clue that something was different.

After enjoying my Italian-style chicken marsala, and while I sipped my strawberry lemonade, I felt a sharp pull in my brain. It wasn't like I heard voices—it was more like vague images filled my head: a house, a woman, gardens, a gate, hills covered in trees, and a pair of eyes. My hands shook, and my glass fell to the floor and shattered. An intense pressure grew between my eyes, and I pinched the bridge of my nose to ease it.

When the tug came, three things happened to me at once.

First, I had the realization that I had an important meeting in Los Altos Hills. I had never heard of Los Altos Hills and even had to look it up on my phone to see if it was real. I would have to check my GPS when I returned to my rental. I knew the address of the house and who I was going to meet. She had blonde hair and mysterious eyes. I knew her, but I didn't understand how.

Second, the waiter came to my table.

"Sorry about the drink," I said.

He gave me an odd look and informed me my meal had been paid for and to enjoy my evening. Flabbergasted, I stared at the server.

I glanced around the café and wondered who paid the bill and why. I wasn't even done yet.

"Mr. Alexander, are you all right?" The waiter scanned me up and down. "Do you need me to call someone? You look pale."

"No." I shook my head. "I'm fine."

How did the waiter know my name? Stranger still, when I checked the table, my drink sat there and nothing had fallen to the floor. I wasn't sure what was happening.

"Are you sure?"

"Yes. Sorry. Just a headache," I said.

"All right. I hope you have a pleasant afternoon." He smiled and started to walk off but turned back. "Oh, I almost forgot. I'm supposed to remind you about your meeting tonight."

A lump stuck in my throat, and I nodded. It was spooky, but I wasn't scared.

The last thing: I got a text from my closest friend, Cindy Martin. *Good luck tonight. I'm sure it'll be you.*

I remember thinking, *What does she know that I don't?*

I've known Cindy for years, and for her to say anything that short and sweet was rare. In fact, I don't suppose I ever got a message from her without any emoticons.

As bizarre as all of this was, I realized that no matter what, everything and everyone I cared about would be okay. Clearly, there was something more to this trip and my being here. I didn't know what. But it wasn't just some free meal. It was bigger than that. If I was selected for what? I had no clue. And if I wasn't, then I would get to see them again. There would be no questions.

Part of me wanted to worry, but I wasn't bothered, which in itself surprised me. I've been a pessimist for as long as I can remember. It probably had to do with the strange death of my father when I was a kid. A death never fully explained. So, for this not to make me worry was one more mystery. What was about to happen was something that would just be. Instead of freaking out and worrying, I was calm and accepting of whatever adventure or fate awaited me.

Even though I was short on time to get to the house in Los Altos Hills, I wanted to enjoy my lunch. Reflecting on it now, I'm pretty sure that was the cynical part of my brain trying to exert some kind of control. I took my time, finished my meal, and when I was done, I tipped the server and left.

I walked back to my rental car. I wanted to take in as much of the classical European architecture and lush landscaping of the outdoor mall as I could. I managed to get a few decent cell phone pictures of the place.

I stopped my lollygagging and got moving. I had someplace to be and what appeared to be no choice in the matter. Before you go crazy, understand this wasn't like one of those stupid movies that you watch, shaking your head, yelling at the screen for them not to go into the dark forest or spooky house or whatever. It wasn't like that.

I'd like to hope I'm explaining this well enough so you don't sit there and think, "Oh this is stupid. I'd never do anything that dumb." It wasn't like I had a choice. I had to go—something compelled me to her. I had to meet this woman, calling me. It was hard-wired into me, no matter how much I tried to slow down or stall, I moved forward.

I moved toward her.

When I finally got in the car and took a breath, I wasn't clammy or shaky, and my heart wasn't pounding in my chest. I should have been anxious, but I wasn't. I was fine.

Knowing without understanding what I had to do, I headed to the freeway.

If I had seen into the future, I would have taken a different route, but I didn't. An accident backed up the freeway. Sadly, I found the onboard GPS wasn't as helpful as I'd hoped. It led me straight into bumper-to-bumper traffic. It was a nightmare, and not something I was used to. I sat in four lanes of cars and not a single one moved. What should have taken no more than half an hour was going to take an eternity.

"I'm going to be late," I chanted as I anxiously tapped along to "You and Me" playing on the radio.

A silver Rolls-Royce cut me off, causing me to stop abruptly. My heart skipped a beat. When my breath returned, I tried to find the Rolls, but it seemed to vanish into the traffic.

"Not possible," I grumbled. The radio stopped for a news break.

I hated being late.

The drive along 280 had lush trees and green hills once I got out of the valley, with attractive homes scattered here and there. It was one of the nicer freeways I'd ever been on and nothing like what I saw in Reno. Well, not until you got into the mountains. I took the S. El Monte Avenue exit and headed up into the hills past a junior college. Who knew there'd be a college out this way?

The road curved and turned till I found the house. To call my destination a house is an understatement. Even from the gate, it was a remarkable size. At least two stories, possibly three. It was an architectural masterpiece situated on perfectly landscaped grounds unlike anything I'd ever seen, not even on TV.

At the massive security gate, I pushed the call box button and waited.

"Mr. Alexander, welcome. Please, drive through," a female voice instructed as the iron gates lazily opened.

I briefly questioned how she recognized me, but I figured there was a camera embedded in the call box.

Before me lay a flawless, recently raked gravel drive hedged by lush beds of orange, red, violet, and yellow flowers, all manicured to perfection. Cherry trees lined the drive and added more color and height.

I drove carefully up the drive and pulled into a circular parking area that surrounded a giant fountain. Spiraling topiary shrubs in massive stone containers invited me to the enormous wood doors sheltered in the portico.

I got out, taking in the sight of the house. It was a cream-colored Tudor-style mansion surrounded by what I thought was an English garden filled with hedges and red and white roses. This estate's upkeep had to be more than I made in a year.

There were several other cars parked near mine. It would seem I wasn't the only one invited to this party. I sensed I was the last to arrive and that bothered me. A few cars had rental tags like mine, and the vehicles that weren't rentals were older with dings and dents. Clearly, none of them fit the surroundings of the estate.

A part of my brain screamed at me, "Leave and run away. You don't belong here." But the rest of my mind and my body overruled this impulse and pushed me forward to the main door. I wanted...no I needed to be there.

I was examining the beautiful gold inlaid carvings, perhaps ancient writing with intricate shapes and patterns on the doorframe, when the door opened and a lovely woman stood there. I was awestruck. She had flawless hair and nails, no more than forty years old, and wore a big welcoming smile, revealing a dimple on her left cheek. She was dressed in an expensive, knee-length dark gray skirt with a light blue cashmere sweater emphasizing her breasts. All of it appeared to have been made to her exact measurements.

"Welcome, Duncan. I'm Amanda Sutherland. You're the last to arrive. Please, follow me." Her tone was gracious but tight. I found it annoying because of its implied attitude.

I mumbled an apology and followed her. My annoyance quickly vanished as I crossed the threshold and a wave of peacefulness filled every part of my body, as if I were a crystal glass.

Still, I wanted to redeem myself for being tardy.

I followed Miss Sutherland and was dazzled by what I saw around me. The floors were highly polished wood with marble inlays, and on the walls were old original paintings, not prints. I could see the brush strokes. They were amazing, like something from the middle ages. Very gothic.

They should be in a museum.

Subtle scents of roses and vanilla caused me to inhale deeply as I followed Miss Sutherland deeper into the house. We arrived at a large reception room where there were three men and two women, all of us about the same age and all wearing similar expressions of puzzlement.

Why are we here?

"Madame de Exter will be with you shortly. Please, enjoy some refreshments." Miss Sutherland pointed to a tray of wineglasses held by one of the uniformed house staff. As the server moved around, she offered each of us a smile with the wine. When finished, she put the tray on the sideboard and walked out of the room.

Our reception room was at the back of the house and anything but simple. It would be like calling Hearst Castle another beach house along the California coast. This one room could probably encompass my entire apartment, bedroom and all. The floors were made of a polished stone I didn't recognize, and the walls had wood moldings and trim. Of course there were more original paintings. The furniture appeared modern and comfortable, not the antiques you would imagine for the space. There was a wall of french doors that opened onto more of the perfectly manicured lawn and another fountain. Tucked away in the back of the yard was a smaller house of a similar style to the mansion along with a swimming pool.

It only took Miss Sutherland's absence for us to start talking, trying to pump each other for information.

"Do any of you know why we're here?" A petite Asian woman asked in a stage whisper as she held up her glass of white wine. Her gaze danced around the room and focused on each of us in turn.

I wouldn't call her pretty, but she wasn't ugly either. Then I noticed that the others were all of an average type.

"No clue," a guy replied. He sniffed the wine and hesitated before taking a small sip. "I'm Doug, by the way," he said with a polite nod to the others. Doug was a bit rough-looking with a scruffy face, and dull brown hair that was thinning on top. He was dressed more for manual labor than a party.

"Duncan," I said as I shook his callused hand. He was definitely in construction work.

It's funny the things you remember. How calm his voice was, and that he wore a blue and green flannel shirt, which seemed a little out of place for the time of year.

"Chui." The Asian woman then sipped her wine.

I nodded at her politely. I don't really remember anything more about her, other than her name, and that she was shorter than Doug and me.

"Janis," the other woman said, glancing at the last two men, who hesitated.

Janis had the best looks and the nicest clothes. Her blouse was silk, and the bag she held was older but it had a Gucci label on it. I do remember her eyes, like pools of water that you could get lost in. Not that I did.

"Hi. I'm Juan," a dark-haired, brown-eyed man said.

The last man was taller than any of us. He was also probably the best-looking guy in the room. Ruggedly handsome with a strong chin and perfect jawline. The rich dark tones of his skin made his eyes pop.

"I'm Erik." He waved a hand toward us as his voice lowered. "If you don't mind, where are you all from?"

Erik, it seemed, had noticed what I saw in our unique group. None of us were dressed in what one would consider proper attire for such a house... mansion... whatever.

"Reno," I said, holding my wineglass but not drinking from it. Even though I felt safe and at ease, still part of me was a tiny bit suspicious. I doubted it was drugged, but I wasn't quite comfortable drinking it.

"Here. The Bay Area," Janis said in a tight voice. She continually scanned the room and the doors. That answer was deliberately vague.

"Morgan Hill. Just south of here," Chui said. She didn't seem to mind sharing or drinking the wine. Her glass was already empty.

"I'm from LA." Erik sipped his wine and made a face, then put it down and didn't touch it again.

"Portland." Juan turned to Doug.

"I guess I win. I'm from Denver." Doug smiled. He had an easy grin and perfectly straight and blindingly white teeth. Smiling seemed to come natural to him. "That still doesn't explain why we're here. I don't recognize any of you, and I haven't been to Reno, LA, or Portland." He chuckled. "Hell. I don't know anything about this place or our elusive host, and yet I feel like I've seen this house and this room before."

There were a few nods from the others.

"We've probably all seen homes like this on TV. That's why it seems so familiar," Janis said with a dismissive wave of her hand. "There are a lot of homes like this in the area. It's not that great."

Erik rolled his eyes as he turned to me.

"I don't know. This place is pretty impressive, and that wonderful scent of roses and vanilla..." I commented.

"The what?" Janis asked with raised eyebrows.

"That scent. I've smelled it all day," I said, glancing around the room at the others.

"I can't smell a thing," Erik said.

Chui looked at me. "I think it's the arrangements in the house. I've smelled it since I got here."

Juan shook his head. "I don't know. I have a bad sniffer so I don't smell much."

"I'm with Duncan here," Doug said. "I started smelling the scent on the drive up here, and normally I don't notice that stuff. It got stronger the closer I got to this place."

"What's that have to do with the house and where we're all from?" Erik asked.

"Nothing, I suppose," I said. "Anyway, I've never been to Denver, and this is my first time in San Jose." I tried to figure out what connected us to this place. "Do any of you work in non-profits?" It was a shot in the dark, but one worth taking. I asked, because that's what I did. It wasn't a big non-profit, with only an annual budget of $8 million, but then Reno isn't a huge area, not that it doesn't have its problems. It does, and the need is great. Like everywhere.

Our group of strangers spent the next several minutes talking and trying to connect the dots. The only things we had in common were: we were all single, none of us were particularly important people when it came to our work or social circles—No CEOs or A-Listers among us, not even Janis— and none of us came from large families. In fact, most of us were only children whose parents had passed on. And lastly, we were all simple folk, meaning none of us were wealthy. Janis was the closest to being rich. At best, she was middle class, thanks to her executive assistant job in High Tech, and as I remember, she was fond of throwing around names of designer labels she enjoyed and made a point of pointing out her Gucci bag.

Why were Chui, Doug, and I the only ones to notice the roses and vanilla? Better question, why was I the only one who had smelled the scent all day?

Chapter Two

OUR MERRY BAND of misfits, as I like to reflect back on, continued chatting away. If any of us had paid attention, we would have realized that much of the late afternoon had already vanished.

By the time the hors d'oeuvres arrived, some of the others had enjoyed more of the white wine. We were served mini beef wellingtons with a red wine sauce, chicken skewers with a paste of peanuts, and mini crepes filled with smoked salmon and caviar.

I felt like something was keeping us all under some kind of spell. Of course, that seemed a ridiculous idea at the time.

Regardless, the evening was better than the plans I'd had for going to one of the local bars.

Miss Sutherland remained absent for the duration. The serving staff told us she was helping the host with the final preparation for our late dinner.

We had two staff tending to our needs—a man and a woman, and they were both beautiful and handsomely dressed in perfectly fitted clothes. I couldn't help but be jealous of them. No one should be allowed to be that attractive. It wasn't natural. They had perfect hair and sculpted features and clothes that flattered their perfect bodies. They expertly dodged any of our questions and turned the tables to keep us in check.

Janis asked the male server, "What can you tell me about our host?"

The server smiled at her. "I'm sure Madame de Exter can answer that better than I can."

Janis started to open her mouth to speak but was interrupted.

"I heard you say you're from here. This is such a beautiful part of the country, don't you think? I love being close to the ocean. There's nothing like lying out and catching some sun." His face lit up and his dimples grew deeper.

Janis nodded, then cleared her throat. "Yes. I suppose."

"Please, try a chicken skewer." He winked at her. "The peanut sauce is excellent."

I had to look away from the exchange. Janis never stood a chance.

You would assume we'd have found this all frustrating or annoying, but none of us did. Honestly, it was fun and a bit thrilling. I can't speak for the others, but I assumed that soon enough our questions would be answered.

It's an odd feeling when time slips away from you. It can be jolting and off-putting, especially when you're around people you just met and know so little about. As the shadows in the room grew darker and the wall sconces gradually got brighter, it confused me as to how and why we were all so at ease. When Doug pointed out that the sun had fully set and we had been talking for a couple of hours, our reactions weren't surprise or bewilderment but nonchalant shrugs.

Cutting off any opportunity to question things further, the double doors opened, halting the conversation. Miss Sutherland entered. Instead of her gray suit and light blue sweater, she was now dressed in a black cocktail dress that showed off her curves and hit just below her knees. Her hair was done in some fancy updo style with tendrils framing her soft eyes; it was perfect for a party. She looked amazing, and I suddenly felt underdressed.

The only saving grace was that the rest of the group weren't dressed any better.

"Madame de Exter is ready to meet you," Miss Sutherland said. "She does apologize for the long delay and hopes you will forgive her as she had an emergency that had to be taken care of."

As much as I wanted to be bothered by us being held in this reception room, I wasn't. All I really desired was to meet her.

Erik summed it up for all of us. "These things happen." His gaze washed over Miss Sutherland, paying close attention to her ample cleavage.

"Indeed, they do," Miss Sutherland said and turned to face us all. "Please, follow me."

Like good boys and girls, we did as we were told. As I passed the spot where she had stood, I picked up the light, clean floral scent of her perfume.

We walked into a grand dining room with a highly reflective wooden table laid out with gold flatware and china that screamed ancient and delicate. The flatware shone like solid gold and the crystal stemware sparkled like diamonds. A centerpiece filled with roses, orchids, intricate small branches, and greenery was arranged around a beautiful candelabrum.

A crackling fire burned in the hearth. Like everything else in this room, the picture of perfect. The walls were covered in a rich walnut paneling. In any other room, it would have made the space dark and oppressive, but here, with the fire burning and the soft warm lighting, it made the room cozy.

At the head of the table, our hostess, Madame de Exter, stood, watching us. I'd never seen anyone like her before, and my body tingled with excitement.

"Welcome to you all." Madame de Exter waved both her hands in a flourish, pointing to both sides of the table. Her dark blonde hair appeared effortlessly swept up with a few strands falling softly to the sides of her face. She appeared young—about my age, maybe early thirties. Instead of being covered in jewels and makeup, she had a natural, timeless beauty about her. She had the most piercing eyes I had ever seen. She wore an elegant cocktail dress, deep emerald in color, which flattered her skin tone perfectly. "Please join me at the table." Each of her movements was precise and seemed planned out, just like everything else had been.

We moved to our seats, which had name cards and a small menu of the meal set out. Again, the wonderful scent of vanilla and roses struck me.

We all glanced around in silence. I didn't touch a thing. I stood there, my hands at my sides, and didn't move. I caught the eye of Miss Sutherland, and she smiled at me.

"Please sit." Madame de Exter slid gracefully into her seat. "I want to thank Amanda for taking such good care of you whilst I was detained this afternoon." She lifted one of the four crystal glasses at her place setting to Amanda, and we checked to make sure we grabbed the same as our hostess. "To Amanda," Madame de Exter said, and we all repeated the toast, then took sips of white wine.

Miss Sutherland nodded.

"I'm sure you all must have questions for me, and it would be rude of me not to do my best to answer them." Madame de Exter put her glass down. "I won't be able to answer everything, of course, but I'll do my best." She beamed at each of us and then again picked up her glass of white wine, enjoying another sip. She focused her attention on me. "Duncan, I'm sure you must have a question or two?"

My face heated, but I nodded. Just like in school, I hated being called on first, but unlike school, I couldn't shrug it off and not answer. I glanced around the table and found everyone watching me.

My palms were sweating, so I took a breath, turned to our hostess, and asked, "How do you know us?"

Her face became thoughtful for a moment, glancing down to the end of the table at Miss Sutherland. "I don't wish for this to sound alarming, but we've been familiar with all of you for quite some time. We've been, in a way, watching you and waiting." She smiled and added, "I understand how it sounds, however, I see no reason to lie about it."

My heart jumped at her bluntness. It was the only explanation that made any sense to me. You don't arbitrarily summon people to your home, especially a home like this, without vetting them.

"You mean you've been spying on us?" Janis asked, her tone sharp, cutting the air in the room.

Since I had arrived, Janis seemed the most uncomfortable and appeared to be the most guarded and unsure of what was happening. Even at that moment, with the rest of us seemingly at ease, she sat with her arms crossed in front of her.

"In a manner of speaking," Madame de Exter replied. "Please, understand it was done from afar and consisted of nothing more than knowing about you and keeping track of what was happening in your life for the last few months. It is much like what anyone would find out about you on one of the social media sites." I sensed the honesty pouring from her as she justified her comments.

I found myself in agreement. I wasn't crazy about the idea of being watched, but considering what we put out there on social media for the world to see, I can't say I was surprised. I remember Cindy and I goofing around one day at work. We checked out each of our names and what came up amazed us.

Once the first question was asked, it broke the ice, and shoulders relaxed around me. Erik and Juan even leaned in closer to Madame de Exter. Chui sipped her wine, almost finishing it off, but stopping just short of an empty glass.

"How can you explain why we all wanted to come here?" Juan leaned in on his elbows. "I mean, I suddenly wanted to take this week off and come here for a vacation. How is that even possible? I don't travel, yet here I am." His attention landed on each of the women in the room. "Not that I mind." He smiled, facing Madame de Exter, then Miss Sutherland. "I mean, you and Miss Sutherland are lovely."

There was a huff from Janis.

Madame de Exter offered a polite half smile. "Thank you, Mr. Herrera. That is kind of you to say. With respect to your question, it requires a much more complicated explanation, and sadly, I'm not able to do it justice tonight." She thought for a moment, frowning at the flustered look on his face. She took a small breath. "I suppose, you can look at it much like a beacon that was sent out, and you answered the call. Does that help?"

He pursed his lips.

It wasn't that the answer was insufficient; the idea of it sounded impossible.

"What about today?" I started. "I was at a late lunch, and the waiter comes to me and tells me lunch is paid for, and he wants to remind me of a meeting I had to be at. What about that? He even knew my name?" Out of everything, even with what I'd been hearing at the table, that question bothered me most. Several of them nodded their heads in agreement.

A small chuckle came from Miss Sutherland at the opposite end of the table, and Madame de Exter had a hint of a benign smile. "That mystery is easier to solve. I told Amanda where she could locate you all today, and she placed the calls. If calls needed to be placed."

"So you really were spying on us." Doug put down his wineglass, his jaw set.

"You know, there are laws to protect people from things like this. We could report you and Miss Sutherland to the authorities," Chui said with a frown on her red face. Janis had a similar hostile look. The women of our group were less susceptible to our hostess's charms.

Doug rolled his eyes and Erik stifled a chuckle. Clearly, they didn't mind the attention. Both men had been eyeing our hostesses in a way that said if either were to suddenly offer them a night of lovemaking, they wouldn't turn it down.

With a heavy sigh, Juan turned to Madame de Exter. "So then, why are we here? Did we do something? What's the deal?" I found him thoughtful and patient. He didn't strike me as the type to ask questions without thinking them over first.

With a warm smile, Madame de Exter grinned, almost pleased. "I was wondering when that question would be asked and of course by whom." She nodded to Miss Sutherland, who stood up and glided over to the heavy doors, opposite those we had entered. They must have led into a different part of the house. She knocked softly as we all watched. Within seconds, it opened and one of the servers stood holding a tray with cream-colored envelopes.

Miss Sutherland whispered something I couldn't hear to the man, and he nodded as she took the envelopes from him. She made her way back to the table and handed each of us an envelope. I ran my fingers over my embossed name in gold leaf. I'd never seen anything that fancy before.

"Please, open the envelopes." Madame de Exter said, a gracious wave of her hand.

I examined my envelope, flipping it over in my hands before opening it. The gold leaf had to be real, and on the back, a blue wax seal held it closed. The seal had a highly detailed image of a dragon sitting on a rock formation. I stared at it for a long moment before breaking the seal and opening the envelope. Inside was a matching cream note card, embossed with the same gold leaf. It was thrilling. I pulled out the note and read the message:

Thank you, Mr. Duncan Alexander. You have been selected to receive this enclosed award. We appreciate all your dedicated work at St. Elizabeth's Family Services in Reno. It is our hope that this small gift will make your life a little easier—Lumière D'espoir Foundation.

I saw the check next and just about fell out of my chair. It was triple my annual salary. A check this large had never had my name on it. I scanned the others; everyone was focused on their checks.

What the catch was and why this gift was for us?

Chapter Three

I GLANCED AT the others as I fumbled with my surprise check. Erik was laughing. Doug and Juan were both giddily chatting about how they wanted to spend the money. Thanks to the awards, the mood of the room shifted from frowns and stiff posture to laughing and pleasant banter. Amazing what a big fat check will do. Even Chui and Janis were smiling and drinking.

No one else seemed to question the award, and for a moment, I thought it odd. I wanted to know about this award. Who nominated me and how they picked the winners, but the thoughts vanished from my mind.

It seemed we each won this exclusive award in our fields. It wasn't clear as to who nominated us, but apparently, it was a little-known award, which would explain why I hadn't heard of it or this Lumière D'espoir Foundation.

All our reactions to the award appeared to be the same, which surprised me. Pleased expressions circled the table. The small part of my brain that kept me from drinking the red wine at first wasn't pleased, but I quickly shut it down. Were we all programmed to be polite, calm, respectful, and relaxed? How is that possible, unless something managed to be put in the food and wine? What struck me was that I seemed to be the only one that noticed. Maybe, it's because I wasn't as impressed with the money as the others. Growing up, we didn't have a lot. My father's mystery death when I was younger left me and Mom living on the cheap. So, the idea of money was nice, but it never motivated me.

I remained quiet and polite, but my mind filled with questions that my mouth didn't seem interested in expressing. Why us? What's so special about these people? How come none of us had heard of this award? That didn't explain the way I or the others happened to be called here. So, I smiled and watched the happy conversation.

As with the hors d'oeuvres, the dinner was amazing. It was a full nine-course meal with a different wine pairing for each one. For starters, we had a champagne toast and an amuse-bouche of halved quail eggs with a cream cheese and salmon mousse topped with Russian caviar. Followed by white wine paired with chilled avocado soup and halibut in lemon-butter sauce. Then we had a sorbet pallet cleanser. Bordeaux accompanied our filet mignon and cheese dish, capped with Sauternes to accompany tiny and elegant pastries/petit fours. I had never eaten like this in my life, and I couldn't even wrap my head around what a meal like this must have taken to pull off.

None of the casino restaurants in Reno aspired to such high levels of dining. The food was expensive, with large portions, and served fast. Diners were never encouraged to linger when slot machines and blackjack tables sat idle.

When the dinner came to an end, I found myself sad. It occurred to me that this meal had been a singular experience, not available anywhere else, even with my newfound prize money, which would go to bills and possibly a new car. I thought about my father's death again and how that went unsolved. Maybe now there was something I could do.

There wasn't a lot of chitchat after the meal, at least not from me.

I kept replaying how nice the evening had been and how it would be amazing to continue. I thought about how boring and plain my life had been, and how a larger world sat right outside my window and I never reached for it. Allowing it to pass me by. Have you ever wanted to replay an event because it was so wonderful? I wasn't envious or jealous, but every time I thought about leaving, my stomach lurched and the back of my neck tensed up.

I wanted to be there, where I belonged.

As Madame de Exter and Miss Sutherland thanked everyone for attending, Miss Sutherland gave everyone her business card just in case we had future questions.

At the front of the house, while everyone else was excited about their award and talking about going home and spending the money, my body dragged. My feet barely lifting off the floor as I walked. I didn't care about what was happening at the front door.

Even though I'd have to pay the taxman a big chunk, I appreciated everything and understood this would help me out once I got home. I had another thought of maybe paying a private investigator to dig into my father's death. See if I could find out what really happened. I'd never thought I would have this option until that night.

"Well, this money is really going to help," Doug said to Miss Sutherland.

"I'm glad to hear it." Miss Sutherland replied.

Doug laughed, a big smile on his face.

Miss Sutherland walked him up to Madame de Exter. He was the last to leave before me.

Distracted by the art and the architectural details of the house, I looked down at the envelope again. "This is it," I mumbled. I was finding it difficult to smile. I guess that was what Miss Sutherland noticed when she walked over to me. I was taking one final look around the grand entry hall as Madame de Exter spoke with Doug.

"Mr. Alexander, Madame de Exter has asked if you wouldn't mind staying for a little while longer," Miss Sutherland said. "She is very impressed with your work and would like to ask you a few more questions."

When I peeked up from the envelope in my hands, a dark shadow covered Miss Sutherland. And I heard the little voice inside my head yell, "No. Don't do it. Run."

I ignored it.

I tried for an appreciative smile. Miss Sutherland escorted me down the hall to another room.

I entered a smaller room with bookcases, two cream-colored sofas, and off to the side, a small oak desk with high-back chair. I decided it must be a drawing room, because not enough books lined the walls to be considered a library. Another marble fireplace filled the room with a warm glow. Red-velvet ottomans flanked the fireplace. Above the fireplace hung another painting, this one a countryside still with the intriguing gothic/renaissance feel to it. The windows had floor-to-ceiling drapes and under the arranged sitting area lay an antique rug, pulling all the colors of the room together. In the background, hints of roses and vanilla filled the air.

"Please have a seat. Madame de Exter will be with you shortly." Miss Sutherland walked over to a decorative golden cart. "May I offer you a drink?"

"No thank you," I replied. "I've hit my limit for the night. I don't normally drink that much." I found a seat near the fire where the warmth radiated out.

"Then some coffee or tea?"

I thought for a minute. If I wanted this fantasy to continue, perhaps having coffee would be a good idea.

"All right, coffee. Thank you." I leaned back, letting my body be absorbed by the soft cushions.

"Very good. I'll have one as well." Miss Sutherland walked to the door. Like magic, there was one of the staff, holding a golden tray with both coffee and tea service.

The woman sauntered in, put the tray down, and poured two cups of coffee.

"Thank you, Elena," Miss Sutherland said.

Elena smiled and quickly exited the room, closing the door behind her.

"How do you take your coffee, Mr. Alexander?" Miss Sutherland pointed to the cream and sugar.

"Both cream and sugar please," I replied. "I prefer my coffee sweet, but I can do that." I leaned forward and started to fix my coffee.

Miss Sutherland took her cup and saucer and sat across from me.

"It won't be long." She took a sip. "Did you enjoy your evening?"

I tasted the coffee and smiled. "This was, without a doubt, the best night of my life." I took another sip of the coffee. The warmth filled my throat, and I chuckled. "Tonight has been a real treat. To be honest, the money will be helpful." I thought of all my bills and this little trip. "Very helpful."

"Wonderful," Miss Sutherland said. "Clearly, your selection was a good one." She faced the door a second before it opened and Madame de Exter entered the room.

"Ah, Mr. Alexander, is Amanda taking good care of you?" Madame de Exter gracefully crossed the room and found a seat before I could stand.

"Oh yes, thank you," I replied, allowing myself to dip back into the softness of the chair. "This whole night has been wonderful. I can't thank you enough, or the Foundation. It's too much. Miss Sutherland mentioned you wanted to ask me some questions about my job?"

Madame de Exter grinned at Miss Sutherland and turned back to me. "I've been impressed with you this evening, Duncan. I hope you don't mind me calling you Duncan?"

Pleased that she wanted to use my first name, a large grin filled my face.

She continued, "I knew from the moment you entered the dining room it would be you. I recognized the pull." She grinned. "I suspect you know what I mean."

"Excuse me?" I actually did understand what she meant.

Her gaze never left mine. "You've felt a connection here, comfortable, like this is the place you wanted to be, correct?"

I wasn't going to lie. "I suppose. I mean, sure, who wouldn't? You have an amazing home and everything is so extravagant and comfortable. How can one not feel connected to this place and to you?"

Miss Sutherland chuckled softly.

"It's not that I'm envious or anything." I leaned forward earnestly. "I know you must have worked hard to have all this. It's wonderful of you to be willing to share it, especially with all of us and mostly with me."

Stop talking! I forced my mouth to shut.

Madame de Exter's beautiful face suddenly seemed to carry a great weight. "Who could ask for a better response?" A playful, mischievous grin transformed her face. "Duncan, would you like this adventure to continue?"

"What?" I was confused by the offer. For the night? What exactly did she mean by this? I tried to pick up my coffee cup, but my hands were shaking and I gave up before I spilled anything or, worse, broke the cup or saucer.

"Tonight wasn't about the awards, Duncan." Madame de Exter watched me more carefully. "But, I suspect you figured that out already."

I suddenly felt like I understood. Why I didn't want to leave. Why I had a hard time walking to the main door with the others. Why I was the only one to smell the roses and the vanilla all day. Why I was so comfortable with everything happening around me.

Madame de Exter sat back in her chair and shifted her feet to the side as her hands rested one on top of the other on her thigh. "Tonight was about me finding someone. Someone I need...someone like you." Her gaze never faltered.

"Need? Me? How do you need me?"

Miss Sutherland cleared her throat. "You were right." Amusement filled her voice.

"I'm sorry, Madame de Exter. I'm very confused. What's happening here?"

"Amanda, please." Madame de Exter didn't face Miss Sutherland. Instead, she adjusted how she sat to move closer to me and her voice was calm and filled with warmth. "Please, Duncan, call me Juliet. The prospect is simple. I'm looking for a protégé, of sorts, and I trust you are the man for the job. I can promise it will be unlike anything you've ever done. It will open up a whole new world to you."

"I... uh... I already have a job." My heart skipped a beat.

"One that does not challenge nor particularly interest you."

How does she know that?

"Is the job you offer dangerous?"

Her delicate hand waved a few times. "It's possible but highly unlikely. However, there are risks. I won't lie."

"I try to avoid difficult situations."

"I know."

"Would I have to move here?"

"Of course." Her gaze still on me. "You'd get to live here. In this house."

I gulped and glanced around the room, the warmth of the fire and scent of the roses and vanilla filled my body with giddy excitement.

"But... um... I don't know anyone here. What about my friends back home?"

"I'll introduce you to people, and you already know Amanda and me."

I was so overwhelmed that I couldn't find any more questions to ask.

"There will, of course, be challenges," Juliet added. "You'll need to learn a lot, but I don't foresee that being a problem, assuming you're interested."

I knew this was a big deal for her. I don't know how I knew, but I knew it. It was something new, however she had a face full of determination. I recognized in no way was this sexual in nature. So, as I saw it, I had two options: play it safe and leave or step out of my habits and take a chance.

I decided to take the money and run. For the first time that day, my body and mind were in 100 percent agreement. I was going to pass up on what was behind door number two. There was too much about this situation that made me uncomfortable.

I stood and faced both Juliet and Miss Sutherland. "I want to thank you for all this; the wonderful evening, the generous award, and the gracious offer."

I took a breath, not moving.

They studied me carefully.

"When do I start?"

Chapter Four

FOR REASONS I could not understand, I agreed to take the job, internship, or whatever it might turn out to be. I still had no idea. What I knew so far was this wouldn't be simple. It wouldn't involve protecting Juliet, although there would be potential danger. I assumed the danger could come from travel, but no one said. And I would probably not get to see my friends often. As enticing as I found it all, something wasn't right, but for some reason, it didn't matter. Every time something made me worry or feel uneasy, it was like the idea was plucked from my mind and flicked away.

So I remained oddly relaxed.

Miss Sutherland and Madame de Exter told me, once I settled into the house, things would become clear and make sense. They wanted me to trust the process. As such, I hadn't left the estate since my arrival four days before. My bags had been brought to the house, my bill at the hotel settled, and my rental car returned. Everything was taken care of.

Amanda reminded me this was my new home, at least during my orientation and training. I was to drop the "Miss Sutherland" and "Madame de Exter" and refer to them as Amanda and Juliet. I even had a vehicle at my disposal. Adam, one of the house staff, showed me to a pristine 1955 Ford Thunderbird, a cheery apple red beauty with a white hard top. It was cool, and I wanted to drive the car but was terrified to scratch it. So, I sat in the car once but didn't drive it.

Most of the time, Amanda had been the one to spend time with me. Juliet was busy with prior Foundation engagements and would see me when she had a break in her calendar. According to Amanda, my position was new for Juliet as well.

I'll admit I was fine with the downtime. I enjoyed the hospitality, and I relished being in the house and the grounds. It was like a luxury resort I would never be able to afford.

Amanda remained vague on how long the orientation at the house would be, but I didn't mind. Why should I? The house was nicer than any place I had ever lived, so this was a hardship I was happy to deal with. And the food was just as good as it had been on the night of the party, albeit not as fancy.

Amanda had only vague answers to my questions about salary and benefits. When I brought it up, she would smile in her welcoming way and say Juliet would go over all of that. I should have been annoyed, but if I was, the feeling quickly vanished from my mind.

So mostly I got to unwind and enjoy. I figured that technically I was still on vacation, so why not? I wasn't worried about a thing, even though deep down I knew I should be.

Then I got a message from my friend Cindy. Cindy is the ying to my yang so to speak. Whenever I'm down, she's right there to cheer me up. So when I looked at the text on my cell, I was a little surprised.

Good luck and much love—Cindy

That was all it said. The only reason I didn't text her or even call her back at that moment was because, when the phone chirped, Amanda, almost on cue, walked through the french patio doors and came out to join me.

"Are you enjoying the afternoon, Duncan?" Amanda sat down next to me under the umbrella.

It was a warm sunny day, and Amanda was dressed in yet another tailored skirt suit in a pastel pink-peach color.

I took in the beautiful yard, and then I glanced at my smartphone again. "I am, but I'm starting to feel forgotten." I tried to sort out my thoughts while getting my point across. "I don't mean any disrespect, but you know, when do I start?"

"Forgotten? Definitely not." Amanda offered a bright smile. "You've already started. You've been on the payroll since you agreed the other night. Juliet wanted to give you ample time to get acquainted with the house, the grounds, and the staff. There is no need to rush into things." She chuckled. "Juliet is patient and never likes to hurry, even when pushed."

"What do you mean 'on the payroll'?" I was surprised. "I haven't signed anything, and we haven't talked about money or my salary. After I agreed, Juliet smiled and left, and you showed me to my room and said good night." I pushed my tea away. I needed to take a breath before I started to yell, assuming I still could. "I've pretty much been on my own ever since. How could I possibly be on the payroll?"

This flustered me because even though I wasn't impressed by money, it was still important. I had always struggled to keep my head above water, financially speaking. I didn't make much money, and I didn't have anyone who could help me out. I was alone.

"You can't just make decisions like that without telling me." The words came out harsher than I wanted them to, but I had bills to pay and, even if I was going to move out there, the credit card companies still wanted their money.

"Of course," Amanda said after several long silent moments. "We never thought...." She shook her head. "I could see how that would be confusing for you, but Duncan, please understand this wasn't done to hurt you in any way. Juliet has nothing but the best intentions when it comes to your well-being. She—well, we assumed that you wouldn't want to have a lapse in your income, so she put you on salary immediately. In all honesty, it's more like a stipend to keep you afloat. Nothing is set in stone, of course, and if you're unhappy with the salary, it can easily be adjusted." She smiled brightly. That always seemed to be her fallback.

My face and neck grew hot. "Ah...um, in that case, sorry." That was about all I could say. I felt like a jerk. I'd been treated so well. The staff and everyone, including Amanda, had been nothing but wonderful to me.

"No harm done." Amanda flipped the few loose strands of hair off her neck, grinning. "I've spoken with Juliet and scheduled a meeting for the two of you for later this evening, once she returns from the office." She stood up, flattening the few wrinkles on her skirt while she viewed the yard. The sun shone down on the ground, filling it with a happy glow.

"Have you gone for a swim in the pool?" Amanda asked.

I was still seated. I should have stood, but I forgot.

"Um no." I wasn't overly comfortable with my body and swimsuits seemed to show more than I cared to reveal.

"You should," Amanda said. "It's very relaxing, and you'll have it all to yourself this afternoon. It's wonderful for swimming laps." She pointed to the pool. "There are men's Speedos in the pool house along with towels."

"Speedos?"

Amanda chuckled. "There's no one around. You could swim nude if you prefer."

"I don't think...." My neck was on fire again.

Amanda winked at me.

I pursed my lips.

"You'll find a new business suit in your room." Amanda started back to the main house. "If you don't mind wearing that for your meeting with Juliet this evening, that would be lovely."

I sat quietly for several minutes, staring where Amanda departed. "A new suit," I muttered with a slight shake of my head.

Everything seemed to be moving so fast and yet at the same time nothing seemed to be happening. I reread the message from Cindy and muttered. "Perhaps, I'll wait until after tonight to respond."

It was possible, after tonight, I would be on my way home because I decided this wasn't for me. It's funny to think of all the lies we tell ourselves. I knew I wouldn't call Cindy later that night. I didn't want to call her. If I called, the dream would be over. I would wake up and be back in my dull, boring life with nothing exciting or adventurous waiting for me. None of this was in my mind at the time. It was only later that I came to understand this about myself.

ONCE I MADE my way back to my room, I found the suit bag on the bed. My room was on the second floor and would be considered a master suite by any standard. It had a king-size bed opposite a stone fireplace. There was a private sitting area with a desk, a laptop, and tablet for my use. The room had a walk-in closet that was bigger than my master bedroom back in my Reno apartment.

The bathroom had granite everything and was clearly designed after some fancy spa because it was beautiful. The shower was a doorless walk-in with a pebble base and solid slab marble walls. There was a full soaking tub with fancy wood accents. All the windows in my bathroom and bedroom had views of the hills and the trees. It was incredibly picturesque.

Off the sitting room, I could walk onto a small balcony that gave way to all the nature around the house. I hoped I could sit out there at some point, possibly even have breakfast or afternoon tea. I laughed.

I walked over to the bed and ran my hand across the suit bag before picking it up. I didn't understand why I needed to wear a suit, but considering it was her house and this was my first official meeting with Juliet, it made sense. She wanted me to play the part and I assumed the new suit would fit my role.

I opened up the bag and pulled out the pants and jacket. There was a small box, which I opened and found gold with onyx cuff links. I wasn't a big suit guy—they all seemed the same to me. I did understand, though, that this was not just any suit. It was expensive. The woolen material softer than anything I could think of, and the colors were dark earth tones, which I appreciated. The Italian shirt and tie complemented the brown tones of the suit.

My foot hit a box, and I glanced down. "Of course." I bent over to pick up the box and opened it to see my new shoes. Polished leather dress shoes with some Italian name I didn't know. A sigh escaped my mouth. "She doesn't mess around."

A knock at the door pulled my attention away. I put everything down and walked closer. "Yes."

"Mr. Alexander," a male voice said. He had a French accent that I quickly picked up on.

I opened the door to find a medium-sized man, older than me. He had a round face and dark thinning hair. He was dressed in a beautiful navy suit with bow tie and pocket square.

"I'm sorry to interrupt you. My name is Fredrick Bisset. I'm here to make alterations to your suit. I was told I would find you here. Is this a good time?" He held a small case in his hand.

"Uh, sure." I moved aside to let him into the room. "Have you been waiting long?"

"Not long, sir," Mr. Bisset replied. "If you don't mind, please, try on everything, and I'll mark it up so we can make the final alterations."

He seemed all business, and I wasn't in any position to decline his request. I was playing by the house rules and this was all part of the deal.

I grabbed everything off the bed.

Fredrick crossed to the window and opened up his case on the desk.

I went into the bathroom, changed out of my comfy jeans and short-sleeved button-down shirt, and put on the new clothes. There was no reason to worry about the tie; it seemed to be standard, so I left it on the counter. I did slip on the socks and the shoes. Overall, the fit was good. I checked the mirror and was rather impressed with myself.

I walked out of the bathroom. Fredrick stood by the window.

"Mr. Bisset, I don't think I'll need you." I ran my hand over the material. This was a nice suit. "Everything seems to fit good."

Fredrick turned and studied the clothes. Then he clucked his tongue. "You're not a tailor," Mr. Bisset said. "Please, if you don't mind coming over here, I'll start the mark-ups."

Again, who was I to deny him his livelihood?

"Do you work here at the estate?" I asked as he helped me out of the jacket and pulled at the shirt and the sleeves.

"No, I work in town at the Los Altos Beaux Vêtements," Mr. Bisset replied, making a few notes on his pad. "Madame de Exter has a standing house account." There was a sharp tug on the back of my shirt. He pulled in the sides to get rid of some of the extra fabric.

"Do you mind?" Mr. Bisset moved me over to stand in front of the mirror on the other side of the desk. Once he had me in position, he made a few marks, checking the mirror, tilting his head back and forth, examining how things fit.

"Now the jacket." He helped me back into it.

Fredrick pulled and tugged and adjusted the material, putting pins in places as well as using marking chalk. It was odd having someone fuss about me like this. I found it unnerving and strangely a lot of work, so I started talking.

"Mr. Bisset...."

"Fredrick, please," Fredrick said.

"All right, Fredrick, is there going to be an issue with getting this back today? I'm meeting with Juliet." I stopped. "I mean, Madame de Exter, and she's requested I wear this."

"I'll have plenty of time." Fredrick paused. "Miss Sutherland has already informed me of the deadline. Do not worry." His French accent danced through the words as he went back to his work.

He made more marks and then stopped. "Take off the jacket, please."

I stood as he circled me, checking my pants. I thought they fit fine, but clearly Fredrick did not. He shook his head and kneeled, marking the length of my pants and then pinned them so that the hem was perfectly set with my shoes.

"The length will be fine, but I'm not happy with the crotch or your bum." He tapped his lips.

"Um...sorry." I wasn't sure what to say to that. I wasn't sure if I should be insulted or not.

"We will make this work," he said, more to himself, and walked behind me. "I'm going to touch you. Do not be worried." He started patting my rear end, pulling the material, and making more marks. With his hand pinching the fabric between my legs, he said, "I need to remove some of the fabric here, or these will not lie right."

I could hear the frown in his voice.

"Will there be time?" I repeated my concern. I didn't know why I was so worried. The trousers seemed fine, but as Fredrick had told me, "you're not a tailor." Clearly this mattered a great deal to him. And Fredrick's nervousness was rubbing off on me because, to my surprise, I found it mattered to me.

"Of course, plenty of time." He faced me.

I began to get a little uncomfortable because he stood there tapping his lip and glaring at the front of my pants. He clucked his tongue.

It doesn't matter who you are. When you have someone standing there examining your crotch, it's nerve-racking. I couldn't take the staring and had to say something. "Is everything all right?"

Fredrick nodded, his attention finally removed from my crotch. "Yes, everything will be fine. I'll need to adjust the inseam so that your pants will lie flat and not make you look *poofy*."

I exhaled.

"Yes, it'll be fine," Fredrick repeated. "You can go change. I'll have the clothes back to you in a couple of hours." He turned, jotted down his notes, then put his tape measure, chalk, notepad, and pencil away.

When I returned from the bathroom with the clothes on their hangers as best as I could, Fredrick was waiting patiently.

"The store will have your measurements on file." Fredrick took the clothes from me. "You'll be able to come in any time and order custom clothing. Or call us and tell us what you're looking for."

"Thank you."

"Or you can pick from what we have in the store," Fredrick added. "We'll be able to alter anything you like and then all you need to do is come in for a final fitting. It'll be much smoother the next time." He gave a professional nod. "I'll bring these back, and we can check the fit when I return."

"Okay. See you in a little while," I said, and Mr. Fredrick Bisset left my room with the suit.

I needed a swim.

AMANDA, DRESSED IN a peach suit, stood waiting at the base of the main staircase.

"Don't you look handsome?" Amanda said.

The suit made me feel like a million bucks and even managed to improve the appearance of my ass. Mr. Bisset really knew his stuff.

"I'm sure Juliet will be pleased. You'll want to go down to Mr. Bisset's shop and pick out a few additional suits and some casual clothes. You'll find that Juliet likes her—" She stopped and tapped her lip a moment. "She likes us all to look our best at all times."

"I see."

"Mr. Bisset's staff are wonderful to work with." She spun around, and I caught another whiff of her light, clean, and fruity perfume. "Everything I own comes from him. They can either order or recreate just about anything you see in a magazine or online."

I stepped off the landing.

"Please, follow me, and I'll take you to Juliet's office."

We walked down the main hall to a section of the house I had not yet seen. Much like the other rooms in the mansion, the space had polished stone floors and deep wood panels all around. A few more paintings hung on the wall. The house always had a wonderful scent of roses and vanilla.

Amanda fussed with an impressive arrangement sitting on a round table under a skylight. "Juliet loves fresh flowers, so the staff makes sure there are always ample roses and orchids in the house."

"The florist in town must love you," I said as Amanda pulled out a white rose, sniffed it, and put it back in a different spot.

"I believe we're their largest client." She winked.

Amanda and I walked the rest of the way down the hall. She knocked softly on a magnificent deep rich walnut door with intricately patterned inlays.

"Please come in," Juliet called.

Amanda opened the door and stopped short of walking in. Juliet smiled at me as I stepped into the office, and Amanda closed the door behind me.

"Duncan, welcome. I'm finishing up." She stood and pointed to a chair in front of her desk, then turned back to her work.

I took in the room as I made my way over to Juliet's desk. In an alcove to the right sat a big oval glass conference table, fresh roses filled a crystal vase in the middle of the table, and chairs circled it. On the wall behind the table stood several bookcases, holding books with tattered covers and barely legible titles. The bookcases flanked a large picture window with heavy curtains in a deep royal blue.

Juliet stood behind a medium-sized wrap-around built-in desk and workstation. It had been made from exquisitely crafted wood. As I studied it, I realized it appeared to be cut from one piece of wood. Wing chairs were placed in front of it. A computer, office phone, and binders filled the space behind her.

The desk held a few knickknacks, paper, and pens. A candle, with no scent that I could smell, burned beneath a melting tray. Considering how modern everything else was, I found it a little out of place.

To the other side of the room, a fireplace crackled, giving the room a nice glow. A sofa and small coffee table sat in front of the fireplace and to the side rested a pedestal with a large shallow emerald container filled with white orchids. The room had a much stronger scent of roses and vanilla than the rest of the house.

Juliet took her seat to finish what she was working on and repeated, "Please, sit."

Dumbly, I stood there as she signed the letter and folded it, then put it in a cream-colored envelope—the same kind we'd gotten when we came here for dinner. Juliet then poured some melted wax over the envelope flap and pressed the seal to close it. She saw me observing.

"Sometimes the old ways are the best." Juliet put the sealed letter with several others. "Or at least the most stylish." I noticed for the first time a slight accent in her voice, similar to Mr. Bisset's. She moved the letters to the side of her desk to be picked up and delivered.

"I'm guessing the post office won't be delivering those." I remained standing.

"No not those. Why don't we sit there?" She pointed to the sofa in front of the fire, then stood and walked to seating area. On the coffee table. a gold serving tray sat with a bottle of red wine and crystal glasses. "Something to drink?" she offered, pouring herself a glass of red wine.

I shook my head. I wasn't so sure that was really red wine.

"I hope you're happy with the suit. Fredrick is highly skilled." She sipped her wine. "Please have a seat."

My brain was slow to process my surroundings. Juliet had already asked me repeatedly to have a seat, and it was finally sinking in that I should sit down.

She raised her glass again and took a sip, watching me.

"Thanks for the suit. It was very kind of you." I sat on the sofa, facing the fire as it crackled and popped. A fire always burned in the common rooms of the house even though it was August. But the house never seemed hot or overly warm, it was always comfortable.

Juliet tapped the rim of her wineglass with her finger. "What do you know of myths?"

"You mean like ancient Greece or ancient Rome? Like their gods? Zeus and all that?" I wasn't sure where this was going, and mythology wasn't my strongest point.

"Well, those are one kind of myth." She paused. "But I mean things like the supernatural?" She watched me carefully.

"I never gave it much thought. I mean, I guess there might be ghosts out there. It's a big world, and I don't imagine we know everything. I've seen some of the videos, and it's hard to believe that they're *all* fakes."

"So would you say you have a healthy skepticism?"

I nodded. I still wasn't sure where this was going. Maybe, Juliet and Amanda were some kind of rich ghost hunters or something. "Well, I guess since I personally haven't seen anything strange happen, then, yes, I guess I'm skeptical."

"Good, that's a fair answer." Juliet snickered. "What are your thoughts on incubi and succubi?"

I laughed.

"Please, Duncan, indulge me."

"I've never given them any thought. I know they're fantasy, not real."

Juliet smiled. "And vampires?"

"I'm sorry. What does this have to do with why I'm here, what I'll be doing? Are you some kind of folklorist or researcher into myths?"

"Are you a religious man?"

"I believe in God," I replied with complete certainty. I didn't follow any one faith, well not since my mother passed away. "I was raised Catholic."

"You believe God created Heaven and the Earth and even Hell." Juliet put her glass down on the coffee table. "He created man and the angels, including the devil and demons. So, wouldn't it be possible that he created other creatures as well?" She paused, taking several breaths. "As you said, this is a large world. Is there no room for the likes of those creatures?"

I chuckled until I got a glimpse of Juliet. Her face was flat with a thin serious smile. I inhaled and found myself standing up. "I'm sorry, Juliet. I'm not..." I stopped and thought. "Listen, if you're looking for a research assistant or someone to help you find these creatures, I'm not—well, I'm not the right guy. I don't know any more about them than what I've seen on TV and in the movies."

Juliet picked up her wineglass again, took a sip, and when she faced me, I felt her stare blazing into me. It was uncomfortable, like I was being examined.

"Duncan, I'm not searching for anything. Well, not in that regard." She stood and gave my shoulder a soft squeeze, easing my discomfort. "Come over to my desk." She walked behind her desk and pulled down a tattered book from the shelf.

I followed, of course, because I was curious.

She set the book down in front of me. "This is a diary of my life. Not everything of course, only the highlights."

The book had a leather binding and was covered with some kind of gold writing that was rubbing off. The pages had a yellow tint of age. As she opened the book, the pages were handwritten in some language I didn't recognize. I thought maybe French, at first, because Juliet was French or so I thought, but this writing wasn't French; the letters weren't right.

"What is this? Code?"

She turned some pages. "As I said, these are the highlights of my life."

I shook my head. "I don't understand. What are you trying to tell me?"

"There are things in this world that you've only heard of in stories." Juliet placed her hand on mine.

I met her gaze, a feeling of complete peace and calm washing over me.

"Until tonight."

Chapter Five

A SHARP KNOCK at the door jerked me from my thoughts. Before I realized what happened, Amanda burst into the room.

"I'm sorry, Juliet," Amanda said.

A tall olive-skinned man in a rich gray suit pushed past Amanda. I was struck by his dark eyes. They drew my attention to his face. Not even the softness of his beard covered his chiseled features. Everything from his perfectly combed hair to his crisp white shirt and bright red tie radiated power.

"So the rumors are true," the man boomed, rushing in and waving his hand at the opened book.

"Victor," Juliet growled as she swiftly closed the book and put it away. She stepped away from her desk and stood between Victor and me. "You have no business being here. This intrusion is unacceptable."

"Oh, spare me, Juliet," Victor snapped, his gaze not leaving me. "When the Head of the Council of Light decides to partake in the Calling, word gets out." His tone mocked her, not even his slight Spanish accent softened it. "Even to those of us on the Dark. Considering that our territories overlap, I'm hurt that you didn't share this information with me. I might have helped."

Juliet moved to greet him. Her small frame filled the space between us.

Victor walked to the gold liquor cart by the door and poured himself a glass of the same red wine that Juliet was drinking. He took a sip and frowned. "You realize it loses something when it's not fresh. How old is this?" He put the crystal glass down.

This was the first time I'd seen Juliet worried. She inhaled deeply and nodded to Amanda, whose expression narrowed on Victor. Amanda closed the office door and took up a position next to it.

It surprised me how Amanda suddenly appeared so dangerous, her hands clasped in front of her, her shoulders perfectly straight. She never took her attention off Victor.

"He's not very attractive." Victor waved a hand in my direction. "Still, he's not hideous. The suit helps."

"Mr. Alexander's appearance is not at issue here. You are."

Victor laughed.

"Victor, none of this has anything to do with you or the Dark," Juliet said.

"Ha," Victor scoffed. "What if he turns to the Dark? Who will claim him? Would you prefer one of my lieutenants?" The corners of his mouth raised. "Or me? I think it's only reasonable that I meet the boy and give him the once-over—maybe even a little taste." He scrutinized me in the same way a farmer would his fattest turkey.

It made my skin crawl.

Juliet offered me a quick comforting smile. "Duncan will not turn to the Dark. It's almost impossible."

"But it has happened, and we've both seen the outcome." Victor turned from me back to Juliet.

"Do you think someone I call to me would even have the slightest chance of turning Dark?" Juliet took a step closer to Victor. "We're not like the Dark. We're careful with whom we chose, so there are no mistakes." Her voice was edged with sarcasm.

"But they have been known to happen, which is why I'm here." Victor met her gaze.

"Regardless, this is not the time. I have every intention of introducing Duncan to everyone when the time is right." Juliet sighed. "When he's ready, not before."

Victor blinked and frowned. "You and your hippie ways, feelings, emotions. You don't need all that, Juliet. You and the oh-so-moral Light make it too complicated." He turned to me with a sinister smile.

The way his deep brown eyes penetrated into my soul made me feel as if I were standing there naked. If there was a blanket, I would have grabbed it and tried to cover up.

"Juliet is a Light vampire and I'm a Dark vampire," Victor said. "You have a choice to make, become a vampire or stay a human." His smile grew, and I thought I caught the glimmer of bright white canine teeth sharpen and grow longer.

His accent mesmerized me in a way I couldn't describe. I'll never forget how he focused on me, watching me like prey. I was lost in his words, not fully understanding them but somehow wanting to hear more.

"Now was that so hard?" He took a seat in one of the room's many chairs.

"Victor, you are in my house, uninvited I might add. You will not speak of these things in front of Mr. Alexander. You're confusing him and bringing more questions to his mind than need be, right now."

"A what?" I asked. "Did you just say you're a vampire?" The words finally made sense as the haze that filled my mind cleared. There was an ache in my chest, and I realized I hadn't been breathing. I took a breath, found the chair nearest me, and collapsed heavily into it. This was insane.

"Victor, please?" Juliet huffed, shaking her head. "You need to leave."

I turned to Juliet, Amanda, and then Victor. I couldn't believe what I heard. None of this made any sense. It was madness. To be honest, it annoyed me that people were talking about me as if I wasn't there.

The more my mind cleared, the more I understood what had been said: the Calling, Light and Dark, Council of Light. What the hell was all that? And Juliet being the head of this council, what did any of that even mean? Not to mention—*vampires*. This was nuts, and I wasn't going to be part of it.

"I think." I stopped. "I need to go." I tried to stand.

"Mr. Alexander—sit." Victor held up a hand in my direction. Two unseen hands pushed me back down in the chair and held me there. I tried to stand again, but I was stuck. Amanda stepped forward and reached into her suit jacket. She pulled out a small silver dagger as she grew closer to Victor.

Juliet held up a hand to Amanda, stopping whatever Amanda was about to do. "Victor," Juliet warned, her eyes growing dark. "You will not harm him. Do I make myself clear?"

Her face had shifted. She was baring fangs, and her face had more of a dangerous, monstrous appearance. Her forehead had ridges that angled down, all of her soft features gone. If it hadn't been for this force holding me down, I would have run. Run or faint, that's about where I was.

Victor remained still but licked his lips.

I blinked, and suddenly Victor was next to me, holding my arm up to his mouth. "Come now, Juliet. How about a little taste? To make up for that swill you drink."

"Victor, enough," Juliet growled.

There was an electrical charge to the room and every hair on my arm stood on end.

Victor kissed my arm and dropped it. The weight on my shoulders lifted, the force that held me had vanished.

"Oh please, Juliet. You sense he's upset or that I'm upset. Who cares? Take your hippie, feel-good magic and get over it." Victor waved an indifferent hand. "The boy needs to listen, and given his current reactions, he would bolt from this room, wetting himself, and then what?"

Juliet walked to me, her face back to normal and her fangs gone. "He will not harm you, nor will I. I'm sorry. This was not supposed to happen like this. I appreciate this is a lot for you to comprehend." She touched my arm.

I suddenly felt calmer and more relaxed, and nodded.

Victor huffed.

"Amanda, you will show Victor out," Juliet said. "Unless, Victor, you want to witness just how far my *hippie* magic can go."

Victor dusted the front of his jacket, a chuckle in his voice. "Very well. But I expect to be invited to his Welcoming, and for the tests. On the off chance he turns Dark, I want to be there to witness it."

"Of course." Juliet smiled at me and faced Victor.

Victor finished his drink and put the glass down. He focused on me one last time, scrutinizing my body.

"Victor, please give Mr. Lancaster my best, will you? He's such an amazing man. Also, inform him to expect my invitation. You realize how much Amanda and I adore him."

Victor froze, and his face shifted just like Juliet's had, but he changed back at once. He forced a polite smile and took a breath. "See you soon, Duncan." He walked to the door where Amanda stood ready to escort him out. The dagger had vanished, her shoulders were more relaxed, and she appeared to be breathing again.

A dropped pin would have shattered the windows in her office after Victor's departure.

What the hell happened? How was any of this possible? If he could hold me down without touching me, then what could others do?

The strong scent of roses and vanilla returned. I didn't realize it had been missing since Victor had walked in.

Juliet's smile had no trace of what I had seen on her face. "Let's move to the sofa."

I sat and the soft warmth of the sofa engulfed me. She continued over to the little bar and poured herself another glass of red wine—although now I knew it wasn't really wine. It was something else. She poured something for me, brought both drinks over, and handed the non-wine one to me. She sat next to me.

"Drink. This will help calm your nerves."

"What is it? Some potion or something?"

Juliet laughed, delighted. "No, it's scotch. A very fine scotch, I might add. I bought it at a charity fundraiser."

I sipped the scotch and watched the fire. Juliet sat there next to me, waiting in silence, never moving. Everything that had occurred swam around in my mind. What had I just witnessed?

"Vampires?" I finally whispered.

"Yes."

"Head of this Council of Light thing?"

"Yes."

"There are Light and Dark vampires?"

"Yes."

"Victor is a Dark vampire?"

"Yes."

"You know how crazy this sounds, right?"

"Yes."

I took a deep breath and focused on the fire, taking another sip of the scotch, allowing it to warm me. "Why do I feel so calm and at ease when I should be scared to death?"

"I'm keeping you calm so you can focus and process all this information." Juliet sipped her red wine. "Please, understand what Victor did was unacceptable, and I will deal with him later. He should never have come here, not like that. The letters you saw me working on were to address the very thing he came here for." She pinched the bridge of her nose. "He never was a patient man, always wanting things his way."

"This is all real. I mean, I saw your faces transform, and there was something holding me down in the chair. I was trapped. I thought he was going to kill me."

"He couldn't hurt you here. My house is too well protected, and he does not want to start a war. Not over this," Juliet said.

"Have you been controlling my emotions from the start? Is that why I wasn't worried or stressed on the day I met you? Is that why all of us at the party seemed like Stepford wives?"

"The simple answer is yes, but there is more to it than that."

I took another drink, the warm liquor soothing my nerves and helping me to relax. "How is any of this possible?"

"As we talked about before Victor arrived, this is a big world and there are a great many things that exist in it." She leaned back on the sofa.

"Are there werewolves and shape-shifters, too? What about witches? What about elves, fairies, and ogres? What about trolls and goblins?"

Juliet laughed, and I understood it was an honest laugh because somehow I detected it. In my mind, I wanted to laugh as well. It was an inside joke and we were both in on it. I actually sensed her good nature and her enjoyment; it was an odd feeling, but I felt it and it made me smile. This was the first time I noticed it, but all my emotions up to this point had been controlled by her. I didn't fully comprehend, or I didn't want to. Now, I wasn't sure if I was smiling because I wanted to or if it was her energy, or whatever, rubbing off on me.

"As far as I know, there might have been, long ago." She took a sip of her drink.

I found myself nodding and my body growing exhausted.

"We survive because we blend in and we are able to hide our true nature." She watched me.

I focused on the fire, the crackle and pop.

"There are witches." Juliet adjusted her feet on the sofa. "I don't know any personally—well, not anymore. Not since I bought this land and had the wards put in place to protect it, just in case. However, they are still out there. We don't mix well, and the gift of true witchcraft is limited, perhaps one in a million or one in ten million. I'm not sure. As I said, I haven't seen a true witch in a long time."

"You have wards on the property and house?"

"It was a long time ago, and I thought it would be prudent. With the complicated relationship between witches and immortals, it seemed like a wise idea. You'll find most immortals, who have been around long enough, will have wards on their homes and even their places of business, as a precaution."

"So, you mean there may be other beings out there?" Between the alcohol, the news that vampires are real and my encounter with Victor, my body was getting heavy and I needed to process everything.

"Anything is possible. However, in all my years here, I haven't had any trouble," Juliet said. "I met a witch a long time ago, and she was powerful, very powerful." She sighed. "As for other beings—" She shook her head. "—no, I've never seen anything like them."

I was quiet again and finding my eyelids growing heavy, so I only had a couple of questions that I really wanted to be answered. "Why me? What if I choose to stay human?"

"The first part of your question will require a little more explanation," Juliet replied. "As for the second, as Victor told you, I'm of the Light, and I will not force you to do anything. If you choose not to take the offer, then I will do to you what I did to the others. I will alter your memory and send you home to your life in Reno. You will not remember any of this ever happening, and you will live out the rest of your life in that simple bliss with the money I gave you."

I went to speak.

Juliet raised a hand. "You will not have to worry about the Dark. You will be off-limits to all vampires. None of them will bother you."

I let the information flow over me as I processed her words, and another series of questions popped into my mind. Amazing how our minds work. "What about my work? What about my friends? What about Cindy?" I cursed myself for not responding to her text earlier. "Did you affect me so that I wouldn't want to contact her or anyone else for that matter? Have you been messing with my mind?"

"I would not make you do anything you didn't want to," Juliet replied. "I'm not allowed, nor is any Light vampire able to force you to do anything against your will. I only enhanced your curiosity and kept you from worrying or being uneasy. Your friend, Cindy, is fine whatever you decide. She will be okay and not remember anything either way."

"But the text?"

"As for the details of you being here, one of Gregor's vampires is with Cindy. Gregor is a friend. He has been watching her and in a way manipulating her ever so slightly to keep her from bombarding you with messages while you've been on vacation. Still, we wanted to ensure you got a couple of messages so you felt like you had a connection and a safety net. In case you needed it."

That actually helped. If anything happened to Cindy because of all this, I would never forgive myself. That would be one more thing I would have on my plate, however, I wasn't worried, which I was starting to find annoying.

"So why me?"

"That is much more difficult to answer. When I decided I needed a companion, so to speak, a series of events and actions, both in and out of my control, were set into play. I can explain that more later. The reason I chose you is because—" She stopped and took several sips of her *red*, as I was starting to think of it. "Well, because, you were unlike any of the others who came to me. Who answered the call. You each had your own unique qualities, but you... When I saw you, I knew." She smiled at me. "Duncan, you picked me as much as I picked you. You wanted to be here. You wanted to be here with me and be my called; becoming what I am."

Did she just tell me I wanted to become a vampire?

Chapter Six

I HAD A lot to sleep on that night. The idea of weighing my life and an immortal life was a big deal. What would it be like? What would I be like? Would I even be good at it? To smooth the transition between that night and the next few days, I shut myself in my room, only opening the door for the occasional checkup by Amanda and when my meals were dropped off.

Why didn't I get in the car and leave? There was nothing wrong with that. Juliet had told me I could go if I wanted. She also said no one would force me to do anything I didn't want to do. Calling Cindy and talking to her was another idea that I didn't follow through on. Hell, I could've called the cops or the media, not that any of them would've believed me. I probably would've ended up in some mental ward somewhere or perhaps something worse might've happened, given what I thought I knew.

The "or worse" stopped me. I didn't want to end up like my father, dead of mysterious causes. Now, realizing there is a world of immortals out there, I pondered the idea of vampires killing my dad, but I didn't know why they would've done it. I doubted my father would leave my mother and me. He was a terrific dad. Of course, I was only eleven when he was found dead. Still, maybe the Dark vampires wanted him for something and gave him no choice. I didn't know and it played in the back of my mind. It was easy to imagine Victor or the others like him killing my father. How he had watched me, how he had held me in my seat without touching me; I couldn't wrap my head around it. How was something like that even possible? I walked through my balcony's double doors and looked beyond, not really seeing the world outside this house.

I learned quickly that many things I didn't think possible were in fact real. Could Victor and his ilk really be bound by the same rules as Juliet? It didn't sound like it, and I didn't want to test it.

I stayed in my room for safety and thought. I slept, ate, and slept and thought some more. I always knew the choice I was going to make. I just had to let my emotions catch up. I wasn't going anywhere in my professional life, and I only had a few friends. Ever since my breakup a year ago, I had remained single, so not much waited for me back home. I glanced at the tray with my half-eaten sandwich of imported German salami and Swiss and the untouched bowl of kettle chips.

Even without Juliet's voodoo, I was drawn there. Perhaps, I didn't have major attachments at home because the universe was setting me up to be a part of this. Was I only a "nothing" because I was to become immortal and fulfill my potential? Until that week, I didn't feel like a nobody and the new realization was bugging the hell out of me. Of course, I tried hard not to think about my life before that week. But there, with Juliet and Amanda, I seemed whole. Also, this estate felt like home, more than I've experienced in a long time.

It was possible Juliet was using her ability to make me want to stay, but I didn't think so. I was frightened, worried, and angry. I also thought, perhaps if I did this, I could find out the truth about what happened to my dad. Juliet or her friends might have resources and theories that I could explore.

On the third night of hiding in my room, I took a nice hot shower, shaved, and made myself presentable in the fancy woolen suit, since I didn't have any other nice clothes. I ran a quick finger over the gold with onyx cuff links. I would need to go shopping and get some nicer clothes since I was going to be there a while, and I wanted to fit in.

I walked down to Juliet's office and found the office door open. I peeked in, and she was sitting in front of the fire with a glass of *red* in her hands.

"Ah, Duncan." Juliet stood. "Would you like a drink?"

"No, thank you. I'm fine."

Juliet nodded and gestured for me to come over and join her on the sofa. "You made your choice?"

"I have." She took a seat, and then I sat. "I have a few more questions if you don't mind."

Juliet sipped her drink. "Of course."

"Are you—are vampires damned?" I know, lame question, but when it comes to matters of your soul, it's always good to be sure. "If I do this, am I in league with the Devil or something like that?"

The edges of her mouth turned up, filling her face with a warm smile.

I realized how this question sounded, but I had to hear the answer from her.

"No. We are not damned. Some might say we are, and I am familiar with the legends, but no, Duncan, we're not in league with the Devil or anything like that. Like with humans, there are good immortals and bad immortals—"

"The Dark," I guessed.

"Not all Dark vampires are evil, as not all Light vampires are good."

"I don't understand."

Juliet hesitated and put the empty crystal glass on the oak side table next to the sofa. "The Dark are capable of cruelty and many of them can be evil. In places like Africa, the Middle East, parts of Asia, they can be very cruel. They are true Dark. Victor is of the Dark. However, I wouldn't call him evil. Maybe selfish. I don't agree with many of his practices, but he is not an evil man per se."

I was about to speak, but Juliet held up a hand.

"The Dark believe that you should be free to live as you see fit. No rules. Do as you please. Victor, for example, would never go out and murder people for fun. Some immortals do that, and it's his job to keep that from happening and to take care of those who break his laws."

I opened my mouth and shifted in the softness of sofa. "But you just said they don't believe in rules."

Juliet thought a moment, "I suppose what I mean is by our rules, the rules the Light abide by."

"Um, okay." I still wasn't sure I understood.

"Even the Dark abide by a basic code of conduct and rules set up by the Dark Leader in charge of the area. So yes, as free as they like to believe they are, they aren't."

I nodded.

"Please, don't ever tell Victor or the others I said that." She smiled. "They like to believe they have no rules and answer to no one, but they do. They answer to Victor, and he is not one to be tested."

"So then, what's the difference?" Now I was confused.

"The Light." She tapped her lips. "Well, the Light's rules are a set of guidelines that we all live by." She stopped. "For example, the Dark will mark people without their consent. People they deem to want or need. They don't give the person a choice. The Light can't do that."

I took a breath, relieved by this. "So, I have a choice? You're not using your abilities on me?"

"No. I've sensed the anger and frustration in you and left you alone. I've also sensed the enthusiasm and eagerness. I don't want to push you. You have to come to this decision on your own now that you know the truth of what I am and what I'm asking you to become. I can't influence that choice."

I glanced at the fire, letting the warmth and the words sink in. "Will I become Light?"

"I believe so, however, I can't say yet. That is what will need to be confirmed."

I frowned.

"As Victor mentioned, there is always a chance that you will become Dark, but I don't believe it is anything for you to worry about." Juliet's gaze met mine. "The Light help to keep the balance of the world, and I sense much of that same balance in you."

She paused, as if deliberating.

Then she nodded as if coming to a decision. "You will learn more about this later. Understand there is good and bad in everyone, Light and Dark. Of course, I'm not saying the Light go out and kill people or cause mayhem. They do not. It is the choices we make that define us as good or evil. Not the group we claim or that claims us."

It was a lot to understand, but I was starting to get it. "Still, it's better to be *of the Light* as you say?"

"I believe so," Juliet replied. "You'll find that the Light are closer to being truly human. We tend to blend into society and work alongside humans even if they don't recognize us. The Dark." She pulled up her legs and tucked her feet under her thighs, leaning back deeper into the sofa. "The Dark have their own way of doing things, not so much here in North America, but in other parts of the world. The Dark can truly be dark."

I sat quietly for several moments, considering all the stuff I didn't understand, and despite it all, I still wanted it. Finally, I raised my gaze to meet hers. "What will it take to become like you. An immortal?"

"There are some tests, and then you will need to be marked."

"Care to elaborate on that a little? Marked? Tests? I'm not going to have to take a written exam, am I? I suck at test-taking." I smirked.

Juliet chuckled. "No, there is no written exam to take. There will be questions you must answer as honestly as possible. Trust your instincts." She tightened her lips and narrowed her eyes. "Duncan, I can't share any more with you right now. I'm sorry. There are traditions and rules that must be followed. I can assure you I will be with you throughout the process. You will not be forced to do this alone. It occurs over six months and can take up to a year. It gives us both time to adapt."

"When does it start?"

"Tomorrow, if you wish to proceed."

"What about my life in Reno? My job? My apartment, and all that?" My leg shook nervously up and down. "I'm supposed to be back at work in a couple of days. Six months to a year?"

"This isn't a simple process. There is much to it, but we must start tomorrow." She reached out and touched my leg, stopping it. "Trust me to the details. No harm will come to you. I assure you it will be fine. After the first Mark, you will understand better."

I frowned at the non-answer. "Will it hurt? I mean will there be a lot of pain involved?" I didn't want to sound like a total wimp. I didn't want to spend six months to a year in pain, suffering some unknown transition.

"This is why movies about such matters shouldn't be allowed. Was being born painful?" she asked.

"I don't know. I was a baby, I don't remember. It's supposed to be pretty painful for the mother."

"It's like being born. There may be some brief pain and some slight discomfort, however, it is quickly forgotten. I promise there is no suffering and no pain in the manner you are thinking."

It was as if my life had been building to this point and there was no backing down. To my core, I knew I needed this. I glanced around the room; the windows reflected the room back at me, the warm tones from the fire giving the image a flicker.

"If you don't mind me asking, are all immortals as wealthy as this?" Asking this was rude, but I wanted to comprehend my financial obligations. If we are judged by credit scores, I'd be in trouble.

"No, Duncan. We accumulate our wealth over the years. We invest and we plan for the future, our future. It's a process. When I came to be, I was not at all wealthy. My first home was little more than a grass hut and some furs thrown about for warmth. Not all vampires are wealthy, but most accumulate money and achieve a comfortable existence over time. It is up to their creator to assist them in this regard. That is why it takes time."

I became silent again and shifted on the sofa. I glanced at the fire, lost in random thoughts.

"Why don't you tell me about yourself, Duncan?"

I wasn't sure what I wanted to say or how to say it. I didn't like talking about myself, so my leg started to tremble again.

"I don't know. There isn't much to tell. I work in Reno. I rent an apartment about the size of this room and I have a few close friends. Both my parents are dead."

That was my life in a nutshell. I froze. Disappointed that my life hadn't worked out differently.

She stood, walked over the gold cart, and refilled her crystal glass. "Would you like something?"

I shook my head and muttered a curse when she looked away from me. I really wished she would stop asking me if I needed something.

She sauntered back over and took a sip of her drink. "What about Cindy?"

"Cindy is my best friend." My face grew warm, not from embarrassment, but from all the reflecting I'd done over the last several days. I realized just how much of my life had been wasted. I existed, but I wasn't living. I stood and crossed the room, then leaned against one of the bookcases with my arms across my chest. Flustered with myself and my life, I marched over to the mini bar and checked what was there.

"If you'd like tea or coffee, we can ring for it."

I shook my head and poured myself some water.

She watched me.

It's hard to talk about yourself, especially once you realize there is nothing interesting to tell. What had I done? Gone to school, worked, ate, and slept. I didn't bother making friends, and as for family, I had none. It was pathetic. It pissed me off, because I never saw it that way until now. I took a couple of sips of water and walked to the mantel. The warmth and light danced around my legs.

"Don't you already know everything about me?" My voice was sharper than I intended. "What more is there to tell? I mean, what do you want to know? I work, I go home, and I do it all over again. I don't travel. I haven't been anywhere. I exist, nothing more. I don't have a life." I didn't mean to sound snippy with her. "My life is uninteresting. Why am I here? What do you want from me?"

"You sell yourself short."

There was a frown in her voice and I glanced over at her. This was the first time I had seen that expression on her face when we talked.

"What about the death of your father?" Juliet asked, changing subjects.

"Wow." My face heated up, and my hand clenched around the glass. "You don't hold back, do you?" I finished the water and put the glass on the mantel. "I don't like talking about what happened to my dad, mostly because there is nothing to tell. He went to work in the morning, and we didn't know anything happened until he didn't come home. We reported him missing. The police showed up at our house a few days later to tell us he was dead." This wasn't quite accurate. At some point, I would tell her, but not now. Not like this. I would be asking for help in solving the mystery of his death when the time was right.

Juliet's voice was soft. I had to struggle to hear her.

"What about relationships?" she asked. "Do you date a lot?"

My heart started to beat faster. When you've gotten all the basics about a person, asking the personal nitty-gritty is all there is to ask. This was why I avoided social media. Still, I didn't like the line of questions, and I didn't understand why any of this mattered.

"No, I don't date. I don't have time, or I don't make time, or whatever. As for a relationship, you won't need to worry about anyone missing me, except for Cindy and perhaps a few people at my office." My voice was curt. "If you don't mind, I'm tired. I'm going to call it a night."

Juliet narrowed her eyes, and there was a frown on her face that quickly melted away. "I understand. There is a lot for you to take in."

I forced a polite smile, and stalked out of the den. I had to leave that room. She wanted to know about the death of my father. Hell, I wanted to know about the death of my father. 'Cause *unknown* was all the police and the medical examiner said.

"The investigation is ongoing, but many things are still unexplained. We're sorry." That was what the investigator had told my mother as I listened from the hall in my dragon pajamas.

What was I supposed to tell Juliet? The truth? That he had gone missing on his way to work and the police found his car and his body four days later? His hair had turned completely white and all the blood in his body had been turned into a powder. They had no idea what caused it, the best guess was some kind of unknown biological or chemical reaction, but who knew?

For the first time in days, all my emotions rushed back. Juliet wasn't making me "artificially" comfortable anymore.

For all I knew, now, it might have been a Dark vampire that did it to him. Maybe it was a Mark that had failed or something? I had no idea. We were left with no answers because the police stopped the investigation when they had no leads and decided there was no foul play. Well, none that they figured out. My mom cremated his body and never talked about it. When people asked what happened, we told them what I told Juliet. It wasn't like there was anything anyone could do. It all happened when I was eleven and it was pretty traumatizing so it wasn't something I wanted to remember, especially in my current mood.

Chapter Seven

BECAUSE OF MY behavior the previous night, I felt like an ass.

The house was alive with activity, and according to Amanda, it was all for my first Mark. Before she left me at the breakfast table, she said that that night's event had a lot of details still to be taken care of. After a good night's sleep, I was kicking myself for how I'd treated Juliet. She didn't do anything more than ask a couple of questions, and I freaked out. It wasn't right.

Juliet entered while I sat in the breakfast room, finishing my fruit and yogurt. My bacon and eggs were still untouched.

"Good morning, Duncan. I trust you slept well." She sat in the chair across from me. Her smile was gracious, but her body didn't have the relaxed grace it normally had.

"Yes, thank you." I sipped my orange juice. "About last night...I apologize. I'm not comfortable talking about myself and sharing personal details. Especially things like dating and my parents."

"I gathered as much." Juliet's tone was polite but tight. She studied me like she was having an internal debate, and she opened her mouth several times before speaking.

"Duncan, it's important for us to trust each other, particularly tonight. I will respect your privacy. However, I do hope you'll be more open with me."

"The first Mark. You still want to go through with it?"

"Of course, I haven't changed my mind. Have you?"

I shook my head.

"Excellent," Juliet said.

I started on my bacon. "I realize today might not be the best day for it, however, I was planning on going out. Pick up a few things and perhaps have lunch or something. I've been cooped up here all week."

She scanned my meal. "Do you mind if I join you?"

"I.... Don't you have things to attend to?" I turned to look out the windows. "What about the sunlight?"

Juliet laughed. "More movie nonsense."

"Oh."

"Anyway, you're my only concern today. However, if you'd like to be alone—"

"No. I would love the company. I'm not familiar with the area, so it would be nice."

"Wonderful." Juliet's face lit up. "When you're finished with breakfast, we'll go out. I'll show you the town, and I know a great place for lunch."

"Are you sure? I mean...I don't want to—"

She raised a hand. "It would be my pleasure. Amanda and the staff are taking care of everything." She leaned in. "I've learned over the years it's best to stay out of Amanda's way when she's planning events. You'd be doing me a great favor if you allowed me to accompany you."

I wasn't so sure I bought it, but I was happy to accept the offer. "All right, it sounds like a plan."

THE CAR JULIET had picked out for us to go exploring in was a 1964 metallic-blue Mustang convertible with a pristine white interior. The car was shining, and the chrome was so bright in the sun I had to turn away.

Juliet stood by the driver's door, dressed in form-fitting jeans and a ruby top. An ivory-colored scarf wrapped about her head and her sunglasses matched the car with white rims and dark lenses. I caught a whiff of roses and vanilla, but I wasn't sure where it came from.

I frowned at my clothes. I was in loose-fitting jeans and a simple button-down short-sleeved shirt that could use ironing.

"This car is amazing," I said as we drove down the road.

"I have to admit it's one of my favorites." Juliet glanced at me. "You can use it whenever you want. Just ask Adam for the keys."

"Really? Thanks," I said.

She hopped into the car, and I took my seat in the passenger side. It had been such a long week, I didn't realize how nice it would feel to be out and about. I felt normal again. It was like Cindy and I were driving over to Truckee for some shopping and lunch—good times.

Los Altos was an interesting town. You wouldn't know it was there. The town was hidden by trees and sitting right in the foothills. We drove onto Main Street and were greeted by boutiques, restaurants, and clean sidewalks. No chain stores to be found. We passed a coffee shop which filled the air with hints of robust coffee.

"Los Altos is one of my favorite places," Juliet said. "It's so insulated from the rest of the world. I know how that sounds, but there is nowhere like it. It has a small-town feel while being in the middle of one of the busiest locations in the country."

Juliet parked and pointed in the direction of some oak and pine trees. "Down First Street is where the Lumière D'espoir Foundation has its office."

I lifted my hand to block the glare of the sun.

"It's where you'll be working once we get through the next couple of nights." She pulled out her purse and dropped her keys into it.

I met her at the sidewalk. I glanced up and down the street. "Wow. This is a nice town. How long have you been here?"

"Let's just say I remember when the town wasn't here." She winked at me, guiding me down the street with her arm in mine, strolling at a nice slow pace. People walked about with bags and dogs. Several of the shops had doggy bowls filled with water, and we even passed a shop that specialized in dog supplies and homemade pet treats.

We stopped in front of the sign for the *Los Altos Beaux Vêtements*, which shone in the morning sun. "Mr. Bisset's shop?"

"He has another shop at Stanford Mall, and I've been trying to get him to open up a shop in Santana Row, but..." She shrugged. "Shall we?"

"Sure, why not?" I opened the door for her.

Everything was clean and organized, with bright spotlights focusing on the mannequins. On one of the walls, brilliantly colored bolts of fabric hung. Near the back, on the opposite side, different styles of men's leather shoes reflected the display lights. A few customers talked to sales associates. They were chatting and smiling as they lingered. No one seemed to be in a rush.

I wonder if I'll ever be able to go to Kohl's after this.

Juliet flitted to the back of the store where a couple of plush purple velvet chairs sat in front of floor-to-ceiling mirrors. She greeted Mr. Bisset. I didn't want to be rude, so I checked the racks with the shirts. Considering my extended stay there in town, I wanted to get some new clothes, so why not look at different shirts for my suit? I nabbed a shirt in my size, if I remembered correctly from the other day. Glancing at the price, my jaw bounced off the floor and hit me in the head. I couldn't afford this store. Who lived liked this?

"Ah, Mr. Alexander, welcome. Welcome to my little shop." Mr. Bisset came over and greeted me with a big smile and a firm handshake. "I'm pleased to see you again. I trust you enjoyed the suit?"

"It's amazing," I replied. "I never had anything so nice before."

Juliet stood next to him, her face cheerful and a twinkle in her eyes. "You did an amazing job, Fredrick."

"Merci beaucoup, Madame de Exter," Fredrick said with a polite nod.

I really noticed his accent at that point.

"Madame de Exter says you are here to pick up some new clothes. How exciting. I've already selected items for you to peruse." He took my arm and led me to the back of the store. "After we met, I thought you might be back, and I took the liberty to order a few things for you to consider."

Juliet was right behind him.

"Oh, Mr. Bisset, I...um...well, we're window-shopping today. I mean, I don't really need anything right now. It's nice to come and see such beautiful things and well..." I cleared my throat. "I don't want to keep you from your other customers."

Mr. Bisset laughed a full laugh that started in his shoes and worked its way out.

It made me laugh as well.

"Mr. Alexander, trust me, you can use new clothes. Everyone can." He wagged his finger at me. "I won't take no for an answer. Now go into the changing room, and I'll bring you a few items to try."

My face flushed and my heart jumped. I panicked as I was being pushed to the changing room. Juliet nodded as if to say everything would be all right. As the curtain closed, I swore I heard a hint of a chuckle come from her.

JULIET SURPRISED ME by eating a salad—well, picking at it was more like it. I hadn't seen her actually eat since the night of the fancy dinner. I don't remember her eating much of anything then either.

While we sat at Maltby's having our lunch, I was in shopping shell shock. "I don't understand what happened."

"It's called shopping." Juliet put her fork down. "You needed some new clothes, and who better to outfit you than Fredrick Bisset? He's the best. Don't you agree?"

"Well, yes, but still. That was a lot of clothes."

"True, I suppose he may have overdone it, but you looked very sharp in them."

"But I can't afford to shop there. I couldn't even afford one of the shirts on their racks," I whispered at her.

"Which is why everything we bought today was put on my house account," Juliet said. "I told you not to worry about these things. They will be taken care of. I have every intention of taking good care of my *Called*. It is up to me to teach you and train you."

"And that includes buying me clothes?"

"Certainly."

"But, Juliet, I can buy my own clothes. I don't need a mother."

"Duncan, that's not my intent. I don't want you to feel uncomfortable. I've never had a Called before, and this is exciting for me. I suppose I got carried away." She took a sip of her iced tea.

Ass, party of one. Ass, party of one.

"Sorry, I didn't mean to be rude. I'm used to taking care of myself and not getting any help from anyone."

"I understand. Please realize that part of this process is making sure you are cared for."

"Is this how your mentor treated you?"

A quick frown crossed Juliet's lips, but before she spoke, it was gone. "No. My mentor was quite different."

"Oh." I cleared my throat, feeling more like an ass than I did before. I forced what I hoped to be a bright smile. "Well, I felt like a giant Ken doll that you played dress up with."

Juliet's eye crinkled, and her cheeks lifted with her wide smile as she spoke. "I suppose that is one way to look at it."

I opened my mouth to speak.

She put her fork down, cutting me off with a wry smile. "I'm a bit of a snob, I admit, and I expect the people around me, who are close to me, to look like they belong." She chuckled. "Plus it was fun. I couldn't help myself. If you want, you can always pay me back, but I hope you don't. I like giving gifts." She picked up her fork and picked at her salad again.

BY THE TIME we got back to the house, it was quiet. Once again, the strong scent of roses and vanilla hung heavy in the air.

Juliet inhaled deeply and ran a finger over the entry table. She checked her fingertip and nodded.

Within moments, Adam, the house attendant or butler or whatever his title was, materialized. Very much the image of a male magazine model, same as the first night I met him. His light-blue polo shirt was tight across the shoulders and chest, revealing his strong frame.

"Everything is set for tonight, Juliet," Adam said. "Is there anything you need at the moment?" He took her bag and scarf.

"No, Adam. See to the car please." Juliet handed him the car keys.

He began to walk off.

"Oh, and Adam, the house is immaculate," she added, and he smiled, his dimples popping onto his face. She turned to me. "He's so handsome, don't you agree?"

I shrugged as my neck and face filled with heat.

Her head tilted in the direction of where Adam had left us. Then she turned toward me. "For this evening, please wear the suit you have. A few people will be here to witness the first Mark."

I nodded.

"There is nothing more I can share about tonight, but if you are worried, you may speak with Amanda. This is a choice you must make on your own—remember that. I have to leave you now. I'll see you later." She reached out and gave my arm a gentle squeeze. "There is nothing to worry about, I promise."

I spent what was left of the afternoon getting ready. Thinking about Juliet's words and how this was a choice I had to make. Trust was part of it. Not only in myself but in her. Considering I wasn't sure what to expect that night, I tried my best not to think about it. I wanted to be there. I *needed* to be there. There was nothing to explain, but I had to do this. It wasn't something Juliet was pushing on me. It was something else. Something about me and who I was and who I was meant to be.

Just like before, I thought about my past and how isolated I had been, but in the here and now, I didn't feel that way. I was ready for a new adventure. I was ready for my life to begin.

Amanda told me to wait in my room until she came to get me, and to understand that the night was important for Juliet and therefore important for me. So, as the time approached, my palms sweated and butterflies did somersaults in my stomach. A tap came from my door and I went to open it.

Amanda stood in a classic powder-blue cocktail dress with lots of sparkle and thin straps at the shoulders. Her hair was done up and her nails matched the dress perfectly.

She smiled at me in her welcoming way. "Don't you look sexy. Are you ready?"

If I spoke, dinner would be coming back up. I forced myself to take a breath.

"You'll be fine." Amanda took my hand and gave it a squeeze. "Relax and enjoy the experience."

We ambled down the hall to the main staircase. Once back on the first floor, the walk to where the reception would be held felt like a death march. Sweat dripped down my back. If Juliet was using her magic on me, it wasn't working.

"Take a breath and relax." Amanda glanced at me as we stopped just outside the dining room.

All I heard was my heart beating and Amanda's words. I forced myself to take a deep breath and exhale.

Behind the door, I imagined thirty to forty people in dark robes chanting at some kind of altar. Perhaps torches on the wall. Animal hides on the floors. Possibly, dead animals or animals in cages.

Amanda opened the door, and we walked in.

Instead, I counted nine of us, not including Adam and Mia. Roses, in all the corners, were highlighted with dimmed lights. Side chairs had been spread along the walls. Off to the side of the room was a sideboard with what I convinced myself to be red wine. On the opposite side was another buffet loaded with all kinds of hors d'oeuvres and beverages.

In the middle of the room sat an ornate carved wooden pedestal with gold inlays and sparkling gemstones in a curvy pattern that resembled ivy. I'd never seen anything like it. Topping the pedestal was a highly polished black stone that served as the tabletop, and on that was a goblet. It was stone and sparkled in the light, causing miniature rainbows to dance around the table.

Next to the goblet lay a wooden blade, and it too was richly decorated with gemstones. I gulped. I didn't want to consider what that was going to be used for. None of the guests paid attention to the pedestal. It sat in the center of the room, out of place and unnoticed by those in attendance.

Once I was able to take my attention off the pedestal, I noticed Adam and Mia were in their formal attire, standing ready to take care of whatever the guests needed. They each held a serving tray of glasses filled with a selection of drinks. They seemed as attentive as they had the night I first met them. It was the only thing familiar to me.

I spotted Victor, standing and talking to another man I didn't know. I assumed he was another member of the Dark only because he and Victor talked. The man was either Indian or Middle Eastern, with dark hair, dark eyes, and a strong jaw.

Across the room, another man was chatting with a tall woman, who had a pleasant enough face. Juliet spoke to two other people, one a rugged man who didn't appear comfortable in the suit he was wearing. He continued to tug at his collar and pull at his jacket sleeves. I could relate. Next to him was a more robust woman, weighed down by the gold and diamond jewelry around her neck and on her fingers.

"Would you like something to drink?" Amanda asked.

"Is it all right?"

"Of course." Amanda flagged Mia over.

I picked up a glass of white wine. "Thank you." I took a sip and the dryness made my mouth pucker.

"Ah, Duncan," Juliet called. "Please come over. Let me introduce you."

Amanda and I walked over to Juliet who was standing beside a man and woman. "Max, Sybil, this is Duncan."

"Very nice to meet ya," Max said. "We've waited for this one to finally have a Calling. Tonight's a big night. I'm sure you're busting a gut to get going." He shook my hand harder than I would have liked.

I decided I liked his down-to-earth nature and his homey way of speaking. He had a very likable demeanor.

"It's nice to meet you as well." I got my hand back and turned to Sybil. "A pleasure to meet you."

Sybil was at least six feet tall, and the heels she wore only added to her height. She was pretty enough, but by the way she looked down her nose at me, I got the impression she enjoyed looking down on people.

"It's a delight." Sybil's voice was deep. "For Juliet to partake in the Calling, she must see great things in you, Duncan." The smile was still on her face, but I wasn't so sure she was as pleased to meet me as she claimed. She turned to Juliet. "None of your lieutenants are here tonight. I would have thought you would have them *all* here."

Sybil drew out the word "all" and scanned the room with a hint of pinched lips.

"My governors will be here for the Welcoming party," Juliet said. "I wanted to keep tonight simple, plus there was no need for so much formality."

Sybil scanned the room. "Yes, I see. It's very *New World* of you." She had some sort of European accent, but I couldn't put my finger on what kind.

Juliet took my arm, and her smile increased. "I like to think so. Now if you'll excuse us, I have to introduce Duncan to the others." She nodded slightly to Amanda who turned to Max and asked him questions about his ranch, which he was more than happy to talk about.

"Garrett, Shannon, this is—"

"Duncan Alexander," Garrett said loudly. "A pleasure to meet you, mate. This is my *dcera*, Shannon." He nodded slightly to the robust woman next to him.

I didn't know what a *dcera* was, but I gathered it meant daughter considering Shannon appeared younger than Garrett. Amanda later confirmed that was correct.

"It seems like only yesterday we went through this process with you, Shannon."

"Oh, Garrett, you make it sound like it was just a few years ago," Shannon said. "It's been well over four hundred years." She faced me. "It's a pleasure to meet you."

Juliet turned to Victor and the man he was talking with. "And you remember Victor," she said with a polite smile. "And his—"

"This is Sahin. He is no longer under my thumb," Victor interrupted with an odd twist of his mouth.

"It's nice to see you again, Victor."

Victor huffed at that so I turned my attention to Sahin.

"I'm pleased to meet you."

Sahin took my hand and we shook. It was a little unnerving the way he focused on me. It seemed like he was sizing me up, or trying to at any rate.

"You're pleased to meet me? We shall see about that," Sahin said. "Who knows, you might end up..." He still watched me carefully as he added, "Assuming you're worthy."

"I um..."

Juliet squeezed my arm.

I didn't understand what Victor and Sahin were doing here, and I didn't understand the remark Sahin made, but I needed to trust that Juliet would take care of me, especially since I didn't know what abilities these vampires might have.

Juliet was able to affect people's emotions, and Victor had some kind of telekinetic ability, but I had no idea what the others' powers were or even if these vampires had abilities. For all I knew, Sahin could shoot flames at me or freeze me.

"Victor," Juliet said in a polite tone with a gentle tilt of her head. It sounded like a warning.

"Oh, very well," Victor said. "We'll play nice. After all, you do me a great honor by allowing me to be present for the first Mark." He glanced at Sahin. "You'll be more respectful to our host and to her—" He stopped for a moment. "Her boy."

I narrowed my eyes and lowered my brows. Before I could speak, Juliet moved us to the center of the room next to the pedestal and glanced around at the assembled people.

"It is best to let Victor's remark go." Juliet faced me.

I took a deep breath.

"Would you like something to eat?" She motioned to the buffet table.

"I don't think I can eat anything. I'm too nervous."

"Of course." She took both my hands. "Shall we do this?"

I bit my lower lip and nodded.

"Friends." Juliet called everyone to attention. "I welcome you to my home and to the first Mark of Duncan Alexander."

Adam and Mia exited the room and Amanda took up a position by the door.

"As you all know, this is the first time I've decided to take part in the Calling, so you can imagine this is a special time for me." She turned to me. "Duncan, tonight you begin a new life. The old life you had will come to an end. Do you come to me of your own free will?"

She waited expectantly for my response.

"Yes?" I replied with a slight hesitation. I wish I'd been told there were questions. I wasn't prepared to answer a bunch of questions.

Juliet grinned, and at once, I relaxed. "Duncan, in just a few minutes, you will receive your first Mark, making you one with me. We will be family. I will be your mentor. I will guide you through the four Marks until you finally become one of us. Is this what you want, and do you understand what that means?"

"Yes. I believe I understand what this means." I only understood portions of what this all really meant. But I was making the right choice and I was ready. I trusted Juliet as she had asked me to, but more importantly, I trusted my instincts.

"Those in attendance, you have witnessed my declaration and Duncan's agreement. What say you?" Juliet waited and the room remained silent. "Your silence is my confirmation."

Juliet reached for the wooden dagger. "It is from nature we come, and it is only from nature we can be born. With this walnut dagger, I offer my blood."

She slit her palm, putting it over the goblet, guardedly filling it with her blood.

I had to swallow hard because I understood what was coming. I wasn't so sure Juliet's blood was going to sit well in my stomach. The blood flow slowed as her wound stitched back together. It was freaky to see the skin actually close up without any outside help.

"In this onyx goblet is my blood. Duncan, will you take my blood and become part of me?"

I breathed and forced myself to focus on the goblet filled with blood. As I stood staring at all that blood, I thought of my life, of my friends, and my home and realized that by drinking Juliet's blood they would all be lost to me. A sudden sadness washed over me. In essence, I was killing myself and now I wasn't so sure.

"Duncan, will you take my offering?" Juliet asked again. The others in the room melted away, and it was her and I.

"I know that by taking what you offer, my old life will be over," I said. "I understand that after I do this, I won't be the same person anymore. I'll be someone different. Something different. I'll be part of a new world. I'll be part of a family again. Your family, and that is something that I want to be a part of."

Yes, my old life would be over. Yes, I would be something and someone different, but I didn't see that as a bad thing, not anymore. I reached for the goblet and put it up to my mouth. The smell hit me instantly. It wasn't the metallic scent of blood but the scent of vanilla and roses. It was Juliet's scent. It filled my nose and my body as I drank. I drained it all, enjoying the scent and allowing it to fill my body.

I finished and put the onyx goblet down.

Juliet smiled.

I faced the others, who watched me, which I found odd. I thought they would clap or something, but they didn't. They were observing me and no one spoke. When I checked the goblet, wondering if I missed something, I started to get light-headed. I shook my head to clear it, but the room and the people swirled around in a haze. I tried to speak and found that the words wouldn't come. Instead, a tingle started in my toes and moved up my body. I sank into darkness.

Chapter Eight

THERE WAS ONLY blackness.

Leisurely the darkness lifted. Something soft and warm cradled my body. A bed, but not my bed. It didn't feel like my bed. Too soft. A room, but not my room. How I arrived in this place, I was clueless, but considering how fuzzy my head was, I doubted I would understand.

A lock of hair tickled my cheek as I moved my head. The hair belonged to the head resting on my chest. A delicate porcelain-colored arm draped over my stomach. A firm leg with a smattering of hair rested on my calf. I didn't wish to disturb them, so I didn't sit up.

A soft brush of lips on the side of my neck ignited my desire and caused a moan to escape from me. The owner of the kiss unknown, but it didn't matter. The lips moved away from my neck. A breath of warm air traveled across my neck and caused shivers in my shoulders as their breath moved lower.

The mix of cool air and a warm body made me realize I was naked.

A hand moved over my chest. "All this wonderful chest hair—it's amazing." The mystery person's soft sultry voice was intriguing and then there was more kissing. The voice was muffled, like an echo in the wind. I could make out the words, but through the haze of my mind, I couldn't identify anything more.

The nibbling at my nipple caused another soft moan to escape me. As my body charged with sexual desire, I got a hint of lilac in the air.

"Do you like this?"

"Of course, he does. Can't you tell?" a second nondescript voice said next to my right ear. "He's so engorged, he's ready to burst." A soft chuckle bounced around the space. "Someone should take care of that for him." This new person teased my ear.

"Oh, I will," a third voice said. This one seemed familiar to me. I didn't know how since I still couldn't tell anything about it, but I recognized it somehow. Hot breath moved up the inside of my left thigh and the fragrance of sandalwood overcame all the other scents.

Sheer pleasure pulsed through me, and my body was alive with each touch, every breath sent bolts of energy through me, all meeting at my groin.

When I tried to focus on who was with me, they disappeared like wisps of steam from a kettle. They vanished without any recognition on my part. Vague human shapes were all I could make out; not even their gender was clear. After what seemed like hours, something changed. I was able to put together a set of eyes, one green and one gray, both beautiful. I wanted to get lost in them. They were home.

A gentle nip on the tip of my left nipple brought a rush of desire with it and pulled my attention away from the eyes.

I tried to participate, but they were phantoms outside of my grasp. When I moved, the eyes followed me. I wanted those eyes. To find out who they belonged to.

There was a soft tweak of the lobe of my ear. All I was able to do was moan softly with delight as these ghosts worked my body. Every touch filled my body with sexual energy begging for an outlet. The actions of the others became frantic. I was losing control. A giant bolt of electricity sent me over the edge. I couldn't breathe or move. It was all I could do to stifle a yell of pleasure or keep from bursting out laughing. I closed my eyes and caught my breath.

When I opened my eyes, the morning sun filled my room.

In my own bed, I sat up. Alone. I ran a hand through my hair and tried to shake the experience from my brain. I needed to know who those voices belonged to, but the harder I tried to recall them, the more they slipped from my mind. The only image my mind recalled was those incredible eyes.

I collapsed back on the bed.

"A dream." I peeked down. "At least the orgasm was real," I muttered, getting up.

I need a shower. Is it possible this dream is a side effect of the first Mark? Drinking Juliet's blood and a sex dream, that's it. That's all the first Mark is.

Other than my intense dream and the feeling of release, nothing seemed any different. I checked my reflection in the mirror. I had a bad case of bedhead, and my mouth tasted gross, but I appeared normal. I was me, which was a bit of a letdown especially after last night. I expected to look or feel different. There had to be more to my first Mark than some crazy sex dream. How was I supposed to be able to check into my father's passing if I was still dull old me? I sighed and pulled off my pajamas and got ready for the day.

Afterward, I headed downstairs, where I was greeted by Amanda and Juliet. It seemed they were waiting for me. How they always appeared right on time could be strange and it was an activity of theirs that, sadly, I was getting used to.

"You did very well last night." Amanda grinned.

My face heated. For a moment, I thought she was talking about what happened in my dream, which was awkward. I wasn't sure how to bring up a conversation about the dream, or even if I should. I doubted Juliet or Amanda wanted to hear about my intense sex dream.

Embarrassment moved through my body for more than one reason. "I passed out," I said. "Sorry if I ruined the event—er...ceremony."

"You would have only ruined the night if you didn't take my first offering or neglected to fall under." Juliet touched my arm softly. "Your body responded exactly as it should have."

I fidgeted with my hands. This didn't help me feel less embarrassed.

"Now, shall we have breakfast? There is much to discuss."

As we walked to the breakfast room, the scent of roses and vanilla seemed different. The aroma came on more pronounced and came from Juliet. I found myself craving it, not feeling complete without it, like her *offering* last night.

"You had us all worried last night when you hesitated." Juliet took a bite of the sliced apple. "Even Victor was surprised. He wouldn't admit it, of course." She chuckled. "He'd blame me for tricking his emotions, but I didn't do anything."

I took a sip of my orange juice.

"It's not allowed to manipulate emotions at the Marking ceremony."

I gulped. "What?"

"That's why Garrett was here," Juliet replied. "He knows when someone is using their gifts or magic and can stop them. It's actually quite brilliant, and I'm envious of it, but please, let's keep that between us."

"But I sensed you," I finally said. "You calmed me down. I was nervous, and I thought I was going to be sick, but you relaxed me. You kept me from freaking out."

Juliet shook her head. "If I manipulated you in any way, Garrett would have called the ceremony off. Victor would have loved that, but no, I was blocked. Only the Dark use their power to manipulate their Called, it's another difference between us."

"Can Garrett block people's abilities?" I asked.

"In a way yes," Juliet replied. "He can be overwhelmed, but yes, he can block our gifts, especially when it comes to my ability. It was the only way to ensure that no one would protest at the selection."

"Like Victor?" I asked.

Juliet nodded.

"Then what kept me so calm?" I mumbled, picking up my toast.

Amanda sipped her coffee, her eyebrows raised.

Juliet grinned.

"Maybe you weren't as freaked out as you thought," Amanda teased.

It gave me a lot to consider. Perhaps I wasn't as worried as I remembered. Or I had assumed Juliet would use her ability on me, and so my mind acted like it would have under her spell, a psychic placebo effect.

Juliet picked at her fruit salad. As I watched her, I couldn't help it. I had to understand because it had been driving me nuts since I started this whole journey. "Juliet, why do you eat food? I thought that immortals only lived off of...um...blood?" I would have to get used to the idea since I was going to be one.

"I enjoy eating. I like food and the texture. I adore the process of eating." She smiled.

"So, you need to eat?"

"No. I enjoy the pageantry of eating. It's not about the food; it's about the community and the artistry. Mostly, the food all tastes the same to me. It's like eating..." She paused, then continued, "I don't really have a base of comparison. There isn't much taste to anything, however, fresh fruits and vegetables are less difficult on my system. Some foods feel better than others, if that makes sense."

I noticed Amanda enjoying my questions.

"So, I can still eat food when everything is said and done?"

"If you want to." Juliet wiped her mouth with her napkin. "It's a good habit to get into, especially when you're in a mixed group or have to spend time with people. There are also places, not many, we can go that do a fusion. These places are owned by immortals and cater mainly to humans, but they have a private menu for us. It's all part of the..." She tilted her head, and a smile curled up at the ends of her mouth. "It's all part of how we blend in."

After that revelation, I decided to start paying more attention to what I was eating and make sure that I enjoyed it. "What happens now?" I took a bite of bacon, focusing on the flavor.

Juliet's face grew serious. "You have to die."

"What?" I almost spit out my bacon.

"Duncan Brian Alexander has to die," Juliet said matter-of-factly. "This has to be done to close out your former life. To give your friends a chance to have closure. It's cruel not to do it. Your friends and coworkers need this. I realize how this sounds, but it's the only way to create a new identity for you. Your old life has to end, so that no one will come searching for you. It will also help us create a clean identity for you."

My mouth hung open, dumbstruck. "So, I don't have to die, just the...the...I don't know, the paper version of me has to die?"

"Yes," Juliet replied. "How you handle it is your choice. The process is part of your transition. If you do not close out your life prior to transition, then you'll always have that tie to it. Does that make sense?"

I thought I understood. I had to own it. "But I don't know—"

Amanda cleared her throat.

"You won't be doing this alone." Juliet pointed to Amanda. "Amanda and I will help to make sure that you don't miss anything. My suggestion is that you keep it simple and believable."

Sipping her coffee, Amanda nodded.

"There is nothing worse than some overly complicated death that raises a lot of questions. We've had to clean up quite a few of these elaborate deaths. They are a hassle for everyone involved."

"Isn't what you're asking me to do illegal?" I realized I was naïve, but it was still something I wanted to know.

Amanda bit back her laugh.

"Yes, however, you must understand—and I cannot stress this enough—humans cannot, now or ever, find out about us." Juliet's tone was firm. "Remember when you asked about other supernatural beings?"

I nodded.

"I didn't tell you the complete truth. There were others, but the humans succeeded in killing them off. The old folktales of werewolves and shape-shifters, fairies, they are based in truth, but they were all systematically hunted down and killed by humans."

Oh God.

"The Crusades were more than what you learned about. Many of the ancient campaigns were all about killing off these creatures. The truth lost to legends and myth. So, it was decided that vampires could not be revealed." She leaned back in her chair. "Humans outnumber us, and even with our abilities, we are no match for them. Some people like to pretend we are the top of the food chain, but we're not, and only an arrogant fool would think otherwise." She shook her head. "If they identified us, they would hunt us down and kill us off, just like they did to the others."

"Or worse, they'd capture, study, and dissect the immortals." Amanda frowned.

I was quiet.

"She's right." A frown crossed Juliet's mouth. "It was not a pleasant time for anyone back then. So, yes, it might be illegal by today's laws, however, it is for the best."

Amanda faced me. "We should give you some time."

Juliet nodded.

"I'll be around if you need me," Amanda said.

How do you plan your own death?

Chapter Nine

MURDER, MY MURDER, was not something I had ever thought about. Not even my own death. Yes, my father died in an odd way, and I saw how much drama that caused. My mother passed away in a hospital, and I understood my own death couldn't be like that. There would be too many witnesses. I didn't want my death to get anyone in trouble.

I couldn't think of anything and needed to clear my head. I went out for a walk to get my thoughts together. Everything in the garden reminded me that life as I knew it was coming to an end. It was fall and the trees were losing their leaves. No more vivid summer colors filled the flower beds, and the days were growing shorter and cooler.

The following afternoon, I took the 1955 Ford Thunderbird and drove to Santa Cruz where I sat and watched the ocean, enjoying the cool ocean mist on my face and the taste of the salt air. The steady ebb and flow of the waves helped me to focus.

On my way home through the zigzagging curves of Highway 17, a brown truck cut me off, almost causing me to drive over the edge into a valley of redwoods. I thought about the accident I'd passed the first day I met Juliet.

Then I remembered how my father's body was found. Dead in the car along the side of the road.

"A car accident," I muttered.

I would cancel my flight home and rent a car, I would tell Cindy I was going to drive home. Highway 80, winding through the mountains, could be dangerous, especially at night. It's not uncommon for there to be accidents, so mine would be no different. The only thing that was different was the car would be rigged to explode. We would need to leave enough DNA evidence to confirm my identity. And as for the rest of the remains, well, there would be one less John Doe to worry about.

I took the basic plan for my demise to Juliet and Amanda. They approved and promised to take care of the various details. As Amanda made notes, she mumbled something about dental records.

Not privy to the final details, Amanda and Juliet took care of the logistics, which was fine with me. The less I knew about my death, the better. My biggest concern was that I wanted no one blamed for the car accident that would take my life. It was bad enough to be involved in this kind of fraud, no matter the reason, and I didn't want anyone else to get in trouble if my planned death, the end of me, went badly and the police came knocking.

FROM THE END of August to the end of September when everything was finalized, I wasn't the most pleasant person to be around. I didn't see anyone unless I had to, and I snapped a few times at Amanda. I would need to apologize to her later. As dull as my life had been, it was still my life, and I needed to mourn the loss of my friends and the life I had.

I didn't hear any more until the end of September. As I sat on my bedroom balcony having lunch, watching the trees, I didn't hear Amanda come out until she sat next to me.

"It's done," she said.

I faced her and nodded. Duncan Brian Alexander was officially dead and Christopher Michael Raymond was born.

"It was a nice small memorial service. The remains are entombed at the Mountain View Cemetery overlooking Reno," Amanda reported.

"Sounds pretty, I know that area. It is indeed a nice view." Leaves fell from the trees beyond my balcony.

She reached out and gave my arm a squeeze and left me to my thoughts.

I was glad I didn't know the details or even when the service was. I decided one should never visit one's own grave, immortal or not. It's creepy.

I couldn't go back to Reno—well, not anytime soon—to get anything from my apartment. Juliet explained that it all had to go, and that I couldn't keep anything—no pictures, no books, nothing from my old life. I hated it, and I became resentful. Especially when I found out that the reason I hadn't been introduced at her Foundation where I would be working, or filled out any employment paperwork, was because I was still Duncan and it kept all those people from having their memories altered.

I FROWNED AT the early morning sun as we pulled up in front of the Los Altos Beaux Vêtements.

"Now when we go in, you'll watch and wait and pay attention to how this is done," Juliet said. "You can't do it yet, but seeing how it works is an important first step." She stood in front of the store in her cream top and a jade scarf draped around her neck. She was beautiful. Since I had to give up all my old clothes, I was in one of my new outfits. Jeans, an aqua lightweight cashmere sweater with the sleeves rolled up, and brown dress shoes. It was a good look for me, and I liked it, as did Juliet and Amanda.

"Are you sure he won't be hurt by this?" I asked.

Juliet shook her head.

"And what about all the paperwork? Security cameras? Won't that cause problems? I don't get how any of this is going to work," I grumbled.

"Chris, relax, I've done this countless times. It'll be fine," Juliet said. "Whatever happens, stay calm and pay attention to what I do."

My hands were tapping on my legs. Before we left the house, Juliet and I had sat in her office, and she'd transitioned for me again. As with the first time in her office with Victor, her fangs extended and her brows grew heavy with ridges, forcing her face into a scowl. It was unsettling, but not nearly as bad as the first time.

"Chris?" Juliet said.

I didn't respond.

"Christopher." She snapped her fingers.

I focused on her and nodded, not used to my new name yet. Getting to pick my name had been enjoyable, but not easy. There are millions of names, and I had to come up with one that was common enough so that it didn't stand out and was appropriate for my age.

It took longer than I thought it would. However, I came up with what I thought was a good name: Christopher Michael Raymond. I googled it and was happy with the number of people who had that same name. I believed it would work nicely. I also, enjoyed all the mug shots. They made me laugh.

Juliet took my arm. "Trust me."

"Of course I trust you," I said. "I just—he's been nice to me, and I don't want anything bad to happen to him."

"He'll be fine." Juliet tapped on the door and waited to be let in. Amanda had called in and arranged to have the store closed for us. The ruse being I wanted a whole new wardrobe. The truth was Juliet needed to do a memory thing, so the fewer people around, the better.

Fredrick appeared at the door with a big smile on his face. "Juliet, Duncan, so nice to see you. Please come in." He ushered us through the door. "I'm excited the both of you are here. Since Amanda's call, I pulled different fabrics and clothes together for Duncan."

"It's always a joy to see you, Fredrick." Juliet headed to the back table that had been pulled out for us to sit.

"Duncan." Fredrick stuck out his hand to shake.

I shook hands but didn't say much. I wasn't sure what to say to him or where to look.

"Come, come." Fredrick shepherded me to the back of the shop. "Can I offer you something to drink? It'll only take a moment."

Juliet stood with her back to us. It was odd for her back to be turned, but I had an idea why.

I let Fredrick pass me so he was centered between Juliet and me.

I took a breath. My hands were damp, trembling at my sides.

Juliet faced Fredrick, her face transformed. She was baring fangs, and ridges angled down her forehead, all her soft features gone. I don't know French so the words that flew out of Fredrick's mouth when he saw her were lost on me, but if I had to guess, it would have been something like: "Holy Shit! What the fuck are you? Please, don't kill me."

Juliet had him by the shoulders, staring him square in the eyes. "Fredrick." Her voice was calm and low, forcing him to stop and listen. The softer she spoke, the harder we both had to listen to hear her.

"Fredrick, this is Christopher Michael Raymond, my friend," Juliet said. "He's always been Christopher Michael Raymond, and he goes by Chris. This is how you know him. It's how you met him when you came to my home to fit him that first time. Do you understand?"

"Yes," Fredrick said. "Of course. Please don't hurt me." His voice trembled.

The poor man was scared to death, but there was something about his voice. It was distant and faraway sounding.

"I have no intention of harming you, Fredrick. We're friends, and I love your store. Tell me, who is the man standing behind you?" Juliet's tone was kind, and her voice warm. It didn't match how terrifying she appeared.

"That's Mr. Raymond, Chris. He's your friend." Fredrick faced me, his brow dripping with sweat. "Chris, you won't let her hurt me?"

I shook my head and forced a weak smile.

"It's good to see you again, Chris. I have a lot of nice things to show you today." Fredrick turned back and faced Juliet.

"That's right, Fredrick." Juliet's voice was level, calm, and just barely a whisper. "Who did you have an appointment with today?"

"You and Christopher Michael Raymond." Fredrick's voice was stronger. "I've closed the store for you both so we can find him clothes without being disturbed."

"And after we leave today, you're going to go and make sure that any documentation that has the name Duncan Alexander on it is destroyed," Juliet said. "You'll create a new file for Christopher Raymond to replace it."

Fredrick licked his lips.

"If anyone were to ever ask you about a man named Duncan Alexander, you have no idea who he is," Juliet added.

"I have no idea who that is," Fredrick mimicked.

"If someone shows you a picture of a man named Duncan Alexander, you won't know him. You won't recognize the picture as Christopher either. You'll see a man you have never met before. Do you understand?"

"Yes, I understand," Fredrick replied, his hands trembling.

"Tell me what you're going to do?" Juliet's voice was soft but commanding.

"After you leave, I will go and destroy the paperwork I have on Duncan Alexander and create a file for Christopher Raymond." Fredrick took a shaky breath. "If I'm ever shown a picture of a man named Duncan Alexander, I won't know him. He will be someone I've never met."

His face was blank, but the sweat soaked his face and concern shone in his eyes. I wanted her to stop but understood how important this was. It was for his protection as much as my own.

"Good," Juliet said. "Now if you are ever confused by this or if you are ever asked about a man named Duncan Alexander, you will call me and only me. Do you understand, Fredrick?"

"I understand." Sweat dripped over his eyelids. "If I'm confused or if someone asks about a man named Duncan Alexander, I'll call you."

"Perfect," Juliet said. "Now, you are going to close your eyes and quietly count to five. When you're done, you'll offer us something to drink, and we'll continue as if none of this ever happened, all right?"

"All right. I would like that." Fredrick closed his eyes and started to count.

Juliet's face turned back to normal, and she smiled at me. She flattened out the creases of her blouse.

Fredrick opened his eyes, life returning to his face. "Ah now where were we? Christopher, would you like something to drink? Juliet, what about you? I can make some tea or I have bottled water." He wiped his forehead and fanned himself. "I'll check the AC, too."

"Tea would be lovely," Juliet said.

Unsure what to say or do at this point, as they had both moved on, I discovered it was hard to get my footing. My heart pounded, and I found my own palms still sweaty.

"Chris?" Juliet asked.

Fredrick stood there, waiting for me to answer.

"Um...tea...fine. Yes. I mean yes, please. Tea is fine, please. Thanks. Thank you." I stumbled over every word.

"Excellent. Have a seat, and I'll be back in a moment." Fredrick happily rushed off.

Once he was out of earshot, I turned to Juliet. "He was terrified, and to be honest, so was I. I thought you might eat him or something."

"He's fine, and I wasn't going to feed off him." Juliet shook her head. "Did you watch what I did and how I talked to him in a calm tone? It's best not to break eye contact, but if it happens, just repeat and reinforce."

"What about his security system?"

"Cameras in the back and on the front only," Juliet said. "I've been here enough I know the proper spot to stand."

"Fine." I tilted my head around, hearing my neck crack.

"The directions were both simple and precise," she continued. "They can't be overly complicated, and it's best to always ask them if they understand you. It's almost impossible to get people to do something against their nature. I couldn't have him harm someone. That goes against who he is. It works the same for when we need to feed off people. Does that make sense?"

"I think so," I replied, my heart no longer racing. I hoped I wouldn't have to do this to anyone. "It's like hypnosis in that regard."

I remembered an article I'd read about a study done on hypnosis, proving that what we see on TV and in movies isn't right. You can't hypnotize someone to kill another person or harm themselves. They have to agree to it. By the time I finished trying to wrap my head around everything that happened, Fredrick had returned with our tea.

"IT'S NOT A process I enjoy, but it has to be done," Juliet said as we passed the various mansions hidden among the trees on our way home.

"Is that why you spent so much money today?" I was more relaxed now that it was over and the worst seemed to be behind us.

"That and you needed new clothes. Plus, he had some really cute blouses and skirts that I wanted." She winked.

When we got back to the house, there were very few bags to be brought in since most of what we bought was being altered. I would go back and pick it up, just as a test to make sure that the altered memories stayed altered.

Taking our usual places on the sofa in Juliet's office, we continued to talk. What I enjoyed most about my transition was spending hours together with Juliet. She explained more about how immortals lived in the world with the humans, and how they had tried to stay out of history's way. It didn't always work. That had more to do with the Dark fighting for power.

"There haven't been any clashes with the Dark here in the Bay Area in over a hundred years. Not since Victor took over. I was lucky—"

A knock came from the door.

"Come in," Juliet said.

I stood as Amanda entered the office with a folder. She sat in one of the overly stuffed occasional chairs and I took my seat again.

"Ah, you have everything?" Juliet went over and poured herself a glass of red and me a glass of water.

I pointed to her glass. "How does it—the blood I mean—stay fresh?"

Juliet smiled and tapped the crystal. "The containers have a special immortal enchantment. It is something I will teach you when you are older, but we have more pressing issues at the moment. Namely, your new identity."

"Okay." I supposed it would be better than having to store blood bags all the time.

"Amanda." Juliet pointed to the file.

"Everything should be here," Amanda replied. "I wanted to wait until after you met with Fredrick, just in case there was something that needed to be altered." She handed me the folder.

"What's this?"

"That folder holds all the documentation for Christopher Michael Raymond," Amanda replied. "Open it."

I opened the folder. It housed a birth certificate, US passport, social security card, California driver's license, an American Express card, and a Visa bank card. There was also a checkbook.

I pulled out a list with my bank account, savings account, investment account, copies of IRS documents. Another sheet of paper had a resume and behind that a high school diploma from Mt. Pleasant High School, and a college diploma with my listed major as business administration from San Jose State University. I even had my own library card.

"Holy shit," I said. "Sorry." I glanced at both Juliet and Amanda. "How is all this possible?"

"All the paperwork you signed a few weeks ago. This is the result." Amanda sat taller and waggled her eyebrows.

"But I never completed college," I said. "And what about these accounts? There's a bit of money in them. How am I going to keep all this straight?"

"Well, you went to college, and I researched the classes you took, and in conjunction with your work experience, you earned the degree," Amanda said. "As for the money, I examined your assets and guessed about what you were worth." She shrugged. "It really isn't that difficult. Anyway, it's all there in your official records. Chris, you were a good student—not the top of the class but you did well. You took a variety of day and night classes because of your work, so it took you longer to graduate."

"I don't even want to think about how many laws you broke to do this." I frowned.

"All right, I'll take it back and you can live in a box under the overpass," Amanda huffed, trying to hide her smile.

Juliet snickered.

"You'd be surprised at how much was handled above board, all nice and legal," Amanda said. "And remember, we have friends and know people. So they help. It's a necessary evil, so to speak."

"Amanda is excellent at this sort of thing," Juliet said. "She helps a few others of our ilk when needed. I've learned to trust her. I believe there should be something else in there? An offer letter and job description from the Foundation."

I scanned the information, pulled out an envelope, and opened it. An offer letter dated a month ago and a job description were now in my hands. "Director of Community Affairs?"

"We needed a position that would allow you flexibility so that, when we need to travel, there won't be any issues." Juliet adjusted her blouse. "It also ties in to your background and experience. You won't need to make things up. It will also give you the authority to run the Foundation when I'm not around."

"Wait. Run the Foundation?"

"Of course."

"But I don't have the qualifications—"

"You do if I say you do." Juliet sipped her red. "Plus, I'll teach you. It's a small organization, so it's not hard."

I nodded.

"As for the salary, I hope you'll find it fair."

"That's very generous, thanks." I couldn't help but laugh. Things seemed so absurd to me. But steps had to be taken and a life had to be built. "I suppose I need to sign all this?"

"That would be lovely," Amanda replied. "I can take it to the office and everything will get filed." She pulled out a pen and offered it to me.

"So this is my new life," I said with raised eyebrows as I accepted the pen.

I went to sign the documents, and before pen met paper, Juliet reminded me, "Sign them Christopher."

I nodded and signed my new name. I had been practicing my new signature over and over again, but the reminder was appreciated.

"I'll leave the rest of it in your room," Amanda said. "You'll need to call and activate the credit cards, and it would be good for you to go to the bank in person so they get to know you. It's the little details that will make the biggest difference."

With everything signed, Amanda stood, as did I.

"Thank you," I said.

"My pleasure." Amanda took the folder with all the paperwork and left.

"I've got to ask, where did you find her?" I asked. "Amanda is amazing. She seems to know and do everything."

"I was wondering when you were going to ask about that." Juliet sipped her drink. "Amanda is my Keeper."

"Keeper?"

"She's the person who takes care of me." Juliet kicked off her shoes and tucked her feet under her. Her shoulders relaxing. "She's my human servant and is tied to me."

I leaned forward.

"But you can go out in daylight. You can do everything anyone else can. You don't need her."

Juliet chuckled. "In most cases. However, if I'm weakened and in need of blood and care, she is there for me. She also provides a link to my humanity."

Juliet raised a hand before I could speak. "Understand, people will come and go and humans grow old and die. Nature, in her vast wisdom, decided it would be a waste to train a new person every fifty or sixty years. So immortals have Keepers, that's what most of us call them."

"Wait. So you mean to tell me Amanda is as old as you?"

Juliet couldn't help but chuckle. "No, I've only had Amanda in my service for..." Juliet tapped her lips. "About two hundred years. When I brought her into my care, she was eighteen." She had a distant look on her face.

"Wow, that's a long time. She doesn't look eighteen, though."

Juliet sipped her red. "No, she grows older, but it's a slower process. At some point, she will grow old and die." Her expression grew sad. "I will have to find a new Keeper. It won't be easy. Amanda is amazing."

"And you can't turn her?" I asked.

"No." Juliet sighed. "I admit that part of me was hoping she would answer the Calling, but she didn't, so there is nothing I can do. In another fifty years, I will release her from her service." She flattened her lips and dropped her gaze. "She will be able to go and live out the rest of her life, well taken care of, and with no memories of any of this."

"That doesn't sound right."

"Perhaps not, but that is the way of things. It won't be that bad for her. I'll alter her memories so she won't be at risk and watch over her until she passes. With luck, she will find love and be happy." She sounded hopeful. "When you complete your transition, you'll need to get yourself a Keeper—not right away of course. I'll help you with the process. They'll need to be someone you trust and care for but will never fall in love with. I can assure you, that causes nothing but heartache and pain. I say this from experience, Christopher."

"If you don't mind me asking, what happened?"

"I don't mind, it was long ago."

I leaned back on the sofa.

"He was my first Keeper, and he was beautiful. He even had all his teeth."

I smirked.

She chuckled. "Trust me, back then that was a big deal. He was perfect. He was a Roman soldier. The Romans had just signed a treaty with the Persians on humiliating terms for the Romans, and Valentinian the Great had been proclaimed emperor."

I opened my mouth to speak.

"I won't bore you, and you don't need a human history lesson. Anyway, I caught his eye. He did everything he could to win my attention. I was young, and my creator, Marcel, sadly, was a drunk and wasn't the best mentor—"

"Wait. Immortals can get drunk?"

Juliet nodded. "Of course. Anyway, when I told him about Giaus, he wanted to check into him and make sure that he was a fitting match. Plus, we had to keep up appearances."

I leaned forward, finding it all fascinating.

"My creator and I, we were both Gauls. That was the part of the Roman Empire that was where France is today. Marcel and I were free Romans. Marcel saw the fall of Rome coming; it was in its decline and he recognized it, but we still played our parts. That was one thing about Marcel. He had been alive for five hundred years and was clever. Despite all his flaws and his drinking, he was smarter than most. He understood how to play the games of men. He made friends with the local powers, bribing them and making sure their pockets were full and any other needs they had were met."

"Not unlike things now." I frowned.

She finished off the last of her red, then got up and poured herself another glass. She refilled my water as well.

"Marcel checked out Giaus to ensure he would make a proper Keeper. Once Marcel agreed, we started the process." She sipped her drink and tucked her legs under her, getting comfortable. "In order for a person to become a Keeper, they must consent. Once that happens, you force your will onto them. It's like what we did with Fredrick today."

I grimaced at the memory.

"You have to convince them that they want to serve you. Keep in mind, they still maintain free will and their independence. That doesn't change."

I was confused, and she noticed.

"Let me explain. Amanda can come to me at any time and tell me she wants to leave. If that happens, then I'll release her. Luckily, that has not been the case."

"In order for the bond to be set, you have to drain your Keeper of their blood, almost to the point of death, and then you allow them to feed off you to heal and replenish them."

I cringed.

"It's not as painful as it sounds. You do need to allow the Keeper to feed off you every so often to keep them bound to you. You'll also need to feed off them on occasion."

I pursed my lips.

"It's a process." She shrugged.

"Wow. It's a bit overwhelming."

"I'll help you through it." Juliet patted my leg.

Her tone was quiet throughout our conversion and as she spoke, a distant look crossed her face. Even with the hundreds of years that she had seen, I noticed this conversation had her the most sullen.

"You'll do fine, Christopher."

"So you had to do that to Giaus then?" Honestly, I was more interested in finding out about Giaus than about the Keeper process.

"Yes." Juliet's face brightened. "Once Marcel approved, I started the process with Giaus. We were married, and everything went smoothly. We watched the Roman Empire come to its end, and we saw the formation of new kingdoms. He even lived long enough to see the beginnings of what would become modern day France."

Juliet smiled, but there were tears in her eyes.

"Juliet, you don't need to talk about this." I placed my hand on her leg, giving it a reassuring squeeze.

"It's okay. It was so long ago it's nice to remember. It keeps me human."

I smiled at her.

"Watching Gaius grow old and die, seeing the life slip from my grasp was quite possibly the most painful thing I'd ever been through," Juliet said. "Even worse than Marcel's leaving this world was realizing there was nothing I could do for Giaus to make his passing easier. We spent all those years together, growing closer and closer. I watched him get old as I stayed young. We went from being husband and wife to father and daughter, to grandfather and granddaughter."

She focused on me, and the room melted away. I actually sensed her pain and sorrow. It was misery.

My eyes filled with tears.

"Chris, that was worse than his death, witnessing him decay before my eyes. I would never wish that pain on anyone, but I wouldn't change it."

"I'm sorry, Juliet." I gulped back my own sorrow as the room came back into focus.

Her hand was soft on my leg. "I will do my very best by you, but I cannot promise you will not have to deal with pain and loss; it is part of being immortal."

Was I strong enough to endure such heartache? I wasn't so sure.

Chapter Ten

"LET ME BE sure I've got this straight." Immortal training was like being back in high school history with a teacher who had no personality. I adjusted in my seat at Juliet's office conference table. "You have three senior governors who you meet once a quarter: Rei, Maria, and Gregor. They each have governors that they work with, and each of these governors has lords or ladies that they work with in their regions." I thought a moment, tapping my pen on my notepad. "You have a total of nineteen governors; three from Canada, four from Mexico, and twelve from the US. This includes your three seniors, whom you work with directly."

"Correct." Juliet nodded. Her tone was flat unlike the previous week when she'd told me the story of Marcel and Giaus. The only things missing from Juliet being a schoolmarm were her hair done up in a tight bun and black heavy-framed glasses. "I mostly only deal with Rei, Maria, and Gregor—it makes running my territory much easier. Back when I took over North America, it wasn't that large a territory. In fact, it had the lowest number of 'civilized' people with the least amount of influence, which is why I got it."

"With how big it is now, why not break it up so that it's not so much to handle?" I asked.

"Vanity, I suppose."

I smirked at her with raised eyebrows.

"They gave me this territory, not thinking much would come of it," Juliet said. "It was out of control and a whole 'new world.'" She smiled and leaned back in her seat. "We've talked about breaking it up, but I suppose the real reason we haven't done it is because it works."

"Makes sense."

"We have our issues, but considering some of the other regions, mine is the most stable. Even the Dark play nice, which is saying something." She pointed to the map of North America. "There are of course problematic areas. Such as the border with the United States and Mexico as well as the parts of Chicago and Detroit, but we do our best to keep them under control."

I nodded.

"Now tell me the reason for the Council of Light," Juliet asked. "Why is it important?"

I shook my head. "All this vampire history is fine, but can't we just talk like normal people, like we did the other day? Can't you tell me what you think my ability might be? Why do we have to keep going over all this?"

We'd spent most of the day and much of the last week going over the history of the immortals and how the two worlds—Light and Dark—had existed in a state of balance for 1800 years. Before that, there was anarchy, and before that, a line of royals controlled all immortals. So, during this time, it had been up to the Council of Light to help keep stability in the world. They worked to keep the vampires from being "outed," so to speak. And they tried to keep the Dark in line.

Like Juliet had said, her area was mostly stable, but that didn't mean there weren't troublesome spots. Only when she talked about her past and her territories did our conversation come to life. She became animated and filled in the facts with her history and her stories.

"You have to understand the past so you don't make the same mistakes."

I stifled a yawn but failed to hide it.

"Chris, we have a history you must understand. This is all significant. This is what and who the Light are."

"A bunch of bookworms." I pushed the books away from me. "What about wars and battles? What about the vampire monarchy? How did immortals affect human history? Did the immortals have anything to do with Lincoln's assassination? What about Kennedy?" I waggled my eyebrows and leaned forward. "What about Elvis? Come on. Immortals must have been involved in that?"

Juliet choked back a laugh. "Chris."

I chuckled.

Juliet straightened her blouse. "It's especially important for you since you are my first-and-only Called. You will be held to a different standard. A lot of people will be on the lookout for you to make mistakes."

I understood. She was the head of the Council of Light, and there were immortals who would be watching her.

"Why not have a king or queen again? It seemed to work before the Council was created? Or, hold an election and have a single president, be more modern about it? That might solve some of the balance issues, especially if everyone got to vote for one leader."

She nodded.

"Plus, I mean, I can't believe there's no one out there that can lead the immortals. What about you?"

"In order for there to be a true single leader of both the Dark and Light, a vampire must unite both groups. The idea you suggest of a simple election won't work. A new ruler must have been created by the queen and have royal blood running through his or her veins." Juliet rubbed her temples. "Since the last queen and her heir were killed by humans, there is no one with that blood anymore."

"Immortals need to be unified in case people find out about them and start a war or something. Wouldn't a united front be better in that case?" The idea of fractured groups, all with their own agendas barely working together, didn't make sense to me. "I still think you should do it, or try."

"I think you've watched too many movies." She smiled. "Thank you for your faith in me, but I could never unite the Dark and the Light. Outside my territory, most of the Dark and some of the Light do not care for me. I'm respected, but they would never have me lead them. And no one on the Council of Light would be accepted by the Dark rulers." She focused on her books as she spoke. "When the queen and her heir died, her ruling Council lasted hundreds of years, but eventually they began to split into the Light and Dark. They battled for years over control."

She tapped the books. "They finally broke into all-out war with one another. That's what hurled the world into the Dark Ages. When the battles were over, a balance was reached. There are none alive today who remember the time of the queen. Marcel would have only been a hundred-years-or-so old and probably too drunk to give it much notice." She sighed. "I know it's not a perfect system and there are issues, but it's what we have. Plus, the world was a much different and smaller place than it is now. I can't imagine how any one person could rule. Especially out of Egypt—well, ancient Egypt, like it was."

"How do you know her only heir died? Couldn't someone be out there in the bloodline?"

Juliet tapped her lips. "It's possible, but they would have to be from her human family, and as far as I know, she had none."

We had several of Juliet's ancient books out on the desk, including her personal journals, and we were looking at maps. Despite the age of all the material, it was neat and had few marks or rips.

I leaned back in my chair and raked a hand through my hair. "So instead of trying something new, we're in a three-way cold war. The humans who have no idea about immortals, the Dark who are kind of vampire anarchists, and the Light who try to keep the status quo while bickering amongst themselves. Does that about sum it up?"

"Well, if you say it like that, it doesn't sound at all interesting." Juliet grinned.

"Juliet, I can't..." I stopped, "Someday, we humans are going to learn that we've been sharing this planet with other species, and when that happens..." I shook my head.

After sitting for so long, my leg had fallen asleep. I got up and crossed to the window. My eyes adjusted to the dark, and my reflection turned hazy and vanished. Two eyes—one green, one gray—stared back at me. A blinding pain shot through my temple.

"Fucking hell." I backed into one of the conference chairs and lost my footing.

"Christopher, what's wrong?"

"I...I saw... Juliet...my reflection, it vanished and was replaced by eyes." My heart pounded in my ears. "They were watching me." I stammered and rubbed my head. The pain faded.

"Chris, your nose."

I reached up and pulled my hand away. Blood.

"Here." Juliet handed me a tissue.

The eyes were the same from my dreams. But there wasn't pain during the dream. In fact, it was the opposite. "Something happened."

"Sit down, please," Juliet said. "What is it? What did you see?" She poured a drink and handed it to me.

The warm burn of scotch traveled down the back of my throat. "The night of my first Mark after I passed out, I ah..." My neck and cheeks heated. "Well, I ah...I had this...um...this dream."

Juliet grinned. "Ah yes, that. You have nothing to be embarrassed about. It happens to all of us. Each Mark will bring with it that kind of reaction, except for the last Mark." She played with a lock of her hair. "That is something completely different."

"No, that's not it." My heart slowed its thundering beat, and I avoided checking the window or my reflection. "I mean yes, that was part of it... wait, you had that kind of dream as well?"

"Yes, Chris, all immortals have erotic dreams. It's part of the bonding we go through with our creator, but that wasn't what had you falling over yourself. What is it?" She reached out and put her hand on top of my arm.

"Right. In that dream, I saw these eyes. They were amazing—unlike any eyes I had ever seen."

Juliet's brow furrowed.

"I just saw them again in the window where my reflection should have been." I finally glanced at the window. "This time, it was like an anvil had smashed into my head. Is that normal, to have someone else's eyes staring at you? What about a bloody nose?" I shook my head.

She was silent, then got up, walked to her desk, picked up the phone, and waited. "Adam, please bring in some lunch right away. The usual. Thank you." She hung up and went still, focusing on me.

"I'm not hungry. I wasn't hallucinating. I'm telling you what I saw, and I'm asking if this is normal. The eyes felt so familiar, but I've only seen them in dreams, and the pain...is this normal?"

"I don't know." She took her seat again. She flipped through her book on ancient European lore.

"There's nothing wrong with me, right?"

Her silence made my heart race, and I had to wipe my sweaty hands on my pants.

"I'm not going to turn into some freak vampire-creature thing, right? What happens if I don't finish the process? What happened during your first Mark?" I tried to fill the silence with something, anything. "Juliet, why aren't you answering me? Maybe we should stop and not go through with it."

"Once it's started, the process has to be completed. Stopping isn't an option." Juliet continued to hurriedly flip through a second book. This one about the magic of Native Americans.

"Why not? Just alter my memories and send me on my way. It would suck but..."

She shut the book harder than I thought even she meant to and studied me. "If we stop, you'll die. I can't alter your memories at this point. I can't force my will on you. It's too late."

I froze where I sat, mouth dropped.

"If we stop the process, the only option is to kill you, and I cannot allow that. If you were not meant to be Called, then yes, we could do that, but you were Called, so we either proceed or you have to..."

"Why didn't you tell me this before I agreed? If this was a risk, why'd you keep it from me?"

My heart pounded again, and sweat beaded on my forehead.

"Because the chances of a bad Mark is—I don't know—one in a billion. I've only seen it happen once." She pulled out another book. "You stand a better chance of getting struck by lightning a dozen times, all on the same day of the week, over a dozen years." She pushed the book away. "It doesn't happen."

"But a bad Mark has happened, right?"

"Once in over sixteen hundred years, that barely deserves a mention. I'm sorry, but I never thought it would be an issue, and I doubt it is now, so please don't worry." She tapped her lips. "I need to figure out what's happening."

I was floored. What was happening to me?

"Chris?"

My body shook. I was about to explode at her again when a knock on the door halted me.

Adam entered with a tray. He crossed the room and placed the tray next to me. He smiled politely and adjusted a few books out of the way so we could reach the tray easily. There was a sandwich for me and a small salad for Juliet. Also on the tray, a bowl filled with chips and a glass of milk.

"Enjoy." Adam started to leave.

"Wait." I jumped up, took a small breath to calm myself, and walked over. I checked his eyes.

"Is something wrong?" He stood there as I stared right into his eyes. He blushed, and I wasn't sure if it was surprise or something else. I didn't care. I had to confirm it wasn't him, even if he was attractive and I was awkward.

"No, sorry." His eyes were blue.

He stood a moment longer, and when I didn't say anything else, he left the room.

"I'm guessing his were not the eyes you saw," Juliet said.

"No." I sat down, shaking my head.

"Eat something."

I sighed. The turkey sandwich looked good and made my stomach growl.

"I'm sorry," Juliet said. "I shouldn't have told you about the failed Mark in that way. I didn't mean to upset you. I've never heard of anything like this, hallucinations, but we'll figure it out."

"It's not a hallucination. It's real."

She picked up her plate of fresh greens and sliced vegetables. "Transitions are standard. I've witnessed hundreds, possibly even a thousand. With each Mark, you become more immortal. Your talent or ability will start to manifest after the third Mark. It won't become fully realized until the final Mark."

I nabbed a chip from the bowl.

"Chris, we can't stop the process. That is why so much went into this before we started. Once you begin, the only option is to turn or die." She pursed her lips. "I'm sorry. I should have told you."

I grabbed a few more chips and popped them into my mouth, enjoying the salty taste. "I suppose the no-way-back clause makes sense, given what I've learned. I get that you weren't hiding that from me." I closed my eyes. "Is it possible that... I don't know if it's possible, but could I be developing my gift thing early?" Knowing my luck, it would have to do with eyes and bloody noses. How was this going to help me find out what happened to my dad and hold the Dark immortals accountable, assuming it was them that murdered him.

"That's what I'm checking into. I've never heard of it happening this soon. I suppose it's possible, but I honestly..." She picked up her journal. "I don't know, and why would you see eyes and not a whole person?"

"Well, in the dream, I couldn't see people's faces either. When they spoke, I understood the words, but all the voices sounded different and seemed filtered, so I didn't even know if they were male or female." I sipped my milk.

Juliet's brows were drawn together, and she bit her lip. "How many people were in your dream encounter?"

"I'm not sure. I heard three different people and I..." My face grew warm. I cleared my throat. "I ah...felt three people as well."

"I know this is a delicate question, but I must ask." She leaned in. "Was I in this dream dalliance of yours? What about any of my staff? Amanda maybe? Mia? Adam?"

"I'm sorry. I don't know. I didn't even recognize the voices. It was..." I didn't know how to say it or even how to explain it. "It was as if people were there but they weren't. I sensed them, but I couldn't touch them, and when I tried to reach out for them, they would be gone or move to a different place."

"If you don't mind, I want to call Victor and talk to him about this." Juliet sighed.

"What? Why?"

"He's the oldest of the Dark rulers and despite his being of the Dark, I trust him, especially in matters like this. The Dark turn people in what you would consider a more typical vampire manner, and he might know something I don't."

I wasn't thrilled with the idea. However, if it meant I wasn't going crazy or turning into something unknown, then I would live with it. "If you think it'll help."

I glanced at my sandwich. I suddenly wasn't hungry.

THE TWINKLING LIGHTS of San Jose reminded me of gleaming jewels. That night, we were driving in a Tesla. Juliet said it was important that we look to future technologies and support them. It was the only way to ensure the survival of all the species. Juliet maneuvered in and out of the downtown traffic and pulled up to a beautiful metal-and-glass modern high-rise.

"This is the Heights."

She turned into the garage where a short, dumpy guard with a fat head was standing.

"Hello. I'm Madame Juliet de Exter. I'm here for Victor Rey."

The guard wobbled off into his small office.

"Victor owns the company that built this building. He wanted something classy and modern to live in, and since he doesn't like San Francisco, he built it here in San Jose."

A sparkle danced in her eyes. I figured there was a story hidden there, but she didn't say any more, and the guard released the gate. She waved to him and drove through.

I checked out the marble columns by the lobby entrance as we drove by. "It's a nice building."

"Very." Juliet found a parking space.

As I got out of the car, my foot slipped. The soles of the black Italian leather dress shoes were slick as ice. I was still getting used to having an upgraded wardrobe. For a meeting like this, Juliet had insisted I wear a suit. She'd informed me it couldn't be the suit that Victor had seen me in already. When you were doing anything immortal related, you had to dress to impress. So, here I was in a ridiculously expensive dark gray suit and burgundy tie to meet with a man I was sure didn't like me. I loosened the knot of my tie.

The elevator doors opened to Victor's penthouse, and I was floored. The foyer had glossy white marble floors. There was a single black wall with a red painting in a brushed nickel frame. It was one of those trendy pictures full of red-on-red smears that any child could do, but the ultra-rich snapped up with no regard for price. Under the picture was a glossy white table with a crystal bowl. My gaze followed the polished white floors the length of the entry to the view of the city. The windows were trimmed in black, giving the effect that each pane of glass was its own painting. The lights of the city grabbed my attention as they vanished into Mt. Hamilton in the distance.

"Welcome, Madame de Exter," a heavyset balding man said with a slight but distinct lisp before offering a graceful bow. He wore a light gray suit with a lavender bow tie and matching pocket square. "Master Rey is expecting you and your companion."

The greeter appeared to be in his thirties, but it was hard to say. Not just because of the whole slowed-aging thing either, it had to do with his balding head. I always considered baldness to make men look older than they actually were.

The man watched me. "You must be Mister Raymond. Please, follow me."

"Thank you, Daniel," Juliet said.

He led us through the penthouse quicker than I would have liked. The black-and-white motif continued throughout. Couches, chairs, tables, all in blacks and whites. The only splashes of color—red—were pillows and knickknacks here and there. The entire home was right off a magazine cover. Clearly Victor had impressive taste.

Daniel motioned us toward two heavy floor-to-ceiling doors and tapped softly. "Master Rey. Your guests." Daniel guardedly opened the door.

Inside the office, Victor stood framed by a view of the city skyline.

"Daniel, do get Juliet and I something fresh. As for Mister Raymond—" Victor glanced at me, then back to Daniel. "Whatever you feel appropriate."

Daniel nodded.

Victor waved his hand, and Daniel was out the door.

"Welcome to my home. Please, have a seat." Victor pointed to the white guest chairs in front of his desk.

"Victor, thank you for agreeing to meet with us." Juliet took a seat.

I followed her lead. The plush white chairs had enough give to make them comfortable. There was a hint of almonds in the air, but none in the room, so I figured the scent was Victor's.

"It's my pleasure." Victor sat down in his black leather chair. "I'm always willing to help the Council of Light. We must keep up our good relations."

His politeness struck me as a bit odd. In the few times I'd been around Victor, he didn't impress upon me as someone who played nice.

"And how are you doing now that you've had your first Mark, Christopher?"

"I'm doing fine. Thank you."

A soft knock at the door interrupted us.

Daniel entered, holding a tray with a crystal decanter and three glasses; two filled with what I was sure was blood, as was the decanter, and a third filled with what looked like wine. Daniel gave a glass to each Juliet and Victor, and then put the wineglass in front of me. His gaze rarely left Victor as if always seeking appreciation from him. Duties finished, Daniel gave one more quick glance to Victor, who didn't seem to notice. Daniel quickly left the room.

"I hope you like the wine. I understand it's very good." Victor took his glass. "Enjoy."

Juliet picked up her glass, and I followed her lead again. I wasn't much of a wine guy, but it was good.

Victor put his drink down. "You mentioned questions for me." His face bore a smug expression.

Juliet needed his help. It was clear from his expression he was listening. However, the longer the conversation drew out, the more opportunity there was for his enjoyment, like a cat toying with its prey.

"Yes." Juliet's body was relaxed, but she had a formal smile. "Christopher has been seeing things since the night of his first Mark. Normally, talents don't start to reveal themselves until the third Mark, and I've never heard of anything like what he has explained to me."

I fumbled with my hands. Juliet didn't waste any time getting to the point.

I took a deep breath. "I don't really know how to explain it. Twice now, I've seen these eyes staring at me. The first time was the night of my first Mark. The second time was this afternoon in Juliet's office, but there was also this sharp pain and I got a bloody nose." I looked from Victor to Juliet. "It happened when I caught sight of my reflection."

Victor sipped his red and put the glass down. "Sounds like madness to me. Perhaps, you should not have put so much faith in the Calling. I suggest you kill him and find another." He lifted his glass to me. "No offense. It's how we Dark handle such things."

"Victor." Juliet stood, and the tone of her voice turned icy and hard. I wasn't sure what to say or do. I was pissed but couldn't do anything, so I stood up as well.

"Relax." Victor chuckled and pointed to our seats. "You cannot begrudge me a little fun. After all, how often does Juliet de Exter come in need of my help?"

Juliet was not smiling.

Victor sighed. "Please, sit."

Finally, she sat and nodded at me. I joined her.

"As to these eyes Chris is seeing, I don't have a clue," Victor said. "I've never heard of such a thing, and I doubt it's Chris's ability. We've sensed nothing special about him." He shrugged my way. "I mean no offense. Sahin told me there were no flashes of strong power about you that he could detect. Your talents are yet to be discovered and that may change, but I find Sahin very accurate about such matters."

"Of course," Juliet said.

"Now, Juliet, do not be miffed," Victor said. "You would have done the same, and in fact, you have. There was nothing disrespectful about us checking him out."

"What about the pain and the bloody nose?" I asked.

Victor shrugged, picked up his glass, and finished his drink. He reached for the crystal decanter Daniel had left and refilled his glass. The crystal decanter must have been a special holder for blood to keep it fresh.

He offered Juliet some more, but she refused with a slight hand movement.

"As you wish." He set aside the decanter.

Juliet picked up the glass of remaining red and froze. Her expression went blank, and her body sat motionless like a statue. A second before the door flew open, she was on her feet.

"What is the meaning of this?" Victor bellowed.

Sahin was out of breath. "Victor, there's been an incident."

"It's more than an incident." Juliet's voice rose.

She faltered forward. The glass dropped from her hand and shattered on the marble floor. Red spilled across the white marble.

Juliet needed my help. I'd never seen her like that, and I wasn't sure what to do. What could I do? Finally, my brain kicked in, and I moved to assist her, but she quickly steadied herself, using Victor's desk.

I wasn't sure what was happening, but whatever it was, it couldn't be good.

Victor's teeth grew sharp and ridges took over his smooth forehead as his brows grew heavier. Sahin was now a foot off the floor, hovering there like a puppet.

"Explain," Victor demanded, his hand outstretched.

Victor was using his power on Sahin, but why? What was this all about? Was it for show?

Sahin peered at Juliet with panic, grasping at his neck.

"My home's been attacked." Juliet's hand touched her temple. "Christopher." She headed to the door. "Amanda and the others...."

"It wasn't us." There was fear in Victor's voice.

Sahin returned to the marble floor with a thump.

"Daniel," Victor shouted. "Have my car ready when we get to the garage. Juliet, I assure you this was not us. I would like to come and see what help I can provide." His face returned to normal.

An attack? What had I gotten myself into? Was I ready for this?

Chapter Eleven

JULIET DROVE IN silence, focused on getting us home. I wasn't sure what to expect when we reached the house. Police, fire, medical—those were what I expected. Perhaps a heap of rubble. When we arrived, the garden lights were on as were a few from the windows.

"Everything looks okay," I said as we pulled to a stop on the driveway.

"Stay close. They may still be here," Juliet warned me.

Victor's Rolls-Royce Silver Ghost pulled up behind us. Victor and Sahin hurried over to join us.

"I don't sense them." Juliet glared at Victor. "If you or any of your people—"

"I did not authorize this." Victor shook his head. "If it's any of my people, we can both enact justice." He turned to Sahin with a frown.

Sahin shook his head.

We raced to the front door, and Juliet ran her hand over the symbols. She pushed the door the rest of the way open. The smell of blood hit me. The copper scent grew heavy as we walked inside.

My stomach lurched. Not in an I'm-gonna-be-sick kind of way but in the hungry sort of way.

Juliet glanced over at me through narrow eyes but said nothing, clearly focusing on something. But I wasn't sure what.

As we followed the scent of blood, we moved through the hardwood doors to the kitchen, pantry, and staff office. The back door was shattered from its frame, and Mia lay on the floor.

The arm still connected to her body had bite marks on it. Her other arm was shredded and torn off. Her legs were bent at unnatural angles and bone stuck through a tear in her trousers. Her head hung to the side, only barely connected by tendons. Blood pooled around what was left of her, a bright contrast to the polished tan-colored floor. I held back a gasp and took a step away, almost crashing into Victor.

"Juliet, I swear to you—" Victor started.

Juliet raised her hand and stopped him.

He frowned.

"What about Amanda and Adam?" I forced the words out and tried hard to not stare at the gore that was once Mia.

"This way," Juliet called.

We hurried to the service hall and the back stairs. She raised a fist, stopping us. "Victor, you and Sahin go through there. You'll find Adam. Christopher, come with me."

We rushed back to the main part of the house and dashed up the main stairs. My arms and legs seemed to move faster than normal. The blood hammered through my body, pounding like a drum in my ears. In no time, we were outside Amanda's bedroom.

"Stay close." Juliet's face shifted into her vampire form.

A crash echoed behind the closed door.

One heartbeat.

Juliet smashed the door off its hinges, shattering the wood and spraying splinters inward.

Another heartbeat.

Juliet crouched on the floor next to a bloodied Amanda.

The bed was ripped to shreds as if a lion had been searching for meat. Feathers and tattered stuffing material lay on the floor. The computer table was still standing; however, the laptop and tablet were in pieces. The glass in the window had been shattered outward, and the drapes hung at an angle.

"Are they—"

"No." Juliet focused on Amanda, but addressed me. "They're gone. The crash we heard was the rest of the window falling to the patio."

The remains of Amanda's pastel-blue blouse were barely visible among the rips and the blood. Everything was covered in blood. Her blood. Her usually perfect hair was matted and disheveled. Her lips were cracked and bleeding, and she had black eyes. Her nose was at an odd angle and dripped blood.

"Breathe." Juliet softly shifted Amanda so that her head was resting on her lap. "I need you to focus and breathe," she repeated.

"I'll call 9-1-1." I headed over to the overturned table that once held the phone.

"No," Juliet ordered. "Come over here. I need you to hold her head."

I did as instructed. I tried not to think about the blood congealing on my hands and soaking into my suit. I had never seen so much blood.

Hell, I'd never seen this kind of bodily devastation before. How could anyone do this?

A small moan escaped Amanda's cracked lips and shattered teeth. "There were too many..."

"Shh." Juliet brushed the hair from her face. "Rest now." Juliet faced me. "Hold her head and try not to hurt her."

"Malcolm," Amanda whispered and tried to move. "Malcolm, he was..." Her breath created a sucking sound as air from her lungs made a gurgling noise.

Juliet's eyes grew dark, her face hardened into a glaring rage. A low growl came from her. She sniffed the air, scanning the room.

Her face shifted back to normal, and she focused on Amanda. "Don't worry. You need to rest."

I quickly positioned myself so that I could support Amanda.

"Hold her," Juliet said.

I held Amanda's head firmly but not too tight. Her body rested limp in my arms. She had bite marks on her arms and her left leg slumped at an odd angle. What kind of monster did this? People can be—Juliet bit into her arm and pushed the bleeding wound into Amanda's mouth.

"Hold her still, please. She needs my blood." Juliet wiggled her arm, getting it over Amanda's open mouth. "Plug her nose."

"But she can't—"

"Do it!" Juliet commanded, and I pinched Amanda's nose closed.

Amanda was forced to take in Juliet's blood. Juliet grimaced but remained silent.

I glanced at the wall where the clock should have been. It lay broken on the floor. By the time Juliet released her arm from Amanda's mouth, both Victor and Sahin were in the room, watching us.

"Help us move her." Juliet's voice was weak.

"What about her bones? Don't we—"

"The blood will heal the body as it should be," Sahin said. "We don't need to set bones or anything like that."

"All she needs now is rest," Victor said.

With Victor and Sahin's help, we managed to get Amanda to one of the guest rooms and placed her on the bed. Juliet ran her petite hand down Amanda's face and pulled a blanket over her gently, covering her body. Juliet's gaze never left Amanda. Every motion of Juliet's body was slow and meticulous.

"She must sleep for a day or two," Juliet said. "But she'll be fine. We got to her soon enough."

I took a breath, and the blood stopped pounding in my ears.

Juliet turned to Victor, "Adam?"

"The same as the woman in the kitchen—there was nothing to be done. We pulled plywood from the storage in your garage and secured the back door. We checked the rest of the house as well. Your home is as secure as possible." Victor offered her his hand. "You need to rest. You gave her a lot of blood. We pulled your stock from the wine cellar and placed it in your study."

"I'm fine." Juliet forced the words out, all the color had drained from her face by then.

"And you should eat." Sahin's voice was oddly kind.

"I said I'm fine." Juliet's voice was a growl. "Now, I appreciate your assistance. Amanda mentioned there were several of them, and one of them she called by name. Malcolm."

Both Victor and Sahin shared a frown.

Victor's face shifted into his vampire form. Ridges angled down his forehead, his canine teeth grew, and I was taken aback by how deadly he looked. "He will soon be dead."

Sahin pursed his lips and rubbed his temple.

"I swear to you—" Victor's face changed back to normal.

"I suggest you leave, now." Juliet pushed her way to the hall.

"Juliet, we had nothing to do with this," Victor pleaded. "Why would I risk the balance we've enjoyed? There is nothing in it for me to gain. Malcolm will be found. You have my word." He narrowed his eyes on me. "It probably has something to do with Chris."

I turned to him and scowled.

"Victor, please go. I'll be in touch." Juliet straightened her shoulders. "I have work to do. I have to call the Council and make arrangements. I appreciate your help tonight; however, now is not a good time..." She took a strained breath.

Victor offered a bow and then peered at me. "You will need to watch both Amanda and Juliet. It is important that Juliet feed. You will take care of your creator or you—"

"Enough!" Juliet demanded. "I will instruct Christopher on what to do. *Now* please."

"I will check on you in a few days." Victor turned to Sahin. "You will say nothing of this, Sahin, on pain of death. Do I make myself clear?"

"Of course," Sahin replied.

"Good," Victor said. "I will deal with Malcolm. No one is to touch him but me or Juliet. Do you understand?"

"As you wish, Victor." Sahin bowed deeply.

Another heartbeat and the main door downstairs closed. They were gone.

I was worried and frightened. Could Victor be right? Was it possible this had something to do with me? "What do we do?"

"Help me to my office," Juliet said. "There is nothing more I can do for Amanda tonight." She buckled but caught herself on the nearby wall.

I rushed to her side and helped her to the office. She moved to the bar where Victor had set out several bottles of red with more in a box by the cart. Juliet quickly poured herself a drink, gulped it down, then a second and a third.

She turned to me and said, "I'm going to need your help. I have to rest, and I won't be able to go out during the daylight tomorrow or the next day in this weakened state."

"All right. Victor mentioned something about feeding. Do you need to...?" I tried to wrap my head around all this. Would she want to feed off me? Was that even possible?

"I'm fine." Juliet finished her fourth drink. Seeing my concerned frown, she amended, "I'll be fine soon. Now please help me to my desk." She was weak, hardly able to walk, and all her weight was on me as we got to her desk.

Should I have carried her?

"Victor could have killed me if that was his plan," Juliet said. "He could have finished me off. I don't believe it was the Dark."

"Who's Malcolm?"

"I don't know what Malcolm's involvement in this is. He's a new Dark vampire, new to the area—and not known for his intellect. I don't think even Victor knows him that well." Her head slumped on her desk.

I hurried over and grabbed the fresh container of blood. It felt light, and there was energy coming off it, like there was an electrical charge to it. I got hints of ozone from it. I brought it over to Juliet, poured her another drink, and raised it to her lips.

"Thank you," Juliet said. "I need to call the Council and my senior governors. I will have to contact Gregor first. Get help here. He won't be happy about this, especially in his territory. Please, pour me another glass."

I did as instructed.

"Duncan," she said.

I stopped and stared at her. She hadn't used that name since I changed it a few weeks back.

"I know this is a lot for you. I know you're scared and worried. I'm not going to lie, things are very dangerous right now, and I've been weakened, but I will do everything in my ability to keep you safe, as will all the Light. You are my blood now, and I will not let anything happen to you." She forced a small smile.

My body tingled with warmth, and for a brief moment, I felt at peace.

She drained the glass and held it out for more. I filled it up again. She sipped it and began to make phone calls.

I sat and kept her drinking. Juliet must have gone through four bottles of blood. I wasn't even sure how that was possible. She talked to different people, but I wasn't focused, so none of the names stuck. My mind was empty. She was putting on her strong voice, but it was taking a lot out of her. My sense of time had to be skewed because within what I thought was a half hour, the bell rang at the front door.

"That'll be Gregor. Please go and greet him. You will know him by his blond beard. There should be several people with him. Please let them in."

Standing, I wiped the sweat from my brow. "Are you sure it's them? What if it's the monsters who did this, coming back—"

"Don't worry." Juliet cut me off. "I can sense whose there—it's him."

"All right."

I hurried out of the office to the front door. Standing before me was a tall handsome man with blond hair, green eyes, and a short trimmed goatee. Behind him were several other people. They all had various expressions of concern on their faces.

"I'm Gregor Russel, and you must be Christopher. Please, take me to Juliet." Gregor's voice was deep and solid.

"She said you'd have a beard." That was all that came out of my mouth.

"I decided to change my look. We do that." Gregor stepped in and faced the others with him. "Secure the house, check on Amanda, and start the cleanup. Be respectful. These were her friends and people she cared for. From this point forward, no one is to come into this home without the approval of Juliet or myself." He turned to me. "Juliet, please."

The others raced off, and Gregor took a step forward.

I stepped aside.

"Sorry. Follow me. We don't know what happened. By the time we got here..."

Gregor's face softened, and he put his hand on my shoulder. "You don't need to speak."

I swallowed heavily and nodded. Gregor's presence had put me at ease. I opened the door to the office. The first thing that I noticed was the empty bottles were gone, as was the case of blood. Juliet must have put them out of sight.

Juliet had another glass of red in her hand. To her credit, she seemed better and more put together. Her eyes were focused, and she had somehow managed to change her blouse. But there was a weakness in her shoulders, and she still had a pale complexion.

"Gregor, come in." Juliet's voice was warm, welcoming.

He quickly walked over and kissed both her checks and then knelt before her with his head lowered. "We will get the Dark for this. Victor, who you've treated with more respect than is warranted, will pay above all the others. He will suffer for this."

Juliet reached out with her hand and lifted Gregor's face to meet hers. "We will not jump to conclusions. I believe that Victor was as surprised as I was. I don't believe he did this nor authorized it." She scowled. "However, at least one of his Dark was here—Malcolm. He will need to be found by us, preferably before Victor finds him."

"It was one of his uncontrolled lot, one of his newbies," Gregor growled. "No one attacks the home of a member of the Council of Light. Certainly not in my territory. We will find him, and he will pay for this."

The muscles on his neck and forehead twitched. His eyes glinted with the promise of vengeance, but he remained controlled.

"You would think we're in the Middle East or Africa," Gregor said. "These things will not happen here. I will not allow it."

He scanned the room before speaking again, his frown was deep. "Have you called the Council?"

"Of course," Juliet replied. "Right after I called you. They will be here by the weekend, and we'll go from there."

"As you wish," Gregor said. "I'm assuming we'll meet with Rei and Maria before you meet with the Council?"

"Christopher, why don't you go and change?" Juliet focused on me. "Perhaps a shower? Gregor and I have many things to discuss."

"But..." I started, but then I got a look at my clothes and my hands. I was covered in blood. Amanda's blood.

"If you need me, I'll be in my room cleaning up."

Arguing would be pointless. I was a mess.

Strangers banged around in the house and chatted softly, but I realized what they were doing. The smell of bleach burned my nose, and I heard water running. They were cleaning up. My stomach churned, again with hunger and not revulsion from the bleach. I couldn't help but think of Mia and Adam. They didn't deserve to die, and Amanda had been nothing but nice and kind. Who would do this to her and why?

Once upstairs, instead of going to my room, I walked to the guest room that housed Amanda. She would probably still be covered in blood. I felt I should do something.

When I reached the door, a tall, young-looking immortal woman with brown hair stood guard.

"I want to see Amanda," I said, not looking at the woman.

She stepped aside, allowing me to open the door. Amanda had already been cleaned and changed. She was still injured, but she seemed better.

"We took care of her already," the woman said. "I suggest you go and clean up. You smell of blood and death." Her nose scrunched.

Amanda's chest rose and fell.

"She doesn't deserve this."

"Of course not," the immortal woman said. "Amanda is a good and noble woman who certainly did not deserve to be brutalized. There can be a lot of cruelty in the world, and sadly, many people take great pleasure in it."

Chapter Twelve

"HOW IS AMANDA this morning?" Juliet leaned against the frame of my door. I closed my laptop and stood. She was dressed in a ruby skirt with a cream blouse. As with all of her clothes they were perfectly tailored. I was sure it was more good work from Fredrick.

"From what I saw, she's still weak, but better than last night for sure." I slipped on my suit jacket. "She probably doesn't even realize I checked on her."

"I'm sure she knows," Juliet said. "Gregor and his team, have they made you comfortable?"

"I suppose. I haven't really interacted with them. I didn't want to get in their way."

"Of course." Juliet gingerly pulled herself to a standing position. "You will need to stand with me at the meeting tonight."

I nodded reluctantly. I hadn't been sure what I was supposed to do, and that had worried me all day.

Juliet had spent the day sleeping in one of the rooms in the basement. Outside her door, an immortal stood guard and told me not to bother her—so I didn't. She finally came to my room after sunset. It was mid-October so the sun went down sooner, but not soon enough for my taste.

"Chris."

"Sorry. What am I supposed to do tonight?" I fumbled with the collar of the suit jacket.

"We'll be meeting with my senior governors," Juliet said. "This will be your official introduction to them, but you won't need to do anything. Still, don't feel like you're just there to observe. If you have something to say, I want you to speak up."

I nodded.

"It's more of a show of unity and support," Juliet continued. "That's why I'm having the meeting here. Against Gregor's wishes." She shook her head. "He wanted us to meet up in the city, but I refuse to be pushed from my home."

I raised my eyebrows. "Well, there's enough security here, that's for sure."

"True," Juliet said. "However, a member of the Council of Light has been attacked where balance reigns between the Light and the Dark. Someone is trying to upset things here. We can't be too careful. Regardless, you being there as my blood will be important to reassure them, show them I'm not worried. I would have Amanda there as well, but she's still too weak." She touched my arm. "Thank you for being with her today."

"But how..." I didn't grasp why this confused me.

"Terrie told me, the woman who's been watching after Amanda."

"Oh."

"She's Gregor's Second and a good woman."

"I didn't feel right leaving Amanda by herself all day. I thought she must be scared and angry."

"Amanda will be fine now," Juliet said. "Her body went through a lot and she would have died without my blood." She squeezed my arm gently. "And she wasn't alone."

My face warmed. "You sure I don't need to do anything tonight?"

"I'm sure." Juliet released my arm, and we sauntered down the hall. "Be your charming self, and everything will go smoothly."

We made our way to the landing for the main stairs.

Amanda stood holding the railing, waiting for us, her arm shaking. She wore flats instead of her typical heels. The marks on her face were almost healed and her rosy cheeks were definitely healthier.

"Amanda." I took a step toward her to help steady her.

"Juliet, you need me—"

"She insisted." Terrie marched over, her hands raised in frustration.

"What I need"—Juliet's voice was gentle—"is for you to get some rest. No one expects you at the meeting tonight. Now, you have a choice. You can go with Terrie and get back into bed and rest, or I can put you in bed myself."

"Juliet." Amanda shifted, her knuckles white from holding the rail. "I'm better. It's my job, and I intend to do it."

"Really?" Juliet crossed her arms. "Release the rail and stand up straight."

"I just need a little..." Amanda wobbled.

Juliet caught her with an arm wrapped around her waist. "Amanda, please rest." Juliet's voice was a mix of strain and worry. "For me. I can't have you wasting your energy on a meeting with my seniors." She faced Terrie. "Help her back to her room."

Terrie nodded.

"Fine," Amanda grumbled.

Terrie took up Juliet's position by Amanda's side.

"Tomorrow, when you wake, come and get me." Amanda pointed at me. "I won't have others doing my job."

"Of course," I said.

"I'll come by and see you in the morning." Juliet's smile brightened as she watched Amanda and Terrie move off.

"She looks amazingly well compared to yesterday," I said.

Juliet nodded and took my arm. "We should get downstairs. They'll be here soon enough."

I SAT BY the fire in Juliet's study. Juliet sipped a glass of red. It was her second since we entered her office. The scent of roses and vanilla remained weak. "What's going to happen?"

Juliet finished off her glass. "I'm going to try to avoid a war."

"Do you want another?" I took her glass and filled it. I poured myself a scotch and took a sip. The fruity finishing taste of cherry tickled my tongue. It was excellent and helped to steady my hands.

"You don't believe that Victor did this." I handed her a fresh glass. "Judging by what I saw of his reactions, it didn't seem like he was involved last night." I sat back down.

"No." Juliet took the crystal glass. "But Malcolm. That is going to be enough for some people." She sipped her red. "Most of the Dark are not known for being as honorable as Victor. He's a strong leader and rules with an iron fist, but he is fair."

"I bet."

"I'm sure some of his people, especially ones who aren't from here, aren't pleased we have a good working relationship."

"Why not?"

"There is prejudice." Juliet sighed. "On both sides, I'm afraid. You may have caught some of Gregor's eagerness to assign blame and move directly on to retribution. Maintaining the peace after something like this isn't going to be easy."

"What happens if there is a war?" The images of Mia and Amanda flashed into my mind. "What does that look like?"

"War is war. People fight. People die." Juliet rolled the glass in her hands. "The balance will be in question, and there is a very good chance that we as a species will be found out. We are not in a place like Africa or the Middle East or even South America where violence of this scale can be easily hidden." She finished her drink. "I don't intend to find out. So we are going to avoid it."

A tap came from the door, and one of Gregor's men walked in. Tall and fair-skinned, he could have been Gregor's Keeper, but I had never asked. "The guests have arrived, Madame. I've shown them to the dining room."

"Thank you, Stephen. We'll be right there." Juliet stood and crossed over to the bar as the door closed. She filled her glass again and drank it down all at once. "I apologize, Christopher. Victor was right. I'm going to need to feed. I had hoped my stocks would be enough, but it's taking too long, and I'm afraid I can't wait."

"All right."

"You will need to be with me when I feed. I hope you'll be up for it."

My face must have shown worry.

"Don't worry. It's not what you have in mind," Juliet said. "I promise, but I wanted to let you know. In case my seniors bring it up in the meeting."

She took my arm; we walked out of the office and headed to the dining room.

THE DINING ROOM was transformed into a conference room. It had been stripped down to the bare basics. A white linen cloth covered the table with pitchers of both water and red sitting there with glasses at each place. A fire roared and the paintings still hung. The heavy drapes were closed, cutting off the view of the backyard.

We moved to the head of the table, all eyes on us. We passed Gregor, who stood, wearing a blue linen dress shirt and khaki pants.

Rei flanked Gregor, his gray suit a stark contrast with his strawberry-blond hair and green eyes. With a black tie and tight jacket, he seemed right out of a Wall Street office.

Maria's dark features were stunning, her chestnut hair flowed past her shoulder and framed chocolate-brown eyes. The dress she wore was covered with bright blues and greens, and cut high and low, showing a lot of leg and cleavage. Her strong shoulders and perfect posture gave her a regal and sophisticated appearance despite her revealing outfit.

"Juliet." Rei walked to her, offering a bow. "We will not let this go unanswered." His voice was solid with a definite French accent.

"Rei, c'est bon de vous voir. Merci d'être venus. C'est Christopher. Il est de mon sang," Juliet said with a tilt of her head to me.

My gaze shifted from Juliet to Rei. I figured it was a welcome and an introduction to me since I caught my name.

"Christopher," Rei said. "I'm sorry to be here under such bad circumstances." He offered me his hand. "Still, it's a true pleasure to meet you."

"It's nice to meet you." We shook hands.

"Juliet, I'm sorry for your loss." Maria walked up and kissed both Juliet's cheeks. "If you need anything, we are all here for you."

"Gracias por venir aqui, Maria. Por favor, permítanme presentarles Christopher, que es mi sangre," Juliet said with a polite nod toward me.

Maria, instead of shaking my hand, kissed one of my cheeks, then the other. "Christopher, it's an honor to meet you." Her Spanish accent was like honey.

My cheeks burned as she pulled away. I'm sure I had a dopey smile on my face.

"With sorrow, I'm here during this difficult time of loss." Gregor's shoulders were painfully stiff and broad. "Thank you for allowing me to help you with this matter." He bowed his head and stayed there until Juliet lifted it.

"Gregor, you are always welcome." Juliet ran a smooth hand along his jaw. "It is I who should be thanking you for putting you out in this way. I feel foolish, but also relieved you're in my life." She addressed the group. "Please, everyone sit."

Juliet directed me with her eyes to the chair next to her. Once she sat, I took my seat.

"So you think the attack has something to do with his Calling?" Rei leaned forward in his seat, resting his hands on the table. "Or his strange reaction to the first Mark?"

My face warmed. I didn't pose a threat to anyone; why would someone from the Dark come after Juliet or Amanda over me? Especially someone I didn't know. I was ready to speak when Juliet moved her hand on the table.

"We don't know," Juliet said. "That is why we need to find Malcolm. Still, I don't want to entertain any half guesses either, so for now, the information about Christopher stays between us. I told you because you have a right to know—as for anyone else…"

"Of course, of course." Rei waved his hand in understanding.

"Do you want us to inform the other governors?" Maria sat back and crossed her legs. She seemed the most relaxed of everyone at the table.

"We shouldn't keep it from them." Gregor turned to Juliet. "Better they get this information from us than to hear through other means."

"If it was the Dark, they will find out soon enough—" Rei quietly tapped his fingers on the table.

"And be preparing for war," Maria interrupted.

"We should be preparing for war." Rei pounded his fist on the table.

Juliet straightened her shoulders and growled.

My heart raced and my bones trembled.

Everyone stopped. Their heads dropped. The only heart beating was mine, and it was going fifty miles per hour.

"No." Juliet's voice reverberated around the room.

Silence filled the empty spaces of the room. I peeked over to Juliet as she watched her seniors. She gave me a gentle nod, and I bowed my head in response.

"Have there been other attacks?" Rei said gently, raising his head, eyes barely meeting Juliet's. "Anything from the other Council members?"

"There have been no other incidents," Juliet said. "The Council will arrive tomorrow. As of now, I'm the only one who has been involved."

I sighed with relief.

"To be clear, no one will be preparing anything." Juliet's voice was level, but there was finality in every word. "The humans and the immortals in the Americas are in no position for war. The world may not survive a war of this nature. Not now. There is too much at stake—"

"But…" Rei said.

Juliet waved her hand. "We are not going to war with the Dark. I've asked them to help find Malcolm and instead to bring him to me."

"And you trust this *Victor*?" Maria's tone was filled with a bite of disdain. She crossed her arms in front of her ample chest. "Gregor, what about you? You did banish him from your city?"

"I didn't banish him." Gregor crossed his arms over his broad chest. "I suggested that perhaps he should relocate. He still has people in the city, and they fall under his control. So he can come and go as he sees fit." He turned to Juliet. "Regardless, he enjoys the peace. It's been good for him and his interests, including those in the city. Those under his charge seem willing enough to play by his rules as long as they benefit from it."

"He does control the largest territory of any member of the Dark," Rei said. "He has been known to deal fairly with the Light, but..." He tapped his fingers on the table. "Juliet, he is still of the Dark, and can we really put this past him?"

"Victor and I work well together," Juliet said. "Yes, he is Dark; however, he is honorable, as are most of the Dark. You've all experienced this." She filled a glass and emptied it. "Consider this: we were with Victor the night of the attack. If it were his wish to kill me, then he could have easily done so. Instead, he helped me. This cannot be overlooked."

"It's true." Gregor nodded his agreement. "He did offer aid to Juliet and has been helpful with the search and the security of the area."

Rei drummed his fingers on the table, and Maria rubbed her temples.

"Also, there are his dealings with Kirtus Lancaster," Juliet said. "No other Dark would allow this. They would have killed him long ago."

All heads shot up and agreeable murmurs spread around the table. This was the second time Juliet mentioned this name.

Juliet must have sensed my confusion. "Kirtus is of the Dark but not really. He is—" She stopped for a moment and glanced at Gregor.

"He is of the Dark but chooses to live by the rules of the Light," Gregor said. "He is a bone of contention with the Dark. Many of them want him killed; however, Victor allows him to live, and as long as Victor offers him sanctuary, Kirtus is left alone."

"We also watch over him," Juliet added. "Well, as best as we can without overstepping."

"I'm sorry, I don't understand," I said. "He is Dark, but he lives by the rules of the Light. Why doesn't he just declare himself Light?"

Maria, Rei, and Gregor were quiet, all looking to Juliet to explain.

It took Juliet several minutes and another glass of red before she responded. "It doesn't work that way."

I furrowed my brow.

"It's complicated," Juliet added. "Both Victor and I do our best to treat him fairly, and that must do for now as an answer."

My gaze dropped to the table.

"We must find Malcolm," Juliet said. "Gregor, please take point on this and work with Victor; however, I suggest you continue working your angles. I doubt very much Malcolm has left your territory yet. As for the other governors, we will notify them together, showing a united front. I'm trusting each of you to be consistent in our message. I don't want a panic, and I don't want to give the Dark any more perceived advantage than they already have."

"Victor did promise to keep this quiet," I said. "He instructed Sahin to do the same—well threatened him is more like it."

"That is true," Juliet said. "If Victor breaks this promise, that will look all the worse for him."

There were nods of agreement around the table.

"In all honesty, nothing about this attack makes sense to me," Juliet said.

"What if it has to do with Christopher?" Rei repeated and turned to me.

All eyes fell on me, and I wished I could melt into the floor. I wasn't sure if I should speak, but Juliet responded.

"Chris had no connections to any of the Dark before he was Called. He was like the others. There is—" She stopped and focused on me. "There was nothing special about him. I'm sorry, Christopher, for how that sounds."

"What about his reaction to the first Mark? The seeing of the eyes?" Rei asked.

"That wouldn't explain why I was targeted by Malcolm," Juliet said. "Victor knew nothing about Chris's reaction until we were at his home speaking to him."

"None of us did until the night of the attack." Gregor crossed his arms in front of himself.

"Still, it is possible." Juliet pursed her lips. "Which is why I'm going to ask the Council to move up his timetable for transition."

"Will they even grant it?" Maria crossed her legs.

"I don't see how they can refuse as long as he passes the Marks." Rei adjusted the cuffs of his shirt.

"We'll find out on Friday," Juliet said. "However, more importantly, do any of you have an objection to my request? Because if you do, now is the time to say."

"No," Gregor replied. "When I met him, I realized he was of your blood. I can't imagine anyone better for you. I told you this then, and I say it again now."

As I sat listening to them, I wasn't so sure I enjoyed being talked about. It was a strange feeling, but I had nothing to add, which I was glad of, because I didn't think I could talk even if I wanted to.

Rei remained silent.

"If you trust him and believe this to be what is needed, then I support you," Maria said.

"I understand I'm asking a lot." Juliet faced Rei and reached out to take his hand. "Tradition means a great deal to you, as it does for me. I don't ask this lightly."

"There are concerns, of course," Rei said. "We employ these traditions for a reason; however, I trust you, and therefore, I must trust your selection. I will support you should the Council ask."

"Thank you all," Juliet said. "This means a lot to me."

I was left to wonder at the current situation, not only what would happen with the Council, but with Juliet and, most importantly, myself.

JULIET AND I made our way back to her office where Terrie sat on the sofa with a young man. Maybe, in his late teens.

"Juliet, this is Ben." Terrie stood up. "He's for you."

I wasn't sure what to expect. What did she mean by "he's for you"? Was she going to kill him?

Juliet walked over to the sofa in front of the fire where he sat. "Hello, Ben. It's nice to meet you." She gained his gaze and sat next to him. "Do you know why you're here?"

Ben had brown hair and hazel eyes with the slim build of a runner. His face was dotted with freckles and he had a straight nose. He wasn't classically handsome, but he was good-looking.

"Terrie said you need to feed," Ben replied without so much as a blink.

His face had a blank expression. He was focused on Juliet, but he wasn't really seeing her.

"This is Christopher. He's going to watch. Is that all right?" Juliet pointed in my direction, but her gaze stayed on Ben.

"Yes, that's fine." Ben's voice was hollow and he didn't look at me. "I don't mind being watched."

"Please, wait outside, Terrie," Juliet instructed. "I'll send Christopher for you if we need you."

Terrie left the room and closed the heavy wood door with a soft click.

"Normally, this would be done in a much different way," Juliet's gaze was still on Ben, but her words directed at me. "However, time is not a luxury I have right now. So, I hope you're ready."

I now had a good idea what was going to happen, and I didn't know if I was ready. My heart pounded, and I had to wipe my sweaty hands on my pants. I swallowed heavily.

"Um…"

"You have to understand, Christopher," Juliet said. "The goal is not to scare him or hurt him or anything like that. Terrie picked him up on the pretense of a first date. He won't be harmed, and she will take him home with the memory of a nice date and a sexual encounter but no desire to see her again. She is excellent at that."

"He looks very young," I said. Would I have put myself in this situation at that age if I were dating? I didn't know. I didn't date until I was in my early twenties. I didn't go out with anyone until I was in college, and that was a disaster. "Is he even eighteen?"

Juliet ignored my question. "Part of why Gregor left Terrie here was in case I needed this. I need to regain my strength, and this is the only option I have now. Typically, I would go out, or if Mia and Adam were still here, they would assist me with this. They are gone and I don't have other options at the moment."

"But he's—"

"Are you going to be okay?" she interrupted.

I took another breath. I trusted Ben wouldn't be hurt and he wouldn't remember this, but he's so young, and this didn't feel right. My head continued to pound. Juliet needed to get her strength, and if this was the only way, then what could I do?

"I need to learn, so I might as well learn the right way." My stomach was doing somersaults. "But, Juliet, he's…. Maybe we—"

"I don't have the luxury of time," she interrupted sternly. "Now, pay attention."

My heart dropped. She was being so cold about it all.

"Ben, come closer to me." Juliet patted the spot right next to her. Ben moved closer to her.

Juliet's eyes became more focused. Her face shifted. Just like with Fredrick. "Where do you go to school? What grade are you in?"

"I go to Silver Creek High School in San Jose. I'm a senior." Ben didn't blink and his voice remained flat.

"All right." Juliet continued to focus on him. "I'm not going to hurt you. In fact, you're going to enjoy this very much. You're going to enjoy this so much it's going to feel like sex. Do you enjoy sex, Ben?"

I wanted to throw up. I didn't want this to be real, but it was. He was in high school, not even college, and she was an adult. It was possible he was eighteen, but I didn't know. But she didn't ask his age. For all I knew, she was a pedophile and I was standing there doing nothing. Allowing this to happen.

"I've never had sex before," Ben replied. "Well, not with another person. I like orgasms, though, a lot."

"This is going to be better than when you masturbate." Juliet's voice was sickly sweet and breathy. "You're going to feel incredible afterward."

Juliet leaned in to kiss him on the cheek. She moved to his lips and kissed him heavily. He quickly reciprocated.

I felt an uncontrollable need to stand there and watch this monster, which had once been Juliet, kissing the young man. She was about to seduce a high school kid. Yes, he was cute, but he was just a kid, someone's child. This couldn't be right. Juliet couldn't believe this was right. How could this be what the Light believed?

Luckily, they weren't actually having sex and their clothes stayed on, which I was glad of. However, they did kiss, and it was passionate, lustful, and deep.

Juliet continued to kiss Ben, moving hungrily to his neck. Unlike Fredrick, Ben didn't seem to mind Juliet's shifted appearance so I suppose that was good. Once Juliet reached his neck and kissed him there, I saw her bite down into his flesh.

Ben's eyes shot open, then closed slightly as his mouth opened, making a slight *O*, and a soft moan escaped from his lips. The scent of sweet apples filled the air and I felt myself start to become aroused. I had to keep reminding myself this was wrong.

He seemed to enjoy it. His hands explored Juliet's body. He fumbled around for the buttons on her blouse. His groping didn't surprise me, considering his age. Finally, he managed to work the buttons and find his targets.

Between watching them and my own discomfort, I failed at stepping up and saying something or stopping them.

Juliet glanced at me as she swallowed a mouthful of blood, and I'm ashamed to admit I found this titillating, which made it that much more difficult for me to stop.

Juliet sucked harder at his neck.

He took a deep breath and moaned again loudly. His chest was heaving and his thighs started to lift slightly. Finally, his body shook in orgasm. Ben chuckled as Juliet pulled away from his neck. She bit her tongue and licked the wounds on his neck—the bloody gashes gradually knitted together, and in seconds, all that was left was a hint of blood, which Juliet licked up.

She kissed Ben again. As he opened his eyes, hers were there waiting for him. "You were amazing, Ben, truly amazing." She kissed him on the lips.

He giggled again, the after-effects of his orgasm well hidden in his pants.

"Now you're going to go with Terrie." Juliet's face was back to normal.

"That was incredible," Ben said. "I've never felt anything like that." He shifted closer to Juliet.

"Christopher, please get Terrie," Juliet said.

I was glad it was over, and I was even more pleased to leave the room. Terrie leaned against the wall across from the door.

"I think we're done," I said.

"Did you enjoy it?" Terrie asked.

I exhaled loudly through my nose and crossed my arms in front of my chest.

Terrie narrowed her eyes on me and gave me a single nod. "I'll take him home now."

We both walked back into the room. She caught Ben's gaze.

He sat on the sofa, adjusting himself.

"Come on, lover boy," Terrie said. "Time to get you home."

"All right." Ben stood up and faced me. "It was nice meeting you. I hope you enjoyed watching, Chris. I really enjoyed having you watch us. I've never come that hard. Thanks."

Once they left the room, Juliet turned toward me, buttoning her blouse. "Are you all right?"

I'm not sure if it was the look on my face or the fact that I didn't respond right away. All I kept thinking of was that poor boy, that he'd never know what happened to him and I wasn't sure if that was a good or bad thing. No one should have that happen to them.

"Christopher," Juliet said.

I wiped the sweat from my brow. Her face wasn't as pale and her eyes had a brilliant light about them, and it was the first time since the attack that the smell of roses and vanilla overpowered me. She was better, but did that make it right? How could this be okay? Based on all that I'd learned about the Light and Juliet, how could any of this be all right?

"Being an immortal means you will have to do things you don't always like," Juliet said. "Sometimes doing them may even cause you pain, but they still must be done."

"But...I...but he..." I tried to speak.

"Ben was not hurt," Juliet said. "He'll have a positive memory. I didn't take anything from him that will not come back."

"You took away his youth." My voice was loud. "You took his innocence." The anger in me built. "I should have stopped you. That wasn't right. He's a child, a hormonal teenager, who has no clue what happened, and I did nothing. I watched and did nothing."

Juliet crossed her arms over her chest. "Then why didn't you stop me? You could have. But I felt your arousal. Are you mad at me or yourself?"

"How dare you," I snarled at her. "I wanted no part of that. I can't..." I stopped, then tried to face her. "I'm sorry, Juliet, but I can't look at you right now. I can't..." I turned and left the office and headed to my room. I wasn't sure if I could ever forget what I witnessed. The worst part was I didn't think I could forgive how it made me feel.

I DIDN'T TALK to anyone for the next two days. I spent that time at the Foundation, working. I toed the company line about Juliet being out of the country and returning on the following Monday. After work, I came home and passed the evening in my room, going over some of the books and tomes Juliet had loaned me before the attack. I tried to forget the incident with Ben.

The only reason I came down on Friday night was because my presence was requested at the Council meeting. As upset as I was, I understood that there were more important issues at hand than my problems with immortal morality. Like the idea of immortal war.

Amanda met me on the landing. She was back to her normal self, dressed in a deep-sapphire skirt suit. "I haven't gotten a chance to thank you for all that you did."

"Of course," I said. "I'm sorry that happened to you. You didn't deserve it." We started down the stairs. "How long before this dog and pony show is over? I'm not in the mood for another meeting."

"You need to understand that things happen for a reason." Amanda took my arm and stopped us. "Tonight is important. You're going to meet the full Council, and they are going to decide your fate. So whatever your opinion may be about what happened, don't let it show. Not tonight." Amanda's hands trembled. "Please."

"Amanda," I started, but paused. Worry danced in her eyes and played on her forehead. "I promise I will put on the best face possible."

"Good," she said, and we were walking again. "I don't know what we would do without you. You're part of our family...or Juliet's family." We reached the dining room door. Max was standing there on point. "They've already been meeting for a while now. They'll let us know when we can go in. I doubt it will be long."

"Good to see ya again." Max shook my hand. "It's really awful what happened."

"Yes, it is." Despite my mood, it was good to see him.

"Amanda, I'm glad to see ya up and about." Max hugged her. "That was a good thing Juliet did for ya."

"I'm very lucky," Amanda said. "Hopefully, the trip over wasn't too rough on you both."

"Nah, it wasn't bad," Max said. "We were at the ranch. So we just hopped on the plane and came out. Still wish it wasn't for something like this." He frowned. It was hard to believe his face was capable of such a thing. "You must be kind of excited to meet the Council. They're a pretty good group. Shouldn't be too long now."

"Well, I don't know if excited is the right word," I said.

Max laughed. "I guess not. I remember my first time meeting with them. They can be a bit much, I suppose."

The doors opened, and Juliet stood in a ruby skirt and cream blouse. "We're ready for you, Christopher."

My gaze dropped to the floor and my feet. *I need to polish my shoes.* I cleared my throat and glanced at Max and Amanda.

"You'll do fine." Amanda gave my arm a quick squeeze.

"Go get 'em," Max said with a thumbs-up.

My temples started to pound as I faced Juliet. *Meet her eyes. Put on a smile. Don't let them see you're upset.* I strode into the dining room, and it didn't look much different from the other night when Juliet met with her governors, except there were eight people besides Juliet and myself.

The others were all new to me. Juliet took my arm, and we walked over to the table where they all sat.

"You remember Sybil and Garrett."

I nodded at both of them.

To my surprise, Sybil smiled back.

Garrett offered a polite nod and a firm handshake.

"Let me introduce the others." Juliet took me to a well-dressed Hispanic man with a deeply tanned complexion and light brown eyes. He was taller than me, definitely over six feet. "This is Fernando. He oversees the South America Region."

He bowed his head in greeting.

"A pleasure to meet you," I said before we moved on to the next person.

"Taqi is from the Northern African region," Juliet said.

"The grace of God shines down on you, Christopher," he said. His black hair and dark features were offset by a brightly colored robe-type outfit. I'd seen something similar in pictures from Morocco, but I had no idea what it was called. He had a distinct scar by his left eye, which stretched to his forehead. It must have happened before he turned into an immortal.

"Thank you. It's an honor to meet you." We moved on.

"This is Anashe, head of the Southern African region." Her hair was in an afro style, which moved with her head. She had pretty hazel eyes and bright red lips. I thought maybe she could have once been a true princess or queen from her perfect posture and how every motion seemed to have a purpose. Decorating her neck was a beaded necklace patterned with small triangles in bold primary colors. It contrasted the red-and-orange brightly colored dress, which accented her curves.

"A pleasure." Her voice was meek and soft. I found that surprising.

"Hello," I said.

"This is Rahim. He oversees that Middle East Region."

He had black hair and dark eyes, but his features seemed more European to me—light skin and a small straight nose. He wore a standard business suit.

Sweat broke out on my hands. Clearly, this was a whirlwind introduction. "A pleasure."

We reached the head of the table where there were two seats. I glanced at the other two women.

"Last but certainly not least are An and Yoi. An oversees East Asia, and Yoi oversees West Asia," Juliet said. An had long dark hair and almond-shaped eyes and wore a gray suit. In contrast, Yoi had short hair dyed a reddish color with a light purple headband the same color as her dress.

"A pleasure to meet you both," I said.

Juliet pointed to my seat, and we both sat down.

"As you all know," Juliet started, "Christopher has answered the Calling to me, and considering recent events, I want the Council's approval to move up his indoctrination. We cannot be sure that the attack on me doesn't have something to do with him and leaving him in this vulnerable state could be dangerous, even deadly."

Sybil leaned forward, resting her hands on the table. "I understand the worry, but don't you think you might be overreacting? Attacks happen all the time. The Dark are known for causing trouble. Especially around a Calling. I'm not surprised in the least. It's not unlike them to remind us that they are relevant and a force to be dealt with." Her attention landed on me as she finished.

I glanced down at my hands and frowned. I really didn't like this woman.

"Is this Malcolm monster caught yet?" Sybil asked.

"No, we're still looking for him," Juliet replied. "However, my people and Victor's—"

"Ha. Victor." The scar became more visible with Taqi's frown. "This Dark you seem to work so well with." He continued with a sneer and a bite of distaste. "You know, back in Africa, we would never tolerate such an attack. He would be dead, his head on a stake for all those to see. This type of thing would be handled quickly and justly. I've always questioned working with the Dark so closely."

"Shoot first and ask questions later." Fernando shook his head with a slight frown. "Perhaps, that is why your region has the problems it has. Hmm?" He turned to Juliet and his expression softened. "These traditions are for a reason. The process needs to be executed carefully, so we don't have the same issues as the Dark. The balance can only be maintained if we stick to these customs. I sympathize with the tragic events you have suffered. I do, however, worry that rushing the process may end up causing more harm than good."

"Not changing and adapting could be what's causing these problems." Yoi nodded and offered Juliet a polite half smile. "If Juliet has a good working partnership with Victor and she believes that moving up Christopher's conversion is important, then we should consider it, not allow our biases to dictate our response. How many of you can say your regions have as few problems as Juliet's? The last major conflict here was over two hundred years ago; she must be doing something right."

Yoi was an elegant speaker with her soft and thoughtful tone. She was quite possibly the most attractive woman in the room. She also showed a great amount of respect for Juliet, which helped me to like her more.

"Let us not forget it was an event that had nothing to do with immortals," Sybil said. "It was a war among the humans."

"A war that could easily have uncovered us all and yet somehow did not," Garrett said. "Let's not forget that either."

Sybil narrowed her eyes at Garrett.

"That is a fair point." An adjusted her suit jacket. "I don't see a reason not to allow Christopher to be brought over sooner, assuming he survives the remaining Marks." She turned to me. "Christopher, what do you think about all this?"

My mouth went dry. I was still upset about what happened with Ben and how cold and callous Juliet acted afterward. Not to mention the sting of what she had said to me right after Ben left. I cleared my throat and took a sip of the water in front of me.

"Well," I started, "since this is all new to me, I hold faith in this Council and in Juliet. She asked me to trust her. She has promised to always do right by me, and I take her at her word." I met the gazes of those around the room. "I may not agree with everything that she does—" I cleared my throat before adding, "I may not agree with everything that all of you do either."

Several eyebrows rose.

"However, it is not for me to dictate." I paused. "But I believe moving my Marks forward is for the best. I would like to see that happen."

Sybil watched me and then shifted her attention to Juliet. Juliet might be the head of the Council, but in this matter, it was Sybil who was elected to be in charge of the proceeding.

"I don't see the need for prolonged debate. I suggest we call for a simple vote, majority rules and no abstentions," Sybil said. "All those in favor raise your left hand."

What do you mean no debate and a simple vote? One question and you're calling for a vote? What the hell?

Juliet reached over and patted my hand.

Garrett's hand was followed by Yoi's. Juliet's went up next, which meant that I needed two more. An's hand went up after a moment, as did Rahim's. I could tell Anashe was going to wait to see how the voting went, and once she saw Rahim's hand go up, hers rose as well.

I took a breath. I think it was my first breath since we'd come into the dining room. It felt like a good victory, so I was pleased.

"Very well. Juliet, your request has been approved." Sybil pulled out her smartphone.

Something about the image of Sybil with a smartphone amused me. Even to this day, it still does.

"We will set his second Mark for the eighteenth of October and his third Mark for Halloween," Sybil said. "His final Mark will follow two days after that."

"You can't be serious. We only have eight more days," Juliet started. "That is—"

"You're the one insisting on moving the schedule forward," Sybil interrupted. "I don't see the need to string it out. Christopher will either pass his Mark or he'll die. Either way, this will be wrapped up quickly, and then we can focus on the larger issue of how to resolve this attack on a member of the Council."

Juliet glanced around the table. If she was looking for support or someone to speak up, nothing came, not even from Garrett or Yoi.

"As the Council wishes." Juliet's voice was soft. Her head bowed in acceptance.

Considering Juliet's reaction to the timeline, this might be a bad thing. Was I ready to face my own death?

Chapter Thirteen

THE COUNCIL'S DECISION to expedite my Marks had my stomach in knots. Would I be ready, or would I die? Maybe I should have said more. I wasn't sure what to make of things, but I had to have faith this would work out.

The house buzzed with activity as the new staff cleaned and a contractor and his crew repaired damage from the attack. The one time I got to speak to Juliet, she informed me the workers had been told the house had been broken into. Which wasn't a lie. It just wasn't the whole truth. I didn't see much of Amanda as she had jumped back into her duties by hiring an estate manager, John Martin. She seemed happy with the selection, as did Juliet.

I held no control over the planning for my Marks or the repairs to the house so I focused on the one thing I had control over: my job at the Foundation.

As the Director of Community Affairs, I had wide latitude as to what my job consisted of. However, it mostly concentrated on what Juliet needed me to do. A big part of my work was to cover for Juliet when she wasn't around, which for the previous couple of weeks had been a lot.

I'll admit that I enjoyed the job and found going to work a nice break. I got to review grant applications for passage by the Grant's Approval Committee, meet with donors, and work with our Director of Communications and Public Relations. I made a difference in people's lives, and that felt great. I didn't mind the long hours, nor did I mind having people come to me and seek my advice. Juliet told me to call her if there was something major, but I hadn't needed to call her yet. As with her immortal life, she surrounded herself with good people who understood what they were doing.

It was unlike the non-profit that I had worked for, where no one seemed to focus on the clients and instead did what they could to make themselves look good. That might not be fair, and we did help people, but working in administration and watching all the petty bickering and whining never made me feel good about my job.

My last meeting of the day concerned our budget, my least favorite part of the job. It finally ended and I was winding down. I leaned back in my chair and looked up at the ceiling, taking in a deep breath. My office phone rang, interrupting my peace. I sighed and hit the speaker button.

"Chris, there's a gentleman here to see you," Rachel, our receptionist, said in a perky pleasant tone.

Rachel was the perfect receptionist. Friendly, polite, and always wore a bright smile. It might have had something to do with her being newly married, but I didn't think so.

"Do you know who it is?" I checked the calendar. I wasn't scheduled to have any more meetings today. Sometimes salespeople were slippery devils and would try to sneak in, but Rachel always sniffed them out.

"Mr. Bodean," her voice bubbled over the speaker. "He says you know him."

I thought a minute. I didn't recognize the name, but then it hit me. Victor's Keeper. What the holy hell was he doing here? "I'll be right up."

I grabbed my suit jacket and slipped it on. I was getting used to my suits and almost felt naked without a jacket...almost.

Mr. Bodean stood in the front lobby, wringing his hands and looking at me with a nervous expression and shiny forehead.

"Hello, Mr. Bodean." I put on what I hoped was a pleasant smile and shook his hand.

"Daniel, please," he said. "Is there somewhere we can talk?"

"Of course." I pointed to the lobby conference room. I didn't want to take him back to my office, in case he was there to cause trouble on Victor's behalf.

"Would you like me to bring in some waters or soda?" Rachel asked as we made our way to the meeting room.

"No. I'm fine. Thank you." Daniel walked into the conference room.

Once the door closed, I lowered my voice. "What are you doing here?"

He glanced out the conference room windows to the parking lot. "Victor wanted me to come here. We found him." His lisp was stronger. I supposed it had something to do with his nerves.

"You found who?"

"Malcolm," Daniel whispered. "Sahin found him." He checked the window again.

"Seriously! Great! But why are you here telling me this?" I followed his gaze out the window. "Wait, he's not here, is he?"

Daniel nodded. "Victor wanted to get him to Juliet, and given the current state of affairs, coming to the Foundation appeared to be the best option."

"Where is he?"

"In the trunk of Victor's car."

That's all it took. I dashed out the conference room door and a surprised Daniel chased after me.

The Rolls-Royce Silver Ghost's window rolled down. "Ah, Christopher, so good of you to come out and greet us." Victor's voice was smooth as silk. "Daniel told you about the gift we have for you?"

"Why the hell did you bring him here?" I questioned. "Why didn't you take him to Juliet or Gregor?" I searched the parking lot, trying to see if anyone heard or saw us.

"Now don't you think I would have taken him directly to Juliet if I could?" Victor grinned. "After the incident, I haven't exactly been welcomed. And, with the Council still lurking about, this was the best course of action."

"Well...still..."

"Now be a peach and call Juliet, will you?"

IT AMAZED ME how quickly everything came to a halt once I called Juliet to inform her about what happened. We all stood around Juliet's driveway, waiting for Gregor. My focus no sooner left the trunk of Victor's car than it drifted back.

"You should never have taken him to the Foundation. My Foundation." Juliet glared at Victor, shaking her head.

"I didn't have any other options. Plus, Malcolm has been nothing but a blubbering idiot since we found him," Victor took a few steps to Juliet.

"You could have called Gregor and worked with him as I asked." Juliet straightened her back.

Victor narrowed his eyes. "As much as I love wiggling my sword in Gregor's face, this was too important. My reputation is at stake, as is my standing in both our communities. I will not be relegated to dealing with your dulled, sword-wielding Gregor."

Biting back my grin, I shared a quick look with both Amanda, who covered her mouth and pretended to cough, and Daniel, who lowered his head to hide the smile.

I turned back on Victor's trunk. Was Malcolm going to burst through the trunk and attack everyone, or was he already dead and rotting in there? Either way, I wanted someone to mention the trunk and the person it held.

"Oh, don't worry yourself, Christopher," Victor said with a wave of his hand. "He's fine, completely mad, but otherwise unharmed."

"We're going to wait for Gregor to arrive." Juliet frowned. "We need to figure out the best way to deal with this, especially now that Malcolm's sitting here in my driveway."

"What's done is done," Victor said in his disarmingly charming way. "I suggest we go in and wait. Daniel can stay with the car."

"Oh, very well." Juliet strolled back to the house.

Focusing on the conversation was an impossible task. A soon-to-be-dead man lay in the trunk of a Rolls-Royce with another man standing there watching it. The idea of small talk made my stomach turn. When Gregor finally arrived, I jumped out of my seat and ran for the door.

"Is he still alive?" Gregor walked into the room, directing his question to Victor.

"What? Couldn't you tell?" Victor asked. "Of course, he's still alive." He sprang to his feet and both men faced each other, their eyes blazing.

"Gregor, please sit." Juliet intercepted him with a strained smile.

"Of course." Gregor prowled to the opposite seat from Victor in the living room. "Good to see you, Chris." He smiled stiffly and nodded toward me.

"You too," I said. I had no idea what was going to happen or how I should even be reacting to any of this. I just really hoped they weren't going to rip the guy's head off there in the sitting room.

"So, now that Gregor is here, we need to decide what we want to do," Juliet said.

Victor leaned back in his chair, raised his hand to his mouth, and rubbed his thumb under his chin. "Well, I would assume you want a full trial and then execution."

"I don't want to draw this out," Gregor said. "We know he did it. We know he's a rogue Dark. We should just kill him and be done with it."

My hands trembled and the image of blood and gore all over the sitting room jumped back into my head. *I vote no.*

Juliet thought a moment before speaking. "There isn't going to be an easy way of dealing with this. I almost wish that you hadn't found him." She turned to me. "This must be very odd for you."

I shifted in my seat as everyone watched me. "It's nothing I'm used to. I can't begin to tell you what the right way or the wrong way to deal with this might be."

"And for that, I'm sorry. It is an ugly reality," Juliet said. "One, sadly, you'll have to learn to deal with." She faced Gregor. "Since the attack happened in your territory, you have final say."

"When are you going to question him?" I asked.

Every eye in the room turned to me.

"Chris, he's insane," Victor said. "There is nothing to learn from him."

"I've reached out to his mind. There is nothing but madness, anger, and hatred for me," Juliet said. "It can happen with new converts, especially within the Dark—"

"Now, Juliet," Victor interrupted. "Please be fair. It has happened within the Light." He tapped the side of his head. "Malcolm has always been a problem and off balance. He finally slipped over the edge and went rogue."

Juliet offered a stiff nod of agreement.

Gregor tapped his finger on the side of the chair. "Crazy or not. Rogue or not, an example needs to be made of him. With your permission, we'll execute him at the event for Christopher's second Mark. I can't have this happening in my territory. I know you would prefer another solution," he said apologetically. "Victor, you'll keep and hold him. Since you'll be a guest at the Marking ceremony, you'll bring him with you as an offering of apology to Juliet."

"Of course." Victor leaned forward. "I would like to have a few of my people attend as well. Sahin, of course, and maybe four or five others to ensure word gets out of the execution. I have no interest in this attack being used to question my power."

"A fair request, but I will not tolerate any shenanigans or grandstanding," Juliet said.

"Of course," Victor said.

"Juliet, you'll make your statement and enact justice, unless you want to delegate it to another." Gregor sat taller in his chair, visually exerting authority.

It was inappropriate, but as I watched, it occurred to me that Gregor and Victor enjoyed one-upping each other. It reminded me of two high school jocks thumping their chests; all they needed to do now was pull out their dicks and start measuring.

"I haven't had to do anything like this in several hundred years." Juliet's comments brought me back to the seriousness of the conversation.

"I suggest you handle this yourself," Victor said. "You don't want to come off as weak. That would be bad for you and the Council, especially with my people present."

"She's not weak." Gregor's voice rose, and he leaned almost completely out of his chair.

"No offense meant," Victor said. "The reality, however, is this needs to be handled with a firm, non-apologetic hand."

"I'll take care of it. Victor's right," Juliet said.

The room fell silent.

"I'm sorry, Chris," Juliet said. "This is not how your second Mark should go. It'll be hard enough for you." She stood, her face pale, a scowl hanging on her lips. "Excuse me." She hurried out the room.

Victor and Gregor shared a raised eyebrow.

"See you Saturday," Victor said with a hint of a smile, giving Gregor a once-over before leaving.

"I still don't know if I believe that he had nothing to do with this, but with Malcolm's madness, there is no way to learn more," Gregor said. "And I'm not the only one." He shook his head. "I hope this works."

MY SECOND MARK rushed toward me. No matter how I tried to slow things down, it was as if I were on a rocket hurtling toward an event I wasn't so sure I wanted to be a part of. I had to go through with this or die.

The night before my second Mark, a note was left in my room, instructing me to go to Juliet's office at 9:00 p.m. When I reached out to Amanda, she told me there was nothing more, and that I should do as instructed.

When nine o'clock hit, I made my way to Juliet's office in one of my new suits.

I knocked on the door, and when Juliet called out, I opened the door and dragged myself in. I was no longer upset with her, so I was happy to be in her presence again. She sat alone by the crackling fire.

"Please, come sit," Juliet said without taking her attention off the fire.

"Is everything all right?" I dropped onto the sofa next to her, inhaling the wonderful scent of roses and vanilla. My muscles relaxed, and the ache at the base of my head eased.

"I dislike the unpleasantness that has surrounded your transition," Juliet said. "The Marks are difficult enough, and to have it soiled by an attack... The timing with Malcolm bothers me, but we've found nothing more. These last few days have given us no more information. Both Victor and I have tried to question him, and there is nothing, only the ramblings of a madman." The fire cast Juliet's face in a warm glow. "Still we have to move forward, so tomorrow night at the ceremony, you will be tested. You'll be on your own. We all must go through this—even the Dark. It is the one thing that binds us together."

"So, no pressure." I frowned, closing my eyes. I wasn't sure I was ready for this.

"Chris." She turned to me. Her face aged with worry and wisdom. The years she'd lived written across her expression. "It will not be easy, so please steady yourself for what is to come." She took the goblet from the coffee table. Thousands of rainbows sparkled around the room when the firelight hit the goblet. "Are you ready for your second Mark?"

"You mean right now?"

"Yes, you must drink of my blood tonight so that tomorrow when you are presented for the test, you will be ready."

Now. Was I ready to do this? The alternative was death, but I'd thought I still had one more day. Finally, I nodded and took the goblet from her hands. "There's nothing in it."

The motion was quick, and I had no time to react. She slit her wrist with her walnut dagger. Her blood filled the goblet. The aroma of vanilla and roses almost overpowered me.

She wiped her wound dry, and not even a scratch was left. She met my eyes. "Do you take what I offer willingly, Christopher Michael Raymond?"

I mentally went over everything that had happened, and any normal person would think my answer would be no, but this was my new world now. Juliet, Amanda, and the others were my family, and even with all the misgivings I had, I wanted it.

The goblet was heavy in my hands, but I drank deeply of the rose-infused vanilla liquid her veins provided. Savoring as it quickly absorbed, leaving a small amount to be swallowed. I put the goblet down on the coffee table.

"It feels different this time." The blood traveled through me, warming my veins and my body. It was like drinking hot chocolate on a cold day.

"Each time, you will react differently," Juliet said. "I suggest we make you ready for bed." She stood and reached out her hand. "I'll help you."

I clasped her hand and an inviting haze crept over my body like a blanket. I don't remember getting to my room, but there I was and much to my surprise—well, I guess I can't say *surprise* given what I went through after the first Mark—I stood naked.

"Soon you'll be one of us. Mind and body." Her voice was soft, so totally different to what I normally heard.

The eagerness of her kiss on my chest caused me to inhale and close my eyes. I reached to caress her dark-blond hair, and I quivered and moaned as she gently nibbled at my chest.

"Finally, I get to feel you. I've been waiting for this. You have no idea how wet you make me," she whispered as her silky hand hastily wrapped around my stiffening member.

"I..." I tried to speak.

"You want to move to the bed? That sounds like a wonderful idea," she said.

Soon, I dropped on the bed with Juliet over me, her naked form pale, soft, and perfect. Her breasts bounced slightly as she shifted on top of me. I wanted nothing more than to get lost in her breasts, inside her.

She smiled at me. "Do you like my body?" She playfully tweaked my nipple.

I groaned in anticipation. This time instead of lying there doing nothing, I reached up and brushed my hands over her flawless breast.

She arched her back with a tremble.

I smiled up at her. "You're amazing."

"You only got to witness a little of my talents with that boy. Wait until you experience what I can do for a man."

I ran my hand down the side of her body.

"I've had hundreds of years of practice," Juliet teased. "You won't be watching this time." She leaned down and nipped at my ear, reaching between my legs, cupping me softly in her hands. "They're so big and full. We've got to take care of that."

Her body shifted, and a soft moan escaped her mouth.

I gasped as I felt the warm, welcoming wetness of her body as she deliberately lowered herself to me. I inhaled a shaky breath.

She grinned at my reaction, leaned down, and kissed the side of my neck. Her hips rocked as she kissed me. "This is for you. I want you to enjoy this, to enjoy me and my body."

We fell into a rhythm. She allowed me to switch positions so that I was on top. I needed to feel her body reacting to mine. Her amazing eyes blazed into me, and I stayed there for what seemed to be years, her eyes offering instructions for me. As we progressed, we were one. Her body responded to our movement, another soft moan of delight escaped her beautiful lips.

My body ached for hers, and my skin was on fire. I craved this and desired her.

I leaned in to kiss her. I needed our mouths to be one. Our tongues danced around as the tempo of our bodies increased. I felt her legs tighten around me and a small cry of pleasure escaped her mouth.

I found myself falling into a comfortable darkness, which no matter how hard I tried to fight, I couldn't resist.

When my eyes opened, I inhaled. "You smell amazing. What is that scent?"

Between the scent and the heat next to me, I realized I wasn't alone. I peeked over, and next to me, where I expected Juliet, lay the strong form and beautiful face of a man I didn't know.

"I'm waiting for you, Christopher," he said, his deep voice welcoming. He had a stunning green eye and a stunning gray eye. It surprised me that they didn't match.

"You!" I realized I had seen those eyes before. They were the ones I'd seen in my other visions.

I shifted in the bed to focus on him better. Juliet was gone, and we were both naked and both very aroused.

"Once you're immortal, we'll be together," he said, with a wonderfully deep voice. He kissed the side of my neck with his full lips. Then he pecked it.

My focus was on my aching body. I needed release. I needed the strong shoulders and hairy chest.

"Do you want that?" he teased. "Do you want me? Do you want to be with me?" His hand moved down my chest and stomach to my throbbing erection. He playfully squeezed it, almost causing me to burst. He chuckled and lowered his hand to my balls and gently massaged them. "So big and so ready for release. I can't wait to taste you."

His gaze washed over my body and then came back up, meeting mine. He moved his strong hand past my balls to the spot before my entry, teasing me. My back arched, and I held my breath.

"I knew you would like this. There is so much more." He breathed into my ear, and I sensed his stiffness near me, the heat radiating off his firm body. He lifted me tenderly, and as I took a breath, he slid into me, my body welcoming him.

Feeling him deep within me, I gasped for breath. I couldn't hold back my body convulsed as I orgasmed. It was intense. I squeezed my eyes shut as a bolt of energy seemed to shoot through me.

When I opened my eyes, I was by myself in my bed. The morning light filled my room as I tried to quickly recapture the images. I sat up and looked around for anyone, sensing nothing but that wonderful sensation of calm that always accompanied my orgasm. I fell back onto my bed.

"More dreams." I inhaled deeply the wonderful scent of sandalwood, wanting to get lost in it all again.

As I showered, I tried to focus on the man in the dream. The more I thought about him, the less I remembered him or his face, but his eyes, I would never forget the green and gray eyes.

Understanding this better now, I realized the vivid dream was all part of the bonding between Juliet and me. The man in the dream was an amalgamation of various men I knew or had seen. A true image created out of my imagination. I decided not to worry about it and chalk it up to a pleasant experience. I got out of the shower to a knocking on the door. I wrapped the towel around my waist and went to answer.

Amanda stood there with a tray of food.

"Good, you're awake and showered. You need to eat this and get dressed." She rushed past me, put the tray down on the table by the window, then hurried to my closet and started going through my clothes.

"I can pick out my clothes for the day," I teased. I felt great this morning.

"Christopher, what time do you think it is?"

I checked the window and shrugged. "Eight, eight thirty, why?"

"It's six in the afternoon," Amanda replied, pointing to the clock. "You have half an hour before you're expected downstairs. Most everyone is already here."

"What?" I glanced around the room and out the french doors to the trees and the hills. That couldn't be right.

"Yep," she said. "You must have had one heck of a great night." She wiggled her eyebrows.

I rolled my eyes. I finally noticed she was dressed for the event. She wore a light-blue cocktail dress with her hair pinned up perfectly.

"Now do you want my help or not?" Her arms were crossed over her chest. "Oh, you might want to pick up the towel." She pointed. "It fell."

"Son-of-a..." My face heated, and I quickly grabbed the towel, trying to cover back up.

After eating some food and getting dressed, Amanda and I walked downstairs. The house had been cleaned and scrubbed. The fragrance of the fresh flowers made it crisp. All the arrangements were in fall colors. The furniture, rugs, and paintings were all beautiful.

"So, what's going to happen?"

"Well, they'll deal with Malcolm, and then you will be tested," she replied. "Since your Marking went well, that is the next step."

"So my Mark went well?"

She nodded. "Anyway, after the test, there will be a reception for everyone to mix and mingle. It should be nice. We've been working on it all week. Thank goodness I found such a capable estate manager in John. And of course, the party helpers are amazing. They can do anything and make life so much easier. I love using them."

We turned the corner and headed out to the backyard

"Look, about my Mark." I slowed down. "I really need to talk to..." I stopped. There was a huge white tent set up with various people milling about the space, both inside and out. I recognized some of them from the Counsel of Light meeting and Juliet's senior governors. Victor was there and what I thought were some of his people, including Sahin. Everyone had dressed to impress. The people I didn't know I assumed were companions or guests. Some had to be Keepers.

"Oh my." I froze.

"Relax." Amanda took my arm. "Everything will be fine."

I forgot everything else and focused on Amanda's face. Juliet wasn't anywhere to be found as we walked into the tent.

The tent included nice paneled wood flooring, not the cheap stuff but the really nice wood that might be installed in a home. In the center of the space was a plastic tarp laid out. Except for the people milling about, the room was a complete void.

"Not good," I mumbled.

No one came over to greet us, and most of the guests had a neutral expression on their faces, while a few had forlorn looks. My stomach did backflips and my forehead perspired lightly.

Amanda ushered me to the side. There was no time for me to say anything because within moments of our entry, the space grew even quieter.

Juliet trudged in. She had on a dark robe with the hood just around her face. Flanking her, Gregor too wore a robe, but his hood was down. They strode to the center of the room and stood on top of the plastic tarp.

"We are here to witness and enact justice," Gregor said. "All present are to bear witness." He paused, allowing the words to sink in. "Bring in the betrayer."

I watched as two members of Victor's group rushed out. There were a few mumbles, but nothing more as we waited. After several tense moments, they dragged in a man bound with silver chains.

His face was bloodied, and what didn't have blood appeared pale. His clothes were ripped and his filth filled my nose.

"Malcolm," I whispered.

Amanda took a breath, and I reached out and squeezed her hand. I glanced at her quickly, and her body tensed and trembled. I had no doubt this was the man that had killed Adam and Mia, and almost killed Amanda.

Malcolm glared at the group and pulled at the chains. The sizzle of his skin and a whiff of burnt flesh made my nose crinkle.

"There will never be peace," Malcolm shouted. "You're all fools. Nature will be in balance. They will ensure it." His eyes were large, and he started laughing.

He's insane.

"Silence!" Victor lashed out, striking the man, and knocked him to his knees. "You should be begging for whatever mercy you imagine you deserve." His booming voice bounced off the tent walls.

Malcolm laughed and then spat at Victor's feet. "You're nothing. You're going to die right along with the others. You think you're powerful. You're not. They're powerful. They are the true power."

"Victor Rey, Leader of the Dark, do you surrender your charge for punishment?" Gregor ignored the man's ramblings.

Victor glanced around the room, met Amanda's gaze for a moment, then settled his gaze on Juliet. "Yes, this man does not speak for me or for those under me. His creator has cast him out and renounced him." He pointed to a stoic woman with long brown hair who had been doing an amazing impression of a statue. "He is yours to pursue the justice you seek."

"Juliet, this is the man that attacked your home," Gregor said. "He killed those under your contract, tried to kill your Keeper, and threatened our ways. What justice do you seek?"

Juliet lowered the hood of her cloak. "I seek blood retribution."

"As this is my territory, I accept your request and honor your wish," Gregor said. "Per our traditions and our rules, I grant you this, Juliet de Exter." He bowed toward her, then raised his head. "Bring the filth forward."

The two Dark holding Malcolm marched forward, but Victor stopped them.

"I shall bring him for justice." Victor snatched the chains from the two men, yanked the shackles hard, and caused Malcolm to stumble. Victor pushed Malcolm to his knees in front of Juliet. "He is no longer a Dark. We turn our back on him."

"Then he shall die," Juliet said.

Gregor pulled up his hood so that most of his head was covered.

"Do you have anything to say, Malcolm, before I take back the gift that was bestowed on you?" Juliet asked.

"You're nothing." Malcolm laughed. "None of you are anything. You're all going to die. The old ones are going to kill each of you and return nature to its true balance."

This guy was nuts.

Malcolm's face went dark, and he started to transition. His loud growl was directed at me. "You're going to bring it upon all of us. He's the one that you should kill. Kill Duncan...Chris before..."

No one would know how Malcolm intended to finish his crazy thought, because the next thing out of his mouth was blood.

I blinked a couple of times in shock. On the floor lay Malcolm's body, and Juliet held his head. Her face was in its true vampiric form, showing her fangs and her stronger ridged brow. She shifted back and dropped Malcolm's head on the floor.

"Remove this refuse from my home and burn the body so that he will vanish from this world."

I wanted to vomit, and I didn't think I was the only one.

Chapter Fourteen

"DON'T LET WHAT Malcolm said worry you. He's insane." Juliet patted my leg.

I winced at the thought. Do or Die. Literally.

After "justice" was delivered, the guests had wandered into the house for drinks. It allowed everyone time to relax while the pavilion tent was prepared for my test and the party after.

Juliet and I had gone to her office. Given what happened, I didn't feel like continuing with my test. I wanted to go and just be alone for a while.

"Can't we postpone the test?" I rubbed my temples. "I can't say I'm excited about any of this, especially after what Malcolm said. Do you really think I can bring about the end of the immortals?"

"Christopher, stop." Juliet held up a hand. "The man was unstable and would have said anything at that point. You need to focus on the coming test. It can't be changed. What is cast must be completed." She poured me a glass of water. "Here, drink this."

I took a sip. It was like drinking air. No flavor and no taste. The only thing to let me know it was fluid of any kind was the wetness on my tongue. Still, to be polite, I drank it.

"So what is this test?"

"Just remember, sometimes we all must do things we don't enjoy," Juliet replied.

"We're ready," Amanda said, opening the door to the office.

"Focus and answer what might be asked of you. Don't forget who you are," Juliet said.

I stood up.

Juliet offered me a warm smile, and then she did something I didn't expect. She hugged me and kissed my cheek. "You'll be fine," she whispered in my ear.

Back in the tent, cocktail tables were scattered around the interior, and candelabra now cast an odd warmth and formality. At the back, there appeared to be the wood-and-stone altar from my first Mark.

Throughout the space were beautiful roses and orchids of all colors, filling the space with what I had grown accustomed to—the strong scent of vanilla and rose. Of course, I knew that had more to do with Juliet than the actual flowers. A familiar scent of sandalwood struck me. I peered around to see where it came from—who it came from—but I couldn't tell. It was too faint and might have been someone's cologne that I hadn't noticed.

The same people from Malcolm's execution watched us. Juliet on my left and Amanda on my right. When we got halfway, Amanda stepped away and took her place at one of the cocktail tables. Juliet and I were alone. I tried to relax, but my neck and shoulders were in knots with everyone staring at me. We marched to the altar, or Juliet's ceremonial table, an ornately carved hardwood pedestal with a black stone tabletop. Juliet and I walked around, now glancing out at everyone.

"We are here for the test of Claiming." Juliet's voice commanded the room to silence. "Christopher, do you agree to be tested in the ancient ways and to live by the results of the test?"

I swallowed, not focusing on the people. "I will." I knew I had to say yes to the test. I wouldn't have gotten this far if anyone thought I'd say no.

"Please, bring in the test." Juliet turned to the side of the tent where a false front hid a hallway.

A figure emerged.

Juliet stepped away from the table, leaving me. "This is your test."

Terrie sauntered toward me, and with her—I froze. It was Cindy. My Cindy.

"What the fuck!" I yelped.

Cindy wore a form-fitting white linen dress, showing off her ample curves. Her brown hair was held up in a simple bun. I couldn't see any marks or bruises. Her makeup, which she rarely wore, could have hidden injuries, but too much care was put into it and it perfectly matched her hazel eyes. She looked amazing, not hurt.

"Why is Cindy here?" My body tensed, and my fists clenched. "Juliet, what the fuck?"

"She is your test. She's learned too much about us." Juliet's eyes were cold and dead. "You must kill her and drink of her. It is the only way."

I didn't understand what was happening. This couldn't be right. Perhaps it was another dream.

"Hi, Duncan," Cindy said. "I thought you were dead. We all did." Her smile blank. "I never believed you got in the car accident. I wouldn't accept it."

Terrie helped her onto the wooden table.

"I kept researching the accident, and things didn't add up," Cindy said. "Then I met Terrie a few weeks ago." Her blank expression mocked me. "I guess I learned too much. I guess I found out things that I shouldn't have."

My heart raced, and my head pounded.

We weren't in a tent anymore. It was a crypt.

"Terrie tried to stop me. In fact, several people tried, but I wouldn't stop," Cindy continued. "I knew I couldn't stop. I guess it has something to do with my love for you." She chuckled. "I knew I never had a chance, you being gay and all. But still I loved you so much, and you never saw it."

Cindy lay back on the table like some kind of sacrifice.

"Anyway, it doesn't matter now," Cindy said. "Terrie told me that you have to kill me so that you can live forever and my dying will keep you protected." She nodded. "That's very important. You can't be found out. I recognize that now. Maybe things would have been different if I wasn't so persistent, but at least I'll get to be part of you. After you feed off me."

I shook my head back and forth. "No." I glanced at the others. "No, I won't. There has to be another way."

I went to move, but Juliet, Terrie, Max, Sybil, Rei, and others had me blocked in. Did I know them? They were all monsters; they just killed a man without a trial. Juliet had fed off a boy, taking his innocence. What did I know about them?

"You have to feed off the blood of one who loves you," Juliet said. "It's our way, and you agreed to be tested, so this is your test." She pulled out a jeweled dagger and placed it in my hand. "You must complete the test. We all must do things we don't like to survive. You must do this."

The others vanished out of my sight. I focused on Juliet and Cindy.

"You mean like you and that little boy you fed off?" I yelled. "The one that Terrie brought you that you made me watch?"

I took a step closer to the altar. "I won't kill her. I won't do it."

"If you don't and she exposes us, we all die." Juliet said, her voice cold and calm. "Do you honestly think humans will leave us alone, knowing that our survival depends on us feeding off them? Or the fact that our blood can heal them? You're not that naive or stupid." Juliet's tone was colder than I ever thought possible.

Juliet and I were alone.

"No I won't!" I snarled at her, and my face ached. "You can't make me do this! Not to her, not to anyone!" My growl echoed off the walls.

My face blazed with pain.

Juliet's face shifted to its true form, the one I remembered seeing when she took on the appearance of a vampire. "You will do as I tell you, or you will die! She will still be put to death. She's learned too much about us, and we can't alter her memories. She'll keep pursuing the truth. If you want to live, then you only have one choice."

"You will not touch her!" I snarled, beating the stone altar. "She's an innocent and you will not harm her!" Every part of my body burned with pain. I wasn't going to let that stop me. I needed to protect Cindy.

Juliet took a step back as I growled at her and jumped on the table that held Cindy and her blank, smiling face. I would die protecting her.

"Understand this, all of you," I roared. I knew they were there, even if I didn't see them. "You will not hurt her. She's mine, and I'll protect her. To get to her, you have to kill me."

My face continued to blaze. When I reached to touch it, the texture wasn't like my skin. It was hard and wrinkled. I didn't care. I needed to protect my friend. The only thing that mattered was getting Cindy out of there and making sure she was safe.

"Enough." The words bellowed from the darkness that surrounded me. "It is done. His test is complete. He is of the Light. Do you agree?"

I checked the space as it came back into focus. Sybil stood to the side, speaking.

"As much as it disappoints me, I agree," Victor said. "You have chosen well, Juliet. I've not seen such strength in a great many years. He would have been a powerful Dark."

My vision started to clear, and my heart slowed. My throbbing face calmed.

Bright light, like a sunny day on the beach, washed over the room. No longer hindered by the darkness of the room, everything was easily seen. Birds chirped outside and all the heartbeats in the room pounded. Not as many as there should have been, but I still managed to glance around the room and tell who had a heart beating and who didn't.

It took a moment, but I quickly made sense of it all. There were all kinds of scents: baby powder, pine, sage, rosemary, lavender, chocolate, sandalwood, roses and vanilla. Everything.

"Christopher, it's over." Juliet stood, her face beaming. "You are of the Light. I knew you would not fail me."

"What's going on?" My shoulders stiffened and I twisted my head around, meeting all the gazes in the room. I peeked down at Cindy, happily blank.

"Please, Christopher, get off the table," Juliet said. "No harm will come to Cindy. You have my word." She reached out with her senses to calm me, and it pissed me off because it was working.

"Amanda," Juliet called, and Amanda stood with something in her hands. "Christopher, look upon your true self."

Amanda held up a mirror, and my transformed face was a mix of pain, terror, and an odd kind of beauty. My brows were heavy, animalistic, and furrowed. My canines were extended. It was my face and gradually turned back to the one I was used to seeing. The face I knew stared back at me, a hot sweaty mess but mine.

I collapsed.

"I gotcha, big guy." Max wrapped an arm around me, keeping me from falling. "You should be proud. I don't think I fully transformed until after my final Mark. Booya, boy, that was impressive." Hints of his Southern accent teased senses.

"Amazing," a gruff male voice said.

"You're going to need to feed—not a lot, just a little—and it should be from someone who cares for you," Juliet said. "It should be Cindy..."

I shook, and my face ached again.

"But you don't have to kill her," Juliet added quickly, forcing serenity into me. "I swear to you, no harm will come to her. I'm asking you to trust me." Juliet took me from Max.

She used everything she had on me. I should have been angry and hurt, and I wanted to be, but she was too strong and she directed all her empathy at me. Amanda helped Cindy off the table. Juliet took my arm and the four of us headed out the back of the tent.

We were in the pool house. We walked past the cozy kitchen, the living room, and bathroom. Amanda moved Cindy onto the bed in the bedroom and took up her position by the door. Her arms resting at her sides with her shoulders straight, she might have looked casual, but I could tell she was ready to pounce if need be.

"If something happens to her…" I wanted to sound menacing, but I wouldn't lie. I needed food. I smelled Cindy and hated that Juliet was right. My stomach grumbled. I needed what Cindy had running through her veins.

"Nothing will." Juliet forced me to relax and trust her. "You've been through a lot. You need this."

I stood there, fixated on a quiet Cindy. Where was the chatterbox I knew? Where was the plucky smile and playful twinkle in her eyes? Juliet picked up Cindy's arm, quickly bit into her wrist, and then handed it to me.

"Your bond to Cindy will help you to stop. If not, I will stop you," Juliet said, meeting my gaze. "I swear on all that I hold holy."

I almost said no, but then I got a whiff of Cindy's blood. It smelled like chocolate-covered strawberries. I wanted it. Something in my mouth popped. I leaned in to Cindy's wrist and began to drink.

The flavor filled me with power and strength. A warm tingle radiated from my stomach to the tips of the fingers and toes. Even my dick ached and my balls twinged with a need for release. I wanted the sensation to last, but a voice in the back of my head told me to stop. As much as I didn't want to, I knew I had to. I took one last drink and pulled away.

"Bite your tongue hard enough to draw blood and lick the wound on her wrist," Juliet instructed.

I did it, and yes, biting your tongue hurts like a son-of-a-bitch but it passed. The wound on Cindy's wrist started to heal. Seeing that helped me relax even more.

I felt like myself again. My heart beat a steady pace and my breathing evened out. What had I just been through? How could Juliet bring my one true friend and use her like this? I tried to fight the anger, but the calm won.

"You did well." Juliet wore a bright smile like a parent whose baby just ate real food for the first time.

"What's going to happen to Cindy?" I demanded. "Is she going to be safe? I can't let anything happen to her." My anger and anxiety kept boiling up, but Juliet smoothed them back down.

"We might have led you to some false conclusions about that," Juliet said. "Cindy was never in any real danger, but we had to make you believe it. It's an awful thing to do." She shook her head. "But, as I've said to you, sometimes we have to do things we don't like. So, yes, it was awful and mean, but she'll be fine. She will wake up in her home and remember nothing. Terrie is very good. That is why I sent her."

"But all—"

"I'm sorry," Juliet interrupted. "It was all part of your test. Even me feeding from the young man, it was all part of the setup for your test."

Confusion, thy name is Chris.

"You can meet him if you like. He's Terrie's Keeper. He only looks young, but I assure you, even when she engaged him, he was over 18." Juliet sighed and continued. "We had to learn your true calling. Would you be of the Light or of the Dark? This test is how it's determined. There are only so many ways to learn the true nature of men."

I rubbed my chin and the stubble gently scratched my fingers. "So now what?" I tried not to sound bitter.

God, I wanted to be annoyed and furious. I wanted to stomp my feet and take Cindy and leave this place, but I was tied to Juliet. There might have been hints of a link in the back of my mind before, but tonight, I felt how strongly bonded to Juliet I was, and I couldn't just run away. Even if at that moment, I really wanted to.

"Traditionally, we celebrate, but if you're not up for it, you can go be alone," Juliet said. "For some people, the second Mark and the test are the hardest parts of the transition. However, it would mean a great deal to me if you would stay, especially with all the negativity that has transpired over the last few hours."

"No guilt." I frowned.

"Cindy could attend." Juliet faced Cindy but focused on me.

Juliet endeavored to be coy and cute.

"Terrie already has a false memory implanted. So it wouldn't affect her, plus..." Juliet paused a moment, holding something back, not wanting to finish that thought. She smiled at last. "You do miss her, don't you? She can stay and be our guest."

It was great to see Cindy again, and I would've loved to spend time with her even just for the night. Part of it felt creepy, and I'll admit if I was a better person I would have told them to take her home, but I missed her. I missed having a friend I knew and understood around. I missed that part of my life. Maybe that was why I couldn't return to Reno, and Juliet knew it.

"Okay, but first, can we put her in something nice? She needs to look as beautiful as all the other women here. I want this to be a magical night for her."

"We can arrange that." Juliet's mouth curved into a full smile. "Amanda, please take Cindy with you and find her something gorgeous to wear."

"I've got just the thing," Amanda said with an excited glance at him, and soon she and Cindy were off to the main house.

Juliet gently pushed me to the bed to sit down. "Thank you."

"For what?"

"I realize how hard tonight has been on you," Juliet said. "I want to say both how sorry I am and how very proud of you I am."

My face blushed.

"I knew when we met you were the one," Juliet said. "I didn't know how strong you were. The depths of your sense of right and wrong. I hope you'll forgive me." Her voice was gentle and warm, and for the first time, I saw the impact and strain this had put on her. The dark circles under her eyes and how her shoulders slumped. I hadn't seen her like this since Amanda had been on the brink of death. "You mean a great deal to me, Duncan, and I want you to be happy in this new life. It won't be easy, and you will always be tested. Some days, you'll fail, and other days, you'll succeed, but never let it break you. Let your goodness shine through and be your guiding light."

Surprised by the tears on her cheeks, I leaned in and kissed her gently. "I promise I'll do my best by you, even if I'm angry and hurt."

I waited for Cindy in the main house. When Terrie, Amanda, and Cindy walked down the main staircase, Cindy wore a peach and silver cocktail dress that sparkled with matching silver shoes. They were all laughing, and my soul filled with joy.

My Cindy was back.

"You look amazing." I greeted her with a hug and kiss on the cheek.

"Thanks. I owe it all to Amanda and Terrie," Cindy said. "It's too bad I won't remember any of this when I get home."

"How are you?" I asked.

"I'm good. I feel fine," Cindy said.

"Can you give us a minute?" I asked Terrie and Amanda. "Thank you for taking such good care of her," I added as they both strolled on. Once they were out of earshot, I focused on Cindy. "Do you realize what's happening to you?"

"Terrie and Amanda explained it to me," Cindy replied, brushing a strand of hair off her rosy cheeks. "They also said I was safe and not to be worried about anything. I'm completely protected here and no one can harm me."

I sighed. They had clearly charmed her.

"I suppose I should be scared out of my mind, but I'm not." She chuckled. Her playful smile and twinkle in her eyes were back. "I guess seeing you again is worth it. I'm really glad you're not dead. I miss having you around. I miss our lunches and all that." She touched my cheek.

I understood exactly what she meant.

"I never knew," I said as Cindy's words of her feelings for me came rushing back to me. It seemed like a lifetime ago, but it was probably at most only an hour.

"How could you?" Cindy asked. "I realized I was barking up the wrong tree. It was my own fault, and once I got over it and started dating, I just wanted you to be happy." She took both my cheeks in her hands. "Are you happy? Is this what you want? Are you going to be happy?"

"The minute I walked into this house, I belonged here. I was home. I don't know if I'll be happy all the time, but I think I'll be happy overall. It's going to be a whole new world for me." I held her hands. "I didn't have anything back home. You were the closest thing to family."

"Still, it makes me sad." Cindy's head drooped.

The muffled chatter and music faded as we focused on each other.

"I'm sorry about outing you in there." Cindy stepped back. "Amanda said she and Juliet didn't know you were gay. They weren't surprised, but why didn't you say anything to them?"

"It never came up." I shrugged. "They didn't ask, and I didn't say anything. I didn't see how any of it mattered. If they wanted, they could've asked." I frowned and repeated, "I don't see why it matters."

"I don't think it does. They were just surprised." She glanced over my shoulder. "Shall we go to the party?"

We sauntered back through the hall and out to the backyard. Nothing had changed other than the atmosphere. Laughing and talking filled the space, and for the first time, I saw servers bringing drinks and food around as well as glasses of red.

"If I'd known you were going to be so powerful, even without your gift, I would have endeavored to impress you." Victor stalked over to Cindy and me, his accent richer as he spoke. "Especially given how nicely you clean up. Who knew we had so much in common. Ah well." He ran his hand along my arm. "I can be very charming when I want to be."

"Victor, this is Cindy." I strained to be polite, moving enough so his hand didn't touch me.

"A pleasure to meet you, my dear." Victor seized her hand and kissed it. "You look delicious."

"Nice to meet you," Cindy said. "You're a Dark, right?"

"I am the Leader of the Dark for this area." Victor straightened up, his chest somehow broader. "It's the largest territory in the world, but don't let that worry you, my dear. The only difference between the Light and Dark is that the Dark actually have fun doing what comes naturally to us all, whereas the Light have guilt and try to suppress our nature."

"Victor." Juliet's tone came right on cue.

"I jest, I jest." Victor held up both hands in surrender.

"Cindy, welcome to my home." Juliet leaned in and kissed both her cheeks. "I'm sorry about the circumstances that brought you here. I hope you will still enjoy my hospitality."

"I should be upset, but I'm not."

"There seems to be a lot of that going around tonight." Victor frowned. "Really, Juliet, must you keep using your parlor tricks?"

"You and your ilk are invited to leave at any time." Juliet glanced to the door. "Especially, if you don't like my parlor tricks."

"You see, my dear, the Light are so touchy." Victor's gaze washed over Cindy as he showed his pearly whites. "Please excuse me. I must have words with Sahin. It would appear that he made an error about Chris."

"Victor can be tiring at times." Juliet shook her head. "Mostly when he's trying to show off. Other times, he can be pleasant enough." She sighed in the direction Victor had gone. "Poor Sahin, Victor doesn't like to be surprised. If you need anything, please ask. Christopher, I trust you'll take good care of your guest."

"Of course," I said. "I'm not letting her out of my sight." I peeked over to the buffet table. "Come on. You have to try the food. It's amazing. I've never had anything like it before."

"I can't wait." Cindy laughed.

As we rushed over to the buffet table, I grabbed two glasses of champagne. The rest of the night was a blur of chatting with different folks and relaxing. I also got a chance to talk with the different Council of Light members in a less formal setting. My goal, however, was to make sure that Cindy had an amazing time, and after we mixed and mingled for a while, we found a quiet place to sit and talk. I got to hear about the latest happenings back home, especially who she was dating, and before long, it was like old times. The two of us sitting, laughing, yakking, and enjoying ourselves as if nothing else mattered.

When the time came for Cindy to go, I realized it would be harder on me than on her, thanks to Terrie's mental tricks.

I pulled Terrie aside before they left and asked if she would please ensure that the memories of the night were beautiful and wonderful. It was the least I could do for her. Even if she only remembered it as a dream, that it would be one of her best.

Terrie agreed, and the weight lifted from my heart. By the time we said our goodbyes, it was just the two of us. Terrie did what she needed to do and even Juliet had left us alone to enjoy our limited time together.

The moon shone down on the driveway, reflecting off the black sedan. Cindy leaned close and gave me a big hug that I returned.

"It was amazing spending this time with you." Cindy said.

"You had a good time?"

"Whenever I'm with you, I have an amazing time." Cindy shivered under the late-night air.

"I don't want you to go, but..." I couldn't finish the sentence.

"Don't be sad. I'm happy. Tonight was amazing, and you're happy. Finally." Cindy kissed my cheek.

Reaching the car door, she turned and waved one last time before vanishing inside the sedan. The tires crackled over the gravel as the car drove off.

Seeing her leave, the gravity of what I had given up burst from my heart.

Chapter Fifteen

TWO DAYS HAD passed since Cindy vanished into the black sedan, her chocolate-coated-strawberry scent disappearing with her. After we said our goodbyes, the realization of never seeing her again had hit me hard. She wouldn't remember any of it, but I would and I got to carry that knowledge with me forever. Sadness hung over me like a rain cloud.

Had I led her on? Was there a part of me that enjoyed the attention I received from her? Or, did a part of me long for the type of relationship my parents had. Only now had I been forced to consider such things. I had to take a long hard look at myself in the mirror to figure this out.

I moped in my office at the Foundation, reviewing the same report for the fourth time and still not reading it. That was my morning. I suppose if I were paying attention I would have noticed sooner, but as it was, a familiar tickle tugged the back of my brain and my gaze shot up before the knock came. I sensed Juliet as she approached.

The last we talked, she'd explained my ability to recognize immortals would grow, and once I completely transitioned, I would be able to sense other immortals with ease. However, it would never be perfect and there were ways for my senses to be tricked. I would have to learn.

"May I come in?"

"Of course." I stood.

She closed the office door, and we met at the small conference table.

"Is everything all right?"

"I was going to ask you the same thing," Juliet took off her mole-hair jacket and placed it over the chair next to her. "You've been quiet and distant."

I poured us both a glass of water. The non-flavor of it had little appeal for me, but I was used to it. I was losing my sense of taste the more I transitioned, so I would need to get used to it.

"I'm all right. My appetite is coming back, as are the flavors, so that's good, but things are still pretty bland."

"It'll be back to normal in the next day or two." Juliet smiled. "After your next Mark, it'll take longer, and then after your last Mark, there'll be no flavor. I suggest you enjoy it now." She played with her glass of water. "I wish I knew what a milkshake tasted like. They look so good."

"They are," I said. "There was this place up in Reno where Cindy and I would go sometimes. It was great." I beamed at the memory.

"I'm sure." Juliet took a sip and put the glass aside. She focused on me, a thoughtful expression crossing her face. "That is partly why I wanted to talk to you."

"Why? Is something wrong? Nothing happened to her, did it?" I found myself standing, surprised at how quickly I moved.

"Chris, relax." Juliet pointed to my seat. "She's fine. Everything went well. Gregor is having Terrie stay up there for a few more days, just to make sure. However, that is why I'm here. I wanted to get your thoughts on having Cindy become your first Keeper? It wouldn't be for a while, but I watched the two of you the other night and she clearly cares a great deal for you, and you for her. The relationship is a platonic one, which makes it a good match."

My cheeks hurt from the smile I suddenly had. I sat back down, letting the chair absorb my weight.

"It's something to consider." Juliet reached across the table and took my hand, smiling at me.

"Is that possible?" I asked, my heart pounding. "I mean I could do that. There wouldn't be a conflict?"

"Of course, it's possible. I don't see why it would be a conflict." Juliet leaned back in her chair and adjusted her sapphire-colored cashmere scarf.

The idea of me being able to keep Cindy in my life, or death, whatever, lifted my spirits. Of course, the worry that something could happen to her, like what happened to Amanda, concerned me. However, that was rare, wasn't it? I would need to think on this. Juliet's voice pulled me out of my thoughts.

"She has gotten over her attraction to you, and clearly you have no interest in her in that regard." Juliet took another sip of her water.

"About that." I cleared my throat, feeling my neck heat up. "I didn't..." My mouth was dry. I needed another sip of water. "It's just not something I talk about. I don't see how it matters. Why should that be the most interesting thing about me? Why should that be the thing people get hung up on?"

Juliet listened to me vent, her face calm and neutral. She was giving me her full attention.

"Why can't I just be a normal guy, and why can't I be thought of that way instead of everyone being interested in who I sleep with or don't sleep with as it stands right now? It's just one part of me."

"I've never really thought of it that way." Juliet chuckled. "For me, I would have done more to make you comfortable."

"Like what?" I asked. "You made me comfortable when you welcomed me. What else? Hire a bunch of go-go boys and pool boys to flaunt around the house? I'm not interested in that. Never have been." I waved my hand, dismissing the idea as I leaned back in my chair. "I mean, would you have hired go-go girls and pool girls for a straight guy, like Doug, from the night we all met? Or would you have brought in only Asian men or women for Chui if she had been your Called? It shouldn't matter if I'm gay or straight, white or Asian. Labels are stupid and shouldn't mean anything. I mean, what's the difference?"

Juliet remained quiet, and my foot tapped nervously waiting for her to speak.

"I suppose nothing," she finally said, letting out a breath. "It surprised me. It did explain a few things once I understood—mainly, why you never fixated on Amanda or me. Perhaps, it's about me and my vanity." She smiled. "Regardless, it doesn't matter."

"Good." I might have said something to her when we met, but I didn't see how any of it mattered and how it was anyone's business but mine.

"I've taken up enough of your time." Juliet stood and put on her jacket, then dusted off a strand of hair. She adjusted her scarf as she spoke. "We'll talk more about Cindy when the time is right. I just wanted to get your feelings on the matter for now. Enjoy the rest of your day."

"Juliet, about that. When are you going to come back?"

"Here, to the Foundation? That's the thing about being the boss. As long as there are qualified people, such as you, manning the ship, I don't really need to be here. Ta-ta." Juliet waved and walked out.

I rolled my eyes as the door closed. A chuckle jumped from my lips. I finished off the water and went back to my desk and the report that waited for me. I needed to get through it this time.

JULIET AND I were going over more scrolls and tomes. And I thought the reports at the Foundation were boring, but this made them seem like the greatest sci-fi novel I'd ever read. Juliet assured me it was all important for my understanding of *the balance*.

Tonight, we talked more about how you need Light and Dark. Nature always worked toward perfect harmony and balance. The immortals were no different.

I found myself drifting back to the night of my test and Cindy. Finally, I couldn't sit there anymore with Juliet. "Why did I react so strongly the night of my test? I would have killed you or anyone who tried to hurt Cindy? I'm not a violent person. Is it part of the transition?"

Juliet took a sip of her red. I had been fixating on chocolate milkshakes since she mentioned it a few days earlier. That was my drink of choice for the night and it was delicious.

"Because she was an innocent, a pure soul." Juliet put her glass down and took a long hard look at my milkshake.

Maybe, it was a dick move to drink it in front of her, but she didn't seem to mind. At least, she didn't say one way or the other.

"You see, Christopher, as a member of the Light, you cannot, by your very nature, harm an innocent." Juliet waved a hand at her books on the bookcase. "It's how you're wired, how all the Light are wired. It is, despite what Victor may say, what makes us different from the Dark."

I rubbed some chocolate off my chin.

"To them, all humans are the same. Food. Playthings to be enjoyed and then cast aside."

My focus changed from the milkshake to her.

"You can see that in the way they treat humans." She crossed her leg and adjusted her skirt. "Some treat them better than others, and that is why Victor is such a good leader for the Dark, in my opinion. He doesn't allow his followers get too carried away, which makes it much easier on Gregor and me." She smirked and picked up her glass of red. "However, Gregor would never admit to it."

"How will I know an innocent, or pure, soul?" I leaned in.

Juliet finished her glass. "Some should take no thought at all. For example, children and the mentally challenged are the truly innocent. Especially those stricken with conditions such as Down syndrome." She glanced to the window. "If there were any on this planet that reflected the light of angels, then it would be them." Her tone was wistful. "As for the innocent souls, they are good people."

"Wait. So, wouldn't that make all humans innocent souls?"

I wasn't being naïve. I knew not all people were truly innocent, but I wasn't talking about your typical psycho or killer. I meant everyday people that you work with, that go about their lives living the best way they can to take care of themselves and their families.

"Correct." Juliet nodded. "Most people are, and that is what separates us from the Dark. For your test, when I gave you the choice to either kill Cindy or die, you chose to fight to keep her safe. You reacted. You were going to try to stop anyone that tried to hurt her. You protected her."

I crossed my arms in front of my chest.

Juliet tapped the side of her head. "It's like the voice you have in the back of your head that told you when to stop feeding off her. You didn't want her dead. You instinctively knew that she needed to live. I like to call that our humanity alarm. It keeps us from harming people."

"So the Dark don't have this alarm?"

"No, they do." Juliet tapped a delicate finger on the side of her cheek. "But they don't listen to it. Well, I suppose, they must, but when it comes to a choice of their life and the life of an innocent, they will choose their own life." She glanced to the coffered ceiling, quietly studying it for a moment. "If you were of the Dark, you would have allowed Cindy to die. Of course, you might have emotional pain in making that choice and you might be upset, but you still would have made that choice."

"So, Cindy would have died?" My hands shook.

"No." Juliet got up and filled her glass with more red. "The test would have been stopped before that happened. The test is all about intent and what kind of person you are. No one has to die and, at least here, no one is sacrificed in that manner."

"I suppose I understand." I finished off the last of my milkshake. I had no idea how I would react with a complete stranger.

"Let me put it another way." Juliet glanced at my empty milkshake and licked her lips, then took a sip of her red. "It's not the same, is it?" She gave a final glance to my milkshake.

"I'm sorry. That was insensitive." I frowned.

"Don't be silly." She smiled. "But, I may have to try to create something like it. It won't be the same, but maybe." She offered a small shrug. "Where was I? Ah, do you remember how you felt when I fed off Ben? You thought he was a minor and that I abused him."

I nodded. How could I forget? I was furious with her, with all of them.

"That was because you thought he was an innocent, a child, and you wanted to stop me." Her face lit up, like she was proud of me. The smile in her voice affirmed as much. "You were angry at me and you even hated me at the moment, because of what you thought I did. It was sneaky and not a very nice way of me testing you prior to your formal test."

"That's how you knew I wouldn't let Cindy die, because of how I acted with Ben." I changed to a more comfortable position in my chair. "That's what showed you I was of the Light? Even though I didn't stop you?" I frowned. I really should have tried to stop her.

Juliet nodded. "Yes, even though you didn't try to stop us."

I wasn't convinced.

"Well, I was ninety percent sure." Juliet flicked the few strands of hair that had fallen back over her shoulder. "I wouldn't know for sure until we tested you and you passed." She stretched and walked over to the window. "Unless there is anything else you want to talk about, we're in a good place, don't you agree?"

I wanted to ask her about Cindy being my Keeper. However, there was something about how she stood at the window. Something was playing on her mind. I didn't know what, but somehow I understood now was not the time to ask.

"I'm good." I stood and twisted my back, as we had been sitting awhile.

"Excellent. Have a good evening, Christopher."

As I left, I glanced back over my shoulder as she remained focused on the window and the outdoors.

THE TIME LEADING up to the big party was routine. I'd asked if I needed to be apprised of anything beforehand, and Amanda had told me that the only thing I needed to decide on was what I wanted to wear to the masquerade. Even though it would be my third Mark, it was still a party and costumes were expected.

It was Halloween, after all. I hadn't been to a masquerade before, so I didn't argue. Plus, it might be fun.

I spent hours online, searching for a mask. I've always considered my eyes to be my best feature, so I wanted something that would really make them pop, so I found a leather mask that had brown accents in it that would do just that.

As for the rest of the outfit, I had no clue. When I went to ask Amanda, she told me I was on my own. Taking my cue from the mask and having limited options, I went to the only person I knew who could help me: Mr. Bisset.

I hadn't been there since I picked up Juliet's and my new clothes after she mind-zapped him. Once I told him what I needed and showed him the mask, he told me to return in three days.

I had no reason to doubt his ability, so I did as was instructed, returning three days later. Sure enough, he had designed this elaborate wool and linen suit for me in the style of a colonial officer. The colors he used pulled from the browns in the mask. It was beautiful and my heart jumped when I saw it. All the detailing was hand-stitched in gold. After he was done fussing over the fit and making sure that everything was picture perfect, he told me to pick it up the day of the party and he would have it pressed and ready for me to wear. I couldn't wait.

With that, I was all set.

Both Juliet and Amanda kept their costumes secret, so I had no need to tell them what I was wearing. It was fun. We were like little kids.

The night of the party, I strolled down the stairs to the main hall and waited. Amanda appeared first, and she was decked out as a medieval bar wench in an embroidered leather corset. A white linen shirt underneath showed her ample bosom. Her light-blue skirt swished about her ankles, catching the light—not right for the period, but she was stunning. She carried her mask of brown leather and blue and white feathers to match her costume.

"You look very handsome." She sashayed up to me.

"Thank you."

"Put on the mask?" she asked.

I slipped it on.

"Is it an earth elemental?"

"I thought it was really nice. I found a dragon as well but thought this would be better. I guess it kind of spoke to me." I lifted it off my face.

"You did an excellent job," Amanda said. "The suit must be Fredrick's."

"Since you left me on my own, I thought I would enlist the help of a pro." I felt great in my clothes. Everything filled me with confidence.

"Well, don't you two look lovely." Juliet streamed down the stairs in her outfit.

"Wow!" I watched her flow down the stairs. She wore a deep crimson full-length sparkly evening gown. Her hair fell to the sides of her face in soft curls. Around her neck, some kind of cascading diamond necklace gleamed. Her mask matched her dress and brought out her eyes.

"I've been excited for this." Amanda smiled at both of us.

Shadows danced along the walls from lit candles, casting a warm glow on the house as soft music played throughout. Every part of the house was polished, decorated, and staged to fit the theme of the party; a masquerade ball. The backyard had a large tent again, larger than the last one. The tent was staged in the same manner as the house. What couldn't be covered in candlelight had well-placed, hidden soft lighting. The space wasn't dark, but it wasn't bright either. It had the perfect warm glow.

"I can't imagine how much work went into this," I said as we walked to the back of the house."

"It was a lot of work," Amanda said. "However, I believe John and the folks from The Party Helpers enjoyed doing it." She turned to Juliet. "It was a good idea to increase the number of staff here, even with the caterer and her staff. It's made all the difference."

"We really need to thank them," Juliet said. "They did this in no time. Please don't let me forget."

Roses and orchids filled every open space as we strolled on.

The music drifted from a band of musicians in the tent. The musicians wore tuxedos and each one had on a black-and-white mask, giving them an elegant appearance.

I felt like I needed to be doing something, but everything was taken care of and my Mark ceremony wouldn't be until midnight. It was odd not to have anything to do but mill about and actually enjoy the evening.

With each new arrival of guests, I was amazed at what I saw. Everyone embraced the idea of a masquerade ball. There were all kinds of nobles and ladies from various periods in time, as well as some more adult outfits. Even though they showed off quite a bit more than I would think appropriate, they were still tasteful.

With everyone in one form of mask or another, I found it a fun challenge figuring out who was who. Although I didn't know a lot of them. Still, I enjoyed the people watching.

Victor arrived in an all-black tuxedo, wearing a bright red leather mask of the devil. Admittedly, it was funny. However, some like Sybil, who was dressed in an evening gown with a feathery glittery mask, didn't seem to approve. Max appeared to rein her in somewhat. He was dressed as none other than a rhinestone cowboy, complete with a rhinestone mask. His had to be one of my favorites for the night.

"You know, I'm not into this whole costume thing." Rei fidgeted with his mask.

We were having a glass of champagne. Rei wore a Canadian Mountie outfit, his modest black mask clasped at the back of his head.

"You did do an amazing job with yours." Rei sipped his champagne.

"Thanks. I figured since I wasn't going to get any help from Juliet or Amanda, I would go simple and stylish." I fussed with my mask.

"Well, I tried that, and you see what I ended up with." Rei pulled at his collar. "I suppose I'm just more comfortable in a suit and tie." He glanced over my shoulder. "Oh, brilliant. Excuse me, Chris, I have to go and see if that French maid over there is really Terrie."

I turned in the direction he was staring, and a tall French maid stood there. It was Terrie. She was with who I assumed to be Ben, her Keeper, in a pirate type outfit. I wasn't completely sure, especially since I couldn't make out his mask from there, although it did have a large pointy nose as part of it. They were definitely an interesting combination.

"Hello," a deep voice said from behind me.

"Hello." I turned around and put on my polite business smile. I took in the thin-framed man in front of me. He wasn't *skinny*, just not big or bulky. The man wore a deep blue jacket with silver-trim, a tunic thing with a white-frilled front, black breeches, and black boots. He had on a blue-and-silver mask with a black Musketeers type hat detailed in blue, silver, and white plumed feathers.

There was something exotic about him and his outfit. Reddish hair peeked out from under his hat. I studied him for a minute, trying to place him.

"I'm sorry. Do I know you? I can't tell with your mask on."

"No, we haven't met. I'm Kirtus. You were talking to Rei, so I figured you must be Juliet's Called. I wanted to come and introduce myself."

He took off his hat, and dipped his right foot forward in an elegant bow.

I tried to place the name and finally it clicked. "Oh, Kirtus. I've heard about you." The minute I said the words, I wanted to shoot myself. They fell right out and I couldn't take them back.

"I'm sure you have." A frown crossed his brow, and his tone became more polite and strained. "Juliet invited me here. I suppose out of some obligation, so I figured the sooner I came to say hello, the sooner I could make my getaway. I wouldn't want to soil the event any longer than need be."

He started to turn.

I'd stuck my foot in my mouth big-time.

"No, wait. I'm an ass." I reached out and grabbed Kirtus's arm softly. "I'm sorry. That isn't how I meant it. Please, don't be offended. It was a poor choice of words."

I tried to dig my way out of the pit I now stood in. I had been raised better than that, and I was deeply embarrassed.

"Yes, I've heard about you, but only good things." I fumbled to make this better. "I wasn't thinking."

He glanced at my hand on his arm, and his muscles relaxed.

"Really? Only good things?" Kirtus's eyebrows rose. "I find that a bit of a stretch." A hint of a smile crossed his lips. "No, it's me who should apologize. I shouldn't have been so touchy. It was rude. Plus, I should be used to it."

"No one should put up with rudeness," I said. "Let me make it up to you. The least I can do is buy you a drink."

"Big spender—one whole drink," Kirtus said. "For the insult you thrust upon me and my character, we should have a midnight duel. I demand satisfaction, sir."

I caught a bit of a Southern drawl.

"Hey, be nice," I said. "You're talking to the guy who knows where the good stuff is. Wait, a minute..." I peeked down at my outfit, understanding his banter. "Very clever. I suppose we count out ten paces and turn and fire on each other?"

I caught sight of one of the servers. She brought over her tray of champagne, and I picked one up for Kirtus.

"Sorry, no duel tonight, but I hope this will suffice."

"Thank you. The champagne is excellent. I suppose it'll do. I like your outfit. It reminds me of—"

"Well, it's a party now." That voice made me cringed. "The rabble has arrived."

Sahin stood, glaring at Kirtus. "Nice outfit. Is it something from your normal collection, or is it something special you picked up at the boy's department at Walmart?"

Sahin turned his back to Kirtus, not waiting for a reply. His focus now on me. "You know, Chris, you really should learn where to step. Who knows what you might kick up?"

I wanted to beat the crap out of this guy. How rude. I was speechless.

"Hello, Sahin." Kirtus stiffened his stance. "It's good to see you too." Kirtus gave Sahin the once-over and narrowed his green eyes. "I see you're still overstuffing your codpiece."

Sahin was in one of those renaissance outfits with the over-embellished codpiece. The outfit was beautiful, but his codpiece was over the top.

"I can assure you it's all real," Sahin said through his joker mask. "I would let you touch it, but you're too much of a *lund k laddu* and I have standards."

Kirtus widened his eyes and bit his lower lip, but he kept his cool. "You keep telling yourself that." He turned to me. "It was nice meeting you. Thank you for the drink. Now, if you'll excuse me."

Shell-shocked by this whole exchange, I didn't know what to say, and as if on cue, Juliet appeared. "Kirtus, you look amazing. I love the blue and silver. It's lovely." She glided closer to us, and her crimson gown caught every light in the room, making her sparkle like the night sky. "I'm so glad you could make it. I see you've already met Christopher."

Juliet leaned in and gave Kirtus a polite hug. I'd never seen her hug anyone, other than Amanda and me, and I think that was the point of the hug for Kirtus.

"Sahin, welcome." Her tone was equally polite and friendly, but she gave him no hug. "Aren't you wearing the most perfect mask? It fits you so well."

"You look beautiful, Juliet. Thank you for the kind invitation," Sahin said through gritted teeth. "Chris, good to see you. Please excuse me." He stalked off.

I wanted to laugh. I really did. It took all I had in me not to. I forced myself to take a sip of my champagne.

Juliet watched him walk off and continued on with the two of us. "So, Kirtus, please tell me how things are going. I understand you've been doing well in your consulting business. I hope you're not overdoing it?"

"I've been busy, which is good. Some days can be a little much, having to deal with people who really don't get it, but I suppose that happens in everything." Kirtus shifted on his heels and pulled at his collar. "How are you doing? I heard about the attack. I wanted to reach out to you and offer my services, but—" He paused and sipped his drink. "—well, you know."

"I do, and I appreciate the kind words and the note. Amanda loved the flowers as well. I'm sure it helped her recovery." Juliet sipped her champagne. "There will always be mental scars, but we got the man behind it, so that was a relief."

"I can't believe that something like that would happen here, especially to you."

"Malcolm was insane," I said. "You can't understand crazy. As much as it saddens me to see that happen to anyone, he's probably better off."

"Christopher's right. Did you know him?"

"Me? No," Kirtus replied. "You know, I try to avoid the Dark whenever possible. I do what I must for Victor, but other than that, I only come out when it's necessary."

"Ah, Juliet, fetching as usual." Victor joined us, glancing over to Kirtus. "Kirtus, nice to see you again."

"Victor." Kirtus offered a polite bow.

"I hope you're representing us well in front of Juliet and her Called and, of course, not telling any stories out of school, as they say."

My heart raced. I was done. What gave these people the right to be so rude to this man?

"Kirtus has been nothing but polite and charming," I defended. "We've been enjoying our conversation. He's really quite interesting. It's refreshing. I wish all your people were like him."

"Really?" Victor watched me with stern eyes through the devil mask. "Interesting. Well, then may I suggest being careful what you wish for and, of course, watching the company you choose to keep, Chris. Remember what happened to Malcolm." He paused and faced Juliet. "As always, a pleasure."

"I'm sorry." My hands trembled. "I really hate *drive-bys*. He intentionally did that. I didn't want to hear any more. The verbal sparring is too much. Haven't we all been through enough?" I shook out my hands to relax them. "I'm sorry. I hope I didn't cross a line."

"Nothing that can't be sorted out," Juliet said. "Victor will be fine."

"Sahin probably ran off and found him," Kirtus said. "I should have held my tongue with him, but sometimes, that man is such an ass." He faced Juliet. "I should leave. I don't want to ruin your night. It was kind of you to invite me. Victor and Sahin aren't the only ones who are unhappy with my presence."

"Absolutely not," I said. "You're an invited guest, and no one can kick you out. They just need to get over it. They all think they're high and mighty, but they're not. You're just as good as them and just as welcome, if not more." I caught Juliet's gaze and my face burned. "I mean unless you think it's for the best... I should shut up now."

"Christopher is absolutely correct." Juliet chuckled. "I invited you and I don't let others, even members of the Light, tell me whom I can and cannot have in my home. I assure you, you will not have any more unpleasant incidents tonight. Now enjoy." She held Kirtus's hand. "Chris, I'll come for you when it's time."

"It's like we've just told the teacher that we were being bullied," Kirtus said.

One of the staff with the trays of champagne passed by, and I nabbed two more glasses.

"I don't remember having champagne in school." I handed him a fresh glass.

"You didn't? You should have gone to a better school." Kirtus took a sip to hide his smile.

Kirtus was a nice guy and interesting to talk with. I didn't understand the big deal, why he didn't fit in, and honestly, I found I didn't give a rat's ass about it. As Juliet promised, there were no more snide comments made to Kirtus. A few glances here and there, but nothing that would cause a riot. Talking about our passion for science fiction and love of old Alfred Hitchcock movies was fun, his favorite being *North by Northwest* and mine being *The Birds*. We chatted until Juliet came to get me for the ceremony.

After excusing myself, Juliet and I made our way to the front of the hall. The same wooden pedestal and black stone tabletop sparkled under the candlelight. On the center of the table, the onyx goblet rested next to Juliet's walnut ornate dagger.

"Please, remove your mask." Juliet set her mask to the side.

I did as instructed and placed my mask on the side of the black stone table. I focused on Juliet's face, trying to block out the others in the room. I took a shaky breath.

The music stopped, and everyone's attention was on us.

"Good evening, everyone," Juliet began. "I want to welcome you all to my home."

There was applause, which was kind of strange but cool at the same time.

"To start, I want to wish you all a happy Halloween." There were a few chuckles as she continued. "Tonight is a very special night for me, and how appropriate it is for this to be the night where we cast off our masks and Christopher receives his third Mark."

I'd relaxed so much with Kirtus that I had almost forgotten why we were there. Maybe that was the point of the party, but now my stomach dropped. Was I really ready for this? With all that has happened, what if I freaked out? Or worse.

"I want to extend a special thank-you to the members of the Council of Light who are all here in support, and of course, to all my governors and their guests." She paused and found Victor. "And of course, I want to thank the Leader of the Dark for his attendance and his assistance in the very recent events that occurred here at my home. It is important for us to build ties and to create bridges wherever we can. To paraphrase someone special to me, we may not agree with everything that each of us does, but it's not for us to dictate what the other does. Still, at the very least, we should have some level of trust and respect for one another, and I have to believe that, moving forward, this will be the case for all of us."

I smiled, recognizing the very words I'd said to her and the Council the night they moved my Marks up and when I was still upset with Juliet after feeding off of Ben. That seemed like ages ago.

"It is time." Juliet picked up the walnut dagger from the table, holding it out to everyone.

I swallowed hard. Ready or not, I had to do this.

"From the time of the first immortals," Juliet started, "we have given our blood to those we see ourselves in. At that time, they only had natural tools around them to welcome their Called. We still honor this tradition. Today, we choose elements from the earth—a wooden dagger to our skin."

Juliet slit her wrist with the walnut dagger.

"And a goblet of stone to hold our offering." She let her blood flow into the goblet. Once the goblet was filled, her wound healed and closed as if willed to do so.

She picked up the goblet. "It is from nature we come, and it is from nature we can only be born. I offer my blood, my essence, and my immortality to you, Christopher Michael Raymond. Do you openly accept this gift that, once given, binds you to our world and all the laws that govern it?"

I surrounded the goblet with my trembling hands and focused on the people in attendance. "Yes. I accept what is being offered with an open heart and an open mind."

"Once you drink this, you will be my blood and I will be yours." A smile curled around her lips, cueing me to drink from the goblet.

The vanilla and roses of her blood caressed my nose, unlike Cindy's blood, which smelled of strawberries covered in chocolate. I wondered if that would always be the case. If my brain would translate different bloods to different things in my memories. It was an interesting thought, and I would ponder it at a later time, but now I drank from the goblet, needing to take in all of it.

Once I finished, I set the goblet down.

"It is done," Juliet said. "You and I are now family. You will always be my—"

The darkness struck like a hammer on an anvil. No longer in the tent filled with guests, I was surrounded by death, destruction, and fire. The metallic aroma of blood filled my nose, then the scent of rotting and burnt flesh.

What happened?

A ruined street stretched before me. The buildings, shops, and cars were all ablaze. I knew this place. I searched for Juliet and the others, trying to figure out what happened.

"Hello," I yelled. As I shoved my way through the rubble and debris, I almost tripped over the mangled remains of a little girl. Her body torn in two. Flesh ripped from her face showed the white of bone and the gray of what lay underneath that bone. Her dress was the only clue I had she was both a child and a girl. She couldn't have been more than nine or ten.

"Merciful God." I faltered back as tears filled my eyes.

A police car burned with the doors torn off. Another car lay upside down in the middle of the street with more bodies, one mangled corpse crushed under the car and another inside with the seat belt holding it.

"Help," a voice called out. "Please, someone help."

I followed the plea and made my way into what had once been a store. Fredrick's clothing store.

"Los Altos," I mumbled.

Shelving and bolts of burned fabric buried Fredrick.

"What's happening?" I ran to him and started to pull the bolts of fabric off him.

"Christopher, thank God." Fredrick coughed. "Please. We need to get out of here before they return."

"What happened? Who did this?"

"I don't know. It all happened so fast. They moved through town. No one had time to do anything. They couldn't die. The police tried, but nothing stopped them. Some of them were holding weapons and others were using..." He stopped, trying to wiggle free. "They were using magic or something."

"Impossible."

His skin paled, and his eyes widened with fear.

Someone was there.

I turned around, and a dark woman stood there at the head of the crowd.

"We're back to finish you off, Duncan." The dark woman crossed her arms in front of her. The white of her smile offset the darkness of her features. "It's only because of luck we missed you the first time, but we've fixed that."

Fredrick's hair turned ghost white and his eyes were now sunken and hollow. I worked to pull him free while backing up at the same time.

"There's no hiding this time." Her voice cracked as she spoke. "Remember, you did this, Duncan. It's all your fault, their blood. Adam, Mia, and Malcolm, it's all on you."

Fredrick shook, or it might have been me, but he had fallen silent. I glared at the woman.

"You're not one of them. Your blood is ours, not theirs, and he won't be able to stop this. None of them will. The die is cast and nature will return to the true balance." Her eyes blazed on me.

"What the hell are you talking about?" The words finally managed to come out.

"Too bad you won't get to see the new world."

My ears filled with screams and burning. Rotting flesh assaulted my nose. Something about the screams struck me. I knew these people.

"You hear that, Duncan?" the woman mocked. "You hear those screams? That will be yours soon enough."

I wanted to yell, but nothing came out.

"And now—" She tilted her head, her face almost sympathetic. "—time to die." She pulled out some kind of metal-and-wood blade. I had an odd sensation of flying through the air. I was. Well, part of me was. My head turned over and I witnessed my body drop to the ground.

"Put him with the others," the woman said in cold, icy tones.

Someone picked up my head, adjusting it till I saw the spikes at the end of the street, rising toward the sky. On top of each of them, a face screamed in agony. Juliet, Amanda, Cindy, Victor, Kirtus, Sahin, Terrie, Gregor, Ben, all of them. They all glared at me, pain and fear on their faces.

I wanted to scream back, but I couldn't. I had no lungs to push air to my mouth, I willed myself to speak and finally sound escaped. "No!" I yelled.

The dark woman gave me an almost amused appearance.

I sensed my body again. I wasn't sure how that was possible, but it didn't matter. I started to fight back, but I was held down by invisible hands.

"You can't do this," I shouted. "We'll fight you. You can't kill all these innocent people. We'll stop you."

I didn't have a body, but I still fought.

"Christopher," a sweet voice said. "Christopher." A familiar female voice called again.

A hand slapped hard across my face, causing my vision to explode in a blaze of white then flash open. I didn't want to see anymore.

"They killed all the people in town," I bellowed. "They killed Mia, Adam, and Malcolm."

"I killed Malcolm," the familiar female voice interjected, trying to calm me down.

"It was because of them. They messed with his mind. He would still be alive if it wasn't for me." I tried to reach out to the voice. I had to make them understand. "They're coming back to destroy us. I heard it. I saw the destruction. Fredrick. They were going to kill him. I tried to help him, but I couldn't." My heart raced and every part of my body ached. "They said it was me. That I don't belong. That my blood is theirs not yours, and once we're dead, only then will nature be in balance."

"He's gone insane," another female voice said.

"I've never seen this happen during a Mark," a male voice said.

"Is it something to do with the Dark being here?" a man questioned.

"No. It's something else, he's seen something," a different voice said.

"So he's a seer?" someone asked. "Impossible."

"I've never seen power like that in someone not turned," another said. "He fully shifted. How is that even possible?"

"Please, give him some room." It was Juliet. "Christopher, it's all right. We're here."

My vision started to focus. Tables were overturned and several people were gathered over to the side, helping someone or multiple people. I wasn't sure. Juliet was holding her arm and there was a small trail of blood running down her cheek.

Tears streamed down my cheek. "Juliet, they've already been here. It was them. I know it was them. They came to kill me. Adam, Mia, and even Malcolm were killed because of me. They would have never messed with Malcolm if it wasn't for me. They're going to come back."

I grabbed Juliet hard, despite the pain I was feeling. I saw her wince, but it didn't register with me. I had no idea of the physical pain I caused her at the time. "We have to stop them. They're going to kill everyone if we don't. It won't matter, Dark or Light. They're coming back to kill us all."

"We'll stop them." She tugged at my hand to free herself from my grip but failed.

"We don't have long," I said, every part ached, my brain was starting to process how much pain I was in. "I don't know how much, but we don't have long. I can feel them. They're close, and they're getting more powerful." My hand dropped from Juliet, and I closed my eyes.

Chapter Sixteen

EACH BREATH I took was like pushing a million pins through my lungs. Each movement was like moving a million stones on each muscle. Each moment in bed was like lying on a million razor blades. My body was beaten and broken. It had to be a dream. That was the mantra I told myself, one fucked-up dream, but it wasn't. It really happened. I lazily stirred from my bed and opened my eyes as I shifted to find a comfortable position—there was none.

"Finally," Amanda whispered next to me. She occupied a chair next to the bed. Her hair was pulled back, and she was in jeans and a simple sweater. It was the most dressed-down I'd ever seen her.

"I feel like shit. Where am I?" My body wouldn't respond to my request to face her, and I didn't understand why.

"Take it easy." She rested a hand on my arm. "You're in one of the basement bedrooms, in case you're light sensitive. You nearly took out Gregor and Rei when you—" She adjusted the blankets "—well, when you were under. Then there was what you did to—"

The door opened, and Juliet rushed in. "What do you need?" She was at my side before she finished the question. She needed to brush the fallen strands of hair behind her ear. "Do you want food, or do you need blood?"

"Nothing. I don't want anything." It even hurt to talk as I adjusted my uncooperative body. "Ugh." I grunted and fell back into the pillow. "What the heck happened to me?"

"I don't know." She nodded at Amanda. "Please, let the others know he's awake."

"Of course." Amanda stood. "I'll bring down some food." She closed the door behind her.

"Chris, what do you remember?" Juliet sat on the edge of the bed. She took my hand, sending a bolt of agony through my body.

"I don't..." I winced. "I remember all these heads on spikes. I remember the screams. I saw a woman, a dark woman, it all—" I froze.

"This isn't normal, is it? I'm a failed *Called*. Something's wrong with me. You're going to have to kill me, aren't you?"

"No, we're not going to kill you." Juliet started to smile, then swallow. "But, Chris, I'm not sure what happened. If you're a seer, then that's very rare. So rare, in fact, that none of us have ever met one. The immortal royal court would have been the last time a seer existed, but that was before any of us and..." She frowned. "Well, that is a legend and one that not too many people believe."

"If it's not that, then am I crazy?"

"No, you're not crazy. That we all agree on."

"We?" I bit my lip as I lifted my upper body. It felt like I was ripping my body in half.

"It doesn't matter." She ran a hand over my head and down the side of my cheek. "Right now, you need to get better."

"Juliet, please, don't try to protect me. Who?"

"The Council of Light and, of course, Victor." She released my hand. "None of them think you're crazy, but..." She paused, taking a breath. "The Council wants to test you, but not until your last Mark, because then your gift will be fully developed."

Some gift. Juliet made it sound like something exciting you wanted at Christmas, but this was so not the case. "You mentioned Victor. What does he have to do with any of this? Why is he involved?"

"Do you remember anything that happened during your vision?"

"I told you all I can remember—Los Altos was in ruin—"

"Not the vision," Juliet interrupted. "What you did during it?"

I thought a moment. I remembered being on the ground and a couple of people around me, but nothing special. "No, I mean, I guess I must have hit the ground hard or maybe your table-altar thing."

"When you blacked out, you started to fall to the ground," Juliet said. "We were all surprised, because that shouldn't have happened. I stopped you from hitting the altar, and I tried to wake you, but you were out. So, Gregor and Kirtus helped me move you away from the table, and we cleared a place for you."

I didn't realize I was under that long. As I shifted my body on the bed, taking this all in, every nerve in my body screamed.

"Everyone was curious but, at the same time, worried," Juliet continued. "It was chaotic to say the least." She licked her lips. "Your body started to twitch. Then your arms thrashed about. You flailed your arms and you started kicking. You began to transform, and I had to use my calming on you, but it didn't work and you struck me, sending me across the room."

"Oh, God." I winced. "I'm sorry." I shook my head. "How is that—"

She held up a hand. "You shouldn't have been able to do that, not to me at least, not really to anyone there. You're new and weak in comparison to the rest of us. Seeing this, both Gregor and Kirtus held you down, but once you turned, you—" She stopped for a moment, then added, "—you knocked them off, hurling Kirtus into some of the guests."

I didn't remember any of this and my heart fell. I hurt people, people I cared about. How was it even possible?

"Sahin and Rei rushed to help."

I wanted to vomit. Had I killed someone?

"You got free, and when Sahin grabbed your arms, I've never seen anything like it, you snapped both Sahin's arms like twigs. You almost ripped them from his body. We were able to get him free, or you would have torn them clean off."

I started to tremble.

"Relax, Chris. Please stay calm." She ran a hand through my hair, and I relaxed. "Sahin is over four hundred seventy-five years old. You shouldn't have been able to do that so easily. Especially since you're not fully turned. It took Taqi, Garrett, An, Victor, Terrie, Max, *and* me to hold you down. Then you went limp and shifted back. It wasn't long after that you came to. When it ended, Kirtus, Rei, and Gregor were injured. But Sahin, you did a number on him and his arms. Since it was in public, Victor needs to respond."

"No, I didn't. I didn't do anything. I couldn't move. They cut off my head. I didn't have a body. I couldn't have been fighting back. I..." None of this made any sense.

"Who cut off your head?" Juliet leaned in.

"The dark lady. She laughed and said that he wouldn't be able to help me."

Juliet narrowed her eyes in confusion. "Who's *he*?"

"I'm not sure and she didn't say anything else about him," I said. "I attempted to fight the dark lady back, but I didn't have a body. They cut my head off." Sweat dripped all over my face. "Juliet, how? It was a dream. How did all that happen?"

"Your body must have responded to what you were seeing. That's the only explanation." She reached for something. A damp cloth. She wiped my forehead. "I can assure you it was you. That's why Victor is involved, as will be Sahin."

"Oh god." I turned from her. "Poor Sahin, his arms, what is he going to do with no arms?"

"Sahin will be fine. He'll need to heal like I did, but he'll be fine." Juliet reassured me. "It's going to take him a few days." She put the cloth down. "Look at me."

I faced her.

"The larger issue is how Victor chooses to deal with such a public assault on one of his own, especially his own Called. There is no way around it. There were too many people present, and I'm limited in what I can do for you."

"I don't understand."

"As with Malcolm, justice has to be served." All the wrinkles on Juliet's face amplified. "You didn't kill anyone, so you're not in mortal danger, but there are other punishments. If you were immortal and this was back a few hundred years, they might remove your fangs, deny you feeding, tomb you for an amount of time."

None of these options sounded good, and I remember reading about some of the other things they did, notably in the medieval times—racks and all that weren't only for humans.

"The other thing is that you're not fully immortal, so that causes its own trouble." She ran her hand through my hair again.

In the back of my brain, I felt peace, but it was far off from my conscious mind.

"Victor is a decent man, and the situation is extenuating. It may be monetary." She frowned. "Of course, knowing Sahin, he may choose to break your arms, which would be most unpleasant, especially since it'll take you much longer to heal. Either way, we have to wait for what Victor decides."

"My arms?" I whispered, glancing down at them. Knowing Sahin, they wouldn't be nice breaks either.

"The other issue is that you're the Called of not only a member of the Council of Light but the Called of the Head of the Council. The Dark love any opportunity to make us look bad or to bloody our noses, so to speak. I'm sorry, Chris. None of this is good."

"What would you do if you had to make the choice?"

"I would like to think I'm enlightened and that I would understand the situation, but—"

A tap at the door interrupted us. Amanda entered with a tray holding a couple of sandwiches and bowl of chips, fruit, as well as a bottle of red. "I brought a little of everything."

Once Amanda entered, our conversation stopped. There wasn't much more to say anyway. I knew what Juliet would do. Malcolm's death sat front and center in my mind. I tried to push it from my mind and focus on the food. The chips smelled good, but so did the red.

By that night, the soreness had completely subsided. So, when I was summoned to meet with both Juliet and Victor, I was only mentally sore and exhausted from the event. The summons had requested us to travel to Victor's home, but Juliet convinced him to meet at hers instead, since she wasn't sure how I would be feeling. She also managed to keep the meeting between the three of us and not include the others.

I knocked on the office door and waited for Juliet.

"Come in," she said.

I checked my suit and took a breath before entering. Behind the desk, Juliet sat, her hair pulled up and her skin rosy. She looked better than she had that morning. Victor sat in one of the guest chairs. He wore a black suit with a light-blue pocket square.

"Please, have a seat." Juliet pointed to the empty seat in front of her desk.

Considering all the time I'd spent in this office, this was the first time my hands trembled and sweat trickled down the back of my neck. I didn't know what was going to happen to me, and I didn't know how much protection Juliet's status offered.

"Hello." I greeted both Victor and Juliet.

"Victor and I were discussing what to do about the assault on Sahin," Juliet said.

I figured they weren't there to swap recipes.

"You've put me in quite a pickle, Mr. Raymond." Victor's tone matched his face—almost sympathetic. "On one hand, Sahin is a big boy and can handle himself. You simply caught him off guard, as you did with us all."

My hands twitched.

"However, on the other hand, he is Dark, and the attack happened in a public setting by a public member, well, soon-to-be member. So tradition requires me to respond, especially taking into consideration the recent incident with Malcolm, which I might add was quite the embarrassment for me."

"I'm sorry," I whispered.

"What am I to do?" Victor asked. "The Light assaulted one of the Dark. There are those on the fringe of my group who would love to see the Light with a nice big black eye." He picked a piece of lint off his suit. "Then there is your vision and your blackout to consider. I will not pretend to understand this. However, it does introduce even more doubt into the situation. How can I hold someone responsible for their actions if said person wasn't in their right mind, or in your case, even conscious?" He narrowed his eyes. "Quite the pickle."

"I'll take responsibility for my actions, and I hope Sahin is all right." I met their gazes. I wanted to show how sincere I was. Yes, Sahin was a prick, but he didn't deserve to have that happen to him, and if I caused it, then I needed to be held accountable."

"Sahin will be fine." Victor rolled his eyes. "He's already recovering. It's more of a flesh wound at this point." He tapped the desk. "Sahin's not the problem here. How I'm going to handle this *incident* is."

I honestly believed that he didn't want to do any of this, but he had to.

"There is only one way to deal with this," Victor said. "I suppose I shall have to afford him the same courtesy I afforded you, Juliet my dear."

"You're not serious." Juliet hit her desk.

"What would you have me do?" He frowned. "If I don't handle this, there could be even worse things to happen, not to me but to Christopher." He shook his head. "I'm sorry, Chris. I get no pleasure in this, but even I have people to answer to."

"If you do this, Victor, what happens will be on you. I expect justice, nothing more, and it will be up to you to ensure that he doesn't get carried away."

"Of course." Victor rose from the chair. "Chris, I will expect you at my home tomorrow night to face justice at the hand of Sahin. If you do not show up—"

"You don't have to worry," I said. "I'll be there."

Juliet stood. "Both Gregor and I will be in attendance as well."

"As is your right." Victor took a step toward me. "Again, I take no pleasure in this."

He moved so quickly that I didn't know what hit me till his teeth sank in my neck. I tried to push him away, but what energy I had quickly drained from me.

"Enough," Juliet commanded.

Victor stepped away from me, wiping his mouth.

I was glad to be sitting in the chair.

"Until tomorrow." He walked out of the room.

Juliet held the phone in her hand. "Bring in a bottle and some orange juice." She hung up and offered me a small towel. "I'm sorry."

"Why did he drink from me?" I took the towel and put it to my neck.

"So he could find you in case you decided to run." She walked from behind the desk, pulled the chair that Victor occupied closer to me, and sat. "Or if I decided to send you away. But don't worry, the effects won't last long. Once your blood works its way out of his system, he won't be able to track you." She patted my leg. "Four days max."

I slumped back in the chair.

"I would have thought my word would be enough, but—"

The door opened and in came Amanda with a bottle of red and a pitcher filled with orange juice. She set it on the desk.

"Thank you, Amanda." Juliet poured one of the glasses half with orange juice and the rest with the red. "Here drink this," she instructed.

I drank it all, but it didn't have the same wonderful flavor as Cindy's blood did. This had more of an almond-milk flavor. It wasn't my favorite.

She took my glass and filled it again.

"Tomorrow night, you will face Sahin, and he will enact justice. As I did with Malcolm. You will not be killed, but clearly, I can't promise you won't be harmed. Sahin is not only cunning and brave but also ruthless."

A shudder ran down my spine.

She sighed and addressed Amanda. "We'll need to prepare for everything."

Chapter Seventeen

IN A BLUR of fretting and pacing, the night of Sahin's justice arrived. The drive to Victor's downtown penthouse didn't last nearly long enough. Juliet told me it would be fine and not to worry, that Victor would keep Sahin in line, that there were laws and rules that governed such things even for the Dark. The ding of Victor's penthouse elevator door pulled me out of my fog. It was exactly like I remembered—highly polished floors and the city view out the window to die for. Juliet stood on my right and Gregor on my left as we marched in.

"Please, follow me," Daniel said, leading us to the living room. That night, maybe twenty-five or thirty people filled the lush space. The moment we entered, the noise volume increased tenfold.

Not-so-nice catcalls and jeers were hurled toward me. I did my best to ignore it, focusing instead on the people. Several immortals dressed in suits, while others dressed in leather with piercings and chains.

A couple of bikers stood, contrasted against the brilliant white walls. Almost all in attendance were people I wouldn't want to mess with. Alone, off to the side, Kirtus stood, frowning in his dark brown suit. He mouthed the word *sorry*.

My chest expanded. At least, I had one friend in the crowd.

"Please, stand here," Daniel said. "Victor and Sahin will arrive shortly."

He scurried off and vanished from the room.

Juliet scanned those in attendance, so did Gregor. Neither spoke.

Silence was my best course of action, and it wasn't like I had any idea what I could say. I managed another peek over at Kirtus, who gave a nod of support.

Three long gongs resonated off the high ceiling and marble floor. It took all I had not to jump out of my skin. On the last gong, Victor and Sahin appeared through the doors that lead to Victor's office. They both wore cloaks. Victor's hood rested around his shoulders, but Sahin's left his face in shadow. Victor shared a look with Juliet and then Gregor. Finally, he faced me.

He turned and addressed the audience. "Juliet de Exter, member of the Council of Light, do you surrender your charge for punishment?"

"Yes, as requested, I have brought my Called for punishment. However, I would—"

"Thank you." Victor cut her off. "Sahin Nayar, is this the man that attacked you, causing you great bodily harm?"

Sahin strained to lower his hood. Both his arms were braced, clearly no longer broken but needing additional support. "He is." He smiled, his expression filled with malevolence.

I didn't realize what I was in for, but one peek into his malice-filled eyes was enough to confirm Juliet's fear that the man had something extremely unpleasant in mind for me.

"You are all assembled to witness justice," Victor addressed the gathered. "As this is my territory and per our traditions and the laws I have set forth—" He faced Sahin. "What justice do you seek?"

Sahin smirked and took several steps forward. He stopped in front of me, his smug gaze burning into mine. I couldn't let my gaze drop from him. I wouldn't give him that kind of power over me.

"How should I make you pay, little worm?" Sahin mocked. "How should I make you suffer? Breaking my arms, almost ripping them off when I tried to help you. You're nothing to me. You're nothing to all of us."

Laughter filled the room. Victor raised his hands, and the room fell silent.

"Sahin, I will ask again. What justice do you seek?" Victor demanded.

Sahin glared back at me. The rest of the room and people faded away as his gaze bored into me. Whatever he had planned, he needed to spit it out. Standing there, staring at me and smirking, was childish. The way his gaze danced around, he got off on it. I wasn't about to give him the pleasure of turning away.

We stood for what seemed like hours. I winced as the mad eyes of the dark woman slaughtering my friends flashed in my mind. The scene of holding Fredrick, his hair turning ghost white and his sunken eyes... It reminded me of what my father must have looked like when they found his body. It made the hair on the back of my neck stand.

Finally, Sahin broke contact and stepped back, his face growing pale. "None, I seek nothing." His voice cracked and his gaze dropped to the floor. "It was an accident."

He took another step back, then faced the wall and turned to look out the window, anywhere but looking at me.

"What?" Victor's voice raised an octave higher than usual.

Sahin's gaze stopped their dashing around the room and set on Victor. "Nothing. I seek no justice from him. It was an accident. He's not immortal and can't be held to our laws. I will not waste my efforts on him." He shoved past several guests and rushed into Victor's office.

I couldn't believe it. Several shouts and boos erupted from the crowd.

Juliet and Gregor both glanced toward me, their expressions filled with uncertainty.

Victor called the room to order with a glare. How someone so charming turned into a barely contained bundle of rage so quickly amazed me. "You have heard the victim's request. Justice has been enacted. We're through here."

"That wasn't justice," a woman called out.

It took me a minute, but I remembered her, Malcolm's creator. The statue woman at Malcolm's execution.

"I demand payback. Break his fucking arms. Better yet, rip them off his fucking body," the woman continued. "No one does that to a Dark and gets away with it."

"Shut up, Cynthia," Kirtus snarled. "Not everyone deserves to die. Sahin has spoken. He wants nothing, and since there were no other Dark injured, it is done."

"How dare you speak to me, you filth, you Lighter." Cynthia twisted around on her heel to face Kirtus. "What are you even doing here? You're not really one of us."

Nods and other comments spread around that I didn't make out.

Victor turned all his attention on Cynthia, and his voice boomed through the space, his Spanish accent definitely thicker. "Cynthia! You'll be quiet, or I shall remove your lovely head from your body. You've heard Sahin's wish, and so it will be done." He addressed the whole group. "None of you will question my choice in witness. Kirtus is here because I deemed it so. Now, since none of you were harmed in the matter at hand, you have no claim to this man." He glanced over his shoulder at me. "If I hear of any of you trying anything against him, you will answer to me. I assure you I will not show the mercy that Sahin showed tonight. Now you will all leave my home. We are done here."

"Victor, is this some kind of—" Gregor stepped forward, his chest somehow doubling in size.

"The three of you will come with me now." Victor waved a hand at Kirtus who stood back to let the others leave. With a frown, Victor called out. "Kirtus, you will stay as well, in case I actually need you."

This didn't surprise anyone but me.

Kirtus bowed his head and joined us.

We followed Victor into his office. Once the doors were closed, Victor found Sahin out on the balcony, a drink in his trembling hand. His cloak discarded on the desk.

"Sahin, what in the seven levels of hell is this all about?" Victor demanded.

We followed Victor to the balcony.

"You demanded this, and I agreed. If this was a ploy to embarrass me, I will remove your head myself, blood or no. What you did—"

Sahin turned, his face pale, eyes hallow with dark circles around them. He seemed every bit his 475 years at that moment. And if I didn't know better, I'd say he was terrified.

He refused to make eye contact with me.

"I changed my mind." Sahin's voice trembled. He hardly met Victor's gaze. "I decided to show mercy."

Victor pulled off his cloak and tossed it back into the office through the balcony doors, "Bullshit! You? You don't show mercy. I've been trying to rein this in since it happened. You wanted nothing short of the life flowing through his veins. So I arrange it against my better judgment because you're of my blood. So what the fuck are you playing at?"

"Nothing." Sahin finally peered at Juliet and Gregor. "You were there. It was an accident. Chris didn't comprehend what he was doing. I wanted to embarrass the Light and Juliet." He licked his lips, his hands shaking. "It was simply an accident. I understand that now. Things should not have gotten this far, and for that, I hope you accept my apologies."

Victor motioned with his hand, and something held Sahin; he couldn't move. The glass with his drink fell to the patio floor, shattering. Victor didn't turn from Sahin.

"Kirtus, hang Sahin over the ledge," Victor demanded.

Kirtus glanced toward us, then to Victor.

"Don't make me ask you again," Victor said.

"No, please, Victor, I..." Sahin started, but Victor cut him off.

"But I—"

Victor turned on Kirtus, his fangs distended and his brows hardening. "Do as I ask. There is wind tonight. Use it. Do not try me, Kirtus."

Wind? What did Victor mean by wind? Did Kirtus's gift have to do with wind or the elements?

"Victor, this isn't necessary. No harm was done. It was inconvenient but nothing more," Juliet said. "You don't need to do this."

"Do you think I'm doing this for you?" Victor barked. "For the Light? Don't be so egocentric. Order must be maintained and an example must be made. I will *not* be embarrassed in my own home by my own Called." Victor narrowed his eyes on Kirtus. "Do as I say, Kirtus. Now!"

Kirtus frowned, but his eyes started to grow gray. He focused, and the winds on the balcony increased. Then a dust devil appeared on the balcony near Sahin, and Kirtus tilted his head. The dust devil twirled around Sahin and lifted him off the balcony and shoved him over the ledge. I wondered what else Kirtus could do. Was it only wind, or could he control other things like water or fire? If it wasn't for seeing the terror in Sahin's face, I would have clapped.

"Please, Victor, mi amor, please," Sahin begged.

"Don't you call me that." Victor's face darkened even more. "You lost that right several hundred years ago. Now tell me the truth. I'm not a patient man, so either talk or you will see the pavement. *Mi amor.*"

Gregor stepped forward.

"Don't you even think about interfering unless you want to start a war," Victor growled.

Juliet reached out and took Gregor's arm.

"Victor, don't do this," Juliet said. "What would you gain? There is no one to witness it."

"I only need one witness, and Kirtus will serve that purpose. Now tell me the truth, Sahin. Why the sudden change of heart? I won't ask you again. What are you playing at?"

Sahin faced me. I hadn't realized until then that he hadn't looked at me once, not since we broke eye contact.

"His power. I've seen it," he stammered, turning from me. "His power, Victor. It's his power. I saw it. There is death and pain. The death of all the immortals."

Victor glanced between Sahin and me. "You saw a dream or a memory. You already checked him. There was nothing special about him, and besides, he's not fully immortal yet. You can't—"

"You don't think I know that!" Sahin yelped. "Victor, I swear to you, I did. I saw it when I focused on him tonight. You have to believe me. I wanted to make him pay for his insult. I was going to have him suffer, but what I witnessed... I saw it when I taunted him. Please, Victor, you must believe me. I would not lie to you, not like this, not now."

"Bring him back." Victor waved his hand in obvious annoyance.

Kirtus nodded, and before he finished his nod, the...well, whatever he used to control the wind...it again started to bring Sahin back over the edge. Once finished, the wind died down, and his eyes returned to their normal green color. He stumbled before regaining his balance.

Victor glared at Sahin and closed in on him. "You have bought yourself more time on this Earth, little man."

"You have to believe me." Sahin fell to his knees. "I would never shame you." He groveled at Victor's feet. I never thought I would see Sahin, or anyone I'd met, do any such thing. They all acted above that sort of thing.

"Unless it's to save your own skin." Victor pulled him up off the deck, and then he studied me. "Well, Juliet, perhaps we should all talk about this. Your boy here has neutered one of my strongest and most trusted men. That is saying something, and I believe it is worthy of at least some amount of discussion."

Victor forced what I judged to be a sincere smile at Kirtus. "You did well."

That seemed to be as close to a thank-you that Victor would pass out.

In my dealings with the Dark, I've found that they run hot or cold with very little in between. Victor changed from being a monster ready to kill his own Called to a welcoming host. Daniel was called in to provide drinks—blood for them and wine for me. It didn't take long before the six of us were sitting around, and per Juliet's request, I relayed my vision to them, trying to remember as many details as possible.

"A seer?" Victor questioned. He played with the crystal glass in his hands. "There are no true immortal seers. It's not possible. Our gifts don't work in that manner."

"Then how might you explain it?" Juliet took a sip of her red.

"I don't." Victor leaned back and his shoulders dropped. "A dream, something his mind created. As for the fit he had, we've all seen newlings react differently. These things happen. Sahin probably picked up on that residual energy. So, he is strong, powerful even, that could be his gift. Strength, it's possible."

"Aren't you listening?" Gregor raked a hand through his hair, his voice sharp. "Your own man saw something powerful and deadly in Chris. So powerful in fact that it terrified him. Are you discounting Sahin's ability?"

Victor's eyes blazed as he stared at Gregor.

"An ability you're proud of," Gregor continued, "especially if it helps you keep control, and now you're going to dismiss it." Gregor stared at the glass of red in front of him, still not drinking from it. "Perhaps Chris is powerful and is going to have amazing strength, but how do you explain away what he saw, what Sahin saw?"

"This is ludicrous," Victor mumbled.

"I can only tell you that I've seen his power." Sahin's gaze dodged around the room. "I witnessed some of what he saw and felt. I don't know about anything else, but I've never seen power in one who hasn't fully turned. Yes, maybe a hint, but this." He finished off his red. "Victor, it's unlike anything. His power is incredible." Sahin's voice softened, and he focused on the floor. "If you wish it, I'll look again, but I hope you do not ask."

"Hold it," Kirtus said. "I'm not so sure that's a good idea. You about flew out of your skin the first time, and you look liked you aged a hundred years." He sighed. "Plus, we don't understand what affect this will have on Chris. For all we know, you could be tampering with his mind."

Sahin glared at him but said nothing.

Victor did not hold his tongue. "When I want your opinion, Kirtus, I'll be sure to beat it out of you."

"Dammit," I said.

I was at the point where I couldn't take it anymore. I didn't care about protocol or any of that damned stuff right then. They were talking about me like I wasn't there.

"Believe me or don't," I said. "I don't really care. What I've told you is the truth. I feel it down to my very core." I paused. They were going to listen to me whether they wanted to or not. "We're all going to be dead. Our heads are going to be on stakes lining the main street of Los Alto. Not only Light immortal heads, but Dark immortals as well. And humans. Victor, your head was there right along with Juliet, Sahin, Kirtus, Gregor, all of them. A dark woman is coming, and she's going to try and kill everyone."

"A dark woman you can't remember and can't describe," Victor snapped. "A woman who is human but is able to do this to all the immortals. And another thing, when is this going to happen, Christopher? Do you have a date or time? What about a month or year? Humans can't do this to us. It's impossible."

"If it's so impossible, then why haven't you tried to kill all the humans and control the world?" I snapped back. I didn't have all the answers, but I wasn't going to be dismissed like a child.

Juliet touched my arm, trying to calm me.

I pushed back. I wouldn't be charmed.

"Why are you hiding among us, them, whatever?" I demanded. "If it could be done and we—well, they are so weak, then why aren't humans in farms being milked for their blood?" I didn't like the image I created. It made me cringe. "Plus, I never said she was a human."

"An immortal then?" Juliet asked.

"No, definitely not an immortal, but something, someone powerful."

"Well, it's not a Moon Child. They don't exist anymore," Sahin said.

"What about the witches?" Kirtus asked. "They're still around, and it's possible they have grown in number without our knowledge."

"We would notice. Trust me," Victor said. "True witches are not known to stay hidden well. They like to flaunt their power, especially when it comes to dealing with us."

"Which added to their downfall," Juliet added. "I haven't seen a true witch in, well, in a very long time."

"But it still could be them?" I asked. "I remember them talking about nature and returning the true balance." Somehow that felt right.

"That does sound like them—nature, balance, and not really big fans of us." Victor tapped the side of his crystal glass, his words and tone even. "Still, their numbers would have to be huge, and then how does that explain you and your vision of them? Not to mention the power they must have. Witches don't have that kind of power. Where would they get it? How would they control it?"

There wasn't an answer to any of this at the moment, like the death of my father, but I feared we would soon get our answer to all these questions, including that of my father.

Chapter Eighteen

I ADJUSTED MY suit jacket as Amanda and I wandered down to our house's media room.

"Are you ready?" Amanda stepped off the landing to the viewing room.

The media room was in the basement of Juliet's house. However, the high ceiling, plush carpet, and bright lighting gave the space an open welcoming atmosphere, which starkly contrasted with the worry and nervousness I was feeling. I faced the hallway that led off to a bathroom and two bedroom suites: the one I stayed in to recover from my vision and a similar one across the hall. I wanted to go and hide behind the heavy cotton drapes that covered the only windows. Part of me wished we were going down there to watch a movie on the flat-screen, but this was it. My final Mark.

"So why down here?" I kicked my foot along the carpet.

"It's private and secure," Amanda admitted. "It's probably one of the safest places in the house."

"Just in case?" I exhaled, and my shoulders dropped.

"Considering everything that's happened, it seemed the best course of action." Amanda rested a hand on my shoulder. "But don't worry—Gregor has some of his most trusted people here. You won't be disturbed."

"And you'll be here." I grinned.

"Yes." A chuckle and a pat on the arm accompanied the word. "I'll be here, right outside this door. We've given the staff the day off, so..." She stopped and tapped on the door.

"Welcome," Juliet said from inside the room.

Amanda gave me a big hug. "See you soon."

"Thank you." I opened the door and shuffled in.

Larger than the bedroom I'd recuperated in, an open sitting room greeted me. Oversized armchairs rested on either side of a walnut coffee table. An oak desk and chair occupied the wall close to me. On the opposite side of the room, I faced three open doors. One led to another bedroom. Through the second door was a bathroom and then through the last door another bedroom.

I focused on all these details, because it distracted me from what was to come, and considering my luck with my Marks so far, I wanted the distraction.

Neutral tan paint covered the walls with a landscape painting of bright blues, reds, and yellows. The floors continued with the plush neutral carpet. As with several rooms in the house, a stone fireplace crackled with life.

"You haven't been in here?" Juliet asked.

"No." I strolled over to the painting, admiring the texture and the buildup of acrylic paints. It gave the painting a three-dimensional look that hypnotized me.

"I used this space when I was healing from saving Amanda."

"Wait, I'm confused. You were here? But, I thought you were in your room upstairs."

"That's what everyone was supposed to think," Juliet said softly. "It was a necessary safety precaution."

I finally noticed that she wore sweats. Her hair was pulled back in a ponytail. "You look comfortable."

"Yes, well, the last Mark can be a bit messy." Juliet laughed. "You can get changed in the other room and hang your clothes up in the closet. I'll be waiting here."

I appreciated not having to change in front of her. Even though in my Mark dreams we had sex, that was all in my head and not real.

The bedroom was big enough to accommodate ten people. I wouldn't have thought the space would be as large. A king-size bed and side tables filled one corner. A lounge chair, a small desk, and a large armoire complemented the other side. Off to the side double doors hid a closet and next to it a bathroom door.

Matching heavy drapes hung from the wall where windows would be expected. I checked behind the drapes and a light box greeted me. A dimmer switch next to the curtains allowed me to turn on the light box, giving me the option for various moods.

"She's thought of everything," I mumbled.

On the bed, clothes laid out waiting for me. To my surprise, it was a pair of sweatpants and a cotton T-shirt.

"I haven't seen anything like this since I lived in Reno."

I quickly changed, walked over to the closet, and opened it. Off to one side of the walk-in closet hung Juliet's clothes. I took a couple of hangers and put my suit away.

I walked around to the sitting room doorway. Inside, Juliet sat on the sofa, facing the fire. My heart pounded in my chest, and my hands trembled.

"Nothing formal tonight," she said. "Are you comfortable?"

"Are you kidding?" I chuckled. "I used to live in sweatpants and T-shirts. They're like a second skin." I shifted my stance, clapping my hands in front of me. "What do we do?"

Instead of Juliet offering me a seat, she stood up and took my hand. "We'll do your final Mark in the bedroom."

We strolled to the opposite bedroom door.

"It's normally a second bedroom for the suite, but we had to clean it out just in case," Juliet said. "There is a bed, of course, so we'll be comfortable."

I gulped and my neck and face heated up, remembering my dreams of Juliet and me having sex.

"Don't worry, Duncan. We're not going to be having sex," she said. "Unless you want to." She waggled her eyebrows at me.

I hated that she could so easily read my thoughts and emotions.

"Um..."

"I'm teasing, Duncan." She giggled. "There are some, like the Dark, and a few of the Light, who choose to make the final Mark a sexual endeavor. I've been told it makes the process easier and more enjoyable. However, I don't subscribe to that."

I nodded.

"Even if you didn't prefer men, I don't see the need for such a bond between us. I've had my share of lovers and partners, and I don't need that from you." She glanced at me, and my expression must have shown insult or bewilderment because she added, "Not that it wouldn't be enjoyable. I believe our bond is strong enough without it."

This second bedroom was exactly the same as the first one I'd changed in. However, in this one, the bed stood alone in the room, dressed with plain blue linens and four pillows.

"What do we have to do?"

I sensed Juliet using her ability to calm me. I supposed if I wasn't as focused on my nerves, I wouldn't have ever detected it.

"You're going to feed off me," Juliet stated. "Then you will fall asleep. You may dream, you may not, but when you waken, the last of your humanity will be gone and Duncan will be dead."

I swallowed hard again.

"You will be an immortal, and Christopher will finally be born. I will stay with you," she reassured me. "My face will be the first you see and my scent will be the first you smell. We will be bonded as Maker and Called. It is a bond that will last between us even once I release you."

"I'm going to die." My voice fell flat.

"Don't be scared. It is painless, I promise you."

I quietly sat on the bed. This was it. Everything led me to this point, but this was the last of my humanity. What if something went wrong and I ended up like my father? I frowned at the thought. If I died, there would be no more me to have these lingering questions in my head about his death. Tears teased the edges of my eyes.

"Are you ready?"

I was either going to die and come back immortal, or I die and be no more. This was the final test, the final Mark.

This was why I had to say goodbye to my old life. This was why I had to cut ties with all my friends and my work, because if I didn't become immortal, for whatever reason, I was a dead man.

I ran my hand over my face. "I think so." I swallowed.

"It's time, Duncan." She sat next to me. "You have to transform into your immortal self. Even if it is only partial, you have to shift. Remember what it was like when you shifted to save Cindy? Once you're transformed, you'll drink from me. I suggest the neck, but you can go for the wrist—either will work." Her voice was a calm ocean of sounds washing over me.

"How will I know when to stop?" My heart beat in my ears.

"I'll stop you when it's time," Juliet replied.

I went to speak, and she raised a hand to touch my face.

"Don't worry. You won't hurt me." She lay back on the bed.

I glanced down at her, seeing her for the petite woman she is. Her body seemed fragile, but I knew, under that delicate frame, she could handle anything. I swallowed hard and took a deep breath. This was it.

I watched her for several moments, and I finally heard an oddly familiar voice deep down in my core. *You must do this if you want the answers you seek. Don't be scared. I'll be here for you.* I assumed this voice was either me, or the link Juliet and I shared.

The pain in my head started off light but quickly grew. Still, it wasn't as bad as the first time I transformed. My vampiric shift came quicker this time. Before I was fully aware, I found Juliet's neck.

I guess I'm a neck guy.

My teeth sank into her lush flesh and a rush of warm liquid filled my mouth. Only the scent of roses and vanilla met my nose. There was no flavor to her blood. My body became aroused as I continued to drink from her.

I wanted to rip her clothes off and explore her body for real this time. However, the need for sex was nothing compared to feeding off her. Drinking her blood from the goblet had nothing on this.

A voice inside of me told me to stop, as much as I didn't want to.

"Enough," I struggled to say. I pulled away from her, biting my tongue to draw blood, and licked her neck.

"Amazing," she said. "I was just going to stop you."

I leaned back, and at the distance, I noted blood on the sheets and on her clothes. Blood covered my shirt. It was a pallet of red.

"Duncan." She pulled me to her. "It is time for you to sleep."

I moved next to her on the bed. My face shifting back to normal. I hardly noticed the pain as I laid my head on her chest.

"Sleep now. When you wake, I'll be right here." Juliet gently rubbed my head and hummed what I thought might be a lullaby. I didn't know for sure, but it had a note of sadness to it.

Sleep, or death, tugged at my core. I suppose I could have tried to push it away, but I didn't want to. I focused on Juliet caressing my head and humming her song as everything slowed down. My lids grew heavy, so I closed my eyes and drifted off, listening to the hum of Juliet and feeling her gentle touch.

Duncan Brian Alexander died.

Chapter Nineteen

THE CLOUDED DARKNESS that was my death hurriedly shifted to a dreamy gray fog. "Soon my love, very soon," a gruff breathy voice said in my ear. "I'll be yours and you'll be mine."

My mystery man.

I met his gaze; the green and gray eyes allowed me to fall into them. They were pools of strength and desire that if I wasn't careful I would never want to leave. I smiled and inhaled, taking in his presence.

I was blinded by bright red-and-green Christmas decorations and holiday music assaulted my ears and filled the mall I stood in.

The gruff voice and eyes vanished.

What was I doing there? I glanced around and realized that Kirtus and I were in a mall, shopping. Of course.

"Thanks for coming with me," I said, facing Kirtus. "I really have no idea what to get anyone, and I hate going to the mall this time of year. It's always insane." I glanced at all the shops with bright-colored lights and signs with big bold letters exclaiming *Sale*.

"No prob."

"Juliet and Amanda have been amazing, and I want to get them something meaningful."

"I'm not sure what kind of help I can be, but I'll do my..."

A woman pushed past him.

"Faggots." She glared at Kirtus and me before stalking off.

"Wow. Rude." Kirtus shook his head.

Only the side of the woman's unpleasant face caught my attention. Her dark brown hair and weathered face only added to her nasty appearance. I shuddered. I recognized her. I didn't know how, but she was familiar.

"Some people." My shoulders trembled, and I turned back in time to stop myself from knocking an elderly shopper to the floor. With quick hands, I kept her steady so only her bags dropped and not her.

"Oh, I'm so sorry."

The woman wasn't elderly, just startled, with dark circles around her eyes and slightly hallowed cheeks. For a second time in less than five minutes, a familiar face stared back at me.

Kirtus picked up the shopping bag and the receipt that fell out of it.

I held her arm and steadied her.

"I guess it's that time of year." Her face glowed brightly. Her dark circles vanished, and her sunken cheeks filled and took on a rosy tint.

"Well, aren't you a real Prince Charming..." She paused, reaching out and taking the bags from Kirtus. Her head tilted. "No, make that a king among men."

Kirtus blushed and handed her the Nordstrom bag and the receipt.

December 3rd in huge letters on the receipt struck me. She slipped the receipt into her shopping bag, grinning at Kirtus. "You're such a handsome man, such fetching red hair and beautiful bright eyes you have, and so unique."

Her smile was infectious.

"You're such a handsome couple." She took my hand as well as Kirtus's. "You know, my son and his husband are about your age, and they are always looking to meet nice new people. They just moved here..."

"Oh, we aren't a couple." Kirtus snatched his hand back from the woman, his cheeks an angry red.

I didn't want to be offended or taken aback by his comment, but I kind of was. He probably wasn't gay, but still I wasn't a three-armed sloth. His remark kind of hurt.

The issue was all my own. I found him very attractive and nice to talk to.

The woman frowned.

Kirtus raised his hand to his mouth and cleared his throat.

"Well, you should be." Her lips were thin with determination. "You're both as cute as a bug's ear." She reached out and patted me on the arm. "He just needs a little push in that direction, Chris. You do make a cute couple, and he's one in a million."

She turned and headed off, humming "You are my Sunshine."

"That wasn't awkward at all." My face and down my neck heated up.

"No. Not in the least," Kirtus said.

A sudden explosion of light and smoke from the second floor landing caused people to scream and knock into each other to get away.

I blinked, clearing out the white flashes from my sight.

Kirtus grabbed my arm and ushered us close to the wall, out of the stampede.

"Keep them from leaving! Round them up!" a female voice commanded. "It's time for you to wake up to the world around you," she bellowed, forcing people to take notice and pay attention.

My sight cleared, and Kirtus and I gazed at where her voice came from. She hovered just above the landing.

"The dark woman," I gasped.

Sparks and fire shot from her hands.

Focusing on her more, I identified her as the woman that ran into Kirtus, calling us fags. She was a witch.

"You live a lie," she barked.

People frozen in place. Some lying on the tile floor in unnatural positions. Dead. Those still alive faced her. Some able to pull out their cell phones to record the event.

"There are monsters around you," she called out. "There are two of them right now." She pointed to Kirtus and me.

We shared a glance.

The sudden pain in my face and body almost overwhelmed me. I started to transition into my true vampire form, unable to stop it. My canines elongated and my brows pushed through my skin. I dropped to my knees, powerless to control my body.

"They're going to destroy the world," the dark woman yelled. "They feed off you. They control you. But we're here to stop them. No more are you going to be cattle for them to feed off of." She cackled.

Another explosion burst from her hands and shot toward the ceiling. It caught some of the Christmas decorations on fire. The fire sprinklers didn't come on. My gut told me the witches did something to keep them from working, just like she and her minions were keeping the people there, watching.

I got a closer look at one of the bodies on the floor. The nice older woman who we had just been chatting with. Dead.

I know that face, a voice in my mind said.

"I can't change back," Kirtus yelped.

"They're recording us." I struggled and tried to shift back.

Kirtus grabbed my arm and turned us away from the cameras, but there were so many people gawking at us, it was impossible to hide from everyone.

"Gaze upon the demons." The witch pointed toward us. "And those aren't the only ones. There are others. See." She pointed to others.

From somewhere, a spotlight shone down on Kirtus and me. We were frozen in place. Screams resonated all around us. I tried to scurry out of the light. I scanned the area and tried to find a way to hide. We weren't alone. Five other immortals in the area each shifted into their vampiric forms, unable to leave or mask their true faces.

Giving up on shifting back, I took in as much of the scene as possible. Eight witches scowled down on us with narrowed eyes, each expression filled with hatred and ugliness. The dark woman was the leader. It became clear to me their goal was to out us. They wanted to make sure that the world saw us.

"Him," one of the male witches shouted.

A flash of lightning hit me and hammered me through the window of a MAC cosmetics store. The sound of screams and glass breaking rang in my ears.

I took a panicked breath and tried to fill my lungs as I prepared myself for the shock of the explosion and the smashed glass. No air came, and my eyes flew open. The scent of electricity singed my nose. The yells echoed in my ears. The glaring laughter of the dark woman chilled me to the bone.

"They're going to expose us." I tried to cough the words out. "They're going to expose all of us and kill innocent people. It's going to happen on December 3rd at the mall." The words rushed from my lips as I gasped for air.

My head twisted this way and that, expecting carnage, but I was on the bed with Juliet. She had me pinned down by the shoulders. My chest burned.

"Chris, what?" she demanded. "What did you see?"

I lifted my T-shirt, revealing the burn marks. My chest crackled every time I took a breath.

"Not possible," she whispered, a hand covering her mouth.

I collapsed into the pillows, my mind and body quiet. We stayed there while I healed. She asked Amanda to come in and allow me to drink from her. I felt bad about it, but Amanda didn't seem to mind.

Juliet tried to talk about my vision, but I shook my head, not speaking. I needed a moment. Hell, I needed several moments. I'd just woken up from dying.

Juliet and Amanda fussed around the bed, their actions not registering. I insisted that Kirtus be present when I talked about the vision, and Juliet agreed. Another meeting was scheduled, but I wasn't sure who with.

I hadn't much time to dwell on what happened to me, becoming immortal that is. Other things occupied my mind, like healing and trying to make sense of my vision. What I did notice was I still felt like me. Juliet's scent of roses and vanilla comforted me. Even when she wasn't present, I sensed it.

Bits of conversation with Juliet included finding out I had been asleep for three days. She'd worried. No one's transition was that long. That was what I decided to call it—in transition. It sounded better to me than dying. I also learned the meeting would include Victor, Juliet, Gregor, and Kirtus. That was all.

After sunset, and when I felt up to company, Amanda and I had a chance to talk. She told me that Juliet hadn't left my side the entire time, which was nice to hear. In a way, I never doubted that Juliet would be anywhere other than at my side. So the confirmation was a relief. Amanda told me that some of the Dark left their Called all alone. That seemed crappy to me.

As I dressed for the meeting, the world seemed different. Night birds sang outside, and small animals scampered in the garden. My senses were like radar for anything warm-blooded. Small details in the paintings and words in books, even the fine print was crisp and sharp.

Things were easier to lift and move. I decided to try it out and lifted my desk with everyone on it, with one hand. I was amazed at how easy it was. I felt tougher and stronger. Of course, I haven't had time to truly test any of this.

In my many hours of preparation prior to my Marks, Juliet explained I would have a preference for different types of human blood. Also, I would be able to sense people who would be more receptive to my "charms." Both traits seemed helpful given the needs of my new life. The other thing—the biggest thing—I was no longer susceptible to human diseases. A great perk of being immortal. The common cold was now a thing of the past. However, there were blood-borne illnesses, such as hepatitis and HIV. They wouldn't kill me, but weaken me and cause internal turmoil with my system. I didn't want to know what kind of *internal turmoil*. Still, for the most part, I was immune to everything.

"THEN ONE OF the witches looked at me and said 'him.'" I closed my eyes as I recounted the vision to the group in Juliet's main living room. "A flash of light or lightning woke me up with a burned chest and broken ribs." I opened my eyes, and Juliet, Victor, Gregor, and of course, Kirtus all stared at me.

I wanted to say more to Kirtus, but his empty face told me it was best to leave it be.

"Assuming your vision is accurate, then we have problems," Victor finally said.

"We have no reason to doubt him," Juliet said. "I was there. I had to fight with him to keep him calm while he was under. I also witnessed the damage done to him. So did Amanda. He could not have done that to himself."

"That may be, but, my dear, we have no reason to believe him." The words flowed like velvet from Victor's mouth. "His talents are unproven, assuming he has the talent of foresight at all. For all we know, it could have been a bad transition. You said it took three days, so who knows how his body reacted. It's possible he got injured during your struggle." He picked a piece of lint off his suit jacket.

"Look, I know it's crazy, but it's going to happen." I slapped down my hand on the edge of the chair. "On December 3rd, the witches are going to attack a mall and Kirtus and I will be there as well as others." I scanned the group, sure to meet all their stares to emphasize my point. "People will see us. They will record the whole event. Then we're going to be exposed." My chest still felt sore as I healed. "Do you need to see the damage? Do you want to see my wounds?" I grabbed the bottom of my shirt and yanked it up, showing them.

Victor sat deeper in his chair, gaping at my chest for the briefest of seconds before turning away.

"We don't even know which mall you saw," Gregor finally said, running a hand through his short blond hair.

I pushed my shirt down, point made. "Well, let me describe it, and then you tell me." My hand absently rubbed my chest. "It had two levels, with a big open space in the center where we were. The woman scowled down from the second floor."

"Wait..." Juliet got up, went to an end table, and pulled out a sheet of paper, grabbing a pen on her way back. "Here, draw it."

"The mall went off to the right and to the left of this midpoint. Then went straight out to what looked like more stores and another big walkway. I had the sense that this was a big mall, larger than anything in Reno."

I drew a basic layout of what I remembered.

"What else? All the malls here are big." Gregor tapped the coffee table I sketched on.

"I don't know, polished floors, all light colors, and decorated for Christmas. Nice stuff, not cheap—this place goes all out." I bit the end of my pen. "Wait. The woman, the older woman, the nice lady, she had a bag that said Nordstrom on it."

"You said the building had two stories?" Gregor rubbed his chin. His goatee scratched against his hands, but I pushed the noise away and focused on the question.

"As far as I could tell, there were skylights when I looked up."

"Well, it wouldn't be the one in the city, especially with what you drew," Gregor said.

"That doesn't help. There are several malls all over the Bay Area. Nordstrom isn't uncommon." Victor leaned in and examined my drawing.

I wasn't sure if he believed my vision, but at least he wasn't discounting it either.

"Still, I doubt it would be out of South Bay. I'm sure it would be local." Juliet picked up her glass of red and took a sip.

She nodded to my glass, and I picked it up and gulped down some.

If fresh blood tasted like chocolate-covered strawberries like Cindy, or buttered popcorn like Amanda, then the bottled blood, or red, seemed slightly less tasty. Hints of pleasant flavors teased my tongue. It just didn't have the strong, truly delicious flavors of fresh blood. What I drank now, kind of tasted like a plain green salad. It wasn't bad, just not *amazing*. The same blood would have a different flavor for each immortal, which made sense.

"It's Westfield Valley Fair." Kirtus dodged my gaze. "Based on what he drew and that he got shot, or whatever, into a MAC store—that's the only place that has a Nordstrom and a MAC cosmetics store."

"Good," I said. "Thank you, Kirtus." I smiled his way. But he continued to avoid looking at me.

"All right, so we have a date and a location." Juliet smiled.

"We're assuming his vision is real," Victor repeated.

"Come on, Victor. This is a lot of detail. At the very least—" Gregor started.

"At the very least what?" Victor interrupted. "What are we supposed to do? Your Council wants to test him. Once he is tested and once he passes, I'll worry about it, but not until then. Detail or no, bruised body or no."

"Victor," Juliet said.

"I'm sorry." He stood. "There is a lot at stake, and I'm not going to put myself out there for some unproven vision. If you haven't forgotten, I'm still in a PR nightmare with Sahin, and let us not forget Malcolm."

Kirtus opened his mouth.

Victor cut him off before he said anything, a frown planted on his face. "I suggest you think hard about even speaking and harder still about your choice of words. Like your life depended on it."

Kirtus dropped his head.

"Juliet, I'm sorry. Please let me know how the testing goes." Victor marched to the door. "Good night."

"We need to stop this." I stared at the floor. "It's going to happen. I know it is."

"I hate to admit it, but Victor's right," Gregor said. "Of course, I'll see what I can dig up, but..." He sighed and stood. "Given everything that has happened, Victor may be right. Let me work my angles. Perhaps, we can force the witches' hand and throw them off guard."

"I should let you two speak." Juliet glanced between Kirtus and me.

"No." Kirtus stood. "That's fine. I should be leaving." He crossed to Juliet. "Whatever I can do, I will, but..." He shrugged and hurried out the room without so much as a nod in my direction.

"What the hell was that all about?" I frowned.

"Chris," Juliet said. "You have to understand, Light and Dark don't tend to mix. So for you and Kirtus to be out together would draw attention, attention that Kirtus probably doesn't want and Victor can't afford. I doubt it had anything to do with your comments..."

I glared, and she changed what she said.

"The comments made by the woman."

"So wait. If I wanted to spend time with Kirtus or Sahin or someone from the Dark, I couldn't? We couldn't be friends? Why the hell not? That's ridiculous."

"I didn't say that. You can be friends with whomever you want."

I crossed my arms in front of my chest.

"It's uncommon. And Kirtus likes to have as little attention shown him as possible. His situation is very unique." She touched my arm.

I relaxed.

"We *will* sort this all out. Have faith and don't worry about Kirtus. He's been around for over two hundred years, he'll be fine."

MY BEDROOM DOOR splintered behind me as it slammed. I tossed my suit jacket on the bed. My whole body trembled, and my neck burned. The Council's test, if you can call it that, was a disaster. I felt like a mouse who had to run a maze for a piece of cheese.

"Unacceptable," I growled.

This wasn't my fault. I didn't ask for this ability. I didn't claim to be a seer. It chose me, and now they had no intentions of believing me. Worst of all, I'd embarrassed Juliet. I couldn't explain how any of my ability worked, and yet the Council thought I would have all the answers and be able to perform on the spot like a trained monkey. It didn't work that way, at least not yet. I might not have known a lot about it, but I knew that much.

I yanked my tie off and flung it next to me on the bed.

"Chris." Juliet softly pushed what remained of the door open.

She calmed me, and I hated it.

"Don't," I commanded. I drew a calming breath and tried to soften my tone. "Please don't. I want to be angry and I want to be mad. They had no right to treat me that way."

She stayed at the door. "They did what they thought was best. No one can design a test for this, they—" She stopped. "We came up with as fair a test as possible."

"You call that fair?" I barked at her. "Cards with shapes? Guessing hidden number? Reading thoughts?"

"It was the best we could do."

"Well, it didn't work. I failed. So congratulations. You have a defective Called. I hope they're all happy." I turned my back on her. My hands still trembled and my teeth ground together.

"That's not fair. We had to test you, and well—"

The anger in me exploded, and I wanted to rip her apart. I turned and lunged at her. My face and body started to transform. There was a pull in the back of my brain. I tried to ignore it, but like a wet blanket being tossed over a fire, I began to die down. When I caught sight of Juliet, she had transformed, and her eyes blazed into me.

"Stop!" she commanded.

I wobbled and, in a less than gracefully manner, reached for the bed and crumpled down.

"You need to relax and listen to me."

I nodded.

"What is done is done," Juliet said. "Just because you failed the test doesn't mean that I don't believe in you. I don't think you're defective, nor do Garrett, Taqi, Rahim, or An. In fact, most of the Council believes you have the gift of a seer. Garrett sensed it and sensed you trying to reach it, but for whatever reason, it didn't work."

"What about Sybil and the others?" I hated it. Juliet had forced her talent on me, and I calmed down, becoming docile; a kitten or puppy could have whooped my butt. The worst part was that it made me realize I'd tried to attack Juliet, my family. Shame poured from my heart.

"Don't worry about them. Your performance today doesn't matter." Juliet glided over and sat next to me. She shifted back—her fangs and heavy brow gone. "Now tell me what you saw."

"I saw what appeared to be a throne, and a man with both a green eye and gray eye there. I stood next to him. I know that's stupid and silly, but it's real. I sensed every part of it. Juliet, I smelled him. It was so strong..." I stopped, trying to remember, then added, "I don't know. A woodsy-earthy-spicy mix. All I know is it was intoxicating. It felt like home."

"What else can you tell me? What about the room? What else about him, other than the scent?"

"My parents were there. They were both alive again. They were happy, along with everyone else. There were others there as well, but I couldn't see them. The building was plain, stone maybe, a hall, but like there was a celebration." I chuckled. "Like a wedding." I lay back on the bed, suddenly exhausted.

"It's possible you saw your soul mate and your wedding celebration."

"Well, if that's the case, then how does that explain my parents being there? They're both dead."

"Perhaps, your visions use symbolism."

"Great, just what I need, more riddles." The test and this crazy new vision of my mystery man, it was getting to be too much. "Why do I keep glimpsing the man with the green and gray eyes, and what about the scent? Do you know anyone like that?"

"I'm not good with eyes. However, there are a couple of people I can think of with that scent or one close enough to it."

"Who?"

"Kirtus is one." She chuckled, her expression and tone playfully taunting me.

I rolled my eyes. "Of course."

"I said it could be several others. Kirtus isn't the only one whose scent might be described in that manner. Remember, as you age, your ability to distinguish scents will improve. It's not like your other abilities." She patted my leg. "You need to get some rest. I'll have the staff bring you up something."

She stood and walked to my broken door.

"Juliet, please, we have to keep the events I saw occurring on the third from happening. Promise me you'll do something."

"I'll talk to Gregor and Victor." Her gaze burrowed deeper into me. "Don't worry. We know that it's coming, and we'll stop them. Now rest."

"I'm sorry about the door and the way I acted toward you." My voice was groggy, the weight of the day draining me. "It was childish."

"I know." Juliet winked at me.

I drifted off to sleep.

Chapter Twenty

IT TOOK A few days for me to come around after the test from the Council of Light and my bout with Juliet. I was emotionally and physically drained from it all.

As Juliet promised, she'd talked to both Victor and Gregor. They agreed to be ready if something happened with the witches on December 3rd. Not privy to what she'd offered them, I still appreciated her standing up for me. She told me it was worth the price if my vision saved people and kept the immortal community from being exposed. What would happen if I was wrong?

She smiled and said, "You won't be wrong." That ended the conversation, and I was left to focus or, in my case, obsess about other things.

My obsession led me to Kirtus's driveway. The simple home surprised me. It was a single-story ranch-style home with a brick façade on either side of the double doors, a large picture window on one end, and three smaller windows on the other. Nothing surrounded the home but trees and open fields.

I stopped my car and checked the navigation system again. My stomach somersaulted and my hands shook. I took a deep breath and opened the car door. The odor of oats and hay assaulted me. I'd thought about calling first, but I didn't want him to avoid me again. Checking my outfit, I pulled at the sweater. I should've worn a suit. The thought made me smile—a year ago, jeans and sweats were pretty much my life. Now taking in my dark jeans and green cashmere sweater, I felt naked.

When I was halfway to the house, the door opened. Kirtus stood in the doorway with a scowl on his face, which made it even harder not to laugh at his Disneyland T-shirt.

"You shouldn't be here," he said.

"I needed to talk to you." I slowed my gait but continued walking. "We need to talk about the other night, and my vision."

"Do you understand how much trouble you're going to cause for me?" His tightly crossed arms gave me no welcome.

"Why? We're just talking. I don't care about what the others think." I stopped and imitated his pose.

"Fine." He ran a hand through his red hair. His gaze was on the hardwood floor but at least he wasn't frowning.

I took this as an invitation and headed up to the house. "Thank you." I brushed past him and strolled into the entry hall. His musky earthy scent sent a shudder through my body. It was that same scent I had smelled in my visions and dreams. All the images of us together rushed back to me.

"Living room's to the left." He closed the door.

My mind blurred.

"Have a seat." He sat in the side chair.

It *was* him. It had to be him. I stumbled and gracelessly landed on the sofa.

"It's you." The words dropped from my mouth. He was the man from my dreams. The images of us flooded back into my mind. The first night I saw his eyes staring at me, the dream of him and me together, his scent. God in heaven, it really was him. I had no doubt—his stronger shoulders, his red hair, his gruff voice, all of it. How didn't I realize it until now?

"What are you talking about?" Kirtus grumbled.

"Your eyes," I finally said. I recognized the forehead and the shape of the eyes and his face, his perfect face.

"What about them?" he asked, then nodded. "Oh right, I'm not wearing the green contacts. I only wear them when I go out."

"You're him," I whispered. "You're the man with the green and gray eyes."

I couldn't believe this. He was a real person and not some crazy delusion my mind created. "It was you all this time, but why? How? Why didn't Juliet tell me? She must have seen your eyes before?"

"I always wear contacts, ever since they've made colored lens, and before that, I wore fake glasses. People got, and still get, weird about my eyes." Kirtus frowned more deeply. "It's not like Juliet and I get together regularly. I couldn't tell you what color her eyes are, or Amanda's."

"But the eyes," I stammered.

"What? The older we immortals get the more we focus on scent and less on what people look like." Kirtus kept his arms crossed and sighed.

"We update our appearance over time so that people don't get too suspicious." He stopped. "You should know all this."

"We're supposed to be together." I found myself unable to stop the words.

"Are you even listening to me?" Kirtus asked.

No, I wasn't. Both overwhelmed and elated, my head swam with details of his naked body. My body tingled.

"Are you crazy?" he demanded. "Chris, what the hell's up with you? Ever since your vision, or whatever, you've been strange." He stood. "You should go."

I shook myself out of my dumb haze. My heart pounded in my chest. Every nerve in my body was on fire. My soul seemed to reach out to him. I needed him to see this too. Every part of me wanted to hold him and be with him. He had to see this. But he didn't. Instead, he stood glaring at me and telling me to get out of his house. With each of his words, my soul crumbled a little.

"You don't understand." I got up. "Kirtus, I've been seeing your eyes and smelling your scent. I've had visions about you and me. If you don't believe me, you can ask Juliet. I've told her about them, even before we met. That's why I came here. I can't get you out of my head, and..." My hands reached out to touch him, to feel him under my fingers. "I can't explain it, but whatever is coming, we have to work together and face it. That's the way it's supposed to be."

He pulled away from me.

"Look, Chris, you're nice enough, a little odd, but nice enough. I don't know if you're a true seer or not, but..." His shoulders softened and his voice calmed down. "Listen, whatever you're imagining, Light and Dark don't mix, especially with me."

"It doesn't have to be that way," I pleaded. I moved closer and he stepped back. There was nothing but air between us. "They did once. It can be that way again. I don't care that you're Dark. All that I care about is if you're a good man, and you are." I reached out to him. "Victor doesn't like you. So what? What's he going to do? Not like you anymore? Big deal."

"No, Chris, he could have my head." Kirtus's voice got stronger, but his posture softened. "There are a lot of Dark who would have done that already, but because of my gift, Victor keeps me around. I do my best to steer clear of them, and they leave me alone. Just like the Light—don't pretend for a minute that they wouldn't kill me if they wanted. They don't like 'messy,' and since my Calling, I've been nothing but messy for them. For all of them. I'm not a true Dark, and I'm not of the Light."

A force unknown to me drew me closer to him.

"Please." He held up a hand, weakly trying to get me to stop, but I heard the sorrow and pain in his voice. It called to me. He was so alone. He had no one. He was just like me, an orphan. I tried to meet his gaze, but he focused solely on the floor. "You really need to leave."

I don't know what came over me. His fallen shoulders and the sadness on his face. I had to comfort him. My heart ached for him. Before I could stop, I reached out and embraced him, forcing a passionate kiss on him.

I was out of my mind, but I didn't care. I loved him. I needed him to understand this. We were meant to be together, to be one. As we kissed, he kissed me back. My pulse raced. More than that, I could feel his soul. Our souls touched, and for a brief moment, we were one.

I pulled away from him and stood. His stare was blazing at me and there was a scowl on his soft lips. Then I caught a whiff of smoke. I furrowed my brow and glanced at my legs as they burned.

"Get out!" He pushed me away.

He'd set me on fire. I never moved as fast as I did at that moment. He controlled the fire because it only burned my clothes, not my skin.

Out in the front yard, the flames on my legs died. Kirtus watched me from the big picture window. Once I reached my car, the drapes closed and he was gone.

I was embarrassed and humiliated, tears streaming down my cheeks. My heart ached. If it wasn't for my enhanced senses, I don't think I would have made it home in one piece. How many people would I have taken out with me?

"What have I done?" I dragged myself into the house, the stench of burned fabric following me like a dark cloud.

Both Juliet and Amanda waited for me. "Let me guess. Kirtus called," I grumbled.

"I'm so sorry." Amanda pursed her lips in a frown.

"Chris, we need to talk." Juliet took my arm and marched us to her office, not caring about my appearance or the stench I carried with me.

"I'm sorry," I stammered.

"Amanda, please bring us a bottle," she said as we moved.

With heavy feet and an even heavier heart, I collapsed into the sofa in Juliet's office. My face warm, not from the fire but my actions. My gaze locked on the floor.

"You should have told me you were going there." Juliet's tone was soft but firm, like a disappointed parent.

"I..." I shook my head and stopped.

"Kirtus wasn't pleased." Juliet sat next to me and rested a hand on my leg. "The only saving grace is he won't go to Victor about this. He is going to let me handle this."

"Why didn't you tell me?" I asked. "When I told you about the eyes and then the scent, you had to know."

"I honestly didn't." She gently rubbed my leg. "Not until he called and we spoke. Then I remembered his eyes. If I'd recognized it, I would have—"

A knock on the door interrupted us. Amanda rushed in, then poured us each a glass of red. She placed the filled crystal glasses on the coffee table.

"Thank you, Amanda," Juliet said.

Amanda nodded and gave my shoulder a squeeze, then left.

Juliet picked up her glass and took a sip. She watched the fire and tapped the crystal glass with her fingernail.

"I really fucked things up, didn't I?" I rolled the glass in my hands. I should have drunk something, but I didn't want it.

Juliet sat quietly. She took another sip of her drink. "It'll be fine. Things will work out."

Hints of tears danced in my eyes. It was the first time I didn't believe her, and my heart sank even deeper.

Chapter Twenty-One

IN A FOG, I did my best to stay out of the way of everyone, including Juliet. She must have realized I was upset and needed time, so she let me be. The real reason for her leaving me alone, I thought, had to do with damage control over my actions with Kirtus. If Kirtus told Victor or the Council of Light members, who knows what she would have to do. She didn't say, and I didn't ask.

As with a great many things, life continued all around me. After Thanksgiving, the estate staff pulled the house together for Christmas. Fresh pine garlands hung over the banisters and a large lit spruce tree towered in the main entry of the house to greet visitors. It was filled with hand-blown multicolored glass balls. Every room in the house had been decorated. A handcrafted ceramic Dickens village lay on the mantel in the living room. The paintings in the dining room had artificial garlands hanging around them. On one of the side tables in the entry, a collection of nutcrackers had been put out to watch the front door. Even in my bedroom, a small spruce tree was decorated in blues and purples with white lights.

As festive as the house was, I felt the opposite. I grew pale and only drank red to keep my hunger at bay. If I was honest with myself and the others, I didn't care if I died. Not wanting to bring the mood of the house down, I spent twelve to sixteen hours a day at the Foundation, hiding.

I dragged myself to the agency holiday party, which was good since Juliet only made a brief appearance to pass out bonuses and to thank everyone for another year of dedicated work. For me, the Foundation represented a safe place. I could work and be left alone, which is what I wanted.

December 3rd, the day of my vision, came, and I didn't bother pulling myself together. It would either come to pass or prove me to be insane, something that I didn't want to acknowledge.

A heavy knock on my bedroom door interrupted my smartphone game of *Beat the Dragon*.

"You were right." Amanda rushed in, giving me a bear hug and kiss on the check. "You were one hundred percent right."

Juliet stood at the door, grinning ear to ear.

I twisted my shoulders free.

"I just got off the phone with Gregor, and they were there—" Juliet said.

"Chris, you're amazing." Amanda grabbed the TV remote, then turned the TV on. "You have no idea."

"A local gang known to target malls during the busy shopping season have been arrested as their pyrotechnics distraction malfunctioned at Westfield Valley Fair today," the newswoman said. "Thanks to mall security and several good Samaritans, the gang members are being held. No injuries were reported and only mild damage to some of the malls Christmas decorations. Let's go live—"

Amanda muted the TV.

"Pyrotechnics?" I glanced up at Juliet and Amanda.

"We had to come up with something." Juliet crossed the room and sat on the edge of my bed. "As for any active electronics that were in the area, the firework display did something that caused them all to fry. Sadly, there will be no videos." She shook her head. "Dreadful, really— all the people in the area are going to need new phones."

"How? I don't understand," I questioned.

"We had to make sure that if things went badly, nothing could be filmed or sent out. That is the one problem with technology nowadays— we have to be so careful," Juliet replied.

"Were any of us there?" I asked.

"Gregor made sure that the witches saw immortals there, but they quickly vanished right before things were about to start." Juliet said. "Sahin was there, Gregor told me, but he stayed clear." She bounced on the edge of the bed. "I think...Victor and the Council can't deny it now."

Juliet's excitement filled the room. I tried to share her joy, but my focus was on my forced kiss with Kirtus and how this news would affect him. "Well, I'm glad that my vision helped. Now maybe we can address the larger issue of the pending attack and immortal armageddon."

Juliet's smartphone rang. It was one of the few times I saw her with a phone. She pulled it out, then glanced at the screen. "I need to take this." She hurried out of the room, closing the door behind her.

"Chris." Amanda clicked off the TV. "I'm worried about you, and so is Juliet."

"I'm sorry. I'm a jackass."

"And it's a well-deserved title," she quipped.

I cleared my throat to hide my smile, but it quickly faded. "I've gone over my visit with Kirtus again and again. I don't act like that. I was totally overwhelmed." I fidgeted with my smartphone. "I've never thrown myself at anyone. It wouldn't surprise me if he never spoke to me again."

"You need to stop." Amanda took the smartphone from me and put it on my desk. "We all make mistakes, even immortals. You're new, and you have been through a lot. Your emotions are all over the place. I can't even begin to understand what all this must be like for you."

I faced my balcony, then closed my eyes and breathed deeply a couple of times.

She put a sympathetic hand on my leg. "It's not as bad as you think..." She seemed to consider for a moment. "Well, not anymore. Juliet talked to Kirtus several times, and I doubt he'll burn your clothes again."

"Well, that's something, I suppose."

"Let's go out," Amanda said. "We've never been out, and I know this great restaurant where you can practice eating with real food, and I can have a great meal. It'll be fun. It's called La Fondue." She stood. "Oh the chocolate fondue is amazing. It's in Saratoga. I promise it'll be a good time." She pulled me out of my chair. "I'm going to see about getting us a reservation, so get yourself cleaned up."

"Sure, why not?" I chuckled. "I suppose going out will be nice for a change."

"Excellent. You don't need to wear anything fancy. Casual is fine." She headed to the door.

I had to admit how relieved I was since my vision did come to pass and Gregor and the other others were able to stop it. I didn't understand how my gift worked, but I hoped, now that people believed me, that I could get some help with it.

By the time I took a shower and got dressed, I had a smile on my face and a spring in my step. I checked the mirror. That night, I wore jeans and a sweater, however I had a white dress shirt and burgundy tie underneath.

The weather was chilly, so I grabbed a light jacket and made my way down to the main entry of the house. The twinkle lights from the Christmas tree gave the space a wonderful holiday feel. Amanda waited for me, her hair pulled back into a long ponytail and wearing a tan overcoat with a delicate Christmas brooch on the collar.

"You ready?" she asked.

"Let's boogie."

The main street of Saratoga resembled downtown Los Altos, with lots of little shops and restaurants. Bright red, green, and gold decorations lined the street, twinkling lights laced back and forth over the main road, offering a lot of illumination. Everything was decorated for Christmas, giving the little town a warm and welcoming feel. A real postcard shot.

As Amanda found parking, I enjoyed watching the people pass by.

At the restaurant, I opened the door for Amanda, and the aroma of cooked food and oil welcomed me inside. Surprised by the kitschy medieval setting, I didn't know where to focus. Heavy velvet fabrics in bright colors lined the walls and windows, enhancing the soft mood lighting. All their holiday décor was silver. Silver wreaths, trees, bells, and garlands gave a nice contrast.

"Hi, Jack." Amanda glided over to the man behind the host stand.

"Amanda." He helped her with her coat. "You look amazing. Do you want me to check this?"

"Yes, please. Thank you." She gestured toward me. "This is my friend, Chris."

"Pleasure."

We shook hands.

"It'll be just a moment," Jack said, and went to put the coat away.

"How did you meet him?" I asked.

"I have a life," Amanda replied with a shrug and smile. "Actually, this is a mixed human and immortal restaurant so..."

"Ah," I said as Jack returned.

"Please, follow me." Jack led us through the restaurant.

A slight haze hovered in the air, and the sounds of sizzling and laughter gave the space life. I wished I had known about this place before my transition. It would've been fun to visit and enjoy. Jack guided us to a more secluded table in one of the back rooms. My eyes adjusted easily to the darker space.

"You need to call me," Jack said. "It's been too long since we've been out."

He assisted Amanda as she slid into the seat next to me.

"I promise," Amanda said.

"Your server tonight is Stephanie. She'll be with you shortly." Jack rested a hand on Amanda's shoulder. "I'm going to hold you to that promise. I'll have a bottle of our best *red* wine sent over for you to enjoy."

He nodded at me. I continued to take in my surroundings. "I can't believe you didn't suggest coming to this place before. It's cool."

"Sorry, it never presented itself before." Amanda picked up our menus and put them to the side. "I'm going to order, so trust me."

Stephanie arrived with the bottle of red and poured me a glass as she introduced herself. Stephanie was a cute twenty-something Filipino girl, probably still in college, but what struck me was her cheerfulness and nice manners. She clearly knew how to work the tip. After explaining the aspects of the restaurant, she offered to fill Amanda's glass. Amanda raised a polite hand in decline.

"None for me, thank you. I'll have an appletini instead, please."

"Of course," Stephanie said. "I'll put the drink order in and be back."

Once Amanda's drink arrived, she ordered, and we had the opportunity to talk about nothing. It was similar to my conversations with Cindy when we went out. A nice break from reality.

"Now—" Stephanie pointed to our salads. "I suggest that you don't eat it all. We can box it up and you can take it home. There are three more courses so you should pace yourself," she said, then left us.

"She's sweet." I glanced at my salad: fresh greens, carrots, cucumber, shredded cheese, and three small pinwheel sandwiches greeted me. I drizzled some honey-mustard dressing over it, and it looked amazing. This was my first real attempt at eating since I transformed. I'd practiced at home, but nothing like this.

I had a forkful of salad when I caught his scent and froze.

"Sorry, I'm late. Traffic was a..." Kirtus stopped and stared for a moment. "Well, that would explain why you picked this restaurant. All the smells would mask our scents until it was too late." He glanced between us. His voice measured.

"Yes, well, now that you're here, take a seat." Amanda pointed to the seat next to her. "We just got our salads, and we're still on the first bottle of red."

"Amanda?" My face heated, and I wanted to run and hide.

Kirtus clenched his fists and eyed Amanda. Still, he looked amazing. Dark jeans that fit him perfectly and a light-green shirt with gold cufflinks that had little snowflakes on them. His outfit was completed with polished back dress shoes.

My heart skipped a beat just looking at him.

"You both need to talk, and it might as well be in a neutral setting with a neutral party." Amanda scooted closer to me. "Now sit."

"I can't believe you tricked me." Kirtus didn't move. "I should go."

"Absolutely not." Amanda raised her voice and pointed to the seat next to her. "You will sit. You two will talk like grown adults and work through this. Unless you want me to..." She twisted a curl of hair around her finger. "Oh, I don't know, make a scene." Then she leaned toward Kirtus and smiled brightly. "Or worse."

Kirtus dropped his shoulders, and his frown lessened as he sat down.

I glanced between Kirtus and Amanda. If there was a rock nearby, I would have crawled under it. "I'm sorry." I picked up my glass of red and took a heavy drink.

Stephanie, right on cue, returned to our table, all smiles and introductions. She put a fresh place setting and salad down in front of Kirtus, then pulled out another glass and poured Kirtus a glass of red before walking off.

"You really went all out, didn't you, Amanda?" Kirtus glanced around the restaurant, then down at the table.

Amanda bit into her salad, chewed, then swallowed. "One does what one must. Let me start our conversation." She put her fork down. "We've established that Chris was a jackass for the way he acted and what he did. You were equally a jackass for setting him on fire."

"I only did that so he would get off me and get out of my house," Kirtus said. "He was acting crazy." He picked up his fork, poked at the salad, and took a bite. "It was only his clothes, not him, I made sure of that." He tasted his red.

"I'm really sorry." My heart raced, and my neck and ears were on fire. I reached up to touch them, to ensure they were not actually burning.

"Well, now that's a start." Amanda sipped her appletini. "Chris has apologized twice now, just today. Don't you think you should do the same?" She tapped her finger on the edge of her glass.

Kirtus tilted his head to the left as he closed his eyes. "Fine," he huffed. "Amanda's right. Setting your clothes on fire wasn't the best way to handle the situation. Especially considering that you may not have been fully in your right mind."

"There." She took another bite of her salad. "That wasn't so difficult, was it? Oh, and eat your salads. Chris needs the practice." She pointed between us, then to our salads.

Kirtus took another bite and made a sarcastic *mmm* sound.

I finished off my first glass and poured another before I tried the salad. I wished it had flavor, because I'm sure it was good. Still, it tasted flat and empty. There was still the crunch of the lettuce and carrots. The squishy wet sensation of the dressing was not what I was expecting and kind of unpleasant until I knew what I was eating. I couldn't believe I never noticed these things before.

Amanda continued on her salad as Kirtus and I picked at ours in silence. Finally, Stephanie came over with small trays of gherkin pickles, boiled potatoes, and other veggies for our cheese course.

"Would you like me to box up your salads?" Stephanie pointed to Kirtus's and my plates.

We declined, and she started to put the cheese fondue together. Once done, she told us she'd be back in a couple of minutes with the bread for us to dip in the cheese.

A soft vibration hummed and I turned to Amanda.

Amanda frowned, reached down to her purse, and pulled out her phone. "Hello," she said. "Of course. I'll be there in fifteen minutes." The phone went back in her purse. "Sorry. I have to go. Juliet needs me."

Kirtus got up and allowed her to stand.

"I expect you to both sit here, enjoy dinner, and talk. Don't make me resort to other measures." She leaned and kissed Kirtus on the cheek and did the same to me.

"Bye." She waved and strolled off.

"Crap." I glanced after her.

"What?" Kirtus asked.

"She drove."

Kirtus laughed. "She's good," he said when he composed himself.

"I can catch her." I stood, ready to make my escape.

"Chris, sit down." Kirtus pointed to my chair. "Amanda went to a lot of trouble to get us here, and I don't want to find out what her *other measures* are." He air-quoted the last part. "I should have figured something was up."

"If you don't mind, how did she get you here?" I was curious because I had been under the impression that he hardly dealt with Amanda or Juliet.

"Well." Kirtus picked up his red, sipping it. "I wasn't completely honest with you the other day. I may not see Juliet often, but Amanda and I get together. Since I don't have a Keeper, she helps me out now and then, especially with community-related issues."

"So, she got you here under the guise of business."

"Yep." He leaned back in his seat. "I thought it was odd that she needed to see me, but I didn't think much of it, given the news today."

"So you saw that?"

"Of course. We all did," Kirtus replied. "You were right, and you managed to keep the attack from going south… so—" He raised his glass to me. "—congratulations."

"Look, about that. I was right about one thing. Even with working on my ability, I'm still not a hundred percent on anything. This other stuff—"

"Can we please not talk about that?" he interrupted and put his glass down.

"Okay." I focused on my hands. "Why don't you have a Keeper?"

Stephanie came by and dropped off the bread for the cheese. She gave the cheese fondue another couple of stirs and turned the temperature down, then added red wine to the cheese.

"You should be all set," Stephanie said. "I'll bring another bottle of wine for you. Enjoy."

She vanished into the haze of the restaurant.

"I don't have a Keeper because of my standing in the community." Kirtus's shoulders stiffened. "I don't want to put someone in danger like that. Juliet lets me borrow Amanda from time to time, and Victor has let me use Daniel now and then. It's helpful, except with Daniel—I always feel like he's spying on me, which he probably is. It's to be expected." He forced a small chuckle. "My guess is Amanda does as well, but that's a little different. I actually enjoy spending time with her."

"She's pretty cool," I said. "I don't want to be nosy, but what happened to the one who Called you? If that's too personal, you don't have to answer."

Kirtus picked up a boiled potato and dipped it in the cheese before tasting it. "Try it."

I picked up my fondue fork, spiked a piece of bread, and dipped it into the cheese fondue. Hints of blood stained it. It added a sundried tomato and basil flavor to the fondue. It was good, better than the salad dressing had been.

Kirtus studied me a moment.

My neck heated. "Sorry, I shouldn't have asked."

"No, it's fine. It was a long time ago. After the accident during my second Mark, he wasn't allowed to finish the process because the Council of Light forbade it."

"What? An accident with your second Mark." I leaned in.

"Yes, there was an accident during my test." Kirtus fidgeted with his hands. "You see, Ryan, the person I was supposed to *kill* and feed off of had a heart condition. Medical science was crap back then, so no one knew. When I tried to protect him, like you did with Cindy, it was too much for his heart..."

"I'm sorry." I glanced back at the table.

"There wasn't anything to be done. He was dead, and I killed him—well, my actions killed him. It took the Council months to decide what to do. They actually met, which was no easy feat back then, and that was that." He watched his glass.

"That doesn't seem right." I wanted to reach out and take his hand so much my fingers twitched, but I stopped myself.

"I've learned since then that Juliet fought to keep me safe. She's always been a noble woman. Anyway, she talked to Victor, who in turn got one of his people to complete the process with the intention of killing me once I was converted."

"Let me guess," I said. "He wanted to see what your ability was."

Kirtus nodded.

"Of course." I frowned.

"When Victor found out, he kept me alive, much to the displeasure of some of the Light and the Dark, of course. Juliet granted me sanctuary in her territories. Anyway, the one who finished my Calling was killed during the American Civil War, and as for the one who originally Called me, I never saw or heard of him again. I guess accidents happen, even to those of the Light." He reached for his red and took a heavy swallow.

"I'm sorry." What more could I say?

"Like I said, it's all in the past." Kirtus sat up and adjusted the collar of his green long-sleeve shirt. "The world moves on, and here we are." He lifted his glass to me. "Cheers."

We continued to eat our blood-flavored cheese in momentary silence.

Kirtus put down his fork. "Anyway, that's why I try not to rock the boat and why I make my home in Morgan Hill. No immortals live there now, but I suppose as San Jose grows, that'll change."

"By the way, you have an amazing home." I wanted to steer the conversation to something more pleasant. "Well, at least what I saw of it and remember."

"Thanks, I can't take all the credit. I had help."

"Amanda?" I said.

"Of course."

"She's talented, that's for sure." I dipped a gherkin pickle into the cheese. Even though it didn't have a ton of flavor, the blood and the texture made it enjoyable. "You should try the pickles and cheese—the texture is pretty good."

"Really?" Kirtus leaned in, found a pickle, and tried it. "I didn't develop the ability to find enjoyment from foods' texture for a long time. It's impressive you have the ability now."

"Huh." I wiped my face with my napkin. "Like, how long?"

He leaned in and checked over both shoulders. "A hundred years." He laughed. "The food is a lot better now than it was back then, so maybe that's why." He smiled, revealing the dimple on his cheek, and settled back in.

We talked and enjoyed the food. The highlight came at the end with the red chocolate. An exclusive for those of us who partake in the red, and it was amazing. I could have eaten the whole thing myself, or ordered another pot of it.

Kirtus drove me back to the house in his Ford Fusion Hybrid. As he pulled into the driveway, the house, every window, archway, and all along the roofline was covered with white Christmas lights. The cherry trees had white and pink lights, giving them the illusion of being in bloom.

"Wow," I gasped.

"Juliet goes all out," Kirtus said.

He stopped the car at the front door and turned to me. "When you're not being all weird and seer-ie, you're pretty fun. Like the first night I met you."

"Thanks." Every part of me was in a heightened state of arousal. I wanted to lean in and kiss him, but before I could make it weird, I decided to get out of car. "I had fun." I waved, closed the car door, and waved some more as he drove away.

Considering how the day started, it ended up pretty good.

Chapter Twenty-Two

"WELL?" AMANDA ASKED, her gaze running over my face.

"I..." I shut my eyes as I tried to call the image forward. "It's in the pool house bedroom in the top drawer on the left side of the bed." I opened my eyes and rubbed my temples to help with the sudden headache.

"Let's go find out." She clapped my leg, a grin on her face.

We dashed out of the living room and headed out to the pool house. The damp chill of the air kissed my cheeks as we made our way. I caught hints of pine as I closed the french doors behind me. The pine reminding me Christmas was approaching.

As with the rest of the mansion, the staff had decorated the pool house with twinkle lights, garlands, and a fir tree. The tree stood well over eight feet, making an impressive focal point. It bore white-and-silver hand-blown glass balls with beaded silver garlands. On the sofa lay an embroidered quilt with a Victorian winter scene. The mantel held a collection of holiday-themed snow globes.

Over the last week and a half, I'd practiced my mental abilities, as best I could, by locating hidden objects; what good was a seer who couldn't control his visions? It was an arduous task, and there really wasn't anyone to get training from. So Juliet and I developed a test: she would hide various items—belonging to different people—around the estate, and I would have to find them. Amanda stayed with me to keep me from cheating. At first, my accuracy was 50 percent, but over time, I'd gotten closer to 80 percent, which I felt pretty good about.

Amanda and I strolled into the bedroom of the pool house. I stopped at the door as she checked the place I saw in my mind. She pulled open the drawer and picked up the dragon signet that Juliet used to seal her personal envelopes. Juliet had even put a small gold bow on it.

I chuckled.

"Clever," Amanda said behind her smile.

"Would have sucked if I couldn't find *that*." I leaned against the doorframe. "How many items did she hide today?"

"Last one." She held up the signet in her hand as she crossed to me. "You did really well. You found everything. That's the best you've done."

"Great. So I can find missing objects." I sighed and rubbed my head. With my ability came headaches. "I don't know how this is going to help us find out more about the witches."

"One step at a time," Amanda said.

I winced and rubbed my temples again.

"How's the head?"

"Fine. It's getting better. The more I use my gift, the better it gets."

"Good. At least the headaches aren't uncommon. Juliet still gets headaches on occasion from using her mental ability."

"Really?"

"Yep." Amanda patted my shoulder and headed for the main room. "Have you talked to Kirtus since the dinner? It's been a few days."

"What does this have to do with my practicing?"

"Nothing. I'm just curious." She winked at me. "You haven't said a word about it since you came home." She stopped and widened her eyes. "Oh, I have an idea. Come on."

We made our way back to the main house. The sitting room had a large fir tree in the corner, covered in all manner of decorations: horns, bells, stuffed animals, rocking horses—but what tied it all together were large red-and-green ribbons draped throughout. Even the lights were multicolored. Miniature buildings rested on the coffee table with a small electric Christmas train running around the edge. It made me feel like I was home.

Amanda closed the doors and shut the heavy blinds. "I want you to try something and you're not going to like it, but we should try it." She raised her eyebrows and an excited smile danced on her face. "Sit on the sofa."

"Amanda?"

She pointed to the sofa.

I shrugged and sat. I pushed the red-and-gold Christmas pillows out of the way, allowing me to lean back.

She pulled over one of the side chairs and faced me. "Okay, you should try to find him."

I looked at her, confused.

"I mean, see if you can visually find him. Focus on him and let's hope you get something. You have some kind of link to him, so maybe you should try it. What do you have to lose?"

"Who him?"

She threw up her hands in amused frustration. "Kirtus."

"I'm not sure that's a good idea." My heart raced, and my cheeks grew warm at the thought of seeing him again. "We should check with Juliet."

"Oh, it's fine. If it doesn't work, then it doesn't work, but if it does, we can try some other things or other people." Amanda crossed her legs and adjusted her skirt before turning an expectant look on me.

I couldn't find a good reason not to do it, especially since it probably wouldn't work. "All right." I shut my eyes and focused. My thoughts turned to Kirtus, the way he smiled, revealing his dimple, and how he smelled. I called up every detail about him, starting with his one gray eye and his one green eye. I sat quietly, mentally painting a picture of him. I tried to reach out to him.

"Nothing. There's nothing."

"Relax. You're trying too hard," she said. "Your face is all squished. Try again. Give it a chance to work. You've barely even started."

I shook my shoulders and rotated my head, hearing a small pop in my neck. I tried again, calling up all my memories of Kirtus.

After several minutes of silence, Amanda groaned. "Oh for pity's sake, take a few deep breaths and relax, Chris. Otherwise, you don't get any of my special red Belgian chocolate."

I kept myself from chuckling and forced my eyes closed. My body relaxed as I tried to find him again. I brought up the image of him and breathed in his scent. A fog replaced the darkness and warm dampness filled the air.

"He's someplace foggy and damp," I said, confused. "It's bright but foggy." I finally started to make out a shape: Kirtus. "I think..." I mentally waved my hands to clear up the fog "I think it's him. He's doing something."

"What's he doing?" Amanda asked.

"I'm not sure." The image cleared. "It's him. I recognize the scent, but there's something else. He's doing something with his hands, and his body is shaking."

"Is he okay?"

I changed my focus and shifted to his face. His eyes were closed, and his mouth hung slightly open, moving like he was trying to catch his breath.

"Holy crap." I couldn't hide my embarrassed laugh. He wasn't in fog but in a shower. Naked. And I knew exactly what he was doing.

I snapped my eyes open and instantly became hot from my neck to the top of my head.

"What? What did you see?" Amanda's voice filled with concern.

"Nothing, I didn't see anything," I lied. "I should have...we shouldn't have..." I shook my head. "I had no right."

"Chris, what did you see?" She touched my leg.

I jerked away.

"Is he alright? Is everything okay?"

A nervous chuckle escaped my lips. "He's fine. Everything is fine."

"Well?"

"Amanda, he..." I thought for a moment, trying to find a polite way to say what I saw. "He was in the shower and having some...um...I guess, alone time."

Amanda froze as her face grew red, and she started laughing. "Oh my." She bit her lip to stop snickering. "Well, I guess there won't be a way to verify that."

"Amanda, we can't say anything to him or the others; that would be flat-out wrong." I cleared my thoughts. Regardless, I wouldn't forget that image, especially with how amazing he had looked wet and naked.

After the vision of Kirtus in the shower, Amanda and I decided we would stop training for the day. That was fine with me. I definitely had a full-on headache. So, the break was appreciated, however, short-lived. Sadly, I still had work to finish from the Foundation before the end of the year and everyone went on Christmas holiday for two weeks.

And much to my lack of excitement, the Council of Light was coming back out to meet.

TWO DAYS LATER, by the night of the Council meeting, I had spoken with Juliet about expanding my training to include psychically checking in on people, then verifying what I saw with them. Trying this new training method, I discovered that I had varying degrees of success. The better I knew the person, the better the vision. The worst results involved trying to locate people I'd never met or had only had seen on TV or online.

Luckily, I didn't have any other visions similar to the one of Kirtus. Really, what would be the odds of that happening again?

"I'M SURE RACKING up the frequent flyer miles, mate." Garrett leaned against the wall, his Australian accent rich to my ears.

The Council members and I milled about in the dining room. The meeting hadn't started, but the room was set up similar to the other times. The only difference tonight was the festive gold tablecloths draping the tables.

"I know. I'm sorry," I said.

"Hey, don't be. We owe you, mate. If we weren't able to stop that display at the mall, we'd all be screwed."

I caught a faint wisp of his scent. It smelled of cedar and reminded me of my times hiking in the mountains. "Well, thank you." I glanced to the floor, my ears heating up. "I hope we're able to stop them."

The doors burst open as Victor charged in with Kirtus and Sahin. "I apologize for being late. We had some matters to attend to." Victor marched to Juliet and greeted her.

"I didn't know they would be here," I whispered to Garrett.

"They're part of this, mate," Garrett said. "So, it seemed only right." He crossed over to the tables that had been put in a circle.

Kirtus glanced over to me, nodding, and I smiled. My face grew warm as my mind filled with the image of him in the shower. My groin started to stir, and I cleared my thoughts and moved over to sit next to Juliet.

There was a slight smirk on Juliet's face as she watched me. I really had to do better at keeping my emotions under control.

As I pulled out my chair, Sybil touched my hand. "Actually, if you don't mind sitting next to Victor and his group, Christopher, that would be lovely." A holier-than-thou smile and narrow eyes greeted me.

"Of course." I hurried to the other side of the round table, and as luck would have it, the only open seat was next to Kirtus, so it wasn't too bad. "Hi." I greeted him and took my seat. I turned to Yoi. "Nice to see you again."

She bowed. "As you. I hope you are well?"

"I'm good, thank you," I said.

She turned to Rahim next to her, and they began chatting.

"How've you been?" Kirtus asked.

He was dressed in a rich navy-blue suit with a pin-striped white, blue, and green shirt. A complementary green tie matched the color of his eyes—he wore his green contacts so both his eyes were the same color. I found this disappointing. He had such beautiful eyes, and it was a shame to hide them.

"Busy, good." It was a challenge speaking to him, knowing what I knew about him. "You know, practicing." I picked at the tablecloth. "Plus, we're getting things ready for year-end at the Foundation."

"I've been busy as well." He adjusted the knot of his necktie. "But things are wrapping up. It'll be nice to have more alone time."

A laugh fell out of my mouth before I could stop it.

He narrowed his eyes and tilted his head in question.

"Sorry."

"Are you—"

Victor cut him off when he cleared his throat. "You can chitchat after the meeting."

"Of course." Kirtus bowed.

"He has no respect," Sahin said, loud enough for Kirtus and me to hear. "Why did you allow Kirtus to attend? Especially with all that is happening. He could be of better use—"

"He was invited. Now quiet," Victor interrupted, narrowing his eyes on Sahin.

Sahin shifted his attention to Juliet.

Kirtus and I both hid our grins and turned to Juliet as well.

"Thank you all for coming," Juliet said.

Juliet was back in charge tonight, and I was grateful. Sybil rubbed me the wrong way. She always seemed to be looking down at Juliet and by extension me.

"You all know what happened and that we are, in fact, dealing with witches," Juliet said. "Since the incident, they have vanished, though. The six witches that were taken into custody have been released, and they too have vanished. No one has been able to track them or pick up any scent of them."

"Human custody, I would like to point out," Sybil added.

"Correct," Juliet said. "They were in human custody and released. Since we didn't want to risk exposure, we had few options. By the time we found out, they had disappeared. We tried to track them, but they somehow vanished."

"If I may?" Victor stood and buttoned his suit jacket. "They had help on the inside. As we have people on the inside of the police, so did the witches. Short of us exposing ourselves to the humans, as Juliet pointed out, there was nothing to do. By the time my people went to intercept them, they were gone, and unfortunately, those that helped them had been under some kind of compulsion spell."

"They got away?" Taqi asked.

"That would never have happened in my territory." Anashe tapped the table while she spoke, as if emphasizing her point.

I tried not to roll my eyes. Anashe controlled Southern Africa, and from my perspective and what I've seen and read, even without immortals, that part of the world was a bit messy.

"What is done is done." Juliet chose to ignore the comments and move the conversation along.

"We have nothing again?" An asked with a shake of her head. "We only know of this impending doomsday that Christopher has seen. Providing us with no day, time, or anything to prepare for. Lovely."

"That's not exactly the case," Juliet said. "That is why I've asked Chris to join us. He's been practicing his talent and has been able to focus on people and find them or at least get hints of their locations, depending on his familiarity with them."

"Has this been tested?" Sybil leaned forward with interest.

"It has," Juliet said. "I've tested him using Amanda and myself. He's been very accurate."

"But he knows you. What about people he doesn't know, people he may not have seen or even know about?" Sybil asked, her gaze falling on me.

"He has had some success." Juliet adjusted her stance, a flat expression set on her face.

"Which means he's had some failure as well." Victor glanced between us. "Juliet, I know I've agreed to work with you and the Council of Light, but we need something. I have my people out there searching, but they need information, reliable information."

"And we'll get it." Juliet focused on me. "I've asked Chris here tonight so that he can try to find them. It's a risk, but at least you will all witness him in action, and we can decide what to do next."

"Very well." Sybil sat back, peering at me and nodding.

"Chris." Juliet nodded toward me.

All eyes were on me, and my stomach dropped to the floor. I took a breath. "Can we dim the lights please, and if everyone can stay quiet. I've...well, I've only been doing this for a short time, so please stay quiet and don't move around."

Kirtus turned the lights down and returned to his seat.

"Thank you." I closed my eyes. "I'm going to focus on the dark woman from my visions. She's the one we need to know about."

With my eyes shut, I became aware of the stillness of the room. Pushing everything from my mind, my body relaxed. I tried the same technique I'd used with Kirtus and painted a mental image of her face at first. The wrinkles, the cruel smile, her flat brown hair, everything I knew about her. Her voice, the way she looked, and how unpleasant she was. My focus stayed on her, trying to call up anything else I remembered.

The dark shifted, and images came together. As my sight came into focus, I relayed what I saw.

"I'm on a road. There isn't any traffic. It's morning, and it feels cool." I mentally tried to take in the information. The images became crisp, and I saw a car coming up the road.

"There's a car," I said.

I knew this car. It was my father's Ford Taurus. I remember him taking my mother and me on long weekend getaways to Lake Tahoe and to go snow tubing over at Donner Pass. We had a lot of good times in that car. My mother kept it until the day she died. It was a lot newer now.

"I don't understand," I said.

I'm not sure if I spoke anymore after that because I concentrated on the car and what happened around me in the vision. The car slowed down. Another car sat on the side of the road. I watched as my father's car came to a stop, and he got out. He looked so young. This was impossible. I glanced at the green Honda with its flasher on. He strolled to the window. There was no sound, but I saw her—the dark woman sat there. I strained to yell out, but my dad couldn't hear me.

She talked and laughed.

My father nodded and stepped back as she got out of her car. With her eyes narrowed, she touched him. He dropped to the ground in convulsions. I ran over to them. I needed to help him but wasn't able to reach him. Every time I motioned for him, my hands went through his body. I heard myself screaming and yelling at the dark woman, but she didn't notice me; she only watched my father in fascination.

I glanced at my dad as his face went pale. Tendrils of blood and energy flowed from his fingers like snakes toward her. She kneeled down to watch him. She brushed the hair from his face, and it started to turn white. The blood and energy trail circled around her, reaching toward the sky. She absorbed it into her.

My efforts to stop her failed. I couldn't and I wouldn't wake up. Even when I turned, I saw it all.

Once his body went limp and she had drained him, she picked him up and put him back into the driver's seat of his car. She laughed as she got back into her Honda. She'd killed him because he stopped to help her.

I had to find them. Stop them. If not for me and the immortals, then for my father.

She started the engine, and her stare blazed into mine. "I have one more stop to make before I see you, Duncan. Your poor mother's so fragile. She's next." She cackled. "Then it'll be your turn." Her mouth turned up into a cruel sneer. "Tell Juliet and the others that they won't find us. Well, not until we want them to. We're well protected this time. It's not like before."

I struggled to scream, but nothing came out.

"Oh, and pass along this message to Victor." She banged the outside of her car door. "Daniel's dead, and Victor really should know better than to send a sniveling little weasel like that out on his own."

My body convulsed. There was no air for me to breath.

"We left his body for him." She waggled her eyebrows. "He might want to get to him before the animals do, winter by the observatory and all." She winked at me. "See ya soon, sonnyboy." She laughed and drove off.

I screamed and my eyes flew open.

"She killed him!" The words finally barreled from me. My whole body shook. That monster even used my father's nickname for me. To taunt me. I couldn't tell if it was tears or sweat dripping from my cheeks. "She killed my father. She said she was going to kill my mother. Then come for me. She called me by my name. She knows me. She killed my father. She's coming after me and the rest of you."

"Shhhh," a female voice said, "Shhh...Duncan I need you to listen to me."

My mother, she was young and beautiful. Her brown hair shone and her cheeks were rose-colored. The sparkle was back in her eyes.

"They're overconfident and you'll stop them." My mother's voice filled my ears. "Honey, I'm so proud of you. I'll help you all I can. Juliet will know, so will Sybil. You have to make them remember. Remind them about Salem." My mother kissed the top of my head.

My body stopped shaking, and air came to my lungs again.

"He's lovely, Duncan. You've chosen well. He'll make you happy. Now relax and open your eyes. I love you, Duncan, always remember that," my mom said. "Now open your eyes. It'll be alright, just open your eyes."

"Breathe and open your eyes. Come on, Chris, open your eyes."

I blinked several times. Everyone stood over me, watching. I lay on the ground, and my head pounded. I scanned around. They were all there, staring at me.

"Chris, are you all right?" Kirtus held my head.

I attempted to sit up, but my body didn't respond.

"Chris, don't move. Say something."

"I need to...I need to sit up." Tears welled in my eyes and my voice sounded weak.

Kirtus and Juliet helped me up and got me back into the chair.

"She killed my father and my mother. She's coming for us."

"We heard." Juliet patted my hand. "And we heard her voice." Her face paled and she looked spooked.

"Where's Victor?" I glanced around the room. "She killed Daniel."

Kirtus was the only one left from the Dark.

Sybil's eyes grew large. "When you, well her, whatever that was, said that about Daniel." She bit her nail. "It would seem that Daniel had gone missing a couple of days ago. That was why Victor and Sahin were late tonight and..." She shook her head.

"They killed him and left his body." My arms and legs were limp.

"We don't know that." Juliet's voice cracked. "But he's going to let us know what they find."

"I don't understand this." My legs trembled, and I reached out to pick up the glass of red. I didn't know when it arrived, but as I peeked over my shoulder, Amanda stood by the door with a bottle. "How long?"

"About ten minutes, maybe longer." Juliet took the glass from my shaking hand. "Chris, what happened after she said 'see ya soon'? We attempted to wake you, but you wouldn't. We didn't hear anything, and we saw the tears. What was there? It might be helpful."

I took several breaths and reached for the red.

Kirtus beat me to the glass. He held it to my mouth so I could drink.

"It was my mother. She was there, holding me. She said that I needed to get you and Sybil to remember that you both know something and that you have to remember." I swallowed.

Everyone shared glances between Sybil and Juliet.

"She said they're overconfident, and we'll stop them. She's going to help. The dark woman said they were well hidden, not like before. I don't know how." I wasn't sure if they believed me or not, but all eyes were on me and no one spoke. "Then my mother said she was proud of me and that she…" I shook my head. "The rest is personal."

"Of course." Juliet squeezed my shoulder. "You should get some rest. We should adjourn for the night."

"No," I said. "Juliet, my mother was very clear. You and Sybil know something. You know about this. What is it? What is it that you and Sybil know? What about Salem?"

They both shared a quick glance, and Juliet tapped her lips.

"Salem?" Sybil muttered and shook her head. "That was a long time ago." She frowned and took a seat. "Juliet, we never found the body, and that would explain what she meant about being hidden better and more protected."

"What body? What about Salem?" Garrett asked. "The Council needs to be informed as to the nature of your involvement with any of this."

"No, it couldn't be." Juliet got to her feet, then sat in the chair near to me. "There was a witch." She focused on me. "Remember when I told you that I hadn't seen a true witch in a very long time? Well, that would have been her."

"She was causing trouble in the Massachusetts colony, getting people all worked up." Sybil clicked her fingernails, then stopped. She poured herself a glass of red. "Her and her coven were…" She took a sip. "They weren't good people, and they got a lot of innocent people killed. They endeavored to release magic into the world."

"We couldn't let that happen," Juliet said.

"Wait." I held up my hands. "The Salem Witch Trials—that was because of her? That was you guys?"

"The 1690s were a difficult time for all of us in the colonies," Juliet said. "We needed to stop her. Allowing magic to come into the world was not an option. It's too powerful, and people back then..." She inhaled. "The ramifications to the world would have been monumental, especially at that time."

"So we took care of her," Sybil said.

"You destroyed this true witch and stopped magic from coming into our world?" Taqi nodded toward them. "What gave you the right to decide that on your own?"

"The Council, prior to several of you joining," Juliet said, a stern expression on her face. "We had the authority. Imagine what would have happened to us if true magic existed. Think of how that would have changed civilization. We didn't have a choice. The witches, well, the true witches, were hell-bent on destroying us."

"The Council decided it was either them or us," Sybil said to the others.

"I remember that," An said. "It wasn't an easy decision at the time. The trials went on for years, into the middle of the 18th century. There were almost 80,000 trials when all was said and done."

"What?" I asked.

"Close to 35,000 people killed because of it, almost all of them innocent. Very few were true witches, and only in Salem was the situation as dire. Not like elsewhere." She frowned. "We did what we thought was best, and sadly travel and communication wasn't like it is now."

"What about this body, or the bodies?" Yoi asked, pulling us back on topic.

"We're not sure," Juliet said. "We found her and her coven. We killed them and burned the bodies. There was something different about the flames. They were blues and whites. We figured it was because their magic was being destroyed. When we went back the next day, the fire had died but..." She tapped her lips. "She had to be dead. Magic was gone and everyone and everything returned to normal. There were whispers, but even those died away."

"But we didn't find any bones," Sybil said. "Just a few pieces of burned material and ash. There were a few hot embers but nothing else. We looked for weeks to make sure. Like Juliet said—things returned to normal. We thought we'd taken care of it."

"So you don't know?" I questioned.

Sybil glared at me. "Anyway, I returned to Europe, and yes, there were trials that continued, but we never found any more true witches or any that had the kind of power to worry us. So I didn't think any more of it—at least not until now."

"What are we going to do?" Rahim asked. "We can't start another witch hunt, at least not like that. The world has changed, and no one would allow it, not even in the most remote parts of the planet."

"I'll have Gregor and his people work with our human allies, and I'll instruct my governors to do a discreet search for our witch friends. Lucky, we have better technology now than we did back then," Juliet said. "In the meantime, we wait until we hear from Victor and learn if what she said is true about Daniel. Then, we wait for Chris's mother to help us further if she can."

"My mother is dead," I said, harder than I wanted. "How is it even possible for her to be in my vision, let alone know things?"

Fernando moved closer to me and kneeled to meet my gaze. "Just because one has moved on from this world, doesn't mean they are not able to help us. I don't know what you saw, Christopher, none of us do, but I believe that your mother reached out and touched your soul to help you. You're her son and her blood. That is a bond that goes beyond anything that can be understood, even by us with our long years." His face softened, and he rested a gentle hand on my knee. "The dark woman may be lying to you, but I feel..." He stopped. "No, I believe that your mother is in fact going to help you and, by extension, us. That kind of love is stronger than any magic, true or otherwise." He gave my knee a gentle squeeze, then stood. "I hope her personal words to you were a comfort and brought you a small amount of peace."

"Chris, because of what she told you, we know who we're up against, and we may even have an idea of their goal and who they're after," Juliet said.

"The dark one, this witch, she's a human by nature. She couldn't be alive, not now, even with powerful magic. How's she still alive three hundred plus years later?" Kirtus's tone was soft but filled with concern. "It's impossible."

"Any more impossible than vampires existing? Yet here we are," I said with a sidelong glance at him.

This gave them all pause, and the room fell silent once more.

I remembered the moment I met Juliet, and she asked me if there was no room in the world for creatures that we didn't understand. That if God had created man and beasts, couldn't he have created other things as well? So a 300-year-old pissed-off witch still around, biding her time and waiting for the right moment to seek out her revenge, didn't seem impossible. My head pounded and hurt, but nothing ached as much as my heart, and what this monster had done to me and my family.

Chapter Twenty-Three

TO SAY THE time leading up to Christmas was holly and jolly would be a lie. Victor contacted Juliet shortly after the meeting with the Council of Light. He confirmed Daniel's body was found on the way up to Mt. Hamilton near the James Lick Observatory.

Victor said that Daniel must have gotten too close or been found out by the witches, and killed as a warning to him and the Dark. Either way, it hadn't been an easy death for Daniel. Somehow, the witches were able to block Daniel's link to Victor, which had everyone with a Keeper worried. If the witches were as powerful as they now appeared to be, it wasn't going to be as easy as it was back in the day when Juliet and Sybil had dispatched them.

Out of respect for Daniel, I went with Juliet and Amanda to the funeral. To my surprise, it was well attended by the immortal community, both Light and Dark. Garrett, Fernando, and Sybil were all in attendance. Not knowing Daniel well, I enjoyed hearing about him through the people that knew him best. At the end of the service, Juliet extended an invitation for Victor to come to her home for the holiday.

I couldn't say I understood the relationship between Victor and Daniel. It seemed nothing like the partnership Juliet had with Amanda. Even so, Victor's pain and sorrow over his loss was palpable.

Even in times of pain and sorrow, life goes on. There were the witches to find and deal with. Juliet informed Gregor, Rei, and Maria what had happened in my vision and asked them to discreetly check into anything odd happening in their territories and report back. Luckily nothing was out of the ordinary in their regions. Everything seemed to be focused here in the Bay Area, specifically the South Bay, which was good, because that meant it wasn't a global event, as it had been back in Salem. However, with the focus here, it meant the situation was even more dangerous, and that didn't have me, or anyone, feeling too good.

I wasn't privy to a lot of the planning as Juliet had been in conference after conference, dealing with all her governors. With the Foundation closed for the holidays, I was left to my own devices. On the plus side, I got to enjoy the house and how it was decorated.

It was so different from what I was used to. In my former life, I was lucky to get a tree set up in my apartment. As for my shopping list, it was small, so I never worried, especially since I did most of it online and never had to actually go to the mall. This year, I didn't have the luxury of online shopping in my underwear in front of the TV. I had to actually head out to the mall, but not Valley Fair. I wanted to steer clear of that place.

"How many malls are here, anyway?" I asked as Kirtus pulled into a parking space.

It was midday on a Wednesday, and I had been promised that this outdoor mall would be less crowded. Judging by all the cars parked, I had a different definition of crowded than the locals. Still, I was glad Kirtus had agreed to come out with me. My plan was to finish my shopping and treat Kirtus to lunch as a thank-you for being there during some rough times for me. Plus, I enjoyed his company.

"More than I care to admit knowing about," Kirtus said.

Even though the witches had been stopped for the moment, I wasn't sure that they wouldn't try anything again, which was also part of why we weren't at Valley Fair. Although it was stupid to believe they would only focus on that mall and not others in the area. I glanced out the car window and my heart skipped a few beats, checking out the Stanford Shopping Center—an outdoor mall near Stanford University. I refused to be held hostage by what-ifs.

Kirtus had promised it would have everything that I needed and then some.

"Thank you for coming and doing this." I got out of the car and slipped on my coat. "It's been a hard time for everyone. I just couldn't sit around and do nothing. It was driving me batty."

"I can only imagine." Kirtus sighed. "I can't believe they got Daniel. He was so much smarter than that." His voice was heavy. "You didn't see anything?"

"No." I shook my head as we walked. "I mean, no one deserves to die or be tortured like he was. I wish there was something I could have done."

"You and me both," Kirtus said.

We fell silent as we walked. People rushed around us with bags and packages. This place had potential to be insanely busy.

"How long had Daniel been working with Victor?" I shrugged my jacket a bit tighter and zipped it up. Maybe an indoor mall would have been a better choice. At least it didn't snow there.

"At least two hundred sixty years, maybe even closer to three hundred." Kirtus stepped to the side, then stopped.

"Wow." I paused. "But he...wow."

"Yep, even longer than Amanda and Juliet." Kirtus's expression softened. "I remember when Juliet found Amanda. Daniel had already been serving Victor for..." He chuckled without merriment. "Well, for a long time."

"I can't even imagine," I whispered. "No wonder it was so devastating for him, for all of you. I wish I had known him better."

"Mind if we don't talk about any of this?" Kirtus's voice trembled. "I realize it's supposed to be healing but..." He shrugged.

"Of course, of course." I looked around at all the stores. "Where do we start?" I forced a smile.

"Who's on your list?"

I pulled out my smartphone and opened up the list. It was quite extensive—well, at least for me. "Let's just say the sooner we get started the better. I don't want to be here all day, especially since I owe you lunch."

"You don't need to do that."

"I know, but I want to. I don't have a lot of friends..." I lowered the zipper of my jacket a bit.

Kirtus nudged my shoulder and smiled. "Come on. Let's get shopping."

The shopping trip went well, and Kirtus had been correct. I managed to find everything I needed. I gave my new credit card a workout, but at least this time, I didn't have to worry about how to pay it off, and that was a great sensation. I still had a couple of additional stops to make shopping-wise, but those I could take care of on my own at the shops in downtown Los Altos.

Lunch was nice. We ate at a bakery called Le Boulanger. The fresh bread smelled amazing, but we settled for salads, which were less than exciting, but we couldn't ask for bottles of red. At least the conversation was pleasant and felt amazingly normal, which was a nice change.

The shopping and lunch gave Kirtus and me time to talk and get to know each other. I found out more about his consulting business and how he walked the line between the Dark and the Light. Even with his protected status, he tried not to upset the Dark. Given that he was out with me, it didn't help matters, but according to him, Victor had assured him that for the time-being he could spend time with me if he chose to do so. I didn't like that Kirtus needed Victor's approval to be seen with me, but I enjoyed the opportunity to spend time with Kirtus, even if we were just going to be friends.

Kirtus brought me home and I found it in the same way I'd left it: empty. Well, I assumed empty, since no one came around to greet me.

An hour later, a tap at my bedroom door interrupted my gift wrapping. "Just a sec." I made sure that everything was put away or out of sight. "All right."

Juliet walked in and saw the wrapped packages. "Someone's been busy."

"I needed to do something." I tidied up the scissors and tape. "With the Foundation closed until the fifth, there wasn't a lot to do. Plus, I didn't want to bother you. You've been busy with other things." Meeting her gaze, I saw an unusual puffiness, and her eyes didn't appear as bright as usual.

"Which is why I'm here." Juliet picked up one of the rolls of Christmas paper and sat on the edge of the bed. "I wanted to know if you would be willing to try to reach out again and see if there is anything more we can learn?" She focused on the red and gold Christmas paper. "We've had no success finding the witches. So you're the best tool we have." She frowned and put down the paper. "I'm sorry."

"Don't be. Anything I can do to help, I'll do it." I started to clear off my bed. "Do you want to do it here or somewhere else?"

"Not right this second, Christopher," She held up a hand. "Prepare yourself. I want to have Victor and Gregor here. I'll have Amanda record the session and..." She glanced up at me. "Would you like me to invite Kirtus?"

I cleared my throat as my cheeks heated up. "Whomever you think would be best."

"Of course. How about in two hours?" At my nod, she added, "Thank you." She walked out of my bedroom.

I had more than enough time to finish my gift wrapping. So once I was done, I decided to go walk around in the backyard to clear my head and try to center myself. I found that being among nature helped. By the time I finished my walk, the sun had set and the temperature was cooling off quickly.

One of the things I noticed about being an immortal was that I felt better, more alive, at night. It was like the sun drained my energy. I was slower and weaker. Juliet explained that was normal and part of reason why immortals gathered mostly in the evening. However, because of the world we live in, we had to adapt to living our lives in the sun, so to speak.

I got back to the house and headed to the main sitting room where everyone was assembled.

"About time," Victor huffed and put down his glass of red. "Perhaps, if you hadn't been out goofing off with Kirtus, we could have done this sooner." He narrowed his eyes on me. "In fact, maybe if you—"

"Victor." Juliet used her polite warning tone. "Chris's abilities seem stronger in the evening. Like many of our talents."

Victor frowned and took a sip of his red.

"Sorry, I needed to clear my head." I tried not to take offense. Victor had been through a lot.

"Are you sure you're up for this?" Gregor rubbed his goatee, his expression filled with concern.

"I'll be fine." I found a seat.

Amanda stood with a camera on a tripod, ready to record. She smiled at me.

Kirtus caught my gaze.

I said, "Long time, no see." I couldn't help the smile on my face. It had been a nice afternoon.

"Indeed."

"Is there anything special you need?" Juliet asked.

I scanned the room and shook my head.

"Then I guess anytime you're ready, Chris."

With my downtime, I'd continued to practice and, as a result, felt more comfortable attempting this. I closed my eyes and forced myself to center. I inhaled softly and focused on the cruel witch, remembering her dark looks and how she laughed as she killed my father and taunted me. Concentrating on her in my vision as she laughed about Daniel and how she left him in the mountains. I pulled up those memories to reach out, but my mind was blank. There was nothing. I needed to reach deeper into my mind and hers.

"This is pointless," Victor grumbled, pulling me back to the room.

"Victor, please," Juliet said.

"He's right," I said, "I'm not getting anything. Sorry." I faced her, shaking my head, then scanned the room and froze.

"Daniel?"

He stood next to Amanda. He looked amazing, young, happy, and smiling. A warm glow accompanied his bright eyes and flawless skin.

"Hello, Chris," he said.

"I don't...but you're..."

"Dead. I know." His smile grew. "I don't mind, well not now anyway, considering I should have been dead a long time ago. I got to witness so many amazing things. I got to see us land a man on the moon and a functioning space station around our planet. Trust me, from when I started my life, that was beyond anything imaginable. I wanted to thank you for locating my body. It was nice to not be left out there to the animals."

"You're welcome." I stood and walked closer to him. I noticed the others were all still not moving. They were there, but not there. It was only Daniel and me talking.

"My time is short, and you need to understand they're plotting again. Chris, they want to bring magic into our world," Daniel glanced around the room. "New Year's. There is something about New Year's, but I don't know what."

"What's so special about the new year?" I questioned.

Daniel nodded. "Victor had me researching the witches from your first vision. The trail led me to Reno, but the clues went cold. There had to be something there, the death of your father maybe, because it wasn't easy for me to find anything. I don't think it's the dark female witch we need to worry about, but I don't know who or what is behind her."

"But she killed—"

He held up a hand. "There is something else—both the death of your father and the death of your mother showed up in my research. There's got to be more there than you realize, but I couldn't uncover anything else before they found me."

"What?"

"Listen, Chris. There is something about your family, something that ties into the witches, but I...I don't know what. I left all the information for Victor in a safe deposit box at the Heritage Bank of Nevada in Reno. He'll remember the name it's under. Also, there are some files in the safe in my office the combination is Left 10-Right 27-Left 70, assuming he hasn't busted into it already. Everything I have will be there. I hope it helps."

So many questions filled my mind, and I wanted to ask them, but a pull in my mind let me know my time was running out. "I'm sorry I couldn't save you."

"How could you?" Daniel asked. "Find them and stop them." He adjusted his bow tie. "I think Victor will really like the gift you bought him for Christmas. I don't know how you managed, but it's perfect. Thank you. I appreciate it. He's not a bad guy. He really isn't. Thank you for seeing that." He winked. "Bye, Chris."

The glow around Daniel got brighter as he started to fade. The yellowish light filled the room, and I had to close my eyes.

When I opened them again, everyone stood watching me. I blinked away tears and raised my hand to my forehead to calm the throbbing. "Did you know he had a safety deposit box up in Nevada?" I asked Victor.

"No, but that would explain why we didn't find anything in his room at the hotel." Victor's voice was shaking.

"Did you get it all?" I asked Amanda.

"I did." She walked over and sat next to me. "You talked right at me, right at the camera, and Daniel's voice came through you loud and clear."

"Amazing," Juliet said.

"Daniel stood next to you right there." I pointed at the camera, then looked at Victor. "I'm really sorry about Daniel. If it's any consolation, he looked good and seemed happy."

"Yes, well, thank you." Victor cleared his throat. "You gave us a few more leads to work with." His voice sounded stronger. "If your family is linked to this, it might explain why they were targeting you the night they attacked Amanda and this home." He gestured for Kirtus to follow and then turned to Juliet. "I'll send Sahin to Reno at once and pull the files from Daniel's safe."

Juliet led Victor to the door. "Please, keep me informed. If this has anything to do with Chris or his family, we need to know. When vetting him, I wasn't able to find much on his family, but then I wasn't looking for anything like this."

"We'll do everything we can." Kirtus gave a firm nod.

"Of course," Victor said. "Thank you, Chris."

Victor and Kirtus left. I slumped back in the chair and rubbed my temples. The pounding in my head softened.

Gregor pulled out his smartphone. It looked so small in his hands. "I'll inform my people. We might be able to duplicate Daniel's research, just in case." He squeezed my shoulder. "We're going to find them and take care of this. Don't you worry, Chris."

Juliet crossed back to me, sat down, and rested her hand on my leg. I felt her energy as peace filled me. "We'll figure this out. I promise you. If there's a link to your family, we're going to find out what it is."

Exhausted, all I was able to do was nod.

"Chris, they will suffer for hurting your family." She inhaled and flicked off her high heels, then tucked her bare feet under her thighs. A soft smile crept over her face. "You bought Victor a Christmas gift. Really?"

"Of course I did. I got you all gifts, including the staff. He's been through a difficult time, so I thought I would show him a kindness, plus he's not that bad—at least when he's not being all dark and ornery."

Juliet patted my leg.

Chapter Twenty-Four

I WANTED TO drop everything, head back home to Reno, and help with the search to find out why and how my family was connected to all this. But I couldn't, no matter how much I wanted it. No one could risk me being found out. It would expose too much and bring up questions that none of the immortals were willing or able to answer.

Sequestered at home, I told my life story over and over again. I wrote it all down, everything about my parents, my grandparents, family friends, past jobs, schools, all of it. I was going to need help with the research, but the help would have to wait for the moment. So, it was just me.

The only part I didn't mind was writing. I got to sit and think about it. At first, the information came out as bullet points with dates, locations, and names. But as I forced myself to remember, I started to paint a picture with details and descriptions, which I found therapeutic.

After a long session in my room, I wandered downstairs. Holiday music filled the first floor, and I was transported back to my youth when my mother would go all out. Even though there were only three of us, Christmas Eve and Christmas Day were big events, and she loved it. Christmas Eve, we would have a fancy dinner and sit around drinking hot chocolate and watching Christmas movies until I fell asleep. In the morning, I would wake up to the wonderful smell of homemade cinnamon rolls. Bypassing the tree and the gifts from Santa, I'd rush to where my parents sat waiting for me in the kitchen.

My dad always wore a big goofy red and white Santa hat and my mom wore an elf hat with pointy ears. They would greet me with big smiles and warm hugs. We would devour breakfast, then open gifts before spending the rest of the morning in our pajamas, playing with toys until it was time to get ready for our early Christmas dinner. How my parents managed to make the holiday so special all on their own was beyond me. It was a magical time.

Smiling at the memories, I walked into the living room.

"Merry Christmas," I said to Juliet and Amanda.

"Merry Christmas." Juliet stood and gave me a hug and a kiss on the cheek.

Amanda hugged me and kissed me as well. "Merry Christmas, Chris."

"The house looks amazing." I gave the grand living room a once-over. A buffet with food and drinks for the non-immortals stood to the side, and across the room, there was another buffet with bottles of red and glasses. A fire burned in the fireplace, and a tree, the largest in the home, was loaded with every manner of decoration, some old, while others new. "Quite the collection." I crossed and took in the ornaments. A clear glass ball with a manger scene put together on the inside. A Santa stuck in a chimney. Several tin angels and crochet snowflakes. The angels and snowflakes looked the oldest and most delicate.

"We all have hobbies." Amanda joined me.

"These are yours?"

She nodded.

"Wow."

"I have a few special ones, but yes, this tree is all Amanda." Juliet poured herself a glass of red. "Would you like something?"

"Sure."

She poured me a glass.

"No staff tonight?"

Juliet handed me my glass.

"Of course not, it's Christmas. I had them leave at noon, and now they have the next few days off to spend with their families and relax." Juliet clinked my glass and winked. "We can all manage just fine for the next couple of days."

"Yeah, Chris, we're not monsters after all." Amanda waggled her eyebrows. "At least I'm not."

Laughter filled the room.

"Whatever I can do, I don't mind," I said. "I still feel funny about having things done for me." I took a sip of my red—it had a nutmeg holiday taste to it. Amazing. It actually brought me back home and I let out a happy sigh.

Amanda grabbed my arm. "That's weird. You don't feel funny. Just a little squishy."

I pulled my arm free and laughed.

"Excellent. You can help with the cleanup," Juliet said with a coy smile as the doorbell rang. "Ah, guests." She put down her drink and headed to the front door.

Amanda leaned close to me. "She loves this time of year. Juliet gives everyone the time off so she can prove how self-sufficient she is. It's charming." Amanda sipped her champagne. "Don't worry. I'll help with the cleanup, so you won't be on your own." She patted my arm.

Juliet reappeared with Gregor, Terrie, and Ben. They were all casually dressed, which was a far cry from how they were dressed for the masquerade and my last Mark. "Terrie, Ben, you, of course, remember Christopher."

"Hi, Chris." Gregor held a Santa-size red velvet bag with a gold tassel rope. On top of his blond head was a Santa hat. He went to the Christmas tree and started pulling out gifts.

"Of course." Terrie reached out a hand. "Sorry we didn't get a chance to chat at your Mark. You remember Ben, right?"

My cheeks grew warm. "How could I forget?" We shook.

Ben cleared his throat. "Ah right, sorry about that. I hope it wasn't too rough for you. Honestly, I enjoyed it, as you remember, I'm sure." He winked and grinned at me. "If it makes it any better, I volunteered. Juliet and Terrie said so many nice things about you beforehand. And you were there for Amanda. That was really classy of you."

"Well, I guess it all worked out in the end," I said. Honestly, I hoped I wouldn't have to go through anything like that again, but considering all that had happened since, I knew it could get much worse. So I counted my blessings.

The doorbell rang again and Juliet excused herself.

"Can I get you something?" I offered. "We have wine and champagne and a whole spread of food. Red?" I led them into the room with the tree and over to the buffet tables.

For a group of immortals and Keepers who had been around for longer than I care to imagine, I couldn't help but be impressed with how much they got into Christmas. Mainly, considering most of them had been around since it started in one form or another. I enjoyed talking with everyone, and Juliet declared that there would be no shop talk tonight. It was a time to get together and share in the joys of the world. Sometimes you needed a break from the real world; all your worries and concerns would still be there waiting for you.

During the merriment, I kept my eye out for Victor. I didn't think he should be alone, so when he finally managed to show up, I was relieved.

Once he was settled in, I made a quick stop by the Christmas tree, then grabbed him a fresh glass of red, and crossed over to him. "Merry Christmas." I handed him the glass.

"*Feliz Navidad.*" He took the glass from me and took a sip.

This would be hard for him. I remembered the first Christmas after my mother died and how alone I felt. I wasn't sure if it was the same thing, but it was as close a comparison as I had.

"I'm really happy you're here." I sipped my own red as I led us over to a more private area where we could talk.

He raised an eyebrow.

"Anyway, I wanted to make sure you got this." I handed him a small red-and-green wrapped box with a gold ribbon and bow.

"Ah yes, the perfect gift that was mentioned in your vision." He accepted the box. "I suppose you want me to open it now?" He put his glass down.

"Actually, I'd like you to open it tomorrow, Christmas Day. In my family, we didn't open gifts until then. I just wanted to make sure you got it before you left, or before I forget."

He lifted his gaze, and there was an honest look of surprise on his face.

"What was said in the vision, I don't know..." I fumbled with my hands. "I really hope you like it. If not, I have the receipt."

Victor smiled at me, and his expression—it was the first time I saw him for how attractive he was. His face was mature and handsome, with hints of gray. This was quite possibly the only time I'd seen him where the creepy factor wasn't there.

"You continue to surprise me," Victor said. "Thank you for your kindness." He examined the gift. "If Daniel says I'll like it, then I have no doubt it will be perfect."

"Well, enjoy the rest of the night." I started to walk off.

"Chris," Victor said.

I turned.

"Did Daniel really seem happy?"

I nodded. "He did. He looked at peace." I grinned. "Young and handsome, too."

"Thank you. I shall always remember him that way."

Victor wasn't an easy person to like, and I felt sure we would continue to bump heads, but for tonight, he was a good guy.

"Kirtus is out on the patio. He doesn't like these types of events but attends when asked," Victor said. "Not everyone treats him as well as Juliet and I. Perhaps you should go out and see how he's doing." Not waiting for me to respond, he walked off with the gift I gave him in his hand.

Taking Victor's cue, I went to the buffet, filled my glass with red, then another for Kirtus. I inhaled, taking in the various scents in the room, but none matched his. I found all the scents overwhelming. With more practice, I hoped I would learn to tell the immortals apart.

The moon danced off the water, along with all the Christmas lights. Holiday music played softly. The scene was peaceful and beautiful. Kirtus stood on the patio overlooking the pool and the pool house. He was wearing dark jeans and a deep green sweater. He looked amazing.

I sighed. "This is where you're hiding."

"Hiding, no," Kirtus said. "Enjoying the view and the night." He turned to face me. "It's hard to believe that there is so much trouble in the world on a night like this. Look around. If people could only appreciate what they have and not try and change things or each other. It's naïve, but why can't we all just get along?"

I didn't have an answer for him. None of it made sense to me. It always bothered me that people couldn't just be at peace with life.

"I don't know." I handed him the glass. "I thought you might need a refresher."

"Thank you." Kirtus took the glass. "Oh, this is different. Nutmeg," he said after taking a sip. "Juliet never ceases to surprise." He leaned against the stone rail. "How are things going inside?"

"Good. Everyone seems to be having a nice time," I said, standing next to him, but not as close I would like. The moonlight cast a white glow around his face. "You don't like these events, do you?"

He shifted on his feet. "They're fine. Everyone is polite enough, and Juliet is always a welcoming host." He glanced over at me. "It's difficult being around people who you know don't really like you and are only being polite. I'll never get used to it."

"You know you shouldn't care what other people think." I took a sip of the red. "I stopped caring what others thought about me a long time ago."

Kirtus raised his eyebrows at me. He didn't seem to buy it.

"Listen, running around and telling people that I'm gay or not isn't the same thing. If people ask, I tell. Otherwise, I don't give a damn. Do you run around telling everyone who you prefer to sleep with? No, it's no one's business."

"You have no idea, do you?" He grinned.

"I don't really think about it." I took a quick sip of my drink. It was a lie and I've never been good at that.

"Liar," Kirtus teased. "I bet you're aching to find out."

He was being a butthead.

"Nope, I already know, just like I know that you have a tiny little mole on your left butt cheek." I waggled my eyebrows. If he was going to be an ass, I was going to be one right back at him.

He furrowed his brow and raised the left corner of his lip.

I probably shouldn't have said it, but the look on his face was priceless. He still had no idea I spied on him in the shower and saw the little mole on his butt, as well as other things.

"How the hell do you... I don't even..." He shook his head.

I laughed. "Serves you right." I glanced out over the pool. "You know what I miss?"

"Nope."

"I miss dancing with Cindy. That is the one big thing I miss. Everything else..." I shrugged.

"So dance. Go out dancing. There are a ton of places here," Kirtus said.

"Oh right, like I'm going to dance on my own." I sighed. "Plus, it wasn't that kind of dancing. Cindy made me take a ballroom dance class with her. We weren't very good, but it was fun and we both got a kick out of it. Over time, we got alright, so we kept it up."

"All right." Kirtus put down his now empty glass on the stone ledge. "Let's dance." He held out his hand.

I rolled my eyes. "Right."

Faster than a heartbeat and with a graceful move, he snatched my hand and spun me around and back into his arms.

"You dance?"

He took the glass from my hand and put it next to his on the stone rail.

"Of course." He pulled me along in time with a Christmas waltz playing in the background. "Hope you don't mind, but I lead," he said, as we moved around the patio. Luckily the music was suitable for this kind of dancing, but being completely honest, it wouldn't have mattered. "You're pretty good." He spun me and my heart raced. Being that close to him was almost too much for my senses to bear.

"Gee, thanks," I said.

We glided in time to the music. He was an amazing dancer and a good leader. I wasn't used to being led. It wasn't something that I'd practiced often, but the class Cindy and I took made us switch up so that we understood how to move with our partner. It sounded cheesy, but I truly got lost in our dancing.

I couldn't be sure if it was destiny or lust, but I enjoyed being held by him and dancing. My body reacted in ways that I hoped he didn't notice. At some point, we stopped dancing, and I found him staring at me. The moonlight made his face glow. I should have taken a step back, but I didn't. I was putty in his arms, and he leaned in and softly kissed me. His sandalwood scent and the way he tasted on my lips felt like home. I pulled back slightly to gaze into his eyes. I was lost staring at him, as he kissed me again, this time deeper.

"We should, I should..." I finally tried to gain some composure.

He pulled away, still staring at me. "I've wanted to do that since the night we first met."

"But you..." I stammered as I tried to put together a sentence. "But the day I came to your house..."

"Was creepy and weird." He smiled. "How would you have reacted if some stranger you just met showed up at your house and did something like that?"

My shoulders dropped. "Fair point."

"Plus, it's nice getting to know you better." He leaned in and kissed me again. "Just don't talk to me about any more visions of us. I don't want to know what is going to happen to us or anything like that. I want this to progress naturally, or as naturally and slowly as possible."

"I'll do my best to keep that promise, but if it's something important..."

"Kirtus, Chris..." Amanda called.

Amanda stood leaned against the door, watching us. We both turned to her, and I realized Kirtus still held me.

"Juliet wants to start the secret Santa exchange." She smiled knowingly before re-entering the house.

"Why do I have a feeling she's been watching us for a while now?" I asked.

"That wouldn't surprise me in the least." Kirtus stepped back. "Shall we?" he asked, and we headed toward the house.

This was quite possibly one of the best Christmases I'd had since I was a little boy running to the kitchen, smelling the homemade cinnamon rolls, and seeing my parents waiting for me.

Chapter Twenty-Five

WITH CHRISTMAS OVER and the New Year right around the corner, everyone went into overdrive. Despite all the resources at the immortals' fingertips, we were no closer to finding the witches or figuring out what they were up to. They remained under the radar and no matter what I tried, I failed to reach them with my second sight. Every time I tried, I got a big fat nothing.

This didn't stop Juliet or the others. They were calling in favors and pulling whatever strings they had, but nothing they did helped. We thought we had a good idea searching out the dark witch, but about the bigger question of how this tied into my family, we had no answer. So, I stayed buried in research.

Juliet introduced me, via video conference, to an immortal in Utah named Gabe. He was blond with crystal blue eyes, very much what you would expect for Utah. Gabe was involved with various genealogy organizations. He helped me examine my family tree and see if there was anything there. The hard part was, I didn't have any living relatives. So, we were going off what I remembered and the photo albums from my former apartment in Reno that Juliet had kept for one of my Christmas presents.

There was the background information that Daniel had on the dark witch. But that trail ended in the late 50s or early 60s. We were searching for links between her and my family, but they remained elusive. All in all, our efforts were slow going, and I feared that by the time we figured it all out, it wouldn't matter.

Not wanting to give up or admit defeat, I cross-checked all the data. Gabe and I did as much as we could. Even if I had an army of assistants, there was only so much material to go through, and Gabe and I had this part of the investigation under control.

I commandeered the dining room for my work and used every square inch of free space. Juliet supplied an extra table, phone, computer, and books. Loads of books. The room was a mess, and it was driving me nutty. I hate having things spread all over the place, but considering the work, I had no choice.

A knock at the door interrupted my reading.

"Yep." I glanced up.

"Having fun?" Kirtus crossed over to the table.

"I thought saving the world, or at least the immortal world, would be more action-packed," I grumbled and put down the book. "I feel like I'm nothing more than a historian, or worse, a librarian." I shuddered.

"Instead, you want to be out there turning over rocks and looking in caves and possibly getting killed?" Kirtus folded his arms over his toned chest. "Trust me, none of this work is glamorous. Movies always make things like this seem much more exciting than they are."

"I suppose." I raked my hands through my hair. "Honestly, Kirtus, I can't find a link to anything. There are too many Alexanders out there. Neither my father nor my mother were into the whole family history thing."

Kirtus glanced at the books as he leaned against the table.

"I don't think it's going to matter," I said. "Whatever's happening is set and no amount of research or digging around is going to make a lick of difference."

Kirtus nodded. "Sahin and a few other Dark have been talking about how they haven't found anything, even with Daniel's research, and they're starting to think that this might be a giant bug hunt."

"Should we worry?" I asked.

"Nah, Victor knows how to handle them. They're just grumbling."

"Can't say I blame 'em." I stood and glanced out the patio window, taking in the view.

I was flustered and so was everyone else. These witches were masters at hiding. I understood there was magic helping them, but from what I'd been told about magic, nothing in this world could hide them. Just thinking about that evil bitch and her minions, out there watching us, really pissed me off. Especially since they were up to something, and the clock was ticking.

I turned to look at Kirtus, but I wasn't in the dining room any longer. I stood in an empty room with a huge domed ceiling. The new place was dark, and there was an eerie green glow and a musty smell.

"What the hell?" I said under my breath.

I knew what was happening and started to make mental notes of everything.

"Duncan, please," a female voice called out. "Please hurry."

I raced in the direction of the voice. I didn't know what this place once had been, but at the moment, it was being used as some kind of meeting place and, from the smell, a holding pen.

"Duncan, here, over here." Her voice led me.

I turned the corner of some temporary wall. The room was huge, and I wondered if the building was some kind of theater.

"Mom?"

She was older and weak. I barely recognized her face, but when she lifted her head and met my eyes, it was her. I rushed over to her. She was held down, chained up like an animal. I looked for a way to free her but saw nothing.

"Sunshine." She smiled at me. "My sunshine." She strained to reach out, but she was held in place. "They know. They know you're searching for them. They've been using their magic to keep you from finding them. They use magic to misdirect you and the others, but using the power to hide has made them weaker than they thought." She frowned. "Still, they can control some of the immortals, not the stronger, older ones, but the weak-minded. You're going to have to be strong. The wards around Juliet's property have kept them from attacking you directly. They've tried several times, but they can't get close, and they don't want to get caught. They're still too weak."

"How is this possible?" I knelt before her, fighting to release her or, at the very least, make her comfortable.

"They're using me," she said. "Like they want to use you, but my blood isn't as strong as yours. They need our blood to bring about the awakening, true magic. They need our blood to complete the spell."

"I don't understand."

"They want to bring in a new age of magic—true magic. That's how they're going to destroy the immortals." She dropped her head but raised it again. "You have to stop them. It has to be you. You have to come here. Juliet and the others won't like it and may stop you, but you have to come. There is no other way."

"How can I fight them?"

My mother licked her lips. "They won't stop with the immortals. They want to rule. They want to take over...the dark..." She coughed and kept coughing.

My mother was coughing up bugs. Only one at first, but then another and another. They were bugs of different kinds; roaches, beetles, slugs. I couldn't help but fall back as she kept coughing. Then she closed her eyes and focused on the bugs until they stopped. "They know you're here. You have to go... Duncan, you have to go right now. Get out of here. Wake yourself up!" She forced the words out as maggots spewed from her mouth.

"Mom!" I was helpless, but I had to do something. I couldn't leave her like this.

"Well, hello there, sonnyboy," the cruel voice mocked.

I turned. "Don't you call me that," I sneered at her. That was my father's name for me, and she had no right to use it and sully that memory.

One by one, I saw others appear from the darkness. "Aren't you a clever boy? And, I thought you were useless. If I'd known then what I know now, things would be much different."

I looked at my mother, and her mouth was a fountain of bugs and pests. "Leave her alone." I made to get to my feet.

"Oh here, let me help you." She waved her hand. I was floating about a foot off the ground and unable to move. "You see, little boy, you think you're safe, that this is only a vision, but you're wrong. We can hurt you."

I struggled, but I was paralyzed.

"I learned we couldn't attack you outright at Juliet's because of the wards, and then because of the security, but I can attack you here. You have no such protection."

With a flick of her hand, I flew across the room and hit a brick wall, and my back cracked. My ribs broke and the air flowed out of my lungs.

"You bring your little friends, we're ready for you." She laughed. "I can't wait to break them."

"We'll stop you." I struggled. "Like before, when Juliet and Sybil stopped you." My body started to heal. Bones snapping back into place, my ribs shifting back to where they belonged. It was a weird and painful sensation.

"Oh, but sonnyboy, I've learned so much. I've had time to reflect and learn. The New Year will begin a whole new world. One where the immortals are gone and the witches take their rightful place as masters of this world."

"Leave my son alone." My mother spat out several centipedes as she spoke.

"Well, aren't you a tough cookie. I can see why Tomas married you." She nodded to two of her companions. They raised their hands and my mother started to convulse and scream.

"Stop!" I yelled, but the dark witch laughed as did the others. "Leave her alone. She's innocent. She hasn't..."

My mother burst apart and all manner of insects crawled and fell from her. Her skin ripped apart as they crawled from her arms and her face, all the while she screamed and the witches laughed. I wanted to kill them. I wanted to rip each of them to shreds.

"Ah, our little sonnyboy is upset," the dark witch said and grinned at me. "See ya soon."

My neck snapped and everything went dark.

How long I was out, I had no clue, but when I opened my eyes, everyone was there; Juliet, Kirtus, Victor, Gregor, Sahin, Amanda, and Terrie. Right next to me, Ben watched me with a smile while rolling up his sleeve. I had the distinct flavor of apples in my mouth.

"They're killing her. We need to stop her!" I sat up and blacked out.

The second time I woke up, only Juliet and Kirtus were with me.

"Don't speak," Juliet said. "You've been unconscious for four days and your body is healing—faster than it should, I might add."

Kirtus kissed my hand and lowered it back to the bed.

"Chris, I don't understand how they did what they did to you, but they almost killed you," Juliet said. "If Kirtus hadn't been there..." There were tears in her eyes, and she quickly brushed them away. "We were lucky he was there."

She reached out and touched his cheek. "Kirtus got me and Amanda when you had your vision. We heard everything that your mother said through you and your description of the location. What they did to you and your mother. I'm sorry."

I shifted around and Juliet put a hand to my mouth. "Not yet. You had a broken back, broken ribs, and a snapped neck, not to mention broken arms and legs." She shook her head. "Chris, by all rights you should be dead. You're going to need to take it slow."

I fought to move. I succeeded, so I forced myself to move a little more, and since I didn't black out, I figured it was time to talk. "We need to find her and go after them. I can't let my mother die, not a second time."

"We have their location based on your description from the vision," Juliet said. "We're pulling together everyone we can, but Chris, over the last couple of days, true magic has begun seeping into our world. We had no idea; we should have known, but we didn't. There have been reports all over the South Bay, cars lifting off the ground on their own, people falling into trances then coming to, random lightning strikes, mysterious dark holes where light is completely void even when light is shined on it." She shook her head. "This all started in San Jose—where they are hiding."

She fussed with my blankets.

"We've had reports as far north as San Bruno and Foster City. The magic hasn't gotten any farther than that, and it's weak, but things are happening and people are scared. No one has any answers, even some of the immortals are scared and leaving the area. The local news, with a lot of help from Terrie, has been keeping this wrapped up, but it's getting out of hand. Social media is on fire with it. We can't hide it for much longer."

"Good. There is no time to waste," I said. "You can't attack them without me. We need to go and we need to go now." I struggled to move, but Kirtus held me down.

"You can't," Kirtus said. "Yes, we understood what your mother said about you being there, but we can't risk it. If they need your blood for the spell, it's too much of a risk." His face was filled with worry and concern. He was scared.

"It's not an option," I said. "New Year is the deadline, and if I've been out of it for four days, we don't have the luxury of time." I glanced between them. "What's the date?"

Juliet and Kirtus looked at each other.

"Please, what day is today?"

"It's New Year's Eve," Kirtus replied.

"That settles it. We need to go now." I pushed Kirtus's hands out of the way and forced myself to stand. I felt ever mending bone in my body. My chest screamed in pain. It was only drowned out by the shrieking in my legs. I wanted to fall back to the bed, but I didn't. This was too important. I took a step and stopped. My body was still healing, but I had no choice. I had to work through the pain. I took another step, and Juliet's hand landed on my shoulder. "We have to go, now." My voice firm and my jaw set.

"If you go outside right now, you'll die," Juliet said. "The sun is high, and your body is too weak."

I glanced around. I wasn't in my bedroom. I was in the basement rooms that we'd used for my final Mark.

"Both Amanda and Ben have been feeding you, but you're still too weak for daylight," Kirtus said.

I didn't like it, but I understood. "Fine, tonight. Once it's dark, we'll go." I made my way to the door. "Everyone's out there waiting?"

Juliet nodded.

"Good, we need to talk." I inhaled and made my way to the door. This was it.

Chapter Twenty-Six

IT DIDN'T MATTER how I felt—tired, sore, battered—at that point; all that mattered was stopping the witches and saving my mother. The image of her wouldn't go away, what they did to her, the bugs...all those damn bugs.

I swatted at my leg, the feeling of bugs crawling up me was too powerful to ignore.

I took one final breath and opened the door to the bedroom. The room was filled with warmth and soft light. There was no outside illumination, which considering the warning I got from Juliet, was a good thing. I checked the room quickly—everyone from earlier was still there.

"We have to stop them and we have to go tonight." I marched over to the small group assembled. If I sat, I wouldn't be able to get up again, so I stood.

"Amazing." Victor watched me.

"Chris, you shouldn't be up." Amanda got up and offered me her seat.

"No, I'm fine." I waved her off.

"You look like shit." Sahin shook his head.

"We're all going to look a lot worse before this is over." I narrowed my eyes at him. We didn't have time for this. We had to work together; we had to work as one.

"You have no idea what we're up against," Victor said.

I saw all their faces. The dark circles under their eyes, the unshaven skin, and the mussed hair.

"Victor, I know exactly what we're up against." I ran a hand through my hair. "The reason why you weren't able to stop them, or even get close to them, was because I wasn't there. I'm the key and the only way through their gate is me. Tonight, I'll be there, and they'll be stopped. No more innocents will be lost." If I had to go alone, I would. Perhaps that would be best even if it would mean my own death, if my vision was any indication. But no, I needed them. We needed each other. My mother said they were overconfident, and I had to believe that. As much as the vision hurt me, maybe that was all they could do. Perhaps, reality would be something different.

I would go prepared. I had to stop the dark woman somehow. Magic or not, she was mortal and she could be killed. I would need to take something. Maybe a gun? No, I wasn't confident enough with guns, but I could take a dagger, maybe the dagger from the Marking ceremonies with Juliet. Assuming I had a chance to get it from Juliet's office or maybe I could attack her with my mind. I didn't know, but I would have to come up with something. And quick.

"Juliet, I don't care how strong he is." Victor's voice pulled me to the conversation. "We should retreat. Leave the area like the Council wants and regroup. Give us time to pool our resources and get more immortals here. I'll contact the other Dark leaders from the Eastern region and the Southern area. There is nothing wrong with a tactical retreat."

"By the time we do that, it'll be too late," Gregor said. "You've seen what's been happening around here. How long do you think we can keep a lid on things?" He rested his hands on the table with the map of the Bay Area. Different zones were marked with various colored circles and then pins in other spots. All of it focused on San Jose. "Chris is right, the first group..."

"The first group didn't even make a dent in them, plus the reports: fireballs, lightning strikes, they tossed cars like they were toys, shadow beasts..." Sahin pointed at the map with a big black circle around it. "These were the reports on TV and online by humans, the ones we couldn't get rid of or cover up. Everyone is terrified. True magic is here, and I don't know how we're going to stop them. They've had time to plan and prepare, we're—"

"I don't care what happened before. It doesn't matter," I said. "I'm going tonight, and I'm going to stop them. They are going to pay for all this." I felt the bones in my chest still stitching back together. "You can worry about the cleanup and how to fix what people saw afterward. It'll be just like Big Foot or UFOs. If we don't stop it tonight, then we're all lost. With you or without you, I'm going."

"Chris," Amanda whispered but didn't meet my gaze.

"You won't be alone." Kirtus stepped up next to me and took my hand. "Someone has to have your back." He gave it a squeeze.

"The Council is wrong, Victor. You know it and I know it," Juliet said. "I'm going tonight. I have to go. Chris is my Called, and I won't let him face this alone."

"He should be dead twice over by now," Gregor said. "You've seen how quickly he's healed."

Victor frowned.

"He nearly ripped off Sahin's arms," Gregor continued. "He almost killed several of us at his second Mark and test. He wasn't even fully immortal yet. He was able to hurt Juliet physically, the bruises on her arm took days to heal. What more proof of his strength and power do you need?"

If all else failed, I could show up and rip her to shreds with my bare hands.

Victor shook his head, then turned to Sahin. "You said he's powerful. You said he had more power than anyone you've ever encountered. Do you still believe that?"

Sahin frowned. "I wish I never met him."

"Sahin..." Victor glared at him.

"Dammit, Victor, we're all going to get killed." Sahin banged his hands on the table. "They can control some of us. I've seen it. You've seen it." He faced me, his stare burning into me like before. "Yes, to answer your question, yes. He's stronger than any immortal I've met, clearly. He's up and walking after that attack, isn't he? You don't need me to tell you that he's different—any one of us would be dead, but here he is." He waved his hands in a grand gesture at me. "He's probably stronger than Juliet or Sybil."

Victor's shoulders stiffened as he stood taller. With a nod, he walked up to me. "I shall be by your side, Christopher. If this is what needs to happen, then so be it."

"You can count on us," Terrie chimed in with a strong nod of her head.

"Can't let you have all the fun." Ben waggled his eyebrows.

"So what's the plan? Go in guns a-blazing?" Amanda asked.

That was the question. I wasn't sure what the plan should be. I only understood that I had to go and I had to stop this.

"That's something we might help with." Sybil strolled over to the table with Garrett next to her.

"We thought, given the circumstances, you might try something, and since the witches can only affect the weaker-minded among us," Garrett said.

"The Council?" Juliet questioned.

"The Council is planning for if we fail," Sybil said. "They've been busy over the last couple of days. They've reached out to the other Dark rulers as well. If we don't stop the witches, they'll be ready." She reached the table and glanced at the map. "They've even reached out to some witches, but..." She shrugged.

There were nods all around the table.

"We should have listened to you at the start," Sybil said to me. "I'm not sure if it would have made a difference, but we would have at least had a head start." She reached out a hand to me. "I'm sorry."

"None of us understood the threat." I took her hand.

"What about the reports of magic?" Gregor asked.

"So far, it's localized to San Jose and the Bay Area," Sybil replied. "There are no reports of anything odd happening outside of the Bay Area. We think it will be spreading out gradually. As you know, we've asked the younger immortals to leave the area."

"Good," Juliet said.

Victor nodded his approval.

"All we can do is hope that, if we stop them, it will stop the magic," Sybil added.

"It will," I said. "We have to kill the dark witch and that will break the spell and seal off our world."

"I hope so, because a world filled with true magic..." Gregor shuddered. "Imagine the destruction and the damage it would cause."

"Enough of this happy horseshit. Let's figure out what we're going to do." Garrett pointed to the map and started to write along the edges of it. "We don't have a lot of time, and if we're it, we have a lot to plan for."

What I found the most amazing about the next couple of hours was how much military experience was in the room. All the men assembled had fought in various major battles around the world. Some experiencing great victory and great defeats, but still they had more experience than I ever would. Victor taught at military schools. Garrett held the rank of general. Kirtus fought in the Revolutionary War. Sybil was a spy during the First and Second World Wars. So, I listened, kept my mouth shut, and offered whatever bits of information I had.

I stayed quiet for another reason—one I didn't talk about. In the end, it would come down to the dark witch and me. One of us would die. I didn't share this with anyone. I didn't want them to try to stop me. Kirtus and Juliet were flanking me the entire time we talked. I didn't know if it was a good plan or a bad plan; I only knew my small part and what I needed to do. I was the map and the key to get in. The rest was, as they say, in the hands of God.

I stretched out my leg and bent it. It was moving much easier now, and it was easier to breathe. I was going to have to feed again because I was still weak.

The group continued to talk and plan. There wasn't anything more for me to do except rest and stay down in the basement until sunset, which was fine with me. I couldn't stand the idea of what lay before us, and what they were all volunteering to do.

Amanda and Ben both came back to the room to allow me to feed off them, and it was helping. I grew stronger, but nothing like normal. I guess the best way to describe it was like having a bad flu or recovering from surgery. I was sore and achy, tired and beat up. All I wanted to do was sleep.

I sat with books spread out in front of me as I went through my family information that still needed cleaning up. I wasn't sure it ever would be, but it was something to keep my mind busy. That was the only part of me that didn't physically hurt. Even emotionally, I hurt, so I welcomed the distraction.

A soft tap on the door pulled me from my books. "Come in." I glanced up as Kirtus walked in.

"I really wish you would let us handle this tonight." Kirtus held up a hand. "I know you have to be there—we all do—but I'm still allowed to wish that."

"It's risky, but it's the only solution we have."

"We've just gotten to know each other," Kirtus said. "There are so many places to see. It would be fun to show them to you."

"Once this is done, you can show me." I smiled up at him.

He crossed over to the bed and sat down. "You're amazing."

"I don't feel amazing right now."

"When I saw your body lift off the floor and I watched you fly against the wall, hitting it hard enough to break it..." His voice shuddered. "Hearing her, hearing her mock you and us and what she did to your mother. Hearing all that through you. It was awful. We were powerless to do anything. Juliet, Amanda, and I, we tried." He shuffled away a couple of the books and scooted closer to me. "There was nothing we could do. When it looked like the attack was over, I held you, then I heard it, I heard the snap of your neck and watched your head drop." There were tears in his eyes. "It was horrible. For all our power and ability, we were powerless to do anything."

"Don't." I reached out and took his arm. "Don't do this. This is what they want. This is what *she* wants. I'm fine. We're going to get that bitch, and I'm going to save my mother."

"I hope so." He wiped at his eyes.

"I know so," I said confidently. "Come here." I pulled him gently into me and hugged him. I kissed his neck and then moved up to his cheek. He was so warm and smelled so good. That earthy scent—sandalwood— it was overpowering and wonderful. My body stirred with desire, and I didn't care; this might be the only time. The first and last time, and I decided that if this was going to be it, then so be it.

I pulled away from him and met his eyes. "Let me love you," I whispered. "Nothing else matters. Whatever's going to happen will happen, so let me love you." I saw the dimple on his cheek as he smiled and leaned in to kiss me, this time with more passion than ever.

When our kiss broke, my heart sank. I needed his closeness. I needed the connection between us. I felt whole when we kissed.

"Are you sure you're up for this? You're still so..." Kirtus started.

I leaned in to kiss him again, allowing him to feel all of me.

His face gleamed with love as he pulled back. "You know, way back when, before the men would go in to battle, it wasn't uncommon for them to engage in a night of passion. In fact, it was encouraged to help keep morale up." Kirtus grinned. "Clearly, you don't need help with keeping anything up at the moment," he teased, his hand massaging my throbbing dick. He leaned to me and kissed me again. We were like an electrical circuit, only complete when we held the other.

My hands ran over Kirtus's covered chest, tugging at the buttons of his shirt and forcing them free. Once his shirt was opened, he leaned back and yanked it off. He quickly helped me remove my T-shirt.

I took in the sight of his broad chest and strong arms. "Beautiful, just like I remember."

Kirtus shifted back. "Do I even want to know?" He smirked.

I shook my head. "It doesn't matter." I reached for his belt buckle and then his zipper. "Here, let me help you with those." I made short work of Kirtus's pants and let them fall. He was flushed with excitement, standing there in nothing but his black briefs that had grown too tight for him.

I wanted to see what was housed inside them, in person this time. I met his beautiful mix-colored gaze, not saying a word. We were both hungry for each other.

It played out in slow motion as Kirtus dragged down his briefs and threw them on the floor.

"Wow!" I said.

He stepped back onto the bed and eagerly kissed my chest. His kisses went lower. I let out a gasp as his touch filled me with warmth and emotions I didn't think were possible. He licked me through my briefs, teasing me with a soft bite that sent a surge of energy through my body. Kirtus glanced up and gave me a coy smile.

All I wanted was our bodies to be together. Being there with him, his scent and the taste of his kisses were all that existed. I could live an eternity with just these.

He continued to work the barrier of my underwear. Every time I would try to lower them, he would push my hands away. He finally took pity on me and removed my briefs, releasing me.

"Very nice." He gently took me into his mouth, working me in and out as he massaged my tight aching testicles. Each nip, stroke, and lick set my body ablaze. I let out soft moans as Kirtus worked his own kind of magic with his mouth.

This level of physical closeness wasn't new to me, but what was new was the emotional connection I felt. I was home. I was where I knew I needed to be. As long as I was with Kirtus, I was safe and loved.

I caught my breath. "I need you to be part of me," I whispered softly.

Kirtus made his way back up to my face and kissed me again.

"Anything for you."

I let out a soft whimper. I couldn't take anymore, and in a graceful movement, Kirtus was lying on his back, facing me with rosy cheeks and a hard cock.

"I guess you're stronger than you look," Kirtus said.

A quick chuckle escaped my lips as I reached back and gently took his member and swollen balls in my hand, giving them a soft squeeze. He groaned and my smile grew.

It was my turn. I deliberately worked my tongue down his neck, but stopped as I heard a gasp to give that spot a little more attention. Then, I moved to his chest. Kirtus wasn't overly developed or toned, but his body was still amazing, with the right amount of hair. I stopped and flicked his nipples, and his dick jerked under me.

"You like that?"

He moaned an affirmative. I teased his nipples but didn't want them to stop me. I was on a mission. So I continued to make my way down. I wanted to work him over, but not get him too close. I didn't want this to end. I wanted our moment together to last as long as possible. It wasn't about the physical desire. My emotions, our emotions needed to connect. We needed to be one, not for release but for our souls. Our souls begged to be joined together, even if for an instant. The physicality was what allowed them to touch.

I took a moment to take in the sight of him, memorizing every detail. When I was finally ready, I worked my mouth down his thick shaft. I made it all the way to the fuzzy base.

He chuckled. "Talented tongue."

I backed off him. "Glad you approve."

Once Kirtus's body was close to exploding, I removed my mouth from his cock and took in his wonderfully tight testicles. I edged him closer to climax, only stopping to give him enough time to calm down. I wasn't in a hurry. It was all about making it last. If this was to be the only time, I wanted it to be something we would remember to our core.

Pausing to calm the yearning of our bodies, I traveled back up to his lips. As we kissed, I changed my position so I could move on top of him. I reached over to the nightstand and pulled out some lotion. It would serve a different purpose now. There was the slightest of pressure against my opening, and with minimal effort, despite how long it had been, I slid Kirtus into me until he was completely seated. I needed to take it slow, not only for my own comfort but to enjoy our emotional bond. We were joined, body and soul. Every feeling I'd ever had for another was gone. It was just the two of us. I was home.

I gently rocked so that I was resting comfortably on him. It only took a moment before our bodies and our heartbeats synced. I was able to meet each one of Kirtus's thrusts but slowed him down when it was needed and tightened around him as desired. He allowed me to work our bodies at my speed and tempo. I was in complete control and enjoyed every second of it. Giving him this pleasure made my heart ache. I didn't want it to end. As we continued our dance of love, I almost completely let Kirtus slid out of me, only to lower myself fully back onto him. A deep aching filled his groans, and his moans finally turned to words, letting me know how close he was. The need grew in him, and I was there with him. With one last thrust, we both released. Feeling our two energies meet and then explode in a physical and mental symphony caused the rest of the world to disappear. It was just Kirtus and me, unlike anything I'd experienced before.

He leaned up and bent lower so that our mouths were one just like our bodies. When we finally broke free and looked at each other, instead of saying anything, Kirtus leaned forward and kissed me. And I knew he was home too.

"I love you," he whispered softly. He was the one. He was who I had been searching for.

He was the reason I had become immortal.

"I love you too."

Chapter Twenty-Seven

THE MOMENT THE sun set, the energy and power rushed back to my body. I still wasn't 100 percent but I wasn't as weak and sick either. I peered out the window once Kirtus and I reached the main level of the house.

"Juliet had every curtain pulled and the doors closed, just in case any light seeped in," Kirtus said. "You have to know how much she cares for you, Chris." He took my arm. "You're her Called, her chosen child, and that is a bond that can never be broken."

"I know." I met his eyes. "I've always known. She's an amazing woman, and I love her, too." I put on what I hoped was a brave face but was still upset about what was coming. Unable to see into future events with my ability, I was worried. I hadn't seen anything since the vision of my mother and the dark witch. I'd tried multiple times, both before and after my dalliances with Kirtus. Still, I understood what I had to do— face her on my own.

I wasn't sure I was ready.

"What?" Kirtus stared at me. There were dark circles under his eyes, and the few wrinkles around his mouth and eyes deepened. "Chris, what aren't you telling me? What don't we know?"

I forced a strong smile. "Nothing. I'm just worried about tonight." It was a lie, but I realized he would try to stop me. They all would. I couldn't let them do that.

He gave me a kiss. "Be careful," he whispered as he stepped back. "Come on. We don't want to keep the others waiting."

If anyone suspected Kirtus and I had been together, no one said anything or even seemed to notice us as we joined them in the sitting room. They were talking and checking their clothes and equipment. It was humorous to see them in jeans and dark-colored shirts, like it would make a difference.

Juliet met us and took my hand. "Please give us a moment," she said to Kirtus.

"Of course." He nodded and crossed over to Victor and the others.

Juliet was dressed like everyone else, in jeans and a plain long-sleeve black shirt, her hair pulled back in a ponytail. Her appearance was more like that of a college student than a 1600-year-old-plus immortal.

She led me out of earshot of the others. "I would prefer you stay here where you'll be safe. I don't want to risk losing you. You're too important to me." She ran her hand down my cheek. "I wish you'd stay, but you won't. I know you won't." She hugged me. "Chris, you're not telling us everything and it's weighing heavily on you."

I met her eyes blankly. I didn't want to lie to her, so I said nothing.

"You don't have to face this alone. You're my family, even more so than Amanda. We're going to be there with you," Juliet said. "We are stronger together. You get that, right?"

"Of course." I took both her hands. "We're all going to be challenged tonight, and I don't know if we're going to make it. It's a responsibility we all have, me above everyone else. I don't know why this happened, but it has to end tonight." I tried to smile. "You look much too young to have a son my age."

"And never forget that, my beautiful boy." A grin spread across her face, and she gave me another hug. "We need to go back to the others and get moving. It's time." She squeezed my hands. "I'm so sorry for all of this."

I HADN'T PAID much attention to the planning, which I regretted now as we arrived at our destination in San Jose. The neighborhood was off a major road, but all of it was empty and dark, like it had been abandoned. The whole area seemed to be cast in a dark fog. If there were any lights on, I didn't see them.

Magic.

"We'll walk in from here." Victor stopped the car. The drive over had been quiet, as had the roads. It was odd for a city with a population over a million to be so dead, especially on New Year's Eve. I didn't ask why, but I had the feeling it had to do with what the witches had been up to. People were scared and either stayed indoors or made plans to be gone.

"They know we're coming." My hands trembled, and I quickly glanced around.

"But they don't know when, or with how many," Juliet said with a firm nod.

"We need as much of a surprise as we can get. Especially now," Kirtus added.

"And they will be surprised." Victor's voice was strong but strained.

Outside the car, extreme blackness surrounded us. Even the streetlights didn't cast much of a glow.

"Magic." Juliet frowned. "This whole area is thick with it."

I nodded. She'd confirmed my thought.

We made our way through the darkness. The veil of fog grew heavier, as we got closer.

"Ah, sonnyboy, 'bout time." The dark voice rang in my head, causing me to stop. "We've been expecting you. Ready to watch your family die?" The cruelty of the words hit me like a slap in the face.

Juliet watched me with big eyes, and I realized she caught it as well. "Try to lock out the voice, Chris." She grabbed my hands and focused on me.

She gave me strength—her strength.

Victor and Kirtus both stopped. No one made a sound as we stood there.

"Focus only on my voice. Keep it from reaching your mind," Juliet demanded, moving her hands to my shoulders, holding me.

I tried to do what she said, but the witch's voice still came through. "She's trying to block me. Such a cute little thing. Too bad you're not interested in her, sonnyboy. I'd tap that in a heartbeat, assuming she had one."

"Get out of my head," I shouted, dropping to my knees, my hands at my ears.

"No, no," Juliet whispered. "Use the voice in your mind. You have to use the voice in your mind."

"Such a disappointment you are," an evil voice said. "Especially letting that monster stick his fat cock up your ass. At least you didn't let that spic do you."

I winced as if hit. This monstrous voice was being disgusting. I tried to push the words out, but he continued his barrage of bile.

"Even though he wants to. Now that would have been humiliating."

I struggled to focus on Juliet, but the voice was stronger. It took all I had to hear Juliet. Finally, in my mind, I screamed out. "Get out of my head! Leave me alone!"

Silence. The voice vanished, and a sense of calm washed over me. Surprised, I realized that I had gone from my knees to lying on my back. I forced myself to sit up. We were still on the street, not far from the cars.

"He's gone." I said, confused. The voice was male, not female? Where is the voice of the dark witch? Who is this new monster I was fighting? Was he a different witch? What was I missing?

"Well, they definitely know we're here now." Victor clicked his tongue. "Oh, and for the record—"

"I doubt now is the time," Kirtus interrupted as he and Juliet helped me up.

Juliet's face was a mix of puzzlement and worry. She spun toward the darkness.

"This is all wrong." Doubt rushed through me like a freight train. "Something here isn't right. The dark witch is messing with me." I was a liability. I really was. How could they allow me to come? "I shouldn't have come."

"That was never an option." Victor frowned, but the frown wasn't for me. It was because of something more. "We need you." He clapped my shoulder. "Come on." He headed off through the growing darkness.

I was glad I didn't know what anyone else was doing, because I realized the witches were using me to figure it out. Even with the dark witch out of my thoughts, there was still a tiny itch in my mind. One I didn't notice before. My relief turned sour. That was how they knew so much about Kirtus and me. She... he...whatever they were hadn't gone, just hidden in my mind. I'd been foolish. I put everyone at risk. I needed to block her, or him. I couldn't allow them to use me anymore.

We reached the exterior of a dome-shaped building. The roof matched that in my vision. "A movie theater. A giant abandoned movie theater," I mumbled.

"No one." Kirtus scanned the surrounding. "There's no one out here."

"They don't need to be," Victor said. "They already know we're here and we're coming right to them. Like lambs to the slaughter." A dark smile spread across his face, and I had a fleeting suspicion that he was up to something. They *all* were, but I had no idea what it was.

We reached the doors, and with uneasy looks all around, we opened the solid double doors and trudged in. I was assaulted by the smell of mildew, piss, and shit. How long had this building been "lived in" by these monsters? The space was exactly like my vision with its domed ceiling and what appeared to be temporary walls. Some seemed more permanent than others, but none of it looked like it was built to last. Was this really where they lived, or was it more of a holding cell for their enemies?

I sensed we were going the right way as we came to an intersection with walkways that led off to either side. I chose to head off to the left. Even with my enhanced sight, the darkness was impenetrable. Some kind of spell or something was keeping the space from having any illumination. We slowed as we ascended a ramp and went through a set of double doors.

I needed to keep my focus and stay calm.

"Where are they?" Kirtus whispered.

It was still dark, but not like the outside. The darkness lifted as we entered the large cavernous space within the theater. White painted markings covered every inch of the floor and the wells. The layout was familiar, just like my vision. I wanted to pick up my pace to find her, but I had already played into what they wanted. The least I could do is try to be smart about this. I would find my mother. I knew I would. So, I made my way to where my mother had been held. I came to a stop right where I knew she should be.

"Where is she?" I yelled.

Even without seeing them, I knew the witches were hiding, waiting like in my vision.

Juliet, Victor, and Kirtus caught up with me, each facing a different direction.

I narrowed my eyes, focusing in on a particularly dark shadow ahead of me. Gradually two eyes emerged.

"Ah, sonnyboy, there you are," a hateful male tone said, and the eyes moved forward, bit by bit revealing his face and body.

Nausea swept up. I couldn't believe this. It wasn't possible. My heart dropped and I wanted to scream. How could this be? How could any of this be true?

"I watched you die. I saw her kill you." The words took all the air with them as they left my body.

He laughed. "Oh, sonnyboy, you saw what I wanted you to see." He beamed. "Just like with your mother. It was simple really, not a complicated spell, but an effective one, just like back in the 1690s."

Two more witches appeared, holding my mother between them.

"Of course," Juliet said. "That's why we couldn't find anything more on your father's death." She stepped forward. "You're the male voice I heard in Chris's head."

"Ah, very good, princess," he said, "and don't for a minute think any of this was easy. That stupid fuck, Daniel, almost found me out. Thank the goddess, I—well, *we* were able to find him and kill him; the little pissant."

My father reached for his own neck as he started to choke and cough.

"Never speak of Daniel in that way, you worthless human shit." Victor held his fingers up. His face had shifted and his true self was revealed. Anger and hatred filled his expression, any trace of his handsome features erased.

"Stop, or the woman dies," a male witch yelled. He was tall with blond hair. He held my mother, and suddenly, fire hovered all around her, not touching them and not burning her—yet.

"Kirtus, if you please," Victor said.

"With pleasure," Kirtus nodded and shifted. He let out a growl. The fire swirled harmlessly in the air, no longer around my mother.

"Witches—so cocky." Victor laughed, smiling even with his vampiric face. "Time for you to pay the piper," he said and returned to crushing my father's neck.

Instead of cries of pain, my father laughed and smirked at Victor. I couldn't believe he actually laughed harder, and with a wave of his hands, he was floating just above the floor. He circled us.

Victor grabbed at his own neck, now the one choking. Victor fell to his knees, trying to pull at the invisible hands.

"Did you really think you could stop me, Victor Rey, the mighty Dark Leader?" my father asked.

Shadows of the man that was my father played out in my mind, him playing Legos with me. My parents playing card games with the neighbors. The three of us putting together the Christmas train that circled our family tree. Him tucking me in at night, checking the closet for monsters.

Now he was the monster.

How could he be torturing my mother and hurting the people I cared about? Where was the happy-go-lucky man with the goofy smile and bright twinkle in his eyes? Where had my father gone? This wasn't him. This wasn't the man who I missed every day since his disappearance. This was Tom. A monster who needed to die.

Tom continued his hovering and circling, addressing not just Victor, but all of us. "Now be a good boy and let the grown-ups talk."

Victor froze in place, no longer able to speak but still chocking.

"Oh, and for your boy toy."

Kirtus became engulfed by the fire he had been controlling. He was unable to move. Every time he tried, the fire would flare up and burn him.

"No! Please," I called out.

"Shhh," Tom hushed. "Now where were we?" He circled us like a vulture until he finally stopped in front of me.

He landed and strolled over. I couldn't believe how much we resembled each other; the only differences were that he was older, a little heavier, and now he had a shaved head with some kind of rune tattoo on the side of his face.

"Why?" I asked.

"Why?" he repeated, the cruelness in his glare blazing at me. He enjoyed mocking me and I hated him for it. Whatever plans I had for him were gone. I was a fool for thinking I could have done anything to stop this. I led us all to our deaths. "Why?" He rubbed his chin. "Duncan—can I call you Duncan? Or do you prefer Chris now? Or is it Christopher?" He stuffed his hands deep into his pockets as if he didn't have a care in the world. "Anyway, Duncan, they killed her. Well, they thought they killed her." He glanced at Juliet. "Didn't you, Juliet?"

Juliet's gaze was locked onto him. She hadn't shifted like Kirtus or Victor and seemed surprisingly calm. "You're her prodigy."

Why hadn't she shifted and attacked him yet? She could easily kill him. I knew she could. But, just like the tickle in the back of my mind, something was off here. A wave of calm washed over me and the anger drained from my mind. I was left with only pain and betrayal. This was my father. The man who raised me. How could he be doing this?

"Bingo!" He pulled his hands out of his pockets and clapped. "Of course, I didn't learn any of this until I was a teenager. That's when my parents, your grandparents"—he pointed to me—"hid us. Moving us around, never really staying in one place too long." He shrugged. "Just like my father's parents had hid them, all the way back to her."

"This doesn't make any sense," I whispered.

"Hush, Duncan," Tom raised a finger to his lips.

I flinched at my old name. It burned my ears like poison.

Tom turned back to Juliet. "We thought we were the only true witches, and we knew about you and the immortals and what you had tried to do her—to all witches." He moved closer to us. "Over the years, my family kept tabs on you and Sybil, watching and waiting. When I was of age, my parents needed me to marry a witch so that our offspring would be strong. Sadly, you saw to that, Juliet." He stopped and pointed to Juliet. "There weren't many of us left, so I had to search a long time. Low and behold, I found Meredith. She was only a quarter witch, of course, and sadly had no idea of her nature, but beggars can't be choosers. Anyway"—he shrugged—"I made her fall in love with me."

"How?" I wanted to fight him. To hurt him. I tried to move my arms, but they were more like concrete weights. All I could do was move how I was held.

"With my charm and pleasant personality. Sadly, I couldn't use true magic. It doesn't work like that. Anyway, bingo-bango." He clapped his hands. "We were married and soon enough she was pregnant with you." He walked over and tousled my hair like when I was a child. I jerked my head and started to shift as I glared at him.

He frowned. "Now, now, sonnyboy." He didn't seem the least bit afraid or worried as he continued, "Anyway, the baby was a boy." He glared at Kirtus who was still trying to get through the fire. Tom scowled and continued, "When I checked my baby Duncan for magic, there was nothing. You were a big fat zero." He stopped and made a zero with both hands.

"I hate you," I hissed. That wasn't true. I hated who he'd become. I hated this thing in front of me, this monster who took my father.

"Maybe so." He shrugged. "Anyway, at that point, I had to do things on my own, especially since your mother couldn't have any more children. So I made do, which was fine, but still, it would have been so much better if I had my boy with me, even though..." He walked closer to my mother. "Did you know he actually lets men fuck him?" He glanced over his shoulder to scowl at me.

My poor mother. Her hair was in tangles and her face and clothes were filthy. It was obvious she'd suffered terribly.

He reached out to touch my mother's face. "How can we have grandchildren with magic if he does—"

"Don't touch her," I yelled. I was fully transformed and moving toward him.

Tom held up a hand.

I couldn't walk and I was transitioning back to my human self.

"So, because I thought you were born without magic, I had to fake my death and make sure no one dug too deep into it. Of course, your mother was devastated. You—well, you were too young and didn't really fit into my plans anymore, so I vanished and went to work. There was a lot to do, and I was doing this all on my own. I was tired of hiding and kowtowing to the likes of them." He pointed at Kirtus, Victor, and Juliet.

As he moved around the space, more of his coven appeared, forming a circle around us. They stood watching him. Attention never leaving him, some of them actually bowed their heads as he got close. Like a cult, they worshiped him.

The power in the space became oppressive and heavy with magic. I could feel it on my shoulders, pushing me down, and even on my chest, making it harder to breathe. The more he talked, the more their power built up and mine seemed to vanish.

"You're an arrogant prick," I said.

"Perhaps, but I'm the one in charge, and I'm afraid the rest of your merry band of misfits, well..." He nodded.

More of his coven entered. They carried limp bodies into the circle. "Make sure they can't get free," he commanded.

Suddenly, both Juliet and I were held by some new force. The energy didn't feel like my father, but some other members of his coven. Knowing the difference should have surprised me, but I was so numb that I just accepted it as a fact.

"But how?" Juliet struggled forward, glancing at the bodies the witches dropped off.

"It was a trap," Sybil said through bloodied lips. They dragged her over and dropped her on the floor in front of Juliet. She looked like she had been run over by a truck. I don't know what they had done to her, but she was weak and broken. On the cusp of death. "We failed. They're keeping us from healing. They have true magic. We're too late."

"Neat trick, right?" Tom puffed up his chest, smiling at the dark faces around him. "What did I tell you all? Vampires are so stupidly confident they don't think anything can touch them." He thumped his chest. "Wrong-oh. We can and we did."

There were cheers and laughs from his crowd.

He waved his hands to silence the group. "Anyway, it wasn't just Duncan's mind I probed." He faced Juliet. "He has a link to you, and of course, you never thought I would reach out to *your* mind. So, because of the link you share, it was a hop, skip, and jump." He crossed to her and ran a hand over her face.

Juliet crumpled to the floor. "No." Her voice sounded defeated and shaky.

This wasn't her. She wasn't some weak child. She was a powerful immortal. This couldn't be happening to her. Hearing her trembling voice and witnessing her in such a state was painful.

"What are you going to do?" Juliet asked through tears.

The shattered bodies of Terrie, Gregor, Garrett, Sahin, and the others they had managed to muster all lay about the floor.

Tom grinned from ear to ear, so arrogant, so full of himself.

"Well, for starters, I'm going to finish the spell that my oh-so-great-grandmother tried to complete back in Salem in the 1690s. Then we're going to kill all of you, including my useless son."

"He's your *son*," Juliet begged. "Your blood. How could you? And what about your wife? Let them go. Your fight's with us. They're innocent." She was trying to grasp for anything to bargain with, but she had nothing.

"Innocent...ha! Anyway, princess—" He stopped for a moment. "You know, maybe I'll keep you around and give you a good fuck or two, in front of that half-man son of mine. Show him how it's done...before I kill you." He grabbed his crotch, then looked at me. "I bet you'd enjoy watching me fuck her."

There were more laughs and chuckles from all around us. His coven was enjoying this. The more he talked, the more of them stepped out of the darkness, surrounding us in greater number.

I wrestled with the invisible force holding me.

"Ah, now, where was I? Right, in order for the spell to work, they both have to die. I've been using my wife's magic to amplify my own and that of my coven. Now that she's brought Duncan here, I have no use for her." He walked to her, lifted her face, and gave her a kiss. "Sorry, love."

"Don't you touch her!" I fought the magic that held me, but it didn't seem like I was using all my strength. Something held me back. I was furious with him and I wanted to kill him, but somehow I didn't have it in me. My body was drained, like I had no energy. So, I just stood there, wanting to listen to my father talk. I hadn't experienced this since I first moved there when Juliet explained the whole immortal thing to me.

"Oh sonnyboy." He dropped my mother's face. "Now, as for good old Duncan, my sonnyboy, his blood is special, but you figured that out already." He glanced at Juliet. "By the time I found out he did, in fact, have magic flowing through his veins—not just any magic but ancient magic, the magic of our ancestors—Juliet Marked him. That's why we tried to get him."

Tom inhaled, shaking his head. "See, I could have reversed the first Mark and trained him to his full potential. I could have even worked with the whole gay thing, but then you kept him nice and secure within the wards of your property. And to top things off, you quickly Marked him again, which made the process irreversible. You and that stupid Council of Light, you really fucked things up for me." He scowled and stalked over to her. "Which flat-out pissed me off."

He slapped her hard enough across the face that it echoed off the walls and the ceiling. "You Marked my only child, who would have been one of the most powerful witches in history." He took a breath and seemed to calm down. "I accepted it and moved on. The trick these days is being flexible and willing to change your plans, improvise. So I am, and I did."

"You need his blood for the spell so you can do...what?" Juliet asked. The disbelief showed in every corner of her face.

"Oh come on. It's not rocket science." Tom kneeled down next to her. "To get his power, of course. Kill him, get his power, and release true magic on the world." He raised his hand, and Juliet lifted off the ground as he stood up. There were laughs and cheers from his coven. "I know all about what you and your group planned. I even know about the Council of Light and how they're building an army. But it's too late."

"I'm going to kill you," I yelled. My face transformed to my true nature, my power building. I could feel it all coming back to me. A trickle at first, but gradually it was building. Something had changed in the room, and I wasn't sure what.

"Of course you are." He lifted me off the ground. His witch lackeys took a step back. I tried to struggle, still unable to break free. "Oh, the power," he said in awe.

He motioned with his hands as he spoke, but it wasn't English, or any English I recognized. He was casting his spell. The witches holding my mother brought her over to him, and he reached out to her. The energy left her body just like I had seen in my vision of my father's death. He was draining her.

"I think we've heard enough," Juliet said, glancing down at him. She smiled, and her face transformed. The ridges, fangs, and the powerful forehead appeared. Her smile turned; she was angry. It made the whole room ripple.

My father glanced around, his eyes narrowing as expression filled with confusion.

"Now," Juliet shouted. The room exploded into chaos.

Victor and Kirtus burst into action, freed from whatever bonds held them. The others, who appeared to be dead or severely injured, roared to life with movements faster than even my enhanced vision processed. A massive melee erupted all around us. The immortals had completely taken them all by surprise. The only ones not able to join the fight were me and my mother. I fought the force holding me, but my father's power was too much for me to overcome, even with all my strength returned.

Fireballs and lightning filled the dome. The bodies of the two witches who held Sybil ripped in half and crumpled to the floor in a pile of blood and gore.

Victor held one a witch's head. "Like lambs to the slaughter." He winked at me.

They had planned this.

Sybil grabbed Victor and lifted off into the air.

She flew.

In awe and complete disbelief, I wanted to cheer. Sybil and Victor were flying low. Every time I thought they were going to hit the ceiling or wall they gracefully dove in an opposite direction, avoiding any attack the witches could throw at them. Sybil held Victor as she moved, allowing him to grab and shred any of Tom's coven that unfortunately got in their way.

They truly had understood the link between me and my mother and father. They used me to feed them false information. It also explained why I felt so meek and calm, just like when I first came to Juliet. Juliet used her ability on me and probably on the whole room, making my father want to tell his story, to act like he had already won. Terrie must have used her ability of mind control to create the illusion of them being defeated.

"No!" Tom shouted.

The bastard was stuck. He had my mother and me, so his proverbial hands were full. He had a choice to make—complete his spell or help his coven. He was pissed, and I laughed.

"What happened? You can't do everything you want!" I mocked. "Have to make some tough choices there, Dad?" I battled to get free. "Hope it's all worth it?"

He dropped my mother and focused on me. "It doesn't matter; they're too late, sonnyboy."

Everyone was busy with the other witches, but I was stuck. On my own, just as I had foreseen.

"I wish things worked out differently." He shrugged, turning his back on my mother. She lay in a crumpled mass. Whatever energy she had left, he had drained from her. "Ah well."

I sensed the blood in my body, every bit of it. Something was happening to it. My fingers started to tingle, and I glanced down. The blood started to flow out from them, heading toward him. As it flowed to him, it transformed into some kind of purplish energy beam, just like with my mother. I struggled harder, but there was nothing to do. The pain of my blood leaving my body grew.

"Chris!" Juliet shouted.

Kirtus and the witch he was fighting stopped. Kirtus created a crack in the earth behind the witch and then pushed her into it. He closed the ground when she was halfway, crushing the woman in a geyser of blood. He started toward me, but another witch caught him and they fell to the ground.

More witches regrouped and blocked the immortals, who were coming to my aid. They were literally sacrificing themselves for my father, to complete the spell. My mother, my father, and I were all cut off from the others. Sybil and Victor, who I'd last seen flying around as an attack force, couldn't get to us. The witches continued to attack them with ball lightning.

"Chris!" Juliet shouted again, her voice reverberating through the space.

Everyone stopped and watched what was happening.

"You lose, Juliet!" my father gloated as the purple strands of energy continued to feed into him.

The energy was gradually replaced by pain.

"All this power... there will be no stopping me," Tom shouted.

"Don't worry about me!" I shouted. "Stop them! Stop HIM!" My voice grew weak, and my body was almost empty of blood. I can't describe the pain of having your blood drained from your body with nothing else replenishing it. My arms and hands grew heavy and my normal pinkish pale skin was turning a ghostly white.

Juliet closed her eyes. I barely understood her. "Now. You need to act now, please. He's my blood and he's your son. I know you love him. We both do. Please."

"Tomas!" A woman called out over the explosions and fighting.

It was my mother. "Leave my son alone," she yelled as she stood.

She lifted her hands, twisted them to the side, and pointed them right at him. A burst of energy left her fingers and shot my father square in the chest. Whatever power she used broke the spell, and he flew back into the wall, accompanied by a sickeningly wet crushing sound.

The second that noise reached me, I dropped to the ground with a heavy thud.

"You won't hurt him anymore," my mother commanded.

There was another bright flash of light.

I wish I'd seen what else was happening around me, but my sight was limited to what occurred in my immediate area. My body was dying. The life was leaving me. My hands continued to bleed, and my blood was still turning to some kind of purple energy, steadily vanishing into the air. There was nowhere for the energy to go and no one to stop it from leaving me. Finally, the blood stopped flowing.

There were a few more loud bangs and yelling, but for the most part, the battle was over. I tried to peek around, but my body wasn't responding. My heart beat and Juliet was there next to me, holding my head in her hands.

"Did you stop him?" I asked.

"He's dead." She ran a hand through my hair. "We stopped him, but Chris. Oh, Chris, I'm so sorry. I failed to keep you safe. I'm sorry, oh my boy, I'm so sorry." Her hands wrapped around me. "Don't move. We're going to get you help."

I knew that expression. She was lying to me, but this time I was okay with it. I was fine. I got to find out what happened to my mother and my father. It wasn't the answer I wanted, but at least, I had the truth.

"As long as we stopped him, that's all that matters." I coughed. "I can go knowing that you're all safe and will continue to be so."

"Kirtus, you better get over here," Juliet called out over her shoulder. Before I blinked, he kneeled next to me, along with Victor and Sybil.

"You're going to be fine. Sybil will take you and get you out of here, get you help." Kirtus forced a smile. "We'll get you home and you'll heal. It'll be fine. There are so many places I want to take you. There is a big world out there for you to explore, and I want to show it to you. So, you better just buck up and um...buck up and..." The façade broke and tears started to fall from his eyes as he grew silent.

Victor looked at me, and every time he tried to speak, he stopped.

That was when I understood the story of my life was over and how bad my condition was.

"Be good to each other. Keep the peace." I started to close my eyes.

"Don't you dare close your..." Kirtus yelled.

Chapter Twenty-Eight

"DUNCAN," A WOMAN said softly.

I smiled. It was my mother. Her familiar voice filled me with joy. I opened my eyes, and I stood surrounded by carnage. It had been quite a battle. Everyone was kneeling or standing around a body. It wasn't the witches. They were all dead from what I could feel and see.

"Ah, my baby boy, you are now and always will be my sunshine." I turned and my mother watched me. Her hair had no gray and her skin had no wrinkles. My mother was young and looked like she did before she got sick.

She crossed over and hugged me.

"Is he dead?" I asked.

She held me tight. "Yes, he's dead. He can't hurt either of us anymore. I thought he was such a good man; kind and wonderful. He treated us both so well, and I loved him so much."

There was so much regret in her voice.

"He tricked me," I said. "Manipulated me with false images. How could he do that to me? To us? For power? I was supposed to save you. I was supposed to free you."

Considering all I had been through, there was no pain, and I wasn't angry or unhappy. Pure peace engulfed me.

"You did." She stepped back. "He's kept me in a state of limbo for years. Not only did he fake his death but he faked mine as well. All that time, I thought it was cancer, but it was him and his coven, they were experimenting on me and my blood, trying to recreate that spell from the 1690s." She frowned. "It doesn't matter. We're both free now."

"Why didn't you tell me?"

"I wanted to," she said. "But his control of me was too strong, I was barely able to reach you, and even that required the help from Juliet."

I glanced over at the group around the body. It was those I had come to know and grown close to, even loved. "Is everyone alright?"

My mother nodded, then looked at them. "For the most part, none of the immortals died, a couple of them are hurt—Sahin, Garrett, and Terrie—but they're being taken care of." She rested a hand on my shoulder. "They all worked together, and that is something that hasn't happened in a very long time. That's all because of you." She stopped. "Well, and him." She nodded to Kirtus and her smile grew.

"He's special, isn't he?"

"Their plan worked perfectly." My mother ignored my question. "They understood your father would focus on you. After the mental attack on you, Juliet figured out that he was linked to you, so while you were recovering, they came up with their plan. When you came to, they told you what they wanted him to know." She chuckled. "Of course what they weren't counting on was you having your own agenda, but they sorted it out."

"But I didn't do anything. Everything I thought was wrong, and everything I was told was a lie, even what Juliet and the others told was just to mislead Dad. I failed."

"You didn't fail. I have to give them credit, especially Juliet. She figured out how to use our bond, and she helped me free myself from your father's grip. She's so powerful, just like you." She waved a hand in front of her, causing the room to grow lighter, "Anyway, it enabled me to stop him. He was so focused on you, getting your power, and completing his spell that I was nothing to him." She sighed. "They played him perfectly."

I frowned.

"Don't be upset with them. They had no choice in using you the way they did. If they hadn't, then your father would have won."

The body on the ground was me. I was the one they all circled. I was dead. The room appeared different now—yes, the signs of battle were all around, but it didn't seem as oppressive as it had before.

"What about the other witches, his coven?" I asked.

"Mostly dead, but some managed to get out. The immortals will search for them, but I doubt they'll find them all. They've become very adept at hiding themselves. And there are other witches out there, but none that are as powerful or as troublesome as your father. Some of them actually want peace with the immortals." She grinned. "Well, as far as I know."

"Are they the ones the Council has reached out to?"

She nodded, took my hand, and led me closer to the group, my new family.

"Are you ready to go back?"

I squeezed her hand tighter. "No, I want to go with you."

"Sunshine, we have different paths." She ran a soft hand over my cheek. "I have to close the window between this world and the world where true magic hides." She left me, crossed over, and touched Kirtus's shoulder, then kissed the top of his head.

He jerked up and looked around, feeling his head. There was no sound, but he said something. The others glanced around the battle zone.

"You have people to return to. They need and love you. There is so much you have to live for."

I stared down at Kirtus. "Tell me it's okay. Tell me you're happy for me." I needed her. I wanted her approval. It would be so much easier if I heard her say it.

"You already know I approve. I was there, remember, at the mall. In your vision, your father wasn't as clever as he thought he was."

"That was you. I remember now. You were the older woman, the one that I thought I recognized somehow but couldn't place. Of course, that was you. You hummed the song."

She touched my cheek again. "Sunshine, I'm so proud of the man you've become. I'm sorry I wasn't there for you after your father left. It forced you to grow up much too quickly. I know it wasn't easy for you, and I'm sorry I did that to you." She inhaled and somehow she grew even brighter and lovelier than before. "It's time, Sunshine."

She hugged me and kissed my cheek, then took a step back. Light, emitting warmth and love, filled her. Her body became brighter and brighter, but I didn't take my eyes off her.

Finally, when she became too bright, I blinked.

When I opened my eyes, everyone was around me. Pain rushed in where there had only been pure light. "Oh, god, I hurt."

The smell of burned flesh and blood filled my senses. There were flashes of fire still to be put out, and off to one side, part of a temporary wall crashed down. I was back in my body, and I felt like shit.

"I told you," Kirtus forced out through tears.

"How?" Sybil shook her head, wiping the sweat and the dirt from her face. "He was dead. It's not possible."

"I don't know." Juliet peered at me, eyes wide, then turned up to the others. "This is the second time he's cheated death. It must be the magic that flows through him, the magic Tom was after."

"It was his mother," Kirtus said. "She touched my soul. She did this; she had to. I sensed her and Chris around us. I swear she kissed my head. It was her. It had to be."

"Let's get him out of here," Victor said. "We can sort out the how and why later." He pulled out his phone and placed a call. His voice started out hard and strong, but it cracked and wobbled as he spoke. He needed to be in control of something that no one had control over, but he was determined to try.

"We'll stay and make sure everything is taken care of, Juliet. Get him home and take Kirtus with you," Gregor said.

I hardly saw Gregor, but his voice was easy to make out. I felt Kirtus's arms wrap around me and pick me up. Every part of my body screamed in pain. I tried to force it from my mind, so I focused on Kirtus and Juliet as they took me out of this cursed place. A flicker of bluish purple light caught my eye.

"She did it," I said, knowing she would be at peace.

Chapter Twenty-Nine

WITH MY FATHER'S plan halted and his coven taken care of, I was back at home and able to rest. Because I lost so much magic, was completely drained of blood, and had died, my recovery was long and miserable. Sure, I got caught up on my favorite TV shows, but if I'm going to be honest, it was a lot of time resting and being bored down in the basement. But I was alive and that was a good thing.

Finally, by mid-January, I was feeling like myself again, and not worried about sunlight, I showered and dressed. I made my way up to the main level of the house, which had all the shades drawn and every drape closed again. I smiled and crossed to the nearest window. Pulling open the heavy cotton drapes and shades, I saw the rain. It was a gloomy day covered in clouds. According to the weather reports, we needed the rain, but I missed the sun and I would've loved nothing more than standing there being bathed in the warm sunlight.

"Chris." Amanda walked over to me and closed the drapes. She had returned to her perfect hair and nails that matched her lavender skirt suit. Her appearance reminded me of the first night we met. I even got a whiff of her clean floral perfume.

"Amanda, I'm fine." I folded my arms over my chest. "It's overcast and rainy."

"Maybe so, but let's not take any chances." She smiled at me. "I'm glad you're better."

"Thanks to you and the others." I'd needed a lot of blood, and if it hadn't been for Ben, Amanda, the house staff, and several others rotating in and out, I would've been dead. I glanced around the entry hall and listened, not hearing anything. "Where is everyone, or do I want to know?"

"Juliet's been at the Foundation since you've been home lounging around watching TV," she teased. "Or, were you just curious about Kirtus?"

"Har-har." I pursed my lips.

Amanda chuckled and patted my hand.

"It seems so quiet. Even the Christmas decorations are down. It's all so empty and plain."

"Well, considering what everyone has been through, I'll take plain and ordinary."

"Do you like it?" I asked, "Being Juliet's Keeper, I mean."

Amanda shifted her stance. Her smile changed and her face grew thoughtful. "It's given me opportunities that I would have never had. I've been able to see our world grow and change in ways I never thought possible—"

"But, you've almost died several times."

"We're all going to die, Chris, I just get to live longer than most." She took my hands. "This isn't about me. This is about Cindy. You're thinking that, if she becomes your Keeper, she may die in some awful way."

I nodded.

"That is a risk for everyone, not just Keepers." Amanda's cell rang. "Sorry, Chris, duty calls." She walked off.

It was a lot to think about. Did I want to bring Cindy into this world? Hadn't she already been introduced to it? Still, it would be the only way I'd get to have her in my life. I shook my head.

I understood how big the house was and that things wouldn't be like they were, but somehow, I had gotten used to all the excitement of the last several months. For it all to be back to normal was going to be an adjustment. The house even smelled ordinary again; roses and vanilla filled the air. I made my way to the dining room that had been converted into my temporary study, and put it back to its typical splendor. With nothing more to do, I decided to move myself back up to my room.

I spent the rest of the afternoon getting myself settled there again. I even managed to work on my family history for a few hours, writing down the information my father inadvertently gave me, keeping it all sorted in case it was ever needed again. His revelations cleared up a lot of missing details, so that was good. I understood why Juliet kept her journals; history, our history, was important. Maybe not today, but in time, who knew what might be needed? So, I worked with Gabe on that, making sure it was all on the computer, making it easy to cross-check and reference.

It was odd knowing that I had witch blood flowing through my veins, what I speculated was that the witch ancestry was what made me a seer. There was no way to prove that, but maybe with research and knowing what to look for, I could learn more.

A tap came from the door, and I saved the file I was working on. "Yes."

"Amanda called and said you were out of the basement." Kirtus walked to my desk and gave me a kiss on the lips. "I would've been here sooner, but my business can't run itself. Plus, it's mid-January and things are picking up."

"No prob," I said. "I've been getting all my family information onto the computer. I just finished a video chat with Gabe. I'd love to go out to Salt Lake and meet him. Anyway, I figured, you never know when we might need it again." I adjusted my neck, welcoming the few pops.

"I thought if you were better, we could go out tonight. I know this great place on the coast. They cater to both humans and immortals. They've done some interesting things with blood. They have this *special* Manhattan clam chowder. It's different."

It was good to see him smiling and not worried—even his red hair had more lift to it.

"That might be nice." I shut down my computer. "I don't want to be stuck in the house anymore. It's amazing, but it's getting old."

Another knock at the door surprised us both. "Come in," I said.

Juliet glided over. As with Amanda, she was back to her perfectly outfitted self—ivory-colored slacks and an emerald-green top.

"How are you?" she asked, then hugged Kirtus. "Hello, Kirtus." She gave him a peck on the cheek.

"I'm better. I got tired of being in the basement, so I moved myself back up here. I hope that's alright?" Even though she appeared better, she still had a bit of worry to her.

"Excellent," she said. "Do you mind coming downstairs? Victor and Gregor are here, and we need to chat."

"Of course." I got up, reached for my suit jacket, and slipped it on.

What can I say? I've found I've turned into a suit man.

The three of us made our way to Juliet's office. Neither Victor nor Gregor seemed happy, and I didn't get why. As far as I understood, everything was back to normal. "Hello."

"Kirtus, please wait outside," Victor said.

Kirtus stared at me, then nodded to Victor. He closed the office door as he left.

"What's wrong?" I asked.

Victor stood at the fireplace, holding a glass of red, and Gregor sat on the sofa, facing me. He rubbed his tightly trimmed blond goatee.

Juliet poured herself a glass of red and brought me one, which I was happy to take. She took a seat in front of her desk, frowning. "Well?" She sipped her drink.

Victor cleared his throat. "There have been reports. Reports of things happening that shouldn't be, considering we supposedly closed the rift. Chris, is it possible that we weren't able to completely stop your father? Is it possible he was partially successful?"

Gregor played with the glass in his hands. "Juliet, I've seen true magic in San Francisco. Not a lot and nothing like what saw here in San Jose, but it's there. Some of us have sensed it."

"And I've seen it here as well," Victor said. "As Gregor said, nothing like before Tom was killed, but still, it's here. We've been able to keep it quiet for now."

I was glad they were working together and not at each other's throats, but I wasn't happy about the reason for their united front.

"Why is this the first I'm hearing of it?" Her frown deepened.

"We wanted to be sure before we brought it to you," Victor replied. "I received confirmation from my people today; without a Keeper, these matters take time." He shook his head. "Chris?" he asked with a hint of a raised eyebrow.

"No." I shook my head. "He's dead and his spell failed. My being alive proves that. I know there are other witches out there, but they are nothing like my father. They shouldn't be able to cause any trouble. My mother sacrificed herself to close the window between our world and the world of magic."

"But, Chris, you were dead. For a short time, you were dead. Is it possible that during that time, some true magic seeped into this world?" Gregor leaned toward me as he spoke.

I nursed my drink. "Honestly, I...I'm not sure." I tried to get my head around the conversation. "So, if some magic seeped out, then what do we need to do to stop it?"

"There is nothing we *can* do," Juliet replied. "There has always been a certain amount of magic in the world, but never true magic, which we didn't know existed until the 1690s. So, if true magic has come to this world, even in a small amount, then we'll find a way to deal with it." She fidgeted with her glass of red.

"I probably should've asked this before, but what is the difference between magic and true magic?" Until this point, I didn't think there was a difference, but now that I had my wits about me, I wanted to know.

"Magic can be learned," Gregor replied. "It's simple tricks, charms, wards, things like that." He pulled a quarter out of nowhere to emphasize his point. "But in order for it to work, the persons involved have to believe in it. It's all simple, nothing powerful or dangerous." He adjusted the pillow on the sofa so he could easily address all of us. "Then there are people who are born with magic, like your parents and you. Unlike learned magic, people who are born with magic can do a lot, and it's not so limited. These people can be psychics, sensitives, witches, people like that, but then, even most of them aren't powerful." He leaned forward. "However, true magic, the real stuff, well, that's a combination of everything, and it's powerful. Your father was able to tap into it, thanks to your ancestors, your mother, and the ancestral magic that flows through you."

I nodded.

"We saw the trouble and pain he was able to cause," Gregor said. "Witches try all their lives to tap into true magic, but to bring it here... We thought it was impossible."

"And then there is you." Victor peered down at me. "You have ancestral magic in you, which is one in a billion. That is why you're so powerful as an immortal."

"If true magic were to come to this world," Juliet said, "people could learn it and use it. True magic wouldn't be limited, and they could wreak major havoc, like the damage you saw in your first vision with the world in ruin. There would be nothing to stop them."

"The part of your vision where you saw our heads on a spike and Los Altos in ruins—that could yet come to pass," Victor said.

"We stopped them once," I said, finishing off my drink. "Maybe, I need to stop them again. It might be the reason I'm the way I am?" I put my empty glass on the coffee table.

"Possible, but understand we got lucky," Victor replied. "Your father was an egotist and loved to hear his own voice. Much like our current president."

Juliet and Gregor glared at him.

Victor raised a hand. "Well, it's true. Anyway, we used that and you against him. I doubt we would be that lucky again. Most tricks only work once."

"You said it's been limited." Juliet crossed to the bar, pouring herself another drink. "I suggest we continue to watch and see what happens. The Council has been seeking out witches and covens that might be willing to help in the event something does happen." She sipped her fresh drink. "At least we know what to look for now."

"My mother mentioned that some of the witches want peace and would be willing to work for that," I said. "She didn't say who, but she said they're out there."

"Good," Gregor said. "What do we tell the others?" He crossed his arms in front of his broad chest.

"Tell them what to look for and let them know that the Council is working on a solution," Juliet offered. "If there is anything urgent, have them notify you and we'll get it sorted." She finished her drink. "In the meantime, I'll talk to the Council and tell them they need to double their efforts in finding these covens that will join the cause. Chris being an immortal born of witches should help our standing. That is the best we can do. I don't want a panic, and I don't want there to be any literal witch hunts. There is nothing to worry about at the moment, and I plan on keeping it that way." She turned to Victor. "I'm assuming you will support this?"

"Considering what we've been through, of course," Victor answered. "Even the most doubtful of the Dark have come around."

"And the fact that it's helping your reputation hasn't hurt either, has it?" One side of Gregor's lip raised.

"I won't deny that the events of the last few weeks have gained me more sway even in areas outside my circle," Victor said. "I would've thought you would be happy about that?" He finished his drink with a slight pucker of his lips.

"Gentlemen," Juliet said, stopping the potential for verbal barbing. "We're all pleased with the relationships we've fostered during this time. Now, unless there is anything else?"

"I suppose not," Victor said and glanced at me. "You know if you get tired of being here with Pollyanna, you are more than welcome to come and stay at my penthouse. I can assure you you'll have a memorable time." He flashed me a wry smile.

I shook my head and bit my lip to keep myself from laughing.

"Always a joy." Victor tipped his head toward Gregor.

Gregor stood up, reminding me just how tall he was, a full head taller than me. "I should be off, too."

"Actually, Gregor, if you don't mind, would you stay back for a moment? Chris, do you mind? Plus, I believe someone is waiting for you."

"Of course not, thanks." I stood. "Gregor, good to see you." I strolled over to the door with Victor. "Have a good evening." I said, and we walked out.

Kirtus wasn't at the door, so I assumed he was in the living room. "Can I show you out, Victor?"

"Please," he replied, and we started to walk, but then he stopped and took my arm. "Chris," he said, watching me carefully.

"Yes." I leaned up against the wall. I wasn't sure what Victor had on his mind, but he seemed different, more thoughtful.

"You and Kirtus being together..." Victor's voice was barely more than a whisper. "You should know that this has come at a very high price, not only for me but for Juliet."

I narrowed my eyes at him.

"Before we realized you were a true seer, I promised Juliet that I would support her on the stipulation that, if you proved not to be a seer, then she would force you to stop pursuing Kirtus."

"I see." I bit my bottom lip. "But, I *am* a true seer."

"And that is where the cost for me came in," Victor said. "I had to promise that not only would I continue to keep Kirtus in good standing with the Dark under my control, but I would also keep any additional harm coming to him from any of the Dark, anywhere in the world."

"I don't understand."

"In a few weeks, I'll make Kirtus one of my lieutenants. This will elevate his status in the Dark and protect him outside of my areas of control."

"Okay," I said, still not seeing what the big deal was.

"He will be posted as my liaison in dealings with the Light, making it possible for the both of you to continue your relationship." His gaze darted over my face.

I went to speak and Victor held up a hand. "This has never been done before. Juliet will support the post. She is the head of the Council of Light, so they will fall in line and back her."

"Does Kirtus know?"

"No. Not yet, and there is still much to do before I tell him, but there are those that don't care for him and will use any excuse to harm him, even with these changes."

"Why are you telling me this?" I asked.

"Because you have a right to know, and if anything is to change in your relationship, if this is just a passing fancy, there is no going back," Victor replied. "I want to make sure you are fully aware of the costs and the dangers you may face because of this coupling." Victor picked a piece of lint off his suit and headed down the hall.

I wasn't so sure he was finished, but since he walked away, I had no choice but to follow him, my head filled with what he'd told me. Why was this such a big deal? Why did it matter who Kirtus or I saw? It was no one's business. We reached the door, and I opened it for him. He stood there.

"Chris." His expression had changed from his normal cocky appearance to an almost friendly one.

I worried what new tidbit he was about to spring on me.

"I want to thank you," Victor said.

"For what?"

He reached out and took my hand. "I will never say this to the others, and I will deny ever saying it now. I owe you a great deal; you found Daniel, and I was able to lay him to rest. It is a debt I will never be able to repay you."

I went to speak and Victor held up his free hand, hushing me.

"You are a good man, and I believe that we would not have succeeded if it wasn't for you and the sacrifice you made. As long as I'm in charge of the Dark, you will always be of us and we will be of you," he said with a firm nod. He released my hand and reached for the door. "Good night, Chris."

"Wow," I said as he headed out.

Victor had completely confused me. He told me about what he and Juliet had done to allow Kirtus and me to date, and now this. The man was unique. Part of me understood why Juliet trusted him. He had honor and a strong sense of what was just. He got into his sporty Mercedes-Benz and drove off.

I glanced at the overcast night. It had stopped raining, and hints of the night sky peeked through the clouds. I closed the door and headed to the sitting room where Kirtus would be.

"How did the meeting go?" He put the book he'd been reading down.

"I really don't want to think about it. Any of it," I said. What we had talked about in the office or when I was alone with Victor. It was a lot to process, and all I wanted to do was go to dinner with my handsome man and relax.

"That bad?" He stood and hugged me. "Hey, whatever it is, we'll face it." He kissed my forehead. "Together." He stepped back. "Why don't you grab your coat and we can get out of here, leave the world to itself for the night." He smiled.

I nodded and we headed out of the sitting room. I grabbed my jacket from the coatroom.

"Ready?" he asked, then walked to the front door and opened it.

I leaned in and gave him a quick peck on the cheek. "Ready."

When I turned to the door, I wasn't looking outside any longer. I stood in some chamber or room. In the center stood a formal table of polished stone with ornately carved chairs around it. On the wall was a mural showing the current members of the Council of Light.

I turned to Kirtus, but he was gone. Alone in the chamber, I turned back to the mural. The wall started to crack and crumble, and I smelled smoke. The chamber was on fire, and the stone table was crumbling to pieces. The chairs burned and everything was in shambles.

I blinked, and everything was destroyed and burned out. In the middle of the space, a large carved wooden chair with inlays of gold and decorated with jewels rose from the ruins, pushing the debris away. A shadowy figure sat on the chair.

A male voice called out, "I've stayed out of the way of history, but it's time to return and bring what is right and just back to this world." There was a flash of a man in some kind of toga with deep-crimson and white stripes.

I blinked again, and I stood in a grass-covered pasture. In front of me rose a hill, and a young girl with long brown hair sat, staring up at an oversized full moon. She laughed and clapped her hands.

I tried to get a better look at her. I stepped toward her, but I tripped and I reached out to stop my fall.

"Are you alright?" Kirtus grabbed my arm to support me.

I held on to the side of the door. I turned and looked at him, not sure what to say or do.

"What happened?" Kirtus asked.

I focused on the details of my vision—I didn't want to lose anything. My head started to pound. "I had a vision."

He took my arm, and we moved to a chair and I sat down. This was unlike my past vision. "Something's coming. Something is changing. Things are already put in motion."

Kirtus kneeled down, meeting my eyes, "Hey, we got this. Let's talk to Juliet. You're not alone. You won't have to face anything alone. Not anymore."

I stood, took his hand, and squeezed it tight, not sure how to explain what I saw. Knowing he was next to me was all I needed. I was—no, we would be ready, no matter what was coming our way.

About the Author

M.D. Neu is a LGBTQA Fiction Writer with a love for writing and travel. Living in the heart of Silicon Valley (San Jose, California) and growing up around technology, he's always been fascinated with what could be. Specifically drawn to science fiction and paranormal television and novels, M.D. Neu was inspired by the great Gene Roddenberry, George Lucas, Stephen King, Alfred Hitchcock, Harvey Fierstein, Anne Rice, and Kim Stanley Robinson. An odd combination, but one that has influenced his writing.

Growing up in an accepting family as a gay man, he always wondered why there were never stories reflecting who he was. Constantly surrounded by characters that only reflected heterosexual society, M.D. Neu decided he wanted to change that. So, he took to writing, wanting to tell good stories that reflected our diverse world.

When M.D. Neu isn't writing, he works for a non-profit and travels with his biggest supporter and his harshest critic, Eric, his husband of eighteen plus years.

Email: info@mdnue.com
Facebook: https://www.facebook.com/mdneuauthor/
Twitter: @Writer_MDNeu
Website: www.mdneu.com

Other books by this author

The Reunion
A Dragon for Christmas

Also Available from NineStar Press

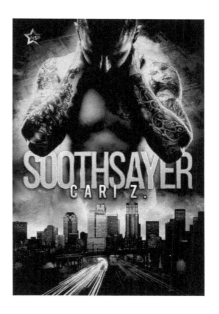

Connect with NineStar Press

www.ninestarpress.com

www.facebook.com/ninestarpress

www.facebook.com/groups/NineStarNiche

www.twitter.com/ninestarpress

www.tumblr.com/blog/ninestarpress